Black Kath's Daughter

Richard Parks

ISBN: 0615594778
ISBN-13: 978-0615594774

Canemill Publishing

DEDICATION

To the Librarians, from ancient Alexandria to Clinton, Mississippi, who have been pushing back against the darkness for a long, long time.

CONTENTS

ACKNOWLEDGMENTS

Portions of this book have appeared in revised form as:

"What Power Holds" - Dragon Magazine #209, 1994
"The Third Law of Power" - Dragon Magazine #224, 1995
"The First Law of Power" - Realms of Fantasy, June, 2001

CHAPTER 1

"There are Seven Laws of Power and, so far as we know, seven immortal Powers ruled by those Laws. Do not confuse the two, for the first is an insight into the nature of power, and the second is power itself. The first cares for nothing, and so is perfectly fair to all. The second cares about something very much, and that something is not you."
—Black Kath's Tally Book

The witch called "Black Kath" stopped to rest along the snowy mountain path. Again.

I don't remember it being quite so steep the last time.

She thought for a moment, remembering to her chagrin that the "last time" was five years before. Not surprising that she'd been in no hurry to return, considering what happened that last time. Yet here she was again, wondering what the new tragedy would be, and whether she was really as old and sick as she felt. Perhaps that was the tragedy. If so, Kath was sure she could deal with it; she'd been dealing with her advancing age and retreating health for years. She didn't think matters would be that simple.

It's Marta you should be worrying about.

Marta, her daughter, was why she was out in the blustery cold instead of warming her old bones by the fire where she belonged. Down at the bottom of the trail her servant Treedle would be tending a nice fire, making their camp ready for Kath's return. He might even have a kettle on for tea. Kath sighed. She could do with a cup of hot tea just then, or hot brandy wine, or hot anything. She pulled her cloak tighter, took a firmer grip on her staff, and kept climbing.

A raven sat waiting on a bit of dead wood clinging to the side of the mountain. "It's not much farther," he said, in a voice as harsh and rasping as one would expect from a raven.

Kath glared at him. "Bone Tapper, 'not much farther' is a different measure for one who can fly and one who cannot."

The wind ruffled the raven's feathers. "About seventy paces, then, before the steps leading to the gate." He rose into the air and flapped off into the crags. "Mind you stay away from the edge of the trail; this wind could blow you over," he shouted back just before it disappeared.

Kath didn't need the reminder. To her right was Mount Karsanmon. To her left was a drop of several hundred feet to the various piles of rubble on the outskirts of the town of Karsan. Separating the two was a stone path barely four feet wide at its best. As she wondered if she would ever feel her toes again, Kath also silently cursed whichever ancient cleric had picked such a dramatic location for the Shrine. She knew that they'd had little choice in the matter, tradition being what it was, but she could still find it in her heart to blame them just the same. Black Kath worked her way along where the path curved around a bend and finally reached the steps. She looked up the stone stairway and into the gateway to the Karsanmon Shrine of Amaet. For a moment she forgot her complaints.

The shrine building itself was just visible through the gate and relatively new, having been built no more than a generation before Kath's time, but the gate was infinitely older. No one living knew if it belonged to the original shrine or who made it. It was a simple thing, two rectangular pillars of granite supporting a carved crosspiece, all perfectly smooth with joints so tight you had to be really close before they were even visible. The ends of the crosspiece swept up on either side like the beginning of an upside down arch; both pillars and crosspiece had each in turn been quarried from a single piece of stone and worked so smooth there was no sign of hammer or chisel on any of them. Snow clung to the top of the gate and covered the steps leading up to them.

Kath put aside her admiration and concentrated on getting up the steps, bracing herself at every step up with her staff. Bone Tapper returned, and landed softly on her shoulder. "Your friend is still following you."
Kath nodded. "I suspected as much. Did you tell him to go away?"

"I did. He didn't."

"Funny. Usually when people get a warning delivered by a talking raven they tend to pay attention."

"He's a desperate fool," Bone Tapper replied. "You know the sort."

Black Kath nodded. She did indeed. Unfortunately. "Well, no sense fretting about it now. Please tell the Priestess I'm coming."

Bone Tapper started to fly, hesitated. "Should I ask her to send someone out to help you?"

"Not unless you want to regrow every feather on your body after I pluck them out. It's rather cold here at night."

"Daytime too. Very well, but I had to ask." Bone Tapper flapped away up through the gate.

By the time she reached the top of the steps, Kath was beginning to regret her pride just a bit. She leaned against the left lintel post of the gate, looking up a the massive sweep of stone above her as she rested. It occurred to her that, if she really wanted to know who had made the Gate, the stones themselves might speak. If she asked them the right way, of course. She decided against it. Some mysteries were not to be tolerated; some were not to be disturbed. Knowing the difference was as close to wisdom as Kath was willing to claim.

The design of the Karsanmon Shrine to Amaet was something like wisdom, too. At least, Kath would have liked to give the builders this much credit: they knew they couldn't match the simple elegance of the Gate, and so hadn't tried. The rest was not wisdom of any sort: the Shrine itself was gaudy, ostentatious, and had a bad tendency to attract fools.

It's bad enough I have to talk to Amaet. Should I have to talk to her daffy priestess, too?

It wasn't that there weren't other shrines, but it was a whim of the Power called Amaet that, if Black Kath wanted to speak to her, the old witch had to do it here. If Amaet wanted to speak to Kath, on the other hand, Amaet would do so wherever she damn well pleased. Life was unfair, and so were the Powers. Kath knew that, but she didn't have to like it. She waited until Bone Tapper returned to report. She sent him back to scouting and then, reluctantly, she entered the Shrine.

Aleeta came to greet her in person. She was a tall, elegant woman just approaching middle years. The Priestess's blue robe of office was arranged so carefully that Black Kath had to wonder how long it had taken her in front of the mirror to manage it.

It must be nice, Kath thought ruefully, *to have so much time.*

"Greetings, Honored of Amaet," she said.

"And to you, Black Kath of Lythos. This is a rare pleasure."

Not rare enough, to Kath's way of thinking. Still, the witch knew that anything she wanted or needed was going to cost, one way or another. Aleeta would have her due; she was no different from a Power in that regard.

"You must be half frozen, poor dear. I've a new recipe for mulled wine I was just trying out. Would you care to join me?"

Kath shuddered inwardly at the "poor dear" comment, but there was no getting around Aleeta and they both knew it. Besides, hot mulled wine sounded very good just then. Kath followed Aleeta through the portal. Just beyond was the huge, echoing Sanctuary, graced at the far end with a gilt statue of Amaet no less than twenty feet tall.

Much larger than the old one. Kath smiled to herself. She remembered the previous statue very well.

"This is new, isn't it?"

Aleeta glanced back, smiled. "New? Hardly. When was the last time you visited us? Your daughter's Presentation ceremony wasn't it? Seven years ago?"

"Five," Kath said. The "Presentation Ceremony" hadn't been the real reason for that visit either. Kath most emphatically did not worship Amaet; their relationship was much more businesslike than that. Aleeta, knowing Kath's relatively frequent pilgrimages to the Shrine and being otherwise blissfully ignorant of just what it meant to be an Arrow Path magician, assumed otherwise. Kath was more than happy to allow Aleeta to keep that misapprehension, since it made Kath's occasional communing with Amaet seem only right and proper. Still, Kath still wasn't sure which excuse she'd use this time.

Aleeta smiled. "Well, there you are. A rare pleasure indeed. No, our old statue suffered a mishap and had to be replaced. The workmen had a jolly time bringing the new one up the pass, let me tell you. Worth it, though. Isn't it splendid?"

"It's very...impressive," Kath said. "Doesn't look anything like her, though."

Aleeta stopped, then turn back to Black Kath with a puzzled look on her face. "What did you say?"

Kath could have kicked herself, if she had been younger and far more flexible. She had forgotten the ironic truth: the High Priestess of Amaet had never actually seen Amaet. "Nothing, nothing at all. Merely a poor joke for which I crave your pardon, Honored One. It was a long trip and I'm very tired."

Aleeta waved it away, magnanimously. "Of course. Now that you mention it yourself, I have to say you aren't looking well at all."

Kath's smile was all teeth. Lovely of you to point out the obvious. Yet you've given me a notion. They arrived at the Priestess's private chambers, if anything more gilt and opulent than all the rest of the shrine, and that was saying something indeed. Out of respect for her guest Aleeta poured the wine herself, dismissing her servants.

Black Kath sipped her portion with honest enjoyment. Aleeta's failures as a priestess and a wit were legion, but Kath did have to admit the woman knew her wine.

"Your observation about my health was, I'm afraid, fairly accurate. Yes, this has been a trying year for many reasons. That's why I've come to the Shrine, to make an offering and, perhaps, take some brief time to contemplate."

Aleeta nodded. "Ah. I thought it might be something of the sort. Many do come here seeking the healing of the Goddess."

Kath wondered how many had actually received it. More than a few would say so, probably. Desperate people could convince themselves of anything, just like Kath's human shadow that Bone Tapper had been following. Kath had learned to avoid desperation when possible, both in others and in herself. She wouldn't be able to avoid this one; he'd made that clear enough.

Kath sighed. *One fool at a time.*

"You'll be wanting the Sanctuary, of course," Aleeta said.

"Actually, I was thinking of the Grotto," Kath said.

Aleeta frowned. "That damp hole in the rock? What for?"

"Call it an old woman's whim. My mother brought me to the Grotto before the new Shrine was completed. It reminds me of her."

"That's rather sweet," Aleeta said, then leaned forward and whispered like one sharing a conspiracy. "Don't worry-- as Priestess of Amaet, I wouldn't dream of telling anyone."

"Too kind," Kath said. "It wouldn't do to let the world know that Black Kath of Lythos is a human being after all."

If Aleeta sensed anything in Black Kath's tone she didn't show it. Kath finished her wine as quickly as good manners allowed and let Aleeta lead her through the sanctuary. They passed by the big gaudy statue of Amaet and through the rear chambers of the Shrine, finally arriving at a plain stout wooden door, braced with black iron. It could have been the door to a storage cellar by appearance. Aleeta unlocked it with a large iron key hanging from her belt.

"Go with Amaet," Aleeta said.

As if I have a choice, Kath thought, but she said nothing more than "thank you" and waited for Aleeta to leave. When she was finally alone, Kath gathered her cloak about her once more, pulled the door open and entered the Grotto.

Someone seeing the Grotto for the first time would naturally think they had left the Shrine entirely and stepped out some unused service entrance by mistake. Kath knew better; this was the real Shrine. The gilt pile behind her, for all its pretensions, was nothing more than a glorified inn. The Grotto was open to the sky, little more than a crack in the stone but, if one thought of the Gate, it quickly became clear that this was why the Gate had been built, why it pointed the way to the path leading here. This was the sacred space that the Gate's presence marked. It was, in short, the place that mattered.

There was a large stone bowl near the end of the crack, placed before a weathered stone statue of Amaet in Judgment, her crossed arms bearing both the ax and the apple blossom.

"You'd think, after so much time, just once I might get the apple instead of the ax?"

No answer, but of course she hadn't expected one. Yet. Kath reached in her purse and produced one coin of gold for the offering bowl. The coin wasn't an offering, it was payment in advance, assuming she wanted to ask a question. She was already in Amaet's debt far more than her ability—or time—to pay. She tossed the coin into the bowl, listening to it clink and rattle around the smooth curved stone before settling silently in the bottom.

"I have come, Amaet."

No sooner had Kath spoken the name than Amaet was there. That is, first she wasn't, and then she was. There was no flash of fire or lightning or rolling thunder to announce her presence. Now the Power—or the Goddess, depending—called Amaet stood with her right hand on the edge of the bowl, radiantly beautiful as only she could be when she chose. Her hair was blacker than Calyt ink, her robe whiter even than the snow that rimmed her offering bowl, and she glowed as if her insides were on fire.

Too bad Aleeta is missing this, Black Kath thought. She'd soil that lovely blue robe. Black Kath considered it worth at least one piece of gold to see that.

WHAT DOES IT FEEL LIKE?

Kath blinked. "I don't understand."

IMMINENT MORTALITY. DYING. DEATH. I ASSUMED YOU KNEW.

Kath took a long slow breath, let it go. "I thought as much. I didn't know for certain."

THEN YOU WEREN'T PAYING ATTENTION.

"I didn't come here to talk about me, Amaet."

WHAT MAKES YOU THINK YOU KNOW WHY YOU'RE HERE?

Black Kath would long ago have asked some friendly deity for patience if there was a single one she considered friendly. The time for patience, however, was long past. She wondered, too, if there was something about immortality that made one tend to be cryptic in every conversation; perhaps the Powers' patience was so immense because they tried everyone else's. Try as she might, Black Kath couldn't remember any Power that would ever willingly get to the point, or at least to the point that she wanted them to get to.

"I concede that the reason I came here and why I am here may be two different things, Amaet. I only know the one. I won't deepen my debt by asking, but you can tell me the other if you wish."

YOU DIDN'T BRING THE LITTLE ONE. I THOUGHT YOU MIGHT.

"Her name is Marta, and she's not so little now. She's almost seventeen. She's what I wanted to talk to you about."

Amaet sat down on the edge of the offering bowl. That is, she crossed her legs in front of her and seemed to perch there. Except she wasn't really touching it, Black Kath could plainly see; she hovered a few inches above the snow. Black Kath wasn't surprised to see that the snow there was melting.

INDEED? WHAT DO YOU WISH TO SAY?

"I want Marta's freedom."

YOU KNOW MY PRICE.

Black Kath shuddered, slightly, but when she spoke to Amaet again her voice was clear and strong. "I accepted the Debt as my mother did before me. As a follower of the Arrow Path I owe you, and so I must serve on your command. Yet even that is not absolute; you may not compel me in matters not related to that service. Marta is one of those matters."

THE NATURE OF THE DEBT IS THAT WHAT REMAINS OF IT WILL FALL ON HER WHEN YOU DIE, AS IT DID WHEN YOUR MOTHER PASSED. MARTA WILL CHOOSE AS YOU DID LONG AGO. PERHAPS YOU HOPED SHE WOULD TURN OUT OTHERWISE?

Kath had indeed hoped for that, and acted accordingly. She had been wrong, and remained wrong even when she had to deny the evidence of her own eyes. Kath wasn't sure she'd ever forgive herself for that, but she hoped Marta would forgive her, once she understood the enormity of her mother's mistake. And she knew Marta would understand, some day. Kath didn't need Amaet to tell her that. Marta's curiosity was already leading her into dangerous ways. Black Kath had done what she could, but her time and Marta's freedom were fast ending.

"You could refuse her," Kath said, barely above a whisper. "You could forgive the Debt."

ALL THINGS HAVE THEIR PRICE. EVEN MERCY. BOW TO ME, BLACK KATH OF LYTHOS.

"You would own me," Kath said.

I OWN YOU NOW.

Kath shook her head. "I am in your debt. That is not the same thing."

TRUE. BOW TO ME AND SHE WOULD BE FREE. SHE COULD MARRY, AND RAISE GENERATIONS UNCONCERNED WITH THE LAWS OF POWER AND THE WAYS OF THE POWERS. SHE MIGHT EVEN BE HAPPY.

"You ask for what I cannot give," Kath said. Her eyes were glistening but her gaze was steady. "Not even for Marta."

Amaet's sigh could have made a rock despair. NO ROOM FOR PRETTY LIES. OUR WORLDS ARE POORER FOR IT. I KNEW YOU WOULD REFUSE, FOR WHAT LITTLE THAT IS WORTH. YOUR MOTHER DID, THOUGH IT TORE HER HEART NO LESS THAN IT TEARS YOUR OWN.

Black Kath turned to leave.

WE ARE NOT DONE.

Kath looked at Amaet almost eagerly. "A command? I'd welcome the chance to reduce Marta's legacy."

Amaet laughed then. REDUCE? NAY, I PROPOSE TO INCREASE IT. I HAVE SOMETHING TO SELL.

"What could you possibly offer that I would want enough to do that?" Black Kath asked bitterly.

There was no kindness in Amaet's beautiful smile. HOPE.

Kath shook her head, slowly. "I am dying, Amaet. What use is hope to me now?"

IT IS NOT FOR YOU.

Black Kath didn't speak for several long moments. It was Amaet who finally broke the silence. YES, I CAN SEE THAT I HAVE YOUR ATTENTION NOW. WELL?

"What do you want in return?"

A SERVICE. IF I CANNOT HAVE WORSHIP FROM MARTA I WILL HAVE ONE GREAT SERVICE FROM HER INSTEAD.

Kath knew the answer before she even asked the question, but hope would not let her keep silent. "I am not dead yet, Amaet. I can do this thing for you instead. What is it?"

YOU TRIED ONCE AND FAILED. NOW YOUR TIME IS DONE, BLACK KATH. YOU ARE TIRED AND SPENT, WORN OUT LIKE A PILGRIM'S SHOE.

It may have sounded like an insult, but it wasn't—it was simple truth. Black Kath brushed it aside. "Yes, I failed. What makes you think Marta will succeed?"

PERHAPS I HAVE HOPE OF MY OWN. AS FOR THE OTHER MATTER...STRANGE. IT'S MY OPINION THAT YOU HAVE NEVER FAILED AT ANYTHING, BLACK KATH. THERE HAVE BEEN TIMES, HOWEVER, WHEN YOU CHOSE NOT TO SUCCEED.

Kath smiled grimly. If she only knew. All she said was, "If you have an accusation to make, then do so."

As she had done once before, many years ago, Amaet gave Kath a vision. Masks floated in the air of the grotto. Kath counted them. One. Two. Three. Four. Five. Six. Seven. The glow from Amaet herself cast shadows through their empty, hollow eyes. As the masks floated, another began to appear. Nebulous. Unreal. But possible. Potential. So easy to give form and substance. To give power.

Eight.

Kath shook her head. "No, Amaet. Not so long as there is breath in my body."

Which, Kath knew, would not be for much longer. Amaet had not given up her scheme, even now. It was too much. "Even if I could do what you want, I would not. You still seek to destroy the balance that holds this world together!" Kath shouted, trying, one last time, to make Amaet see reason. "Even a Power should not speak of such things!"

GREAT RISK FOR GREAT GAIN. I WILL DO AS I HAVE SAID. THERE IS NOTHING YOU CAN DO ABOUT IT.

Not much. But not nothing, Black Kath thought. She asked another question. She had a feeling that Amaet would answer this one, coin or no coin. That was Amaet's privilege. It was also, Kath feared, her pleasure. "What if Marta refuses, or fails at the final step as I did?"

THEN, UNLIKE YOU, SHE WILL DIE IMMEDIATELY. I WILL SEE TO THAT. MY PATIENCE HAS LIMITS.

"You ask too much, Amaet."

PERHAPS. WILL MARTA REFUSE ME, DO YOU THINK? WOULDN'T IT BE BETTER WITH JUST A BIT OF HOPE?

Kath didn't know. She wanted to, and Amaet was all too aware of that. She knows me. She's won more times than not, with that. Damn her.

"Very well. What is this 'hope' you offer?"

IF MARTA IS WILLING AND ABLE TO PERFORM THIS SERVICE FOR ME, ONCE THE GREAT MATTER IS SETTLED SHE WILL BE FREE.

Black Kath frowned. "You increase the Debt over this?! That is no more or less than what you offered me!"

Amaet shrugged. AND MY GIFT IS THAT THE OFFER STILL STANDS. THE CHOICE WILL BE MARTA'S TO MAKE. THAT IS SOMETHING LIKE FREEDOM, YES?

Kath nodded. Yes. Something very vaguely and remotely like freedom. At least, to Amaet's way of thinking.

"Goodbye, Amaet," was all she said. In another moment she was alone. Kath left the Grotto, but she did not go back into the Shrine. She was just too weary to deal with Aleeta again. All she could think about was Marta. Kath had waited too long, where Marta was concerned. There were reasons and she had meant well, but she had been wrong, she knew that now, and Kath did not think there would be enough time to make things right. Not for Marta, and not even for herself.

Forgive me, daughter. I have no right to ask, but I will ask just the same. Forgive me...

Kath picked her way carefully through a rubble-strewn gap between the rock wall and the Shrine, using her walking stick several times to avoid falling. She finally emerged from behind the Shrine and made her way back out to the Gate. Bone Tapper was perched there, his black feathers standing out sharply against the snow on the top lintel.

The raven called down to her. "He's still lurking about." If Bone Tapper intended to comment on Black Kath's choice of exits, one look at the expression on her face must have dissuaded him. "I can still send Treedle to take care of it," was all he said.

"I imagine that service could weigh heavily against his debt," Kath said, "but, knowing Treedle, it will weigh even heavier against him. I will not ask this."

"He does lack a certain taste for blood," Bone Tapper said, as he fluttered down to her shoulder. "Perhaps it will not be necessary to be so...final."

"You told the man to go, and he would not. You told him we know his intent, and yet he waits our return. Is the man insane?" Kath asked.

The raven seemed to consider the question very seriously. "If the word means anything, then yes, I think he is."

"Then his life is not in my hands. Let's go."

Kath wasn't halfway back down the narrow trail when the man appeared out of a crevice in the rocks. His clothes were of good quality but much worn and ill-kept. His black hair was uncombed, and his beard had seen neither razor nor shears in months. That didn't mean he lacked a razor, by any means. He held it in his right hand, but it wasn't gripped for shaving.

"Black Kath of Lythos," he said blissfully. "At last I've found you."

"Since you took great pains to arrange it, I think it unlikely you could have lost me. What do you want?"

His eyes were fixed on her as if she were the only fire in a blizzard. "You know what I want."

Kath nodded. "You want to kill me."

"Of course," he said, and freshened his grip on the razor.

"May I ask why?"

He frowned then. "You dare ask? Why would anyone seek to kill those who hold the Powers in fetters? Nay, name those rather who would not. Don't speak foolishness, nor take me for a fool. We understand each other, oh yes."

"Ah. You think I command Amaet against her will. And you do worship her, don't you?" Black Kath took one step back up the trail.

The man frowned, and advanced one step himself. "You can't run from me."

"One step is not running," Kath said, calmly. "Neither is this." She took one more careful backward step. "You didn't answer my question."

"Amaet? I worship her more than life itself," the man said.

"Good."

Black Kath reached out with her walking stick and tapped the side of the mountain, right at the spot she'd passed earlier and worked her way back two steps to reach. In that instant a chunk of rock larger than the two of them together broke loose directly beside the would be assassin. He barely had the time to glance in surprise and horror at what was bearing down on him before the stone flipped over the edge and took him with it. In a moment all that was left to remind Black Kath and the raven of his presence was a high pitched scream that lasted for several long seconds before ending rather abruptly in the ravine below.

"Go with Amaet," Kath said, without a trace of sarcasm, or emotion of any other kind.

Bone Tapper ruffled his feathers. "And they call ravens cold blooded."

Kath strode past the broken rock without another glance. "How many chances did we give that poor deluded fool, Bone Tapper? And do you really think he would have believed the truth if he'd heard it? No. He had his own truth. Mine is that I do what I have to. I'd advise you to remember that."

"I'm unlikely to forget," the raven said, peering down into the distant haze. "Your reminders do tend to get a person's attention."

Kath shook her head, looking thoughtful. "I don't think I was giving a reminder just then, Bone Tapper. I think I was getting one."

Bone Tapper seemed to know that a comment was neither required nor welcome. He perched in demure silence on Black Kath's shoulder until they reached the welcome campfire waiting for them down in the valley.

CHAPTER 2

"The difference between a Power and a Deity is mostly prescriptive. You worship a Deity. With a Power, you negotiate."
— Black Kath's Tally Book

It was the evening of Marta's seventeenth birthday. She sat before the fire in her mother's hearth and ordered the flames to dance.

Black Kath sat at her table a few steps away, enjoying the warmth of the fire on her old bones but not really expecting anything else of it. She'd been writing intently in her accounts book a few moments before, when Marta's disagreement with the flames got her attention, and she put her quill aside. The raven on her shoulder seemed content to doze and took no notice of either of them. Black Kath started to peel an apple.

"Daughter, why did you do that?" she asked.

Marta turned her face away from the fire. It was a lovely face; Black Kath had noted that fact with some concern a long time ago. A lovely face indeed, framed by hair only a shade yellower than the red of the fire itself. A face that was going to be trouble for Marta, sooner or later. No help for that, Black Kath knew. She tried to be what help to her daughter that she could.

"I wanted the flames to dance," Mara said simply. "So I told them to. I waited till Bone Tapper was asleep; I didn't feel like listening to his insolence."

"Bone Tapper is what he is, as are flames. Flames already dance. By their nature they can do little else. I rather admire them that; there are far worse ways to spend a brief life than dancing." Kath's own time for dancing was

12

long past. She winced. The pain was back in her chest; she knew what it meant. Marta would know soon enough. Black Kath was sad about that, but only a little. There was too much yet to be done, and Kath had begun far too late. "Marta, lambkin, if you know they dance, why did you tell them to do it? Isn't that rather like telling a snowflake to be cold?"

"I wanted a pavane," Marta said. "Something with a little form and dignity. They just leap about."

"I see. And the flames' leaping, that offends you?"

Marta reddened. "You've been so quiet lately, and when you choose to speak you're mocking me! You could make them do it."

Her mother thought about it. "I suppose."

Kath looked at the fire. She said nothing. She did not wave her hands or command. Yet in a moment the wild flames were suddenly chastened. They separated into two lines with but a spark separating a crown of fire on each side, as if the flames were holding hands. They processed side by side to unheard music. After several long moments Kath yawned as if losing interest and the flames settled back to their former chaos.

Marta stared at the fire long after the flames reverted to nature. There was a tear in the corner of one eye. "Mother, why won't you teach me? I want to learn!"

It's too late to lead you, daughter. I will have to goad instead.

"Daughter, why won't you learn? I want to teach you."

"You're mocking me again!"

Kath finished peeling the apple and sliced it neatly in half. "No, I am not mocking you. I really would like to know. Have you been listening to anything I've said for the past seventeen years? What are the Seven Laws of Power?"

"How can I tell you that? You've never told me!"

Kath sighed. "You are my darling daughter and I love you dearly, but you are a trial. First of all, I can no more teach you the Seven Laws of Power than I can teach your heart to beat. Second, I didn't ask you for a sodding list! I asked you what they *were.*"

Marta blushed again, but her mouth set in a firm line. "The Seven Laws of Power are the well from which a sorceress draws her art. A hedge witch might know one or two. A true sorceress would know all seven."

"Almost accurate, but not quite. Never mind that now. There's one thing I can teach you, Marta, so please learn: the Seven are not keys to power. They simply reflect the power and understanding you already have."

Marta looked away. "I have no power or understanding. That's the problem."

"No, the problem is that you're too full of anger and self-pity to hear yourself think." Black Kath handed her daughter half the apple. "Eat this. You're too thin. So was I, at your age."

"Thin, or too full of anger and self-pity?" Marta took the apple half and bit off a large chunk. She chewed sullenly.

Black Kath sighed. "Both."

"So tell me: what did your mother do about it?"

Black Kath laughed gently. "What I'm doing now. First, she made me eat something. Then she gave me this."

Her mother reached around her neck and removed the silver pendant she wore there and handed it to Marta. Marta studied the silver emblem; it was an arrow bisecting a circle. The nock and the point of the arrowhead just touched the edge of the circle.

"It's a nice piece of jewelry," Marta said. "But I don't understand; what has it to do with the Laws of Power?"

"You do keep to the point, Marta, as best you understand it. That's good. You don't understand the point very well, however, and that's not so good. You think this is just a piece of jewelry?"

Marta frowned. "Isn't it?"

"It's the symbol of the Arrow Path. The Arrow Path is not the only way to acquire the Seven Laws, but it's the way I chose, and my mother before me."

"Does this have anything to do with a 'debt' you keep mentioning?"

"Not 'a' debt. *The* Debt. A Power called Amaet established the Arrow Path. Those who follow it owe her debt service, just as Treedle and Bone Tapper serve me. When I die you will inherit the Debt, Arrow Path or no."

"That hardly seems fair," Marta said.

"It's not, lambkin. The Powers aren't interested in fair, and Amaet less than most. Please remember that; it's important."

Marta considered this. "Why are you telling me this now?"

"I had hoped to never have to tell you at all." Kath held up her hand and Marta, about to protest, fell silent again. Kath nodded. "You who want flames to dance for you will not understand why. Neither did I when I was your age, but that doesn't matter now. You've turned seventeen, and it's time to choose. If you choose the Arrow Path, you might find what you need to bear the Debt. Perhaps...perhaps even to repay it, which I could not. I hope so. What happens now is up to you as your will and the fates decree."

"Is it magic?"

"The pendant? It's a symbol, and that's much more powerful. The Arrow Path itself is magic, at least in one important respect: it gives you the ability to recognize a Law of Power when you find one. That's not a gift, by the way. It's a service that is owed to you under the terms of the Debt. The arrowhead touching the circle represents the beginning of a journey that has no end. Do not undertake this lightly."

"I don't understand, Mother. If this way leads to the Seven Laws, won't that be the end of the journey?"

Black Kath shook her head. "The Seven Laws are not the end, Marta. You won't see that now; I didn't. Nor do you have to understand. All you have to do is decide."

"What lies beyond the Seven Laws?"

"I don't know. Perhaps you'll find out; I never did."

Marta hesitated, but only for a moment. She hung the pendant around her neck.

"How does it feel?" her mother asked.

"Heavier than I thought. Yet it feels...right. Good. Like an old ache that's finally gone away."

"When you get to be my age, then speak to me of 'old aches,'" Kath said.

"What now?" Marta asked.

The door of the kitchen creaked open. Black Kath's servant hob, Treedle, stuck his homely face into the room. "Mistress, you have a visitor."

"There's your answer, Marta. Life goes on. The world turns and events unfold. Just like before. If there's a difference, you'll have to make it yourself." The Powers know there's little enough I can do for you now. She turned to the hob. "That will be a messenger from King Alian, yes? Ask him to wait for a moment and I'll see him. Fetch him a goblet if he's so inclined."

Treedle nodded and closed the door softly. Marta didn't bother to ask how her mother knew who was at the door; that was one of the least of what she had seen over the years.

Kath poked the sleeping raven. "Get off, you lazy thing!"

The raven croaked once, blinked, and then hopped down to the table. It eyed the apple peelings Kath had left there, and then ignored them. "You interrupted a very lovely dream," he said.

"I'll do more than that if you leave a mess on that table. I have a guest to see now, but I think you should prepare yourself for a journey."

"Delighted," said the raven, clearly not delighted at all.

In a very short time Kath was back, accompanied by a young man with long blonde hair and a self-important air. "The Queen's pregnancy is proving to be a difficult one; she's ill and there's fear for the babe she's carrying. I am sent for," she said.

"You're not a midwife, Mother," Marta said. "And you just got back from Karsan yesterday!"

"It was the midwife who examined her and sent for me. I tend to trust her judgment in this. The fact that I've just returned is annoying but entirely beside the point." She turned to the messenger. "You needn't stay. Tell Mistress Thornap I'll follow as soon as I can."

The man nodded once and left without speaking at all. Marta watched him go. "I don't like him," she said.

Kath raised an eyebrow. "Oh? Why is that?"

15

"I didn't like the way he looked at me. I didn't like the way he studied this room as if there might be something here that belonged to him."

Kath shrugged. "He's on his way back to Karsan and, with luck, you'll never see him again." She turned to Bone Tapper. "Tell the horse to get ready. You and Treedle will be going with me. As always, I'll have need of your eyes and his strength."

"What about me?" Marta asked. "Do I start seeking the Laws of Power now?"

"You already are, though you don't seem to realize it. No, as much as there is to do here I was thinking that perhaps you should go with us this time. If you've chosen to follow me there's more to learn than the Laws."

*

Marta closed the door leading to the back of the wagon and climbed up onto the driver's bench beside Treedle. She didn't know his real name. She knew that he had been a human man once, and when his debt was paid he might be one again. As it was, her mother had found the shape he currently held, that of a creature no more than four feet tall yet extremely quick and strong, with brown skin, pointed ears and elongated face, to be most useful to her. Marta felt her breath turn to steam in the cold air and she pulled her cloak tighter. The hob didn't look at her. "How is your mother?" he asked.

"Just tired, I think," Marta said. "She's sleeping."

"Best thing for her, then. We'll be at Karsan soon and she'll have work to do. Bone Tapper's gone ahead to tell them we're coming, and to scout the road."

Marta blinked. "Scout? For what?"

"Anything. It's always a good idea," Treedle said. "There are those who do not wish your mother well."

"Why? What has she done to them?"

"Usually what they asked her to do."

"That doesn't make any sense," Marta said.

"You're right."

Marta looked at Treedle, then looked back at the road to Karsan. The White Mountains rose in the near distance to the north; Marta was so used to seeing them there that she barely noticed them now. The road itself was wide and well maintained for a cart path. Closer to her home it was little more than two ruts through the snow. Still, there were trees on either side of it, deep and dark enough for anyone to hide in despite the bare limbs and snow. Marta looked at the world around her with more suspicion. "Lately I feel as if I'm seeing everything for the first time again. I'm not sure I like it."

"Hmmm," said Treedle.

"Is that all you have to say?"

"What do you want me to say, Mistress?"

She frowned. "My name is Marta, as you well know."

Treedle nodded affably. "I do. Just as I know our relationship is that you are mistress and I am servant. If you want me to call you by your first name I will, but there was no insult in addressing you by your proper title."

Marta just stared at Treedle for several long moments as the forest passed by on both sides. "Treedle, I thought you were my friend."

"Does one normally own one's friends?"

"But I don't...I mean we don't..." Marta stopped. It occurred to her that she'd never really understood what it meant to have a bond-servant. As long as she could remember, Treedle and Bone Tapper just were. A part of the household no different than her mother or herself. Yet there was a difference, one she had never really seen before now. It was just one more thing that was different, since her birthday three days before. Marta felt the Arrow Path pendant heavy against her skin. Perhaps the change had something to do with growing up, but Marta didn't think that was all of it. She reached under her cloak, touched the pendant for a moment. "You owe my mother debt service because you did not have the price of the magic you needed, yes?"

"Yes," Treedle said.

"So it was your choice," Marta said.

"And I would make the same choice today, if it was mine to make again. The one doesn't change the other."

"But...owing service to someone is not the same as being property. You're not a slave!"

"A matter of perspective. My life is not my own, so it amounts to the same thing in my view."

Marta didn't argue the point. "Do you hate me, Treedle?"

He laughed then. "Never. Nor your mother, either. As I said: my choice. You chose to follow your mother's road. No blame to you for that, and I will serve you well when the time comes as I have served your mother. But I cannot be your friend, Marta. Perhaps I was once, when you were smaller and needed one more than you knew, but it's too much to ask that of me now."

Marta considered this. "What...what if Mother forgave your debt? I could speak to her."

Treedle smiled, but it was a sad smile. "Marta, I know you mean well, but what makes you think Black Kath controls the rules of the Debt? I will be free when my debt is paid. Not before."

"When will that be?"

Treedle turned the wagon away from a treetop that had fallen onto the edge of the road. "I don't know," he said, looking very serious. "I'll know when it happens."

Marta shook her head. "I don't understand this. You mean Mother wouldn't tell you?"

The hob shrugged. "I think she'll know when I do. I suspect that the price of a service in gold does not equal the price of the service in time. You'll have to ask your mother about that if you want to know. I don't, since it wouldn't change anything."

"It doesn't sound fair. Yet I'm told the Arrow Path isn't about being fair."

Treedle sighed. "You'll forgive me if I'd rather not talk about it. The Arrow Path has crossed my road once already. If it never does hereafter I'll count myself fortunate."

"Oh," Marta said, turning a little red. She didn't say anything else until they arrived on the outskirts of Karsan.

It had been five years or more since Marta had been to Karsan. She knew it wasn't a large town; the largest structures in it were the king's castle at the north edge and the various taverns and inns that served the pilgrim trade to the Shrine to Amaet on Mount Karsanmon just beyond. Still, all she had to compare Karsan to was an isolated village or two near her mother's solitary holding and by that measure it was like a beehive. So many people coming and going at once made Marta both nervous and excited. Most of the folk going about their business paid her mother's brightly painted cart little attention, but Marta did note that there were some who either averted their eyes and hurried away, or stopped whatever they were doing to watch intently as they went by.

Marta frowned. "What are they staring at?"

Treedle grunted. "What the others choose not to look at. Us. You. The promise of your mother's presence."

"Why should anyone care about that?"

Treedle stared at her. "Mistress, surely you're aware that Arrow Path magicians—or any other kind—aren't exactly thick on the ground? For a kingdom the size of Lythos to have one in residence is a source of pride to some. For others it is a worry they would gladly do without."

"But why should they worry?"

"Suppose they have need of her services and can't afford the fee?"

"Then they should weigh that need against the cost," Marta said primly. "No one forces them to seek her out."

Treedle just shrugged. "Need often trumps sense, and some people can resist all save temptation. If your mother had to be sought in some distant land like Wylandia or Morushe... Yet she is here, and her power is here, and the thought of what that power could do for them is never far away with some folk."

"No matter how we turn the knife lately, the edge always seems to be pointed at us," Marta said, looking disgusted.

Treedle smiled then. "Wasn't it you who said something about the Arrow Path not being fair? Yet I think in this case it is completely fair. If a blade with two edges can be said to be fair, that is."

Marta started to say something, thought better of it.

"Almost there?"

Kath stood in the open doorway behind the driver's bench.

"Yes, Mistress," Treedle said. "Shall we stop by the Apple Branch first?"

Kath shook her head. "I charged Bone Tapper with letting Master Lokan know we were coming; our beds will be ready tonight. We'll go to the castle first; one common trait of kings is that they don't like waiting."

"Won't you need Bone Tapper?" Marta asked.

"I'd prefer to have him handy, but I don't think taking him to the castle is a good idea."

Marta frowned. "Why not?"

"For the queen's sake. If you were in your sickbed, would you want a carrion raven staring at you?"

"I didn't think of that," Marta said, then quickly changed the subject. "I hope the queen will recover; I'm sure the king is worried about her."

"What makes you think so?"

Marta frowned. She had met King Alian once. It was on her previous trip to Karsan five years before. It seemed a very long time to Marta; surely the king was a very old man by now. "The Queen is much younger than he is, I understand, and very pretty besides. I've heard he dotes on her."

"Her or the need for an heir?" Kath said dryly. "He already has a wife, and if need be could get another. What he lacks is a son."

"That seems rather unfeeling," Marta said.

Her mother smiled, suppressing a yawn. "Well, perhaps. But I did want you to consider possibilities other than the first one that occurs to you. When we get to the castle you can read the king's face and tell me which one you think is true."

*

King Alian was worried, that much was certain, though Marta couldn't tell much more than that. Kath and Marta had gone directly to the Queen's side upon their arrival, though of course King Alian had been notified. He came into the queen's bedchamber soon after, unannounced and unescorted, as Marta could imagine any expectant father might have done. He didn't look quite as old as Marta imagined he would. Oh, she knew he was about forty, and there was gray here and there in his beard and hair, but his step was firm and his manner vigorous.

"How is my Lady?" he asked.

The king rose a bit in Marta's estimation with that. Perhaps it wasn't his real question, but it was the one he'd asked. Kath straightened from where she had been examining the young queen along with Mistress Thornap, the midwife.

"As well as may be expected, Your Majesty. I need more time to be sure of what that means," Kath said. "I'll bring word to you as soon as I know more."

Kath then allowed Mistress Thornap to politely but firmly shoo the anxious man out of the chamber so they could get back to the matter at hand. Marta felt very sorry for the young queen. She didn't look very regal. Rather she looked small and pale and frightened, almost lost in the huge canopied bed, but then Marta guessed she had reason to be frightened.

Kath smiled at her. "The pain comes and goes, Majesty?"

The girl nodded, for she was little more than a girl. Perhaps Marta's age or even less; Marta wasn't sure. She was a dark-haired princess from Junland on the southwestern coast. Not so far from home, but more than far enough from family and friends. She'd brought only two attendants upon her marriage, one being her old nurse who had since died. The other, Lady Dolwyn, was a plain, brown haired, stolid woman who watched Kath and Mistress Thornap alike with equal suspicion.

Marta had liked Mistress Thornap almost instantly upon their first meeting; she was a round, happy sort of person. Or rather she looked as if being happy was her normal state; her face was made for smiling, Marta thought, though in truth Mistress Thornap wasn't smiling now. She conversed in low tones with Marta's mother, with the Lady-in-Waiting hovering on the edge as if a stray word might escape her. Marta tried to pay attention, but despite her best efforts she was getting bored. There was nothing for her to do, and no reason for her to be there so far as Marta could see.

Marta's gaze went to the open window in the round tower that held the Queen's bedchamber. Beyond that she could see Karsan spread out before them, and to the right the road leading through the town and up into the mountain pass that held the Karsanmon Shrine. Marta had been there just once before, but remembered the wonder of being in the mountains, the giddy feeling of looking down on the world. She'd like to do that again; perhaps if there was time on this visit —

"Marta, come here."

Marta looked up. Both her mother and Mistress Thornap were looking at her. There was a twinkle in Mistress Thornap's eye but Black Kath was almost glaring.

"Please pay attention, Daughter, though I know the view is lovely. And close the shutters; we don't want the Queen catching a chill."

"I'm sorry," Marta said, blushing. She hurried to obey and then went over to the bed. "Yes?"

Kath had the bed coverings pulled down; the Queen lay in her shift, shivering slightly, though Marta didn't think it was very cold in the room at all; there was a fire in the grate and the other windows were shut tight. If anything, Marta thought the room was a little warm.

"Forgive me, Majesty, but there's something I want my daughter to examine."

"As you see fit," the Queen said, and tried to smile. Marta smiled too, though guiltily. Examine? Why? Marta had no skills of magic or even the more common but useful knowledge that Mistress Thornap boasted...not that Mistress Thornap ever did any such thing. Marta felt her confusion growing, but tried to keep it from showing on her face. She walked calmly to the beside as if she did this sort of thing every day.

Kath took her daughter's hand and guided until it rested lightly on the queen's very slightly swollen belly, just above her thin hips. Marta didn't claim to know much of the ways of the world, but she was pretty sure that any birth such hips could manage would not be an easy one.

"I want you to keep your hand there for a moment...yes, just there. A light touch as you are doing now. Don't move until I tell you."

Marta nodded, but didn't understand what the point was. She glanced at the queen, who in turn looked curious. Still, Marta think she preferred the queen's curiosity to her fear, and she knew her mother seldom did anything without a reason. Marta took deep, slow breaths. She wanted to at least look as if she knew what she was about, for the queen's sake if nothing else.

"Do you feel that?" Kath asked.

Marta almost panicked. Feel what? She didn't feel anything except... "Oh," she said aloud. She spread her fingers slowly, then moved her hand from side to side over the queen's belly despite her mother's instructions to stay still, but if Kath noticed or minded she didn't say.

Her mother leaned close and whispered to her. "You may not understand what just happened, but that's not important. Keep silent for now."

Marta just nodded. Kath did not ask her what she had felt, or why she was sure it was something other than her own imagination. Marta knew it was not imagination, but a very clear and precise feeling. There was something wrong with the queen. Something...broken. That was the image and word that came to Marta, even though she didn't know just what might be broken or how to mend it. If it could be mended. Even as Marta knew her impression was accurate, she also realized that it was incomplete. Something was broken. Something was missing, as well. Marta had the sinking feeling that she knew what that something was.

"Majesty, you're going to be fine," Kath said.

The Queen looked at her for a moment then turned to her Lady in Waiting. "Lady Dolwyn, help me sit up, please."

Lady Dolwyn pushed past Mistress Thornap and Marta's mother to gently raise the queen to a sitting position, carefully placing the pillows behind her back to support her. The queen winced, once, but kept her expression blank otherwise.

"Thank you," she said, then, "Would you and Mistress Thornap leave me alone for a moment?"

"Majesty, you need your rest..." Lady Dolwyn began, but the queen stopped her.

"Thank you for your concern; I will rest soon, I promise. Please wait outside."

Reluctantly, Lady Dolwyn obeyed. Mistress Thornap followed looking, to Marta's eyes, oddly relieved. Marta started to follow but the queen shook her head. "Lady... I'm sorry, Marta? You may stay as well. I think you know something of what we must discuss."

Marta knew something, but not much. Still, she just bowed slightly to the girl in the bed and kept her mouth shut. The queen turned to Marta's mother.

"Mistress Kath, you know what is wrong. Please tell me."

It wasn't a question, but it wasn't a command, either. To Marta, it sounded almost like a plea. A plea to make things other than they were.

"I think you know as well, Majesty," Kath said. "I said you will recover your health and I believe that to be true. I am seldom wrong."

The queen just looked at her. There were tears in her eyes, whether from the pain or something else, Marta wasn't sure. "My baby?"

Kath nodded. "The child is dead, Majesty, and even I cannot change that. What I do from this point on I do for you alone. I am truly sorry."

The queen closed her eyes, and her small hands balled into fists. "I hoped...I hoped I was wrong. Well then, I've failed. Better I had died." Now she was sobbing openly. Marta wanted to go to her, but her mother was there first. She took the queen's hands in hers and held them there until the queen looked at her.

"Majesty, first quickenings often go awry. There will be others."

The queen managed a weak smile, but quickly turned away. "Thank you. Please leave me now."

Black Kath nodded and, without another word, left the chamber with Marta close behind. Mistress Thornap was nowhere to be seen but Lady Dolwyn, waiting impatiently in the corridor beyond, hurried back in and quickly and firmly shut the heavy chamber door. Marta frowned when she heard the bolt being slid behind them.

"What did she do that for?" Marta whispered.

Kath looked distracted. "Hmm? Oh, that. Lady Dolwyn is just doing what she should be doing now, and that's protecting the queen's privacy. Her Majesty is handling it better than I expected, but still best the king doesn't see her until she's had time to grieve a bit. Alian won't be any use to her in any event until he's had some time to come to his senses again."

Kath was already several steps down the stone corridor and Marta had to hurry to catch up. "Come to his senses? But he doesn't even know yet!" Marta whispered.

"Which is why we're going to tell him. You don't think Mistress Thornap asked him to send for me to heal a dead child, do you?"

Marta just stared at her mother for a moment, and it was clearly all Kath could do to keep from laughing. "No, she's not a magician, if that's what you think, but she has a talent in these matters. She knew, or at least suspected, and arranged it so she wouldn't have to tell the king herself. Since King Alian is the one who sent for me, the cost will fall on him alone. Quite clever, really."

Marta was thoroughly disgusted. "And to think that I liked her! That sweet, smiling face... Damn, I didn't know she was so devious."

"Don't swear, daughter, at least not with so little reason. And don't think too badly of Mistress Thornap. There isn't a bone of harm in her, but she's kept her position at this court for a long time, and in a backwater kingdom like Lythos that's especially hard. Unlike places like Morushe or Wylandia, few positions here besides the higher nobility are hereditary."

The reached the spiral stairway on the outer wall of the tower and started down. Marta still seethed. "So she arranged for you to travel all this way to do her dirty work."

Kath shrugged. "That's one way to look at it. Another is that it was wise of her to reassure both the king and the queen that all that could be done, had been done, considering the result. Don't hold it against her, Marta. In her place, I'd have done the same."

That was as close to a compliment as her mother ever gave, in Marta's recollection. She grudgingly accepted the logic of Mistress Thornap's actions, but she still didn't like them very much. Yet something else came to mind then that rather pushed her annoyance deep into the background. "Mother, what happened in there? How did I know what little I knew?"

"You're on the Arrow Path now, remember? That means that you recognize a manifestation of the Laws when you experience one."

Marta grasped what her mother was saying and felt a rush of excitement. "Which Law?"

Kath shook her head. "I can't tell you that for two reasons: One is that I don't know. There is more than one Law that could have told you. The second, and most important reason, is that telling you what the Law is called won't help you, or I would have named them all already. You can't be taught the Laws, Marta, as I've said more than once. The name of a Law comes last, not first. Be patient."

"I'll try, but it's hard," Marta said. "Are you going to see the king now?"

"We're both going. I don't expect a proper curtsey and he won't either, but do bow when you're introduced. Otherwise I again suggest you keep silent unless an answer is needed. This may be delicate."

Marta didn't know much about kings or queens either, for that matter, but she rather thought her mother was right about that. As glad as she was to be included she was worried, too. She hoped she wouldn't have to speak at all.

The king's private chambers were on a lower floor of the castle, below the towers. Kath spoke briefly to one of the guards on station outside, who disappeared through the door and returned almost as quickly. "His Majesty will see you."

As if there was any doubt, Marta thought, but she kept the thought to herself. She followed her mother inside.

The king's chamber wasn't quite what Marta had expected. It reminded Marta of her mother's kitchen. Not that there were pots and pans and an iron spit in the fireplace, but it was clearly a work space, just as her mother's kitchen was. It was always at the table there that Kath worked on her accounts, and wrote in her big ledger book. There were ledgers here, too, and a massive table to hold them. Neither the heraldic tapestries nor the weapons displayed on every wall did anything to hide the room's main purpose. Across the table from the king were other open books, and parchment and writing tools, and two chairs now empty. Marta didn't need the sound of a closing door across the room to tell her that Alian had only just dismissed a pair of clerks so he could grant the private audience her mother had requested.

King Alian looked up from his books. "Mistress Kath." He didn't say anything else.

"My daughter, Marta, Your Majesty. I believe you've met her before."

Marta bowed awkwardly and the king nodded at her. "Of course. I remember you; you've grown up well."

Marta found herself blushing despite her best intentions. She stammered a thank you, since it seemed rude not to, but the king had already shifted his attention back to her mother.

"That is a very grave face you're wearing, Mistress Kath."

"The child is dead, Majesty," Kath said.

So much for delicacy, Marta thought, frowning, but she kept silent, and watched, and listened.

The king sat back in his chair, almost as if someone had pushed him. "Blunt and to the point, as usual," the king said finally.

"A quick, clean wound heals fastest, in my experience," Kath replied.

"Yes, of course you're right. And since we're alone it's not indelicate to be told the truth," Alian said. "I would ask if you are certain, but that would be foolish, wouldn't it?" Her mother didn't say anything, and it was plain King

Alian hadn't really expected an answer. "Perhaps if Mistress Thornap had been quicker..."

"It's tragedy enough, Majesty. Blame will not make it better."

"It would make *me* feel better," Alian said. "And I am the king."

"You will still be king tomorrow and the day after, and your queen may yet bear you children. You will need Mistress Thornap then."

The king grunted. "Tell me, Black Kath of Lythos--do you ever tire of being right?"

"Every day. This one has been particularly grueling."

Alian rubbed his eyes. "I must go see her. Forgive my haste, but please name your fee."

"Nothing."

King Alian had started to rise, but at that he sat back down. "Mistress, I'm in no mood for riddles."

"Neither am I," Kath said. "There was nothing I could do save confirm what all suspected...including yourself, unless I am very much mistaken. Else you'd have been even more upset than I judge you to be. Still, I have worked no Power on your behalf. Yet."

Alian frowned. Marta could see the lines on his face then, and that sense of age that had been missing when she'd first seen him in the queen's rooms. "Mistress, you haven't told me the worst, have you?"

Kath shook her head. "Majesty, the queen's womb should have expelled the unfortunate infant on its own by now. It has not. If that does not happen soon the corruption of the dead child's flesh will spread to your lady. She will die."

The king didn't say anything for several long moments. "Now we come to the real transaction and the real price. You can correct this, I know. How soon?"

"As soon as possible, though I would have the Queen rest for a little while first. This will not be easy for her."

"I will want to see her first."

Kath shrugged. "I think Lady Dolwyn can be persuaded."

The king smiled then, very faintly. "Please wait and rest here, Mistress. My guards will bring you anything you require."

"I need nothing save some water and the use of your chair. Your queen will require brandy wine, and as much as she can drink. So. Aren't you going to ask my price?" Kath said.

The king hesitated. "I think I must."

"Five hundred in gold."

Marta almost gasped. The king did gasp, and his face turned bright red. "Mistress Kath, have you taken leave of your senses?!"

"Your Majesty, my senses are among the few things I have not taken my leave of in the last few years. I am well aware how high the price is. I know that the queens's own bride price could not have been so high. I know what I am asking, and I am sorry. The one doesn't change the other."

Marta finally realized where the 'delicacy' her mother mentioned came into play. Marta had the distinct feeling that King Alian was a hair's-breadth from calling for an axeman and a good stout wooden block.

"Your services have always been dear, Mistress. Even a king should not trade with you without need, and Lythos is not a rich kingdom. This is the income of at least an earldom for a year!"

"You have one or two still vacant, as I recall. You can manage."

"Mistress, that is not the point—"

"Your pardon, Majesty, but it is precisely the point. For my own part I would help your lady for nothing, and gladly. The price is not up to me; I always know what it will be, but I do not set it. I am of the Arrow Path, and this is how it must be. All I can say, Majesty, is that you must ask yourself if your lady's life and the future heirs she will bear are worth the cost."

The king frowned. "What about catweed? I understand it can be useful in some...predicaments."

"True, Majesty, but it works by poisoning the mother a little and the child she carries a lot. Since the child is already dead I doubt it would serve, nor is your wife strong enough to risk it in any case. Killing her outright would be more honest."

Marta had seen no king other than Alian, and she had certainly never seen a king engulfed in stone cold fury. She wanted to change herself into something very small, if only she had the skill, and disappear into a crack in the wall. Yet she watched her small, frail mother bear the fury of the king's glare without flinching and Marta felt ashamed.

"Mistress Kath, I warn you—"

"Forgive me, Majesty. I have this bad habit of saying what I think. Yet I realize I am your subject and you have the right to compel me to your service at any time. Yet the price will be paid, one way or another. I have no more say in the matter than you do."

"I don't understand that part of it all," the king said. "Yet people who know far more of the matter and in whom I have trust say this is so. That is the only reason I haven't called my guards. The notion tempts me still, Black Kath."

"Your counselors speak the truth. You can believe me as well so far as this: I wish it were otherwise. I know the King's problems are great, and I do not wish to add to them any more than I presume to judge them."

The king said nothing, did nothing for several long moments, time that, to Marta, felt as close to eternity as she ever wished to judge.

"You've said the queen may conceive again. If you speak truly, then Mistress Thornap may need me to summon you again. My resources are not limitless, Mistress. Do you see my problem?"

"I do," Kath conceded. "Is there a solution?"

"That's up to you... or the one you serve." Alian looked grim. "If you agree now as part of the price to be present and aid at the queen's next confinement, I will grant you the income of all rents from the Earldom of Lutnal for two years. I think you'll find that comes to somewhat more than you're asking now. I'm not sure how I'll manage short of new taxes, but I will do what I must. What say you?"

Now it was Kath's turn to be silent. She closed her eyes, and after a bit Marta thought that perhaps she had gone to sleep, but finally she opened her eyes again, and there was a strange expression in them that worried Marta. Her mother only nodded. "It is acceptable, Majesty."

If the king was relieved he didn't show it. Or much of anything. "I'm going to see my lady now," he said coldly. "Please wait here."

"As you wish," Kath said, but Alian wasn't listening. He was already striding fast toward the door, as if he could not wait to get away from Kath and anything to do with her. He slammed it behind him.

"Well," said Marta.

"Well, what?" Black Kath was already on her way to the chair King Alian had vacated.

"Five hundred?" Marta was having trouble imagining the sum. She could count that high, easily enough. She had seen the number written down before, recognized its shape and form, the sound it made it her head when she spoke it. Yet she tried to picture it as five hundred medallions of gold and felt a little dizzy.

Kath lowered herself into the king's chair. "You weren't the one who had to tell him," Kath said. "I was afraid he wouldn't pay; a new queen would be cheaper. Old Junland has more daughters than a dog has fleas. Alian still might take that door, I suppose. The queen could slip away quietly while he is alone with her."

"Mother!"

Kath yawned again. "I didn't create this world, daughter. I do try to understand how it works."

"I can't believe the king would do that," Marta said, though no sooner had she said the words she pictured Alian smothering his child bride with a feather pillow. She shivered. "I hope he won't do that..."

Kath smiled, faintly. "If he does, I've misjudged the man."

"What if he had refused?"

Kath looked unhappy. "The truth? I'd have saved the poor girl anyway," Kath said. "And in so doing, been liable for the price myself and thus increased the Debt I would have passed down to you. That act of charity would have harmed my own daughter, and yet I would have done it. I'm sorry."

Marta shook her head. "Don't be. I'd do the same, if I were in your place. I wasn't sure it was possible, though."

Kath smiled then. "It's one of Amaet's cruel jokes. You can use Power on your own behalf however you wish. Any use of Power to help another brings a high cost, in some form. You'll find that a conscience is an inconvenient burden along the Arrow Path. Yet it persists…in some people."

Marta was still having trouble at the thought of all that money. "What are we going to do with five hundred pieces of gold?"

"Oh, that? Nothing. I didn't tell the king, but most of the price is to be paid to the Karsanmon Shrine, where doubtless Maleet will commission an even gaudier statue. You'll find that most of the time the bulk of a payment in gold will go directly to one of Amaet's shrines, somewhere. And before you ask: no, this was not my decision, any more than the amount was. One virtue of the Arrow Path is that you always know what a use of Power on another's behalf will cost. Don't worry about it now."

Marta tried not to worry, but she couldn't help thinking about it. The more she understood about the Arrow Path, the more Marta wondered if it was such a good bargain. Even so, she asked herself if she would have chosen differently, knowing what she did now, and the answer came to her in the image of the flames in her mother's fireplace, dancing their pavane for her alone.

Despite his anger King Alian didn't forget the water; a guard brought a tin pitcher of cool well water and two cups. Marta poured for her mother. It didn't seem very long at all until the summons came. Marta followed her mother as she walked slowly back up the staircase to the queen's chamber.

The king, Mistress Thornap, and Lady Dolwyn were already there, of course. Kath whispered something to the king who nodded, curtly, and slipped out the door after kissing his queen once on the forehead.

The queen's eyes were red and puffy; she'd clearly been crying but she wasn't crying now. Rather, the queen seemed to be trying to remember the words to some old Junland nursery rhyme; she sang the words in a high lilting voice, just a bit slurred.

"Clever is my darlin' o, carving shells for a cameo,
Knock three times and enter o, quickly does my garden grow…."

The queen frowned. "Doly, love, is that how it goes? I con' remember."

"Perfect, my girl," said Lady Dolwyn, as she poured out another cup of the dark red brandywine.

The queen sighed and leaned over and whispered conspiratorially to Marta as she and her mother approached the bed. "'s really about getting a baby. They thought we didn't know. Garden growing. We knew what that meant." She giggled.

Marta tried not to laugh. It was hard at first, but then she remembered why they were all there. After that, it was easy. Marta glanced at the half emptied bottle on the tray and hoped the queen had drank enough.

Kath whispered something to Mistress Thornap, who nodded once and hurried from the room. Kath looked at Marta. "Help me turn the covers back down."

The queen protested. "'s cold."

"Just for a few moments, Majesty," Kath promised.

The queen emptied the dregs from her cup and put it aside. Lady Dolwyn started to fill it again, but the queen shook her head. "'No more, please, Doly. Stuff makes me dizzy."

"One more, my girl," Lady Dolwyn said.

"I'm your Queen!" said the girl crossly.

Lady Dolwyn didn't even blink. "That too, and still my precious girl, Mysona. Now drink up."

Marta now knew the queen's name, Mysona, and it seemed as if that knowledge brought Marta a little farther from the Queen of Lythos and a little closer to the frightened girl in the bed. Marta realized that Lady Dolwyn had been seeing that girl all along.

"Very well, but if I stain these sheets 's not my fault," the queen said. She took the cup and sipped, made a face. "Doly, I con'. No more. Please?"

Lady Dolwyn took the cup away. "All right then." She glanced at Marta's mother. There was a question in her eyes. Just then Mistress Thornap returned, bearing bundles of cloth that looked like swaddling, and a plain stout covered basket. Kath nodded.

"I'm ready. Lady Dolwyn, hold her hands..rather, let her hold yours."

"Take my hand, Mysona," Lady Dolwyn said. The queen reached up and Lady Dolwyn enveloped the girl's small right hand in both of hers.

"Marta, help on the other side," Kath said.

Marta hurried to the far side of the bed and took the girl's left hand. The queen's grip was surprisingly strong.

"Your Majesty, grip as hard as you want. They'll just have to bear it," Kath said. She turned to Mistress Thornap. "Be ready."

The queen suddenly looked around. "Where's the king? Where's Alian? He should be here!"

No one said anything for a moment, then Kath looked at her. "I sent him away, Majesty. I can bring him back if you wish. Do you really want him to see this?"

The queen finally shook her head. "I want him here...I don't want him to see." She thought of something. "We could blindfold him."

"Your Lord would look silly in a blindfold," Lady Dolwyn said, smiling.

"I know," said the queen, and she grinned wickedly. "Very silly..." She yawned then. "'m tired."

Kath placed both hands on the girl's belly. She took a long, slow breath. Marta knew something was coming, but she knew better than to listen for chants or look for flashes of light and thunder. It was always thus in an invocation of true Power: touch? Sometimes but not always. Touch would be the case here. Focus? Always. Concentration. Intent. Then the thing was done and the consequences, whatever they were, quickly followed. There were always consequences.

"What was that song you were singing, Majesty? You have a lovely voice," Kath said.

"'Clever Darling,'" the queen said. "I con' remember it all."

"Please sing what you know," Kath said.

The queen started the song again, but she hadn't gotten past the first line before her eyes went wide and her face as white as the sheets she lay on. She opened her mouth to scream but just as quickly whatever had struck her seemed to pass. Slowly, the color began to return to her face, but she was still very pale. Her mouth worked slowly up and down, but no words came out. Two great spasms passed through her body and Marta's hand began to ache where the queen gripped it. Mistress Thornap came forward with her baskets and her winding cloth and in another few moments all was done.

"My garden..." the queen said, and that was all. Her head fell back on the pillow and her eyes closed. Lady Dolwyn's face turned almost as white as the queen's and she started to throw herself on the still form, but Kath grabbed her firmly by the shoulders.

"Stop that! She's only sleeping. See?"

In a moment Marta, too, could see the slow rise and fall of the queen's chest even as her grip lessened. Marta lowered the queen's hand carefully. Lady Dolwyn was weeping and Kath shook her gently. "The bleeding has already stopped. She'll need to be bathed and her nightclothes changed. Do it gently and she'll sleep through all."

Marta and Kath followed Mistress Thornap out, and again Marta heard the bolt being slid, but she took it as nothing amiss this time. Kath spoke to Mistress Thornap for a little while, but Marta and her mother left the castle as soon as they could politely do so. They joined Treedle and Bone Tapper at the Apple Branch Tavern that evening. Master Lokan the almost insufferably jolly innkeeper had their rooms prepared and supper ready.

"My, how your little girl has grown!" he said, beaming at Marta, who found herself blushing at the attention.

"Like a weed," Kath said dryly. "Is it well with you, Master Lokan?"

"Quite passable. And yourself?" He asked the question as if he really did want to know. Marta had the strange feeling that he was more interested than perhaps he should have been, but couldn't say why. Kath, for her part, just shrugged.

"I yet live."

Master Lokan nodded, his smile never wavering all the time they were there. Marta couldn't say why, but she was a little relieved when they left the inn early the next morning for the trip home.

Treedle was a little surprised. "No visit to the archives this time, Mistress? Brother Akaen will be disappointed."

Her mother merely said, "I think I should spare the king the sight of me for a little while. He has more important concerns."

Marta, remembering the king's anger, wasn't surprised at all.

CHAPTER 3

"Hard as it may be, try not to be afraid. Frightened people do stupid things."
— Black Kath's Tally Book

By the end of March word had come that the queen was with child again. Marta would have said a prayer for her, but somehow the idea of praying to Amaet or any other Power made Marta extremely uneasy. She settled for wishing the queen well.

The months made their slow, stately progression through spring and into summer and then into fall. Marta, despite the Arrow Path, wouldn't have said that this summer and fall was any different from the last, nor the spring. Nothing happened. After her brush with a Law of Power at Karsan, Marta fully expected something—anything—to happen. That 'something' stubbornly refused, and continued to refuse until the summer days ended and the nights were getting colder again. Marta, frustrated, asked her mother about it as Kath made an entry in her ledger which, as usual, was spread out on the kitchen table. Kath just shrugged.

"That's all? Nothing to say?"

"What would you have me say, Marta?"

Marta thought about it. "I don't know... I've been on the Arrow Path for almost a year! I mean, well, how long did it take you to find the Laws?"

"Years," Kath said. "It never occurred to me to count them."

"But was it years until you found the First Law?"

"Oh, that. Don't fret, Marta, because it's not worth fretting about. Even those on the same path don't necessarily take the same steps. You'll find what you're seeking; there's no avoiding it. But if you think it'll help, I will tell you where I found the First Law."

Kath described a cave less than a mile from her home. Marta was a little surprised. She knew that hill where the cave was and she knew the cave, too. She had never dared to go too deeply inside it, but she had played near the entrance and just inside the cave many times.

"The First Law is there?" Marta asked eagerly.

"I said I found it there, which isn't the same thing at all. You may find it somewhere else. In fact, I wish you would. It's a dangerous place."

It seemed a strange thing to tell Marta about the possibility and then as quickly warn her away. Marta started to question her mother further about, but Treedle interrupted. "A messenger from the king, Mistress."

Marta knew who had come. She knew it the instant Treedle announced his presence. She didn't know if that was important. Maybe she was merely quick to expect what she did not want, and this time the fears were justified. Treedle brought the messenger in as Kath directed, and Marta nodded.

It's him.

The young man from before. The same intent stare, the arrogant manner, the way he looked at her and, Marta realized, at her mother, were all just as she remembered. Marta had an impulse to step between her mother and the messenger and strike the young man, preferably with something heavy. Kath, for her part, didn't seem disturbed in the least.

"The queen?" she asked, and the young man nodded.

"Mistress Thornap believes her confinement is near," he said. "I was told you would understand."

"Indeed I do. Are you to return with me or shall I follow?"

"You may follow as quickly as possible," he said. "I'll take word that you are coming."

She may? How sodding considerate, Marta thought, but if Kath was offended by the man's tone she didn't show it.

"Well then. Be it so."

The news of the Queen's new pregnancy hadn't been a surprise when it had come, but Marta had known the silence that followed since would not last. The messenger—any messenger—had been expected. Marta felt a chill, nonetheless. She was very relieved that this particular one would not be accompanying them. She watched him leave.

"I don't like him," she said. "No matter, he's gone. We leave in the morning?"

Kath shook her head. "No. Treedle, Bone Tapper, and I will be leaving in the morning. You're staying home."

Marta argued, of course, but didn't get very far. The next morning she was out in the chill helping her mother get ready to leave.

"The babe is impatient, unless I've miscounted the days," Kath said. She looked thoughtful. "Not that I blame him. Too much to be done and life is short. Best he gets to it."

"So the king's child will be a boy, then?" Marta asked, as she helped Treedle pull her mother's travel cart out of its shed.

"If it lives. Few things are certain and that one thing almost least of all."

Marta saw to the harness while Treedle, patient as stone, went to fetch the horse. He came back leading a very unhappy beast, with its ears flattened and eyes rolling. Steam blew from its nostrils, despite the fact that the morning was fairly warm.

"Yssara doesn't appear to be in a good mood," Marta said.

"He never is," Treedle muttered darkly, "though I'll admit he's worse than usual."

"It's not time yet," Kath said. "No matter what you think."

Marta frowned. "Time? Time for what?"

Her mother didn't answer, and after a moment Marta realized that she hadn't been speaking to either of them. She was talking to the horse, who apparently understood. It immediately subsided, looking sullen but resigned. Marta slipped the harness over its head and down on its shoulders while Treedle quickly fastened the buckles.

Black Kath frowned. "I forgot to make a note about that..."

This time Marta didn't ask; since her mother was clearly speaking to herself and no one else. Kath got off the stump she'd been resting on and made her way back to the house. When Kath returned, Bone Tapper was riding her shoulder. Treedle helped her climb up onto the bench before he went to the other side and clambered up to the driver's side.

"I should go with you," Marta said.

"Yes," Kath agreed. "In fact, I'd prefer it if you were going. But you can't. I've left a list of things to be done while I'm gone and, since you're the only one who can do them, I don't see a good alternative, do you?"

Marta started to suggest leaving those things, whatever they might be, undone until they returned, that they could not be so very important as this. She saw the expression on her mother's face and decided against it.

She's just waiting for that one.

"Yes, Mother," was all she said.

Treedle shook the reins, once, and Yssara started off instantly at a brisk walk. Marta wasn't sure, but as the cart pulled away she thought she saw her mother smile. Marta sighed and went back into the house, looking for the chores list. She found that list on the table, pinned to the top of her mother's big old accounts ledger by a small plate of bread and cheese.

"'Eat something now and then. Pick the apples if you want cider this winter. Read this book,'" was all her mother's note said.

That afternoon in the orchard a cool breeze was blowing, chilling the sweat on Marta's brow as she reached up into the branches. She shivered. Funny how, with great mysteries to be solved, and important matters to attend, the apples still have to be picked.

She reached for another apple, perfectly ripe by the look of it, and hesitated. A thought came unbidden, as they almost always do, but this one told Marta something she hadn't known before. It's about to fall.

Marta blinked, and in that space of time the apple did, indeed, fall. She had enough presence of mind to open her hand and grab it before it could hit the ground and bruise itself. She held it in her hands for several long moments, wondering. "How did I know that?" she said aloud.

She hadn't guessed the apple was about to fall; anyone who knew a ripe apple from a green one could have said as much. No, this was different. She knew. But how?

Marta froze in place, listening. There was a jingling sound on the breeze, something out of place in the normal background of creaking branches and rustling leaves that marked the apple orchard. Marta kept very still, wondering for a moment and then rejecting the notion that she'd made the sound herself. She wasn't wearing any jewelry except for the pendant her mother gave her back when she first joined the Arrow Path, and that was safely tucked under her jerkin. After a moment Marta heard the sound again, closer, but with a definite direction attached to it.

I can't let him see me.

Another certainty, and just as unbidden. In one corner of her mind Marta realized that what was happening to her now was important in ways she couldn't even begin to understand, but mostly she was thinking about the best place to hide. From whom? She didn't know, but that didn't seem important just then.

Marta very carefully set her bag of apples near the base of the tree where they would be less conspicuous, then jumped up to catch the lowest branch and pull herself up. The tree wasn't especially large, but the leaves were thick and would make good cover, especially if whoever was nearby didn't think to look up. Marta moved quickly and carefully as high up as she thought prudent, and then kept very still.

The jingling sound, closer now, was easily identifiable as a horse's bridle. She could hear the clopping sound of the beast's hooves just at the edge of the orchard, but she still couldn't see who it was. Marta tried to peer around a clump of leaves and reached for a branch to steady herself. Three things happened in quick and precise order: The first was that instant flash of knowing, or rather of recognition, that the branch Marta reached for was not sound. The second thing that happened was that the branch broke. The third thing was Marta fell out of the tree.

Yet even as she fell, Marta was thinking primarily of the first happening. It was important. She didn't know why, but she didn't question her certainty in the least. Then Marta hit the ground, and for a while didn't think about or question much of anything.

When Marta's vision slowly passed from darkness to glaring light again she found herself lying on her back on the ground under the apple tree, staring up into the face of the handsome young messenger from the day before. At least, Marta thought he was handsome. She didn't have much to compare him to, so she wasn't entirely sure. She did know that she had detested him at both first and second sight and her present situation hadn't done much to endear him.

"I suppose you meant to do that?" he asked.

Marta glared. "Of course I didn't mean to, you fool!"

He grinned. It was an extremely unpleasant expression, to Marta's way of thinking. "I'm a fool? I'm not the one tumbling out of trees like a drunken squirrel."

Marta started to get up, felt dizzy, sat back down. The 'drunken squirrel' remark cut a little closer to home than she would have liked to admit. She managed to glare at him. "What are you doing here? You delivered your message and my mother obeyed."

"She forgot something. She sent me back to fetch it."

Marta wasn't impressed. It wasn't even a very convincing lie, as lies went. Perhaps if she hadn't still been a little woozy from her fall Marta might have made more of an effort to pretend otherwise, but just then it was too much trouble. "No she didn't. She'd have sent her own messenger."

She tried to sit up again and this time she made it, with the man's hand on her shoulder to steady her. She tried to brush it away but he merely tightened his grip, making Marta wince. "You're hurting me!"

"That was your choice, since your honesty has left me no other. Get up." He didn't wait for an answer; he just grabbed her by the arm and pulled her upright. Marta was so dizzy she almost fell down again, but she was determined not to let that happen. She didn't fight his grip; she used it to steady herself until the world stopped spinning quite so much.

"Where are they?" he asked.

Marta blinked. "What are you talking about? What do you want?"

He sighed, affecting a slight air of affront. "What indeed? If your mother was a jeweler, I would be asking about jewels and gold, would I not? For a brewer, ale and beer. Your mother is a witch. I suppose you are too. So what am I asking for? Think carefully and the mystery will be revealed."

"I have, and it isn't. You've been rude and I no more care for that than my mother will when she finds out. Speak plainly."

He stepped back a bit as if to get a better look at her, though he was careful not loosen his grip. "Oh, I'm sorry, I clearly didn't understand. You're simple, aren't you?"

Marta just stared at him, stunned into silence. He apparently took that silence for assent. "Well then, I will speak plainly. First, what your mother discovers or doesn't is of no concern to me... or rather, soon won't be. Second, since it's not obvious what I want, I shall tell you: I want your mother's books."

Marta frowned. "Books? You mean the one she uses for accounts? There's nothing else but a few histories." It was true that her mother loved to read and used her trips to Karsan to visit the Royal Archives whenever time allowed—not often—but she had few books of her own. Besides the expense and the space they took up, they were too distracting, her mother said. For all that, she had made certain Marta had her letters and numbers, and could even read old Lyrsan, with difficulty.

"Accounts....!" the man looked to heaven. "I mean her books of magic, you dolt!"

Marta blinked. "There aren't any."

Now it was the would be thief who was speechless, but only for a moment. "Girl, don't lie to me!"

"But...It's the truth. Why would I lie about it?"

"You'd lie to keep me from finding the books, of course. Good thing I'm not so simple as you are, so I don't believe you."

Marta found her anger again. "I'm not simple, and what you believe is between you and the Powers. I've told you..."

The man sighed and pulled a dagger from his belt. This he held to Marta's throat. "Do not trifle with me. I'm taking a considerable risk here, I know what I want, and you're going to give it to me. Now, then: Do we understand one other?"

Marta took a deep breath, let it out. "I understand perfectly. Yet I can't give you what doesn't exist."

He looked grim. "Shall we see now just what does exist? Take me to your mother's rooms."

The thought of being alone inside the house with this lunatic wasn't especially appealing to Marta, but she couldn't think it would be much worse than being in the orchard with him now. Besides, the point of his dagger, now pressed to the small of her back, was very persuasive.

Marta knew her life was in danger, but that wasn't the worst. She also knew beyond question that the young man was even more afraid than she was. This did not make her feel any better. Quite the opposite. Black Kath had taught her long ago that people who are afraid are capable of nearly any stupidity. Marta barely needed the lesson; she had seen as much in herself.

If he's so afraid, why is he doing this?

She hoped she could get at the answer before his fear caused him to do something horrid. She knew it was only a matter of time before that happened.

"I'll take you there," she said and the man nodded, for the moment, content.

His name was Laras. He got around to telling her that somewhere during the search. "Not that it matters, you understand, but you probably should know. You have the right, I think."

There was so much there, said and unsaid, that made Marta's fear grow like a strangling vine. It was only a matter of time, she realized, before she did something crazy and stupid herself.

If that happens, I'm lost, she thought to herself, knowing it for simple truth. Marta tried to think. She couldn't give Laras what he wanted because it didn't exist. Could he be made to understand? A man with so much invested in an idea would be loathe to give it up, yet she had to try. "Why do you think the source of my mother's power is a book?"

He just looked at her, in that condescending way he had when he clearly thought she was being simple. "The priests of Amatok recite their liturgies from a book. The King's household accounts are in books. All the wisdom of the ages is contained in books, or so the clerks say. Your mother knows spells, incantations, charms...she can turn people into animals! You can't tell me that such things don't take great care and preparation and formulas impossible to remember." Laras stopped riffling in her mother's linen chest and pulled Marta closer. "There has to be a book. Where is it?"

Marta finally understood. *Maybe I'm as simple as he thinks.* "Oh. You want my mother's power."

"Of course."

Marta blinked. "But why?"

He just stared at her for several long moments, and Marta couldn't help but blush. She knew what she'd said sounded foolish, but with what she had seen of the burden her mother bore it was hard to imagine anyone not driven, as she herself was, to take the Arrow Path to choose it blindly. She was certain that this was exactly what Laras was doing. "I mean, you can't understand what you are asking!"

Laras drew himself up to his full height, towering over Marta. "Not understand? It's you who do not understand. I'm a messenger, girl. A servant, and if things are left to their normal course that's all I'll ever be. Yet I see the ability to shape the world all around me. I've seen what it can do. Political power. Magic. The King gains his power from his birth, your mother from her knowledge. I can't change my birth, but I can learn. I will learn, and I need that book. I knew your mother would be away and I made my choice."

"You need to make a different choice. You need to learn. There are many fine things in a book but what you want to know isn't there."

"Girl--"

"Marta."

"Marta, I'm not a fool, so don't play me for one. If magic was a simple matter you'd have turned me into some small crawling thing and stepped on me out in the orchard."

"That's not the way it works," Marta said.

Laras fingered his dagger. "Very well, then. Tell me how it works, and then I won't believe you and we can proceed without wasting any more time on your nonsense."

"What you're really seeking are the Seven Laws of Power. They are the beginning of mastery; once you have those there's no need for a book, except an accounts ledger. That's what my mother has, as I told you."

"An accounts ledger? Pray, how does one work magic with a tally book?"

Marta glared at him. "You don't, of course. What you do is keep track of what you are owed. Magic costs. When you work magic on behalf of someone else, that person owes a debt. Debts are very powerful; for all I know that's one of the Seven Laws. I-I don't understand it fully myself, but I've seen how it works. If someone comes to my mother for help, she gives it. But the service must be paid for, even if it is a dear friend. Even if it is a king. If the price is beyond their ability to pay, my mother takes payment in kind."

Laras shook his head. "It all sounds very practical; there's something appealing in that. Yet what has that got to do with turning men into animals?"

"Everything," Marta said. "My mother accepts service where it's needed most. Bone Tapper is a crow because mother's eyes are weak and she needs someone to see for her. What better than eyes with wings? Then there's her cart horse—"

"   Enough! Are you saying that it is only the debt that gives her the power to transform?"

"She has to have permission, in a way, from the person transformed. The debt gives that assent. I'd tell you how that links to the Seven Laws but I am not my mother and there's much I do not yet understand. You may believe me or not, but I'm telling you the truth."

Laras just looked at her for several long moments. He finally sighed, deeply. "I believe you."

Now it was Marta's turn to stare. "You do?"

Laras looked at her pityingly. "Of course I do! Even the King's finest bard couldn't have made up such a ridiculously unlikely tale on the spur of the moment. You're certainly not that clever. Damn."

"   I'm sorry, Laras." To her own surprise, Marta realized she did mean it. She understood what it was to be disappointed.

"As am I." Laras didn't release his grip on her arm. If anything it was tighter than before.

Marta read his intention. There was a hollow, sinking feeling in the pit of her stomach. "You intend to kill me, don't you?"

"Yes."

Marta struggled to keep her voice calm, if nothing else. "May I ask why? I'd have given you what you wanted if it was mine to give. If it existed. Would you have killed me then?"

Laras looked insulted. "I'm not a monster, Marta, whatever you think of me. If I had the books I could have fled far away. Perhaps taken a job in a stable or something, at least long enough to learn what I needed to know to guard against your mother's revenge. What choice do I have now? A king's messenger is not so grand a thing, but it's far more than I had. If I lose it I lose everything, yet if I stay now...well, we both know what would happen."

"Suppose I don't tell her about you?"

"Suppose I believed you there, too? I'm not such a fool as that, Marta. I knew what a risk I took coming here. I'm not going to take another for no gain. If it helps, tally that in your book."

Marta's mind raced. "Wait...there is no book. That doesn't mean there is no power."

"Don't waste what little breath you have left, Marta. We both know you'd say anything to save your life."

"Of course I would. Even the truth. The Seven Laws of Power."

Laras hesitated. Then, reluctantly, he spoke again. "I'm listening."

"The Seven Laws of Power will give you what you want, and their nature is that, once you learn the first, the others will come. For all I know it's the only way witches and sorcerers gain their power. I just started what my mother calls 'the Arrow Path' yesterday, but I know where to go to find the First Law. If you have that you can start over anywhere, and it won't matter if I tell tales on you."

"So why haven't you done so already?"

Marta looked grim. "Because my mother told me to harvest the apples first. You don't argue with Black Kath of Lythos, even if you're her daughter. Maybe especially if you're her daughter."

Laras frowned. "Not to rain on the flame or anything, but how do you know I won't kill you anyway? That way I'd have the First Law and the leisure of my position to find the rest."

"You said you weren't a monster, and only you know if you're telling the truth. I have to gamble that you are."

Laras smiled then. "Lead on."

For all his jovial appearance, Laras wasn't taking any chances. He took a length of stout rope from his saddle and tied it securely around Marta's waist, knotting it at her back so it would be difficult for her to reach. Marta felt like a dog on a leash.

Laras put one more loop on the final knot. "How far is this cave you're talking about?"

"About a mile. Well concealed, though," Marta added hastily. "You'll never find it without me."

"Assuming I'm willing to tramp these woods for days looking? Not likely. Let's go."

Marta knew that Laras didn't entirely believe her, yet his need forced him to take the chance. And it wasn't entirely a lie. Black Kath had discovered the First Law of Power in that very cave, or so she had said. Yet Marta had been to the cave herself many times looking for the First Law, ever since she was old enough to know that the Seven Laws existed. If the First Law was to be found there so far Marta had entirely failed to do so. This would be her last chance.

What reason do I have to think this time will be different?

ALL YOU HAVE TO DO IS DECIDE.

Black Kath's voice. A memory from the day before. Marta felt the pendant representing the Arrow Path next to her skin. She'd almost forgotten about it.

I have decided, Mother. I hope that's enough.

Marta made and discarded a dozen wild schemes as they walked, Laras over a score paces behind her, she leading the way at the end of his taut leash. Laras was half a head taller than she was and twice as heavy; she couldn't overpower him and, with the rope tied around her, she couldn't run. Marta reached behind her, touched the knot. Laras pulled once on the rope, jerking Marta painfully.

"Don't," he said.

Marta didn't know why she'd done it in the first place. She knew she couldn't untie it with him watching her. For that matter, Marta wasn't sure she could untie it at all. And yet why, for just a moment, had she seen an image of the ropes parting easily, almost as if cut?

For that matter, how did I know that apple was going to fall, and that branch to break?

Perhaps she was imagining about the rope, but she was sure that wasn't the case for either of the other two. She was as sure of both as she was of her own name. It was important, and no mistake. But what did it mean? She looked for the pattern as she walked, all the while not even certain if there was one to be found, or if it would matter if there was. They would be at the cave soon, and when Laras didn't find what he was looking for, he would kill her and that would be that. Laras's fear would make him into a monster after all.

"Apples ripen and fall. It's their nature," she said aloud.

Laras frowned. "What?"

Marta ignored him. There was no time. She was on the trail of something, perhaps something important. "So do apple branches, eventually. All living things grow old, lose their strength, grow weak..."

"True enough," Laras said. "Your point is?"

Marta didn't know. She found what seemed an insurmountable obstacle, like a rock fall blocking her path. Something that didn't seem to fit. "Ropes aren't living things."

Laras sighed deeply. "Marta, I'll thank you not to go mad with fear before we reach the cave."

Marta wasn't mad or even, at the moment, afraid. Her thoughts proceeded with the clarity of well polished crystal. Ropes were not alive and yet they still aged, grew weak, developed imperfections. Eventually a rope would fail, even though that was not what it was designed to do.

"Strength always yields to time..."

Laras just shook his head in disgust, but Marta wasn't looking at him. It was as if he no longer mattered. She could think only of what she had just said, knowing it was true enough but also knowing that it wasn't the answer. Close. Very close, like a name known in childhood or the words to a song she could almost but not quite recall.

Time was the problem. Or rather, it wasn't the answer. Something else was, a word she had spoken but now couldn't name. "It isn't Time," she said, finally.

"I disagree," Laras said. "This would appear to be your cave."

Marta had been so deep in her own thoughts that she'd quite forgotten about the cave, though apparently she had led Laras straight to it. It was nestled in the bottom of a high, wooded hill, looking no more than a darker patch of shadow until one was quite close. The opening was no more than five feet across, though it widened considerably further in. No stream flowed from it; this was merely a break in the rocks where part of the roof had reached close enough to the surface for a small cave in to create an opening.

Laras surveyed that opening with satisfaction. "Well, at least I know you were telling the truth to this point. Now you will show me where the First Law of Power can be found and you'd better not be lying about that."

"Of-of course," Marta said, and tried to sound like she meant it.

Yet she didn't. Marta was lying. She didn't know where the First Law of Power was, or what it was. Just because her mother had found the First Law here didn't mean that Marta would; she knew enough to know that it just didn't work that way. She was close to it; she felt it. She could almost taste it, but still she could not name it.

Damn, I'm out of time.

Marta already knew that time wasn't the answer. Time destroyed power? Yes...and no. Apples fell. Branches broke. Ropes rotted. Power ended. Was it just time? Did time alter the sun, wear down the seasons? Perhaps, but she knew the answer was not time...necessarily. What was it? Marta walked very slowly toward the entrance, with Laras following at rope's length. She put up her hand to brace against the stone so she could peer into the gloom. Neither of them had thought to bring a torch.

What is this?

The stone. Marta touched the stone, and she knew something about it, something she couldn't see before then. Just like the apple, and the branch of the apple tree.

"What are you waiting for?" Laras demanded. "Go on!"

"If I go first, I might find the First Law before you do. In fact, I will."

Laras looked at her intently. "Are you saying I should kill you now? You are mad."

"Not at all. If you kill me, likely you won't find it at all. It's hidden in a place not so easy to see."

That part, at least, was no less than truth.

Laras hesitated. "We seem to be at an impasse."

"May I make a suggestion?"

Laras didn't bother to hide his suspicion. "You're being much too co operative."

"Am I? If, as you say, you're no monster, then you'll let me go once you find the First Law, the one that will, in time, unlock all the others. I want you to find that bloody Law as much as you do."

"Well..."

Perhaps he was going to confess what Marta already knew, that she was dead either way. There was a certain annoying honesty in his character that might push him to it, but Marta didn't give him the chance. Better the pretense than the truth, when the pretense kept her alive. "Hobble me," she said. You have enough rope. Even if I could untie the knot around my waist I couldn't get loose from the hobble too. Not before you catch me. That way you can enter first without worry about me getting away, and I can direct you."

Marta gambled that Laras's need was stronger than his suspicion, and this time she was right. Laras shortened his leash by a few feet and then cut off the extra. Marta eyed the change.

Close...but it might be enough.

"Stand still."

Marta obeyed, and Laras tied one end of the hobble to her left ankle and then the other to her right. "Now, then. Show me which way to go."

"Inside, of course. The passage will go left and right. Go toward the right."

"Very well, follow me."

"I don't have a lot of choice, Laras."

He laughed then. It was a hollow sound. There was neither mirth nor cruelty in it. Marta fancied she saw a little of what drove Laras then, and what might have could have been different for him. For both of them.

Your need drives you to become something you are not. With a better choice that could have served you well.

"We don't have a torch," Laras said, it apparently just having occurred to him that they might need one.

"It's not so very far from the entrance," Marta said quickly. "There's enough light to see."

Laras frowned but kept walking, and bent over to enter the cave. Marta approached the entrance again, pulled by Laras's rope as he worked his way deeper underground. Marta reached out, slowly, praying her hand would find the place she knew must be there, that she would feel, would know, what she needed to know.

There.

Something amiss in the rocks. A potential that would take but the slightest push to manifest to great affect.

"The rock looks very strong here, held in place by forces greater than a hundred men. But it isn't strong," she said, too softly for Laras to hear this time. "It's weak."

The feeling was sudden and powerful, more so even than before. It was the word. Not Time. Weak. Weakness. The rock would not hold. Would not? Could not, for anyone who knew the secret. Marta took a deep breath and struck one stone above the entrance, just the one. In a moment, the hill rumbled. Marta threw herself backward against the rope as several massive blocks of limestone fell from the roof of the cave at the entrance. The first one just missed her as she struggled against the rope. The next cut the rope cleanly in two as it smashed against the first and Marta went sprawling and fell, hard on her back. The roar and rumbling continued for several long moments as she struggled to regain the breath that had been knocked out of her and to untie the hobble. When Marta rose again all was silence. She leaned close to the mass of rubble blocking the entrance to the cave.

"Laras?"

"Damn you!"

The reply was muffled but unmistakable. Laras yet lived. Marta felt some relief at that, but for the moment she couldn't say why. He had been going to kill her; there was no question of that. By all rights she should wish him dead, but she did not.

She shouted to be heard through the blockage. "Are you all right?"

"Oh, well enough," he said. Then, "Of course I'm not all right! I'm trapped!"

Marta smiled then. Laras was unhurt. If he'd died in the rock fall then, well, so be it. Since he wasn't dead, then undamaged was better. It would make things simpler. "Shall I get you out? I can do it," Marta said, and knew she spoke the truth.

Muffled laughter. "Now, how could I persuade you do to that?"

"I would do it freely, Laras. But then, you see, you would be in my debt. Remember what I told you about debts?"

Laras made a sound. It might have been a curse, it might have been an expression of pure terror. Marta was certain it was one or the other.

"Yes, you do understand. How would you like to be a snake? They can crawl out of tight places easily enough. I think you would make a fine snake."

"You're bluffing!"

"Are you sure?" Marta asked, sweetly.

Silence.

He believed her; Marta knew it. Yet she wasn't sure herself if she could do what she threatened. Once the obligation was incurred, could the fulfilment of the obligation be achieved by the rights she acquired under the terms of the Debt itself? Well, why not? Once the mechanism of the Debt was in place—which according to her mother's tally book required only agreement with the terms—then Marta's perogative became means to an end, just as any other. Why not use them to fulfil her end of the bargain? Marta believed this might be possible but, no, she was not certain. Yet Laras didn't know that...

There it is again. That same feeling.

Marta had touched another Law. Not the First Law; she had tucked that one away securely into the fullness of her understanding. She would recognize it from then on, but not as a new thing. Not like this. Yet the meaning that had brought this new recognition eluded her. She'd touched another Law, and recognized it for what it was as the Arrow Path promised. Yet that wasn't enough in itself. She didn't understand. At least, not yet. Marta shook herself, forcing her concentration back to the here and now.

Marta nodded, even though he couldn't see her. "You see we have a problem," she said quickly. "Or rather, you do."

"What are you going to do?" he asked.

"I'm going to take your horse and go find my mother. She will be very interested in all this, I believe."

"The First Law of Power was never here, was it? You lied to me!"

"No, Laras. The First Law is indeed in that cave. If you look for it, you might even find it. Perhaps in time to escape before we get back. I'd advise that, I really would."

"It's not that I have a choice," Laras muttered; Marta barely heard him.

Yet hear she did, and knew he was wrong. He had a choice, and so far he'd made all the wrong ones. There was still time to make the right one. For, when he finished stumbling around in there, he would inevitably find the other entrance that she knew lay on the far side of the cavern. If he was wise, he would use it to be long gone before Black Kath heard of this day's work. Marta's choice was that she would not go around to the other side and seal that entrance as well, trapping Laras there in truth rather than assumption.

Why am I letting him go?

Marta didn't have to think about it too long. It was because she owed Laras a debt, and she had to repay it just as those who sought her mother's help had to repay her. Whether he had meant to or not, Laras had done her a service. With his unwitting help, Marta had found what she was looking for.

"Strength gives way to weakness," she whispered to the stone, too softly for Laras or anyone else to hear. "It's a paradox, but it's true." She played with the words, liking one sound better than another, feeling them out, going for the concept's best expression.

"What Power Holds, Weakness Frees."

Marta smiled. It was the First Law of Power. She had it now; her journey begun. Her mother had said true about the Arrow Path, for when Marta found the law, grasped it, understood it, there was no question in her mind. Marta knew she was right; she knew what she had won today and that knowledge made her almost giddy.

Now it really begins.

Despite her happiness, that thought was like a drenching of cold well water. Now that she had the First Law there were more questions. Such as what all the implications of the Law were. How best to apply it. What it's limits were. There was so much she wanted to ask her mother when she returned, so much she had yet to learn. She hardly knew where to begin. Her mother would know; Marta was sure of it, and she could barely wait. She backtracked to where Laras's horse was patiently waiting for him and took the reins.

"Your master's not coming. Let's go home," she said. The horse, for want of another option, followed without protest.

CHAPTER 4

"In magic, there is no such thing as a 'little' power. It all leads to either mastery or destruction. Or both."
— From the Chronicles of Dommar the Beast

Laras cleared as many of the stones as he could, but soon came to larger ones he could not move. More, even if he did manage to shift them, it appeared that all this would accomplish would be to bring down the crumbling ceiling on his head. Now and then he heard the ominous crack of stones fracturing in place, yielding to the heavy stress placed upon them. After the third such he was so skittish that he managed to bang his head against a low hanging boulder. He scuttled back until a solid stone wall stopped him.

"Well, Laras my lad, you've made a royal mash of it one more time."
It was dwelling on the obvious, but it occurred to Laras that perhaps he should have killed Marta while he had the chance. Yet, even now, there was something about that course of action that bothered him just a bit. Perhaps it was the fact that he'd never killed anyone in his life. Oh, he was pretty sure he could do it if the need arose, but that need hadn't been so clear before. Or perhaps it was more due to the simple truth that the point had been to discover this "First Law of Power" that Marta had spoken about. Marta's life or death had always been secondary to that.

If Laras could have accomplished what he'd set out to do without harming anyone, then that would have been fine with him. He had nothing against Marta; she was a pretty young thing and he'd have regretted killing her. It's just that he hadn't thought he could get what he wanted otherwise.

Now, his back to a wall of stone there in the darkness, he was thinking that he'd been right. He was certain it was too late, either way. There he was, and all his brooding about what he should or could have done didn't change that one bit.

"I'll bet she was lying," he said aloud. "There's no power here."

The words seemed to hang on the air, along with his breath. Laras thought about that. He could see his own breath; where was the light to see anything coming from? Not the entrance just ahead; that was blocked solid. Laras got up slowly, turned to put his back to the entrance and looked right and left.

The dim light was coming from the left. Laras followed it and soon came to a place where the right wall of the tunnel was broken away and he looked out over a cavern. The light didn't get much brighter and after a moment Laras understood why; the source wasn't very large, or was very far away. It was a little hard to tell which, but Laras did know it was high on the wall on the other side of the cavern. Yet light meant an opening, and that meant a way out. Laras looked down at the edge of a waterfall and studied the rocks there, looking for a way down. He finally shook his head.

More bad luck. The rocks are wet and the light dim at best. I'd kill myself trying that way.

He wondered, idly, if this was some torture that Black Kath's bastard daughter had prepared for him: full sight of an escape that he couldn't possibly reach. Well, he'd fool her yet. He would reach it. Somehow. The tunnel leading from the entrance went both right and left. He'd have to try the other way. There was no light there; it might not even open into the cavern proper. Laras studied the rocks again, and the clusters of stalagmites further down waiting to greet any falling body with sharp spikes. Laras remembered that Marta had told the truth about the branching tunnel, and told him to go to the right which, coming in, would be the opposite of the way he'd just come.

She must have been lying, yet this way clearly leads nowhere.

He decided he'd take the other branch of the tunnel, and darkness be damned. He didn't know what was waiting for him, if anything, or what other surprises Marta might have prepared. Yet, even assuming she had the power to lay traps, why would she? Wasn't being entombed alive bad enough? Perhaps and perhaps not. Whatever the facts turned out to be, Laras did know one thing for certain—there was a way out of this trap, and he was going to find it.

I'm going to live, Black Kath's Daughter. Count on it.

Laras worked his way down the tunnel going the other way. He passed the entrance, now just a dark patch in the wall to his right. A few steps beyond that, the darkness was almost absolute. What little had filtered through from the other opening of the tunnel was almost gone now. Now and then Laras saw patches of lesser shadow that might have been light, might have been his imagination. The floor was slanting down sharply and he had to maintain contact with the left side of the tunnel to keep himself oriented properly. He wasn't sure how long he'd been walking when his fingers suddenly brushed against nothing, and a freshening breeze touched his face. Laras groped for the opening, found it, and found the light again.

He stood on the floor of the cavern, looking across to the light on the other side. There was a river between them, too wide to jump. He didn't see anything but a forest of stalagmites further down the river; certainly nothing as sensible and useful as a bridge. Laras kneeled down and put his right hand into the water, feeling for the bottom. The water was cold, but no worse than the cave itself. Yet, feel as he might, the bottom of the river was out of reach. Laras considered. It might only be a few feet deep, but then again he might have to swim. Assuming he could reach the exit he could now clearly see across the cavern, there was no way he could get very far on foot in wet clothes. It wasn't yet winter, but he was chilled to the bone in the cave as it was, and the nights outside were chill enough to give him his death if he didn't take precautions. He started to strip down.

There was a splash out of tune with the waterfall, and the occasional drip from a stalactite above. Laras hesitated, peering at the surface of the river. Did something move in there? He shook his head.

Couldn't be.

Oh, he had heard the stories as a child, of demons and hobs that dwelled in caves and came out at night to snatch children for supper, but he knew they were just stories told to persuade the little ones to go to bed quietly. Yet nothing could really live in the darkness of this place, with nothing to eat. He pulled off his boots and jerkin.

UNLESS IT ONLY ATE OUT OF HABIT. AND CAN HUNT BEYOND THE CAVE IF NEEDS MUST.

Laras hesitated, then slowly stepped out of his breeks. He wouldn't go mad, not so close to escape. He hadn't heard that, whatever it was. He wouldn't listen to strange voices. He would leave this place and he would survive. Laras wrapped his boots and the rest of his clothes up in his cloak and tied the bundle securely before carefully tossing it across the stream. He waded into the water, shivering. The drop-off was sharp and he almost stumbled, but he found his footing quickly despite that; there was a layer of sand on the bottom that kept it from being too slippery. The water rose quickly to his waist but no higher.

Could have been much worse—

Something grabbed Laras's ankles and pulled hard. His feet were snatched out from under him and he went down, flailing; the cold water closed over his head. He tried to shout before he remembered and got a mouthful of water. He opened his eyes in the murky dark; he saw nothing at first save what appeared to be two flashes of pale white, like small fish. Then further away a pair of eyes opened. They glowed red with malevolent intent and in the light they shed Laras realized the two white fish were a pair of cold pale hands, attached to arms long and thin as bone, pulling him toward a face framed with drifting green black hair, toward a gaping mouth set with sharp white teeth. He tried to kick but his feet were held fast, he tried to reach down but couldn't get a grip on his captor. His vision began to dim again.

I'm drowning!

The thought came as if from a distance, shrinking further from him even as the balefire of those eyes came closer still. He was going to die after all and, despite the rage, despite the fear. Once again his bad luck struck him down, despite his best efforts. Deep down Laras had known he was doomed, because everything he did came to nothing at the last. This was just the final failure.

LET HIM GO, CRAJA.

T   he voice again. The one he hadn't heard before. He wasn't hearing it again, not really, but the thought it had expressed seemed friendly enough despite that. The answering hiss was anything but.

"I won't! He's mine--I caught him!"

HE BELONGS TO ME. IF YOU'RE HUNGRY, GO HUNT THE WOOD.

"Not fair...not fair! No flesh so clean, no meat so tender! Mine!"

There was no answer from the other voice, just a brilliant flash of light, and a howl like a hundred wolves. It pierced the distance to wherever Laras was drifting and brought him back, for a moment.

That was strange, he thought, and that was all he thought for a while.

When Laras came to himself again, he was lying on cold stone, shivering. He blinked several times, and coughed, spitting up water. After a moment or two he could breathe properly again. He did that, and nothing else, for several long moments. There was a dim shape lying beside him, and he finally realized it was his clothes bundle. He glanced behind him to the underground river where he had very nearly died, then grabbed the bundle and drug it and himself as far he could from the water until a massive crystalline formation near the far wall stopped him. He eyed the river nervously as he unwrapped his clothes with numb fingers. He saw nothing. After using the cloak to dry himself a bit, got dressed again, never taking his eyes off the river, expecting at any moment to see a bone white face with red eyes peer and grin at him from the riverbank.

"What was that thing?" he muttered.

A CRAJA. SURELY YOU'VE HEARD OF THEM?

Laras had to hear the voice now. He didn't want to, but he had to. "Nursery tales...I didn't know they were real."

THEY'RE NOT...ENTIRELY. JUST A STUBBORN MEMORY, A SORT OF GHOST THAT GROWS OLD ENOUGH TO FORGET THAT IT NO LONGER LIVES. IT THINKS IT HUNGERS, AND SO IT EATS. YOU, IN THIS CASE. ALMOST.

"You saved my life...where are you? Who are you?"

COME TO THE TO THE TOP OF THIS SPIRE AND I WILL ANSWER BOTH QUESTIONS. IT IS, AFTER ALL, THE WAY OUT. YOU DO WANT TO GET OUT, YES?

Laras started climbing immediately. The light got stronger the higher he climbed, and the way was fairly easy; it was plain to see that the biggest part of the rock formation was one huge stalagmite, more ancient than any other in that very old place.

Part of the glow that marked the way was coming from the entrance, a sort of friendly yellow light. But there was another light, blue white, almost like the light of the sun filtered through ice. Laras reached the top of the stalagmite and found the source of the blue white glow: a woman with long black hair and white skin, glowing as if with an inner fire.

I AM AMAET, CALLED BOTH GODDESS AND POWER AND I AM HERE NOW, BEFORE YOU. WHAT SHALL YOU CALL ME, LARAS?

Laras fell to his knees and bowed low. He averted his eyes which was just as well, since Amaet's smile was blinding.

A VERY GOOD ANSWER. SO. WHY ARE YOU HERE, LARAS? WHAT IS IT YOU ARE SEEKING?

It took Laras a few moments to find his voice again, and he was still unable to look at Amaet directly, but he knew the answer to the question and he spoke it clearly. "Power."

WHAT WOULD YOU DO WITH IT?

That was a harder question, but he also had an answer. It never occurred to him to lie about it. "I would take revenge on Marta, Black Kath's daughter, for trapping me here. I would seek my independent destiny."

Amaet smiled again. Laras didn't see it, but he knew it was so when he saw the light intensify; he wondered why he hadn't already been burned to nothing by the glory of it.

TWO SEPARATE MATTERS BUT PERHAPS LINKED, AS MOST THINGS ARE. YOUR DESTINY IS UP TO YOU. REVENGE IS EASIER TO ARRANGE. HOLD OUT YOUR HAND.

Laras did as Amaet commanded and a glint of gold appeared there in the gloom of the cave, floating in the air about Laras's hand. Something small and heavy fell into his palm and his fingers closed on it, reflexively, to keep from losing his grip. When he opened his fingers again he saw a small circular pendant of gold with an engraved arrow bisecting it. The pendant was attached to a thong of black leather.

"Goddess, what is this?"

A TOKEN OF ME. WEAR IT ALWAYS.

Laras quickly looped the pendant around his neck and Amaet leaned close and whispered the name of the First Law of Power. She held out a stone. TAKE THIS.

Laras did as she directed. The stone lay flat on his right hand, barely covering the palm.

WHAT DO YOU HOLD?

Laras frowned. "It's a stone, Great One."

YET IT COULD BE SOMETHING ELSE, IF YOU WISH IT. IF I COMMAND YOU. I WANT YOU TO TURN THE STONE INTO PEBBLES.

"How?"

BY APPLYING WHAT I HAVE TOLD YOU, LARAS. INVOKE THE FIRST LAW OF POWER.

"'What Power Holds, Weakness Frees,'" he said, feeling a little foolish. Surely there was more to it than that...

There wasn't. The stone crumbled in his hand, and rained down to the to the top of the stalagmite as a shower of pebbles. Laras's face lit up like a beacon.

DO ANOTHER, Amaet commanded.

Laras shattered another rock. A big one, this time. This time he said the words with full intent, concentrating hard, and the rock flew apart with a rumble like thunder and pebbles rained down far into the cavern. There were lines of blood on his face and hands where rock shards had cut him, but Laras giggled like a happy child.

IS IT EVERYTHING I'VE PROMISED?

Laras closed his eyes. "Wonderful!"

MERELY A BEGINNING. YET YOUR WORSHIP IS NOT ENOUGH PAYMENT FOR THIS. WHERE YOU ARE CONCERNED I AM THE SOURCE OF ALL THINGS, TO DISPOSE OR WITHHOLD AT MY WHIM. DO YOU THINK EVERY HEDGE ROW PRIEST OR GILDED SHRINE PRIESTESS COMMANDS THE POWER THAT YOU HOLD NOW?

Laras just bowed. He didn't understand that, or much else. He also felt that there was no reason he had to understand. His motives, from that point on, would be elegantly simple. "Command me, Goddess."

WELL SAID. YES, IF YOU WANT THE NEXT MORSEL, THERE IS SOMETHING I WANT YOU TO DO FOR ME.

"Anything," Laras said, without thought of hesitation. Kill, rob, cheat, steal, he didn't care. If the First Law gave so much power, what would the Second do? And the Third? He had to find out, and as soon as possible. He only hoped that the Goddess's errand didn't take so very long.

GO TO MORUSHE. USE THE SEAL YOU BEAR AS ALIAN'S MESSENGER TO GAIN ACCESS TO THE LIBRARY AT THE SHRINE OF AMATOK. I WANT YOU TO ACQUIRE A BOOK FOR ME.

Laras's smile died. Morushe was a long way from Lythos, at least two weeks from the border, and it would be two days to reach that. Longer, if he didn't buy or steal a new mount. After his first taste of real power, it seemed forever.

"I will go, of course," he said. "What book shall I take?"

I WILL MAKE IT KNOWN TO YOU AT THE PROPER TIME. WHEN YOU HAVE ACQUIRED IT, BRING THE BOOK TO THE KING'S LIBRARY AT KARSAN.

Laras felt a chill. "But...I can't go back there! When Black Kath finds out what I almost did to her daughter..."

YOU FEAR BLACK KATH? EVEN WITH YOUR NEW POWER?

Laras couldn't bring himself to look at Amaet directly, but he did force himself to speak. "As yet I know only one Law. Black Kath knows all Seven, or so the stories go, and she has had their use for many years. I can't challenge her...yet."

SO YOU'RE NOT A TOTAL FOOL. GOOD, THAT WILL HELP...BUT ONLY UP TO A POINT. DO YOU FEAR THE WITCH MORE THAN YOU FEAR ME?

"No, Goddess."

THEN DO AS I SAY. YOU'RE A CLEVER LAD. FIND A WAY. AND DO IT BEFORE THE FIRST NEW SNOWFALL BLOCKS THE PASS TO MORUSHE, OR I SHALL BE VERY CROSS WITH YOU.

"May...may I ask why you want this book moved?"

BECAUSE SOMEONE WILL NEED IT, AND VERY SOON. ONE MORE THING, LARAS--DO NOT MAKE A HABIT OF QUESTIONING ME.

Laras bowed even lower. "As you wish it, in all things."

Amaet smiled again. It was as if the sun had come in full to that deep dark place.

YOU WILL DO WELL.

Laras smiled. He was determined, in fact, to do very well indeed. And why not? It had turned out to be so very easy. He left the cave without further delay but he couldn't resist, just for fun, breaking one more big rock on the way out. He liked the sound. It felt like thunder itself was in his hands.

CHAPTER 5

"I know my wants, but I require counselors, nobility, clergy, and learned folk of all description to reveal my needs. I tend to trust what I want more than what I need."
— Bruga X of Borasur, Called The Deliberate

The next few days were a blur to Marta. She felt groggy and out of sorts as if she'd both slept too long and woken too early. She finished picking the apples for want of something else to do. On the third day, with nothing left to do and her mother still not returned, Marta decided to take a walk. She was at the cave's mouth before she even realized where she was going.

The first entrance was still sealed, as she'd left it.

What if he didn't find the other way out?

Possible. It wasn't immediately obvious and he'd had no torch. She knew she'd given him a chance to escape, but that's all it was and it might not have been enough. Marta wanted to see for herself. She` didn't know why, except perhaps to make certain that Laras's life wasn't on her head.

It wouldn't be my fault.

But it would be, she understood without question, her responsibility. Marta's wasn't sure which was worse. Marta hiked around to the far side of the hill. The melting snow had made the ground muddy in spots; she picked her way up the hillside carefully until it was more rock than dirt. Even then she had to take care; some of the stones were wet and slippery. There was a gnarled old juniper clinging to the hillside where the cavern opened; Marta used a branch to pull herself up the last few feet. She noted, almost without thinking, that the old tree was fairly solid, despite its age and twisted condition, and the fact that it grew on little more than a pocket of earth left in a hollow in the rocks.

Marta wondered what her mother would say about the tree. Perhaps nothing. Perhaps something along the lines of "life wants to live." Sometimes matters were simpler than she tended to credit them. Marta wondered if her encounter with Laras was one such. Somehow she didn't think so. She didn't really believe that he was dead. She didn't even believe she had seen the last of him. She did wonder what it all meant, if anything.

Marta peered into the cave, but it was hard to see. The change from the bright outside to the gloomy cavern made it hard to focus. Marta stepped just inside and waited for her eyes to adjust.

"Laras?"

Her voice echoed back to her from the far side of the cavern. She heard nothing else but the distant splash of water, and the occasional single drips from the stalactites above. Her eyes were better accustomed to the gloom, and there was a good deal of light streaming in from the outside now; Marta could even make out a faint glow from the high end of the far tunnel. If Laras were still here she would see him or, more surely, hear him.

He got out.

Marta felt a little relief, even though it was only what she'd expected. Yet sometimes she thought it quite pleasant to receive what she expected; so often that didn't happen at all. Marta turned to leave; she felt no compulsion to linger in that cold damp place. Something on top of the stalagmite summit near the entrance caught her eye, and Marta got her first good look at the Shrine.

The statue was to Amaet in Judgment, with the Axe and Apple Blossom in opposite hands. Despite her surprise and wariness—Black Kath's warnings had not gone unheeded—Marta couldn't help but admire the artistry she saw there. The statue was, there was no other word, exquisite.

"Who built this?" she asked, softly.

ARE YOU SURE YOU WANT TO KNOW? THERE'S A PRICE.

Marta looked around her, saw nothing that she had not already seen. "Who's here?"

DO YOU REALLY NEED TO ASK?

Marta did not. She looked at the statue of Amaet set in that deep dark place and she knew. Marta took a deep, slow breath and let it out. It turned to mist in the cold dark air.

"Amaet. You are the Power called Amaet."

YOU MAY ADDRESS ME AS 'GODDESS.'

Marta shook her head. "No I may not. You are a Power, not a goddess."

I COULD BE. ALL YOU HAVE TO DO IS WORSHIP ME.

"I cannot."

Amaet appeared then. She seemed a rather ordinary, if beautiful, young woman only a bit older than Marta herself. The blue-white glow that surrounded her did seem to set her off a bit, though, from anything to do with the word "ordinary."

I SEE THAT OUR RELATIONSHIP IS GOING TO BE A COMPLICATED ONE.

"As it was with my mother?" Marta asked.

Amaet smiled then. It was all Marta could do to keep from looking away. Come to that, it was all Marta could do to keep from throwing herself on her knees and bowing to the splendid creature before her. All that saved her was her mother's warning, and the certain knowledge that, if she did as she wanted to do, she would be lost.

YOU WANT ME TO EXPLAIN. CLEVER. NO, I DON'T THINK I WILL INCREASE YOUR DEBT JUST YET. YET YOU MAY KNOW WHO MADE THE SHRINE, IF YOU CHOOSE.

Marta frowned. "You said there was a price."

CERTAINLY. BUT I DID NOT SAY YOUR DEBT WOULD BE TO ME. MY LANGUAGE SKILLS ARE RUSTY, FOR ALL THAT I SEEM TO BE USING THEM A BIT LATELY. PERHAPS "COST" IS THE MORE CORRECT TERM? YES. THE KNOWLEDGE WILL COST YOU. HOW MUCH? I DON'T KNOW.

Now Marta smiled. "You have limits."

OF COURSE I DO, AS DOUBTLESS YOUR IRASCIBLE DAM HAS TOLD YOU. DO YOU, CHILD? DO YOU EVEN KNOW WHAT THEY ARE? I DOUBT IT.

There was a great deal Marta didn't understand, but she knew a challenge when she heard one. "How can I find the answer to the shrine?"

GO DOWN TO THE RIVER IN THE BOTTOM OF THIS CAVERN, BUT DO NOT TOUCH THE WATER. WAIT A WHILE. THE ANSWER WILL APPEAR.

Marta looked down at the river, but she went no closer. She did want the answer. Yet not so much that she was willing to go blindly to get it. She remembered what Black Kath had said about the Powers more than once: that they were not neutral in the affairs of the world, that they had interests and biases and deep passions. That they were very much like human beings in that regard and this more than anything was what made them so dangerous and unpredictable. "I'm sorry, Amaet. I...I do not trust you. I can not."

Marta braced herself, and found her hands balling into fists, her heart racing. Yet Amaet's reaction was simply to smile wider, and even more radiantly than before. Marta felt an odd flutter at the pit of her stomach and, for a moment, all she could think was how beautiful the Power called Amaet was. It took her a moment to push the thought aside so she could concentrate on what Amaet was saying.

YOU ARE WISE, AND THAT'S SELDOM A CAUSE FOR REGRET. WHILE I SELDOM HAVE NEED TO LIE, I CERTAINLY CAN IF IT SUITS ME. HAVE I? THE ANSWER TO THAT IS ALSO DOWN BY THE RIVER. SEEK IT OR NOT.

Marta shrugged. Amaet had summed the situation very well and, try as she might, Marta could not find a flaw in what she had said. And Marta did want the answer. She was partway down the stalagmite before she was even aware that she had made her decision.

I don't feel very wise.

Climbing down the stalagmite was both easier and harder than Marta expected. Easier, because the sunlight flooding in past the broken stone reached far enough to light the way almost adequately. Harder, because the pull of the earth itself seemed intent on helping her climb down, even when she didn't want or need any help. She almost slipped more than once, each time at a point where the bottom of the stalagmite and the cavern floor beyond were entirely too far away. When she was finally down on the slope that passed for the cave's floor Marta had to take a few moments to catch her breath and wait for her heart to stop beating quite so hard.

When she was more rested she looked at the river again. It was pretty much what it appeared to be from the top of the stalagmite, a dark flow like liquid obsidian weaving its way through a forest of stalagmites at the far end of the cave before straightening out to go slow and deep toward the opposite end and disappear further underground. She walked slowly down to the water, but not too close. The rocks looked slippery and Marta wasn't in the mood for a cold bath.

"I don't see any answers, Amaet," she said aloud.

YOU WILL. IF YOU DO AS I SAID.

Marta reddened. She'd forgotten about the "wait" part of her instructions. Not too surprising; Marta knew her patience mostly by the lack of it. She didn't call upon it any more than needed. And what did 'wait' mean to an immortal Power anyway? A few minutes? A year? A lifetime? Marta sighed gustily and watched the river. Nothing happened for a long time. Marta was beginning to think nothing would happen, and Amaet was just having an odd joke at her expense. She hadn't yet lost her fear of Amaet; Marta wondered if she ever would. That didn't stop Marta from being annoyed and she was about to tell Amaet the same when she finally did notice something in the water. Something that moved.

Fish?

At least, Marta thought they were fish. They were small, and white, and there was more than one of them. How many? Marta wasn't sure at first, then decided there were two. Just like the two eyes watching her from the water.

Marta stared. There were eyes in the water, she was sure of it. Red eyes, just below the surface and back a bit from the two white fish. Only they weren't fish, were they? Hands. Small, bony hands.

I THINK ANOTHER FOOT CLOSER WOULD DO IT. SHE DOESN'T LIKE COMING OUT OF THE WATER, BUT SHE'S VERY HUNGRY.

Marta felt a cold spot in her stomach as if she'd swallowed a stone, and she quickly moved a step back.

"What is that thing??"

A CRAJA. IT'S A SORT OF GHOST...WELL, REVENANT REALLY.

"You mean it's dead?"

IS THERE ANOTHER MEANING OF 'GHOST' I'M NOT FAMILIAR WITH?

Marta reddened. "Has that thing been there all along?"

NOT ALWAYS. NOR WAS SHE A "THING." HER NAME WAS KESSA.

Marta finally understood. "She's the one who built the shrine!"

CLEVER GIRL. IF A BIT SLOW.

Marta didn't have to look to know that Amaet was smiling again. Marta imagined it was a rather unpleasant smile.

"And this is why you wanted me to come here, to feed me to your pet? Is that your price to settle the Debt?"

Amaet laughed, and the stalactites overhead hummed in ominous harmony. IF IT WAS, YOU'D BE CRAJA FOOD AND NO ARGUMENT. I DON'T THINK YOU UNDERSTAND JUST HOW GREAT THE DEBT IS.

Marta was beginning to think Amaet was right. She didn't understand a great deal, but she was going to learn. If she lived long enough. Whether she would or not remained to be seen.

"What now?" Marta asked.

GO TO THE WATER IF YOU WANT TO DEVOURED. LEAVE IF YOU DO NOT.

For several long moments Marta did neither, though she could certainly see the sense in leaving. "How did she wind up like this?"

WHAT BUSINESS IS THAT OF YOURS?

"She might have snapped me up like a minnow. I think that gives me the right of some curiosity."

Amaet didn't say anything for a while. Marta felt the silence weighing on her from behind, as if it were some hungry thing itself, slipping up on her with stealthy tread through the gloom of that deep place. Marta wanted to look at Amaet, to keep her in sight as she would anyone whose motives and actions were suspect, but to do that she'd have to look away from the terrible, pitiful gaze coming from the creature in the water. Marta was very reluctant to do that.

YOU'RE A STRANGE ONE, MARTA.

Now Marta did look at Amaet, for a moment. It was easy. Amaet was standing just a few feet behind her. At first she'd been on top of the stalagmite, and now she wasn't. Marta wasn't surprised at all. "How so?" she asked, making sure that the craja was still where it had been. It wasn't. It had slipped a foot or so closer, but that was all. Marta eyed the creature warily.

YOUR FIRST FACE TO FACE MEETING WITH A POWER, AND YOU BARELY BLINK! YOU MEET A CREATURE THAT DEVOURS THE LIVING TO KEEP ITSELF CLINGING TO THE MEMORY OF LIFE, AND RATHER THAN FLEEING IN HORROR LIKE A SENSIBLE GIRL, YOU LOOK ON IT WITH PITY—DO YOU THINK IT WILL PITY YOU IF CATCHES YOU?

Marta shook her head. "What it feels has nothing to do with how I feel. And this may be new to me, Amaet, but my mother hasn't left me totally ignorant of you. I knew we would meet sooner of later."

S O YOU ADDRESS ME WITH A TONE YOU'D USE ON A FISHWIFE?

Marta almost laughed, but she was able to squelch the urge. It was a close thing as it was; whatever her bravado with Amaet, she at least had some idea of what she was capable of, and didn't want to find out in any more detail than necessary. "Sometimes a person has to speak clearly to be sure she is heard."

Amaet sighed. I HEAR YOU, MARTA BLACK KATH'S DAUGHTER, BUT I'M NOT SO CERTAIN YOU'VE HEARD ME. STAND UP, KESSA. LET THE GIRL SEE YOU.

In response, the creature scuttled backward in the water like a crayfish. Marta could almost swear she'd heard it whimper.

OBEY ME, KESSA. FOR THE SAKE OF WHAT YOU ONCE WERE.

Amaet walked past Marta, if "walk" was the proper term for gliding a few inches over the mud and stone without touching them. She held out one slim hand and waited. Marta thought she understood something about patience then; she knew without question or thought that Amaet would stand there, waiting, for a year or a dozen, and sooner or later she would get what she wanted. Fortunately for Marta this time it was sooner. The top of the creature's head appeared. There was still hair there. It grew long and black and tangled, but there was more skull than scalp, and the long thin arms were only a little less bare than a skeleton. The nails were long and ended in ragged points. Amaet took the creature's hand and helped it to stand upright. It rose dripping from the black water, shivering. Marta could see the thing's ruined body, and it was all she could do to keep her gorge from rising.

NOT TOO MUCH LEFT NOW. WHAT WERE YOU, KESSA? DO YOU REMEMBER AT ALL? THINK.

The creature shimmered like mist in sunlight, then changed. Marta looked at a woman of about thirty, with long dark hair and gentle brown eyes.

Marta shivered. "How did she come to this? What did you do to her?"

SHE DID THIS TO HERSELF. WOULD YOU LIKE TO SEE WHAT YOU'VE DONE, KESSA?

The woman shook her head, and the hunger Marta had seen on the creature's face before was replaced with sheer terror. There was a mirror in Amaet's hand. It hadn't been there a moment before. LOOK, she said. The woman turned her head, crying out in anguish.

"Stop!"

They both turned to look at her. Marta took a step forward. "You're hurting her," she said, more softly.

THERE IS NO 'HER' TO HURT, MARTA. JUST A STUBBORN MEMORY THAT WILL NOT FADE. KESSA MADE A LOVELY SHRINE IN THIS CAVE. SHE WORKED HARD, GAVE IT THE DEVOTION SHE NEVER GAVE HER HUSBAND, HER CHILDREN. ALL FOR ME. OR WAS IT FOR YOURSELF, KESSA? YOUR PRIDE IN YOUR SKILL, YOUR ARROGANCE IN BEING SELECTED AMONG ALL THE STONE CARVERS IN A VILLAGE THAT HAS BEEN DUST FOR HUNDREDS OF YEARS? WHAT KEEPS YOU HERE, FEEDING ON THE SCRAPS OF LIFE?

There was no sound from the woman. Marta couldn't even be sure she understood what was happening, except on some primal, basic level that only hunger or fear could reach.

"Let her go," Marta said. "Please."

BE CAREFUL OF WHAT YOU DESIRE, MARTA.

Amaet released the woman's hand, in that instant it wasn't a woman at all. It was the craja, all hunger and appetite, and Marta was much too close. It sprang forward, faster than a snake, and it was only Marta's good luck that she managed to catch its bony arms as it reached for her. As it was she was overborne and fell hard against the stone behind her. The thing's teeth were inches from Marta's throat, its eyes glowing red.

"Mine!" it shrieked, like a demented child.

Fool!

Marta barely had time for the thought. It was all she could do to keep the thing's teeth away from her, and its fetid breath was sickening. Marta could feel her strength failing.

It's too strong...

But how could it be? It was nothing but bone and hunger. How could it be there at all? Marta forced herself to think, concentrate. Amaet was smiling at her from a few feet away and Marta used the anger from that knowledge to bolster her aching arms.

Amaet said Kessa did this to herself. What if she was telling the truth?

There was the answer. Marta spoke the words even as their true meaning gave her what she needed to know. "What Power Holds, Weakness Frees."
Marta let go off of the creature's left arm and its hand shot forward, tightening around Marta's throat. She could feel the ragged talons cutting into her skin, but she ignored it just long enough to reach out to the creature's chest, in to the creature's body. She pushed her hand between crumbling bone and rotted sinew until her fingers closed on something small, hard, and cold. She gripped the thing she found there, and she broke it.

There was no sound for several long moments. Marta felt the thing's grip tightening on her and wondered, just for an instant, if she had been wrong, but the doubt didn't last any longer than that.
I wasn't wrong.

The grip went away. The touch went away. There was nothing left of the revenant except for a few moldering bones and what might have been a scrap of cloth. Marta took a deep breath, looked at the broken thing she held in her hand. It was a talisman, a small female figurine clutching an axe and apple blossom.

Amaet. As if there was any doubt.

Marta sat up, and held out the broken talisman. "She did it for you. You were what Kessa clung to, why she would not leave this place."

The Power looked strangely thoughtful. PERHAPS.

"She almost killed me!"

AND YOU KNEW WHAT SHE WAS BEFORE YOU TOLD ME TO LET HER GO. STILL...

Marta blinked. "Yes?"

IT WOULD HAVE BEEN A WASTE.

Marta didn't get a chance to ask what Amaet meant by that, for in a moment Amaet was no longer there. Marta wasn't fool enough to try and call her back; she'd been fool enough for one day and still managed to live through it. More, she had learned that the First Law was good for more than breaking rocks and hinges. It could break chains, too. Even ones that could not be seen.

A hard lesson but, to Marta's way of thinking, well worth learning. However, the one lesson was quite enough. Marta left the cave as quickly as she reasonably could. She did pause to bow stiffly at Amaet's shrine, but it was not a bow to Amaet. She fervently hoped that she never would bow to Amaet. No, her homage was to Kessa alone, along with a wish—if not a prayer—for her peaceful sleep.

CHAPTER 6

"Anyone fool enough to hunt for a dragon deserves to find one."
—Bruga the Deliberate

Bone Tapper was the first to go.

He snapped to attention on Black Kath's shoulder like a soldier receiving an order, then lifted its wings and flapped away into the quickening woods, sounding a cry too much like a human voice.

"Done! Done! Done!"

Kath took a firmer grip on the reins and stopped her small wagon. The horse was already getting restless. Kath had seen the signs clearly, hoped that she might yet outrun the shadows one last time. Apparently, that was not to be. "Bone Tapper, you return this instant!"

Of course it did no such thing. Its cries turned to echoes that quickly faded. Black Kath listened to the silence and realized there was no chance of getting home now. She was out of time. She slapped the reins once and pulled the wagon off into a small clearing. The bushes lining the cart trail closed in behind her just in time. Another moment and the cart-horse's outline grew indistinct, then shimmered, then changed. Something that was no longer a horse slipped out of the harness that no longer fit and slithered off into the woods. Black Kath did not bother to call after it. Yssara already had his instructions, such that they were. Since they only required him to do as he was inclined anyway, only more so, she had no doubt he would obey her. Even though, right now, it did not have to obey her in anything.

What Power holds Weakness frees. The first of the Laws of Power. Black Kath had long thought it a paradox, but it actually made perfect sense. Here was the proof.

Sodded prince fouled up everything.

The queen's second pregnancy was nearly as troubled as the first, which was no more than Kath expected. Mistress Thornap probably could have handled it herself, but a deal had been made and so Kath had come, for all that her time was short. There was no arguing with kings, and babes who would be king. Poor Mysona nearly bled dry from the womb twice and all the royal oaf could think to ask was "Is it a boy?" Yes, Majesty, it sodding well is. A fine fat suckling boy and yes, if you ever get around to asking your lady will live, thank you exceedingly but I really must run off and die now.

Well, it hadn't gone exactly like that. Alian had shown more than a little concern for his lady, and angry as Kath was, many things went well thought but equally well unsaid, which is the way of most of life. Not a Law of Power but true enough as such things went, right up to the end.

Which is almost here.

She had hoped for more time, but that wasn't to be. The witch gingerly lowered herself from the cart before the first spasm hit. She managed to collapse with her back to a nearby oak before the second wave of pain nearly washed her away. She sank to a sitting position on the soft grass as the covered cart began to hum like a choir preparing for song. The cart, with its red and gold markings did not change; it was one of the few things that served Black Kath in its own nature. It was just a cart. Unlike the horse that had pulled it, or the one who remained within. Black Kath thought it very fortunate that she had been driving now and not Treedle. There was a good chance the cart would have been left on the road. At least here her death would have a little privacy. Kath wasn't alone yet, but she knew she soon would be.

Enjoy it while you may, Darlings. You're still not free...

"Your servants have departed, Mistress."

A squat little man stood before Black Kath. His features were broad and ugly, his back stooped, his arms thick and long.

"All except you, Treedle. Well, don't hang about. You won't have much time."

"I know," he said, and began to change. His back straightened, his legs lengthened, his features refined and reformed into that of a tall, broad man with curly red hair. He was still young, despite the years he had spent in Kath's service. Kath wondered if that was because his time belonged to her for so long, and he only retained what had belonged to him? Possible, but there was no leisure to sort it out now. He looked exactly as she remembered, so many years ago.

Black Kath smiled. "You understand even this? Well, I'm not surprised. You always were a clever sort. Far more so than I was. I should never have answered the summons, deal or no."

"A servant knows a command when he hears one, Mistress."

Black Kath laughed, but not for long. She hadn't the strength left for it. "Impertinent, too. Well, it's true enough in its way. And close to a Law of Power," Black Kath said, wincing at a new pain. "Not quite, but close. Off with you, then. Be free as long as you can."

The man who had been a hob for so many years still hesitated. "Is there anything I can do for you, Mistress?"

Black Kath didn't answer for several long moments. "My death frees all who have obligation to me until Marta claims her birthright. I thought you understood that. You are your own man until Marta finds you. Go."

Treedle drew himself to his full height, considerably more than it had been as a hob. "I'm my own man now, as you say. And as my own man I repeat—is there anything I can do for you?"

She smiled at him. "Treedle, even now you manage... to astonish me."

Black Kath felt the black tide rising within her, fought it back as she turned over the spark of a notion in her mind. Death waited while Treedle waited. Finally Black Kath smiled again. "Marta is young. There is much she doesn't understand... Yssara has agreed to help me just a bit, but what I ask of you will be much greater. Lean close, Treedle. If it suits your whim, perhaps there is something you can do for Marta, if not for me."

Treedle listened and Black Kath Spoke quickly before the tide of pain rose again and would not wait for either of them.

*

Marta woke from a very dark dream. She sat up suddenly in her bed, pushing the blankets aside. Her mouth opened and closed several times. She could not form words, or do anything except sit there and shiver. It was some time before the fear ebbed enough to let her senses return to her. She tried to remember what had happened, what had frightened her so, but she could not.

"Mother...?"

She remembered. There was no sense in calling out; Kath had not returned from Karsan. For one terrible moment Marta imagined Laras ambushing her mother unawares at any one of a number of places along the road to Karsan, and her act of foolish charity—if such it was, Marta wasn't convinced of that—had led to her mother's doom. Yet the more she thought of the idea the more ridiculous it seemed. Laras? He wouldn't have been able to get near Black Kath of Lythos, even if he were fool enough to try. Bone Tapper would have spied him and Treedle, if need be, could rip Laras limb from limb, if her mother didn't turn him into a pile of ash first. He was no threat.

So why hasn't my mother returned? It's been weeks!

It was the first time she let herself admit that her mother was overdue. Marta didn't think for a moment that Mistress Thornap could have misjudged the time so badly. Had something gone wrong, and the king taken vengeance on Kath? Marta dismissed that. He wouldn't dare...or if he had, Marta would have heard.

"Would you? When was the last time you were anywhere you would hear?" Marta asked herself. The answer wasn't very satisfactory. A week or more since she'd gone in to Molbrook to sell Laras's horse. She'd thought of keeping it, but for some reason she wasn't sure if she would be ready to talk to her mother about the First Law, considering the foolish risk she'd taken soon after. Explaining the strange horse in their stable would have taken the matter out of Marta's hands. Marta knew all that, though true enough, was just an excuse. The real reason was that the wretched beast reminded her of Laras, and she wanted no part of it. Koman Tol had offered her a fair enough price—for Kath's daughter he wouldn't have dared otherwise—but if need be she would have given it away.

Marta shivered again. She thought of pulling the blankets up again and trying to go back to sleep, but she was afraid the dream was still there, waiting for her. She waited as long as she could stand it, then got up and got dressed. The embers in the kitchen grate were well banked; it only took a few minutes to get the fire back to life. There was still a faint scent of apples in the air; Marta had finished preparing the last batch for storage only a few days before, and she'd sent the rest to Molbrook for pressing. Marta opened the accounts book, then closed it again. She'd read it through twice already; she didn't understand everything that was in it, but she understood more than she ever had before. She hoped the rest would come in time. More than that, she hoped her mother would soon return to answer all the questions she had about the Debt; especially that bit about how she might win free of it. There was nothing more to do but wait, and Marta had been doing that. Now she was done with waiting, too.

"I can't wait any more," she said.

Marta took her cloak from its peg by the door and went outside. The air was crisp and cold and all the stars sparkled brightly; it wasn't quite winter yet, but close enough. The first snowfall could come any time now. Marta looked to the east and judged dawn to be an hour away, at most. She went back inside and by the time dawn came she was ready to leave. She quenched the fire and made sure all the lamps and candles had been properly snuffed out. She locked the doors behind her; not that she expected anyone would be foolish enough to rob them. It was just sense. You locked your house when you weren't going to be there and, if someone was missing, you looked for them. Simple.

It wasn't a short walk to Molbrook, but Marta arrived there just before noon.

There's not much to the place.

That hadn't been true all of Marta's life; she was so used to her home with just her mother and Bone Tapper and Treedle for company that Molbrook, with its one road and no fewer than twelve buildings had seemed quite amazing. Now Marta knew it for what it was: one small market town barely existing to serve the farms around it. Many people came to Molbrook for business but few lived there, and now that the harvest was in it was even quieter than usual. Marta went into the Black Ox for a bite of lunch and mostly had the place to herself.

Old Nath was sitting before the fire as usual; he glanced at her when she came through the door but otherwise took little notice. That was only slightly less true for the brewmistress herself. Mistress Pala came out with the same fixed smile she might have used for any customer. She brought Marta what she asked for, a bit of bread and soup. She glanced at Marta's pack but said nothing about it, nor asked after her mother except to note that she hadn't seen her in a bit.

"She's been away on business. I'm going to meet her," Marta said, as if it were all arranged and nothing out of the ordinary. She found that she didn't want to talk about her mother to Pala or anyone else in Molbrook, and she felt distinctly uncomfortable about even being there. She wasn't sure why, at first. She'd been coming to Molbrook most of her life, and knew most everyone there. Except...

Except there's not a single one I would call my friend.

Marta had never thought about it before. Molbrook was just there. She went to the town now and then with her mother, and almost never alone. She'd never played with the children who lived there when she was growing up, nor spoken to anyone except on business, hers or her mothers. She'd never questioned this, never really thought about it at all. It just was, as her mother and Treedle and Bone Tapper just were. Everything in its place and as it should be. Only now it wasn't as it should be. Her mother was gone and she realized there wasn't a single person in Molbrook she could turn to for help. Her mother had no friends, and this she had no friends either.

Best not to need help then, Marta thought, and tried to feel that this, too was just the way things were and not some flaw that needed mending, if it could be mended. There wasn't time to think about that now.

"Is Koman Tol about?" Marta asked after she'd finished her soup.

Mistress Pala, wiping out a mug, didn't even look up. "I believe he took a string of horses out two days ago. Heading to Karsan, I imagine."

Marta thanked Pala for the information and placed two bronze coins on the table. She picked up her pack and left without another word, though her heart was sinking. If Koman Tol had gone to the market in Karsan, then there was no chance she'd be able to buy back Laras's mount, or any other. It only took a few minutes for Marta to find Koman Tol's wife at the stables and confirm what Mistress Pala had told her; the only horses left were two pregnant mares, neither in any condition to travel. Marta started to leave, but Koman's wife stopped her.

"Mistress..."

Marta blinked. It took her a moment or two to realize the woman was talking to her. No one had ever called her that before. When she was with her mother it had always been "Marta," if anyone needed to refer to her at all.

"Yes?" Marta asked.

The woman hesitated. Marta knew she was afraid, and couldn't think why. Then she realized that the woman was afraid of her. Marta just stared, dumbfounded, but the woman was too caught up in her own conflict to even notice.

"This mare," she said, pointing at the smaller of the two, a gray with a black streak on her nose, "she got out yesterday and ate something that looked like catweed. I'm afraid for the foal."

With good reason, Marta thought. Catweed had many beneficial properties when used correctly, and its effect on pregnant women could sometimes be one of those benefits, but that surely wasn't the case here.

Marta shook her head. "If it was catweed, the foal will drop in a day or so, ready or not. I don't even think my mother could prevent that, and she won't be back for a while."

"I know, but it would be worth it to me to know if the foal is poisoned. If you'd name your price I would know if I could afford it."

"I'm not—" Marta started to say that she was not her mother, and there was nothing she could do. Then she realized that, perhaps, there was. A pregnant mare was not much different from a pregnant queen, in at least one very important respect. Yet if Marta did this, what would be the price? Her mother said she would know, but how?

Marta tried to recall her mother's meeting with King Alian, when the price was named. Kath had gone into a sort of trance then, but Marta hadn't a clue what it meant. She closed her own eyes, but didn't know if would make any difference.

If I do this, what if the price is more than the poor woman can pay? I can't just name one if I don't know —

Marta blinked. She did know. Beyond doubt or question. It couldn't have been that easy, yet it was. As if...well, as if she couldn't avoid knowing, once the question was asked. It was only after the fact that she remembered what her mother had said about a very similar situation. If she didn't use power directly, then there would be no fee for simply reporting what her understanding of the First Law told her. It was exactly the same as Kath's first examination when she knew Mysona's child was dead.

"I'll tell you if I can," Marta said. "That will not cost you anything, except I would wish that you watch her closer from now on."

The woman agreed at once and Marta, since there was no help for it, walked over to the mare. It snorted once, but otherwise didn't protest when Marta laid her hands gently on its rounded girth. It even seemed to be enjoying the contact. After a few moments Marta straightened up and then patted the mare on her shoulder.

"It seems that it wasn't catweed after all. The foal is healthy and should drop in its own good time," Marta said.

The woman thanked her profusely, her relief evident, but Marta barely noticed. A little while later Marta was back in the street, alone, with the road to Karsan stretching before her in all its vastness. Marta wasn't sure she was ready for what was coming next, but she was certain about the mare. She wasn't quite sure how she knew that the foal was all right, any more than she knew how she'd understood that something was deeply wrong with Queen Mysona's child, or that the cost for the understanding that came with the First Law was not the same as using Power. She realized that she could have named a price of her own to the horse trader's wife, if she chose, but that was a separate thing. Not that any of it really mattered to her at the moment, but it was something to think about later.

I still have to walk, Marta thought, and shrugged. "Then I'll walk," Marta said aloud to no one in particular, and set out by herself on the road to Karsan. As much as she dreaded the trip, she was still happy to be out of Molbrook, and she didn't look back at the place once she'd left it behind.

Marta walked for three days. She rested or slept when she was tired, ate when she was hungry. When a cold rain came she walked through that too, grateful that she'd had sense enough to bring her oilskin cloak even though the one lined with rabbit fur was warmer. When she heard someone coming on the road ahead or behind her Marta ducked into the trees or whatever cover was available to her until she was certain of who it was. Sense, again, to Marta's way of thinking. She was alone on the road and not everyone would know or believe she was Black Kath's daughter. There might even be those who did not care. Once she stopped an old peddler driving his cart on the road from Karsan, but he had not seen her mother, or heard of any unusual happenings at the palace since the birth of the King's son.

Marta blinked. "The King's son is born? Is the queen well?"
The man smiled, showing three missing teeth. "Oh, yes. A fine healthy boy and the queen right as rain. Had a bit of trouble, poor thing, but Black Kath pulled her through it fine, as I heard it told."

Marta thanked the man and hurried on her way. The child was fine, the queen was fine. There would be celebrations, probably still going on. Perhaps her mother remained behind...?

Marta shook her head. This was Black Kath of Lythos. She wouldn't have remained behind for a party, king or no king. At least poor Mysona's second child had fared better than the first; that was something. Marta tried to take some comfort from that, but all she could think about was her mother.

On the fourth day, Marta found her mother's cart.

The recent rains had already covered the wheel marks leading from the cart track to this hidden clearing; Marta wasn't entirely sure how she'd managed to find it in the first place, but she'd turned off the main road without hesitation and walked almost straight to it, led by some new instinct that seemed to say, "if this is what you seek, here it is." The certainty hadn't come in words, but it was no less real. It was a new feeling, a new experience. Marta had another hunch about why it was this way, and it was all too easy to put into words. She avoided doing that for a little while, refusing to see what the mound of newly turned earth clearly told her, but she was too tired and too numb to resist for very long.

"Is it...because the cart is mine now?"

Seek what is owed, what is due, what is yours. You will always know.

The words were from her mother's account book, written on the very last page.

"Mother is gone. They're all gone...Treedle, Bone Tapper... I'm alone."

No, that was wrong. Treedle and Bone Tapper had left, but they weren't gone. The same sense that told her where to find the cart told her that much. Of her mother it said nothing. Marta thought of a column totaled, a page completed, an account closed. It was easier than thinking of death. She would not think about death at all. There was too much to be done and Marta was sure that she wasn't ready, perhaps not even yet able, to do it.

"Mother..." Marta felt the tears coming, and she fought them with a ruthless ferocity. "No. No tears. I am the Witch of Lythos now."

Marta didn't know how long she stood there, fighting for all she was worth. She would not give in to tears; she would not give in to anything. Marta was alone now, alone in a world that did not love her or her kind; she'd seen the proof often enough and barely acknowledged that before now. Now she would do nothing else. She fought her grief to a standstill with nothing except will and cold fury. It was all on her now, ready or no. Marta did nothing else until she trusted herself not to waver, not for a moment. Dry eyed and fierce, Marta finally gauged her mother's grave against the only Law of Power she knew, and every time the measure came out wrong.

There should be no grave.

She remembered the day Black Kath departed for Karsan, and her own dismay at being instructed to read the accounts book. To her surprise, there had been more to it than she'd thought. Not, perhaps, the power that Laras had sought, but certainly more than the dry figures, debts and obligations she'd expected. There was a fair bit about the workings of the Debt, and more about the time of Transference, when a witch or magician's heirs inherited both the services owed and the services due. Most of that information had been recently entered in the book.

Was it all for this, Mother? Did you know?

Yet if what she had read was true, then none of Kath's servants would have done anything except flee until the time when they were reclaimed, and certainly none would have paused so long as to bury her.

Mother, why didn't you tell me?

Foolish thought. Marta had known, and just refused to see. Her mother's infirmities had been getting worse for years. Marta hadn't wanted to deal with what was happening to her mother before; it was far too late now. She forced her concentration back to the business at hand.

Now then, Black Kath's passing would have freed her bond-servants for a time; surely none of them would have paid her the courtesy of burying her. And if they had, why? Fond as she was of Treedle and, despite his surly disposition, Bone Tapper, Marta knew it was neither love nor loyalty that had bound both to her Mother's service. Yet if a passing farmer or such had found the cart and buried her mother, why was the cart still here? At least they would have taken it for safekeeping or salvage. Yet here it was, and here the grave was, and one or the other should not be. It was something she didn't understand, and by the Laws of Power that was a very dangerous thing. One who controlled power had to understand it, else it was as like to control her. Or worse.

Marta looked at the sun. It was low in the sky, but not yet at the treetops. There was a little time left in the day, and Marta was fairly sure that at least one of her mother's former servants was not so very far away.

Marta sighed. "Let's test my understanding, shall we?" she said to herself and no one else in particular.

Marta tried to remember the summoning words from the account book, and was a little surprised to find that she didn't have to try at all. The words came, without hesitation. Perhaps it was a function of the Debt, not the Laws of Power; incantations had nothing to do with the First Law, so far as Marta had seen and her mother had taught. Marta could see that there were advantages as well as obligations enshrined in the Debt, like all true agreements.

Marta felt a little foolish, but she said the words with every ounce of command she could muster. "Bone Tapper, oldest. Tie binds strongest. I sing to you. Now sing to me."

Reluctantly, and from deep in the forest, there came an answer like a cry of despair. Marta slowly smiled and then followed the sound, leaving the clearing as she slipped through the woods as nimbly as a doe. Now and then she repeated her chant to give direction until the sound was quite loud.

"What was your trouble?" she asked then.

The voice answered out of a grove of aspen. "Murder."

"And what was Mother's promise?"

"To hide me from the noose," the voice sounded more raucous with every passing moment, as if the throat that bore it changed and shriveled by the moment.

"And was it done?"

"She made me a raven!"

"And was it done?" Marta repeated, an edge creeping into her voice.

"It was." The voice was a harsh sigh.

"What do you owe Kath and her own?"

"My life."

"And what will repay that?"

"My life."

"So shall it be. Come, then."

A figure that was almost like a man stepped through the ghostly trees, then it was less like a man and hopped along the ground then at last nothing like a man as it flapped slowly through the growing darkness on broad black wings. The creature called Bone Tapper lit on Marta's left shoulder.

"You will serve me as you did my mother," she said.

"As you become your mother," replied the raven, and the sound it made then was as much like a laugh as a raven could manage. Marta clamped a hand over its beak, looked straight into its beady black eyes and smiled a smile like honey dripped in poison.

"Right now you will hold your tongue while you still have one. Tonight at my command you will tell me everything you remember about the time my mother died, and if you leave out anything I'll pluck you like a Midwinter goose." She let go of his beak. "Nod if you understand."

The raven did nod then, slowly and unmistakably.

Marta nodded herself, satisfied for the moment. "And so for today. Tomorrow you will help me find the others."

*

Marta had been cold before. In the snowy woods near her home. In the cave. This was different. She shivered and pulled the blanket closer about her, keeping as close to the small campfire as she dared. Bone tapper eyed her from a nearby branch.

"It's not that cold. A little chilly, perhaps."

Marta glared at him. "Don't presume to tell me how cold I should be. I'm freezing."

"It would be warmer in the cart."

Marta sighed. "Which is not here, and thank you for reminding me that I will be sleeping on the hard ground again tonight because we have no horse to pull that sodding cart and had to leave it! I hoped we'd find Yssara today."

"He's nearby, I'm certain. We'll find him tomorrow."

Marta thought so too. It was strange and new to her but, as when she was seeking Bone Tapper, Marta was certain she could sense the creature's presence. Almost as if she could sniff him out, like a hound, though it was nothing so easily expressed as a scent or sound. She said as much to the raven.

Bone Tapper just ruffled his feathers, looking desolate. "We're bound to you, Marta. Tethered. Maybe the chains aren't visible, but they're there."

She snorted. "You can spare me your woeful countenance of martyrdom. My end of the chain's heavier than yours, from what I can see. Yet the idea of a tether is close enough to the mark."

Marta knew a little about the time of Transference; whatever bonds her mother had shared with her servants were being recreated with Marta. She'd rather thought it merely meant the transfer of the debt relationship, but clearly there was more to it. Marta almost wished she'd brought her mother's accounts book from home; she didn't remember anything specifically about this matter but she wasn't sure enough of her memory to say there was not.

Yet even more than that, Marta wished she had never left home at all. That right now she was in her own warm bed and could stay there, snuggled deeply content, until her mother rousted her out for breakfast. Yet there was no warm bed and probably no breakfast either. She had planned for a trip to Karsan but now her food was fast running out and, in the places they had been forced to wander, there were no inns or even friendly homesteads where she might find more.

In addition to all that there was the fleeting thought, roughly shoved aside, that if she hadn't found the grave her mother wouldn't really be gone.

"I wasn't prepared for this," she said to no one in particular.

"Your mother wasn't in good health for some time," Bone Tapper said.

"I didn't mean that," Marta said, though it occurred to her that perhaps she did, in fact, mean that. She pushed that thought aside too. "I mean this infernal chasing."

"You haven't wept," Bone Tapper said.

Marta blinked. "What are you talking about?"

"Your mother is dead."

"I'm well aware of that. Do you think I am not?"

The raven slightly raised his wings, which Marta knew was his way of giving a shrug. "I wonder."

"Wondering or worrying about me doesn't finish the task at hand. We have to find Yssara. Then Treedle."

"I'm not your mother," Bone Tapper said. "She worried about you. I do not. I do wonder, however."

"Keep it to yourself, then."

"There's nothing in the Debt that says I cannot have an opinion," the raven said. "In fact, your mother encouraged it."

For the first time in a while Marta forgot the fact that she was cold. "My mother is gone, and I have to do what she did, yes, and with less than a fraction of her power and skill! I may not be anything approaching what she was. Not now, perhaps never! Yet whatever you think of me, Bone Tapper, you doubt this at your peril: I will have what is mine."

The raven cocked an eye at her. "I was a raven three days ago. I was a man two days ago. Now I am a raven again. Marta, I have every reason to believe what you say. I was just—"

"I'm going to sleep," Marta said, though she wasn't sure if she would or not. "I don't want to hear any more about it."

"It's going to be chilly tonight. If I were a man I could keep the fire burning," he said.

Marta rolled the blanket around herself as tightly as she could and lay down on the unyielding ground, her back solidly to fire and raven alike.
"Let it die," she said. "Everything dies."

Bone Tapper didn't say anything after that, and eventually Marta drifted off to uneasy sleep. She dreamed of being on Laras's rope again, only now it was tied around her neck. She clawed at the knot but Laras only pulled it tighter. She struggled to get her fingers around the rope, and finally managed just as she happened to glance back. It wasn't Laras holding the rope. It was Amaet.

WHOSE END OF THE ROPE IS HEAVIEST?

Marta woke up breathing as hard as if she'd been in a footrace, and every muscle in her body seemed to ache. She groaned as she sat up, slowly disentangling herself from the blanket as her breathing began to slow down to normal.

She put her hands to her throat, unsure for a moment if she would fine a rope there. Marta was relieved to find that there was not.

Just a dream.

Perhaps, but even without the presence of the choking rope Marta wasn't quite able to convince herself of that. After all, if the debt forged a bond between her and her servants, wouldn't it do something similar between herself and Amaet? Marta knew enough of how the Debt worked to know there was no reason to exclude herself from the rules that bound others; she too was a servant. Marta shook her head. True enough, yet too dreadful a thought for first thing in the morning, even on a wretched day like this one.

This would be a wretched day; Marta had no doubt. It didn't exactly look the part, in the hopeful time just after dawn; the morning sun was clear and strong. Marta would have appreciated it more if it hadn't hurt her eyes so. At least it was driving off the night's chill...a little. The birds were calling but even that bit of natural cheerfulness annoyed Marta for reasons she couldn't quite name.

Fine thing for them to be cheerful. Snug in their nests, breakfast to be found when needed, no Powers trying to run their lives...

Marta stared at the cold ashes of last night's campfire. Breakfast. What was she going to do about that? Maybe Bone Tapper could find something, but where was he? Marta looked around, saw nothing that looked even vaguely ravenish.

"Bone Tapper, where are you?"

There was no answer, and she called again, louder, "Bone Tapper!"

The answer came, faint and distant. "—finish breakfast in peace?"

So he had found something, the sneak. Marta set off in the direction of the voice, striding purposefully. "What have you found?"

"A young deer." The answer came from much closer now.

"And I don't suppose it occurred to you to share?"

"You're very welcome to share, if you want. There's more here than I can eat."

"There better be—"

Marta stopped. A freshening breeze had just brought her a smell that wasn't very fresh at all.

You don't mean...

"Bone Tapper, how long has this deer been dead?"

Bone Tapper flapped up out the thicket just ahead and settled on a branch to groom his feathers. "About four days. Or maybe five."

Marta felt her gorge rise. "Urgh," was all she said.

Bone Tapper looked at her. "What did you expect? If I am to be raven, shall I not take the advantages as well as the limits?"

"But carrion..."

"Has a piquant aroma and a sharp, bold taste to one suited to the fare, such as I. There's plenty left."

"Your generosity is beyond words."

"Not at all. Part of my obligation is to counsel you from my perspective. My perspective is that of a bird that eats whatever it can get. I hope it was useful to you."

Marta realized she was still carrying the sodden blanket. She found a tree limb on the edge of a clearing and threw it over the branch to dry a bit. "Is it always going to be like this? Sarcasm? Seeming to yield in all things and yet actually yielding in nothing? Every word of counsel a thinly veiled complaint about your portion in this transaction? Is this how you pay your debt?"

"I am a poor thing of feathers, beak, and appetite. I do my best."

"Yes, but at what?"

Bone Tapper just shrugged and continued grooming. Marta would gladly have wrung the bird's neck, if he'd been within her reach. On the positive side of the tally, she wasn't nearly so hungry now as she'd thought she was a few moments ago. All thoughts of food now inevitably raised an image of crawling maggots, and meat painted with the vivid colors of putrification. She was still thirsty, however.

"Is there any water about? I mean, water that doesn't involve fetid stumps or floating mosquitoes?"

"There's a natural spring at the base of that rise just ahead. I can't smell anything interesting in it, for what that's worth."

"One instance where a raven's perspective actually has merit," Marta said. "Watch my blanket. If there's so much as one bird dropping on it when I get back, I'm going to assume you were responsible. Is that clear?"

"Unfair," Bone Tapper said, "but clear enough."

Marta left him there, sulking. She walked about fifty yards to a hillock and found the spring where Bone Tapper said it would be. It bubbled out of a crack in a stone, and pooled where the rocks made a natural basin. Marta drank deeply and splashed her face and neck with the cold, clear water. The potential of the day began to look a little better, although now her stomach was rumbling again.

If I don't find that wretched horse today I'm going to have to return to the cart for more provisions, and I'm not sure how much is there.

The alternative would be to find a town, but she'd have to do that even if the horse did turn up. Which so far it had not. Marta knew it was nearby, but that is all she knew. And so far nothing of what she had felt, or heard, or seen spoke to her of a horse...

Marta swore colorfully. She wasn't looking for a horse, was she? Just something that had once been a horse. Strange, she'd had no problem keeping the idea of form and function separate when she'd been seeking Bone Tapper. She knew he was really' a man, whatever form he'd taken in her mother's service. Yet what was Yssara, really?

Not a man.

Marta knew that much about the creature, whatever it was. Yssara, with his strange golden eyes and the habit of breathing steam even when it wasn't cold--

That was the answer. It had all been right before her all this time. Marta began to wonder if she were as big a fool as she sometimes suspected. She went back to where Bone Tapper was waiting with her blanket. The blanket wasn't yet dry but it was, she was pleased to see, spotless.

"Bone Tapper, is Yssara a dragon?"

He stared at her in surprise for a moment before answering. "Certainly. Didn't you know?"

"Not exactly...well, to be sure I never gave it much thought. A dragon? Mother made a dragon into a horse?"

Bone Tapper shrugged. "And why not? Yssara owed your mother debt service and she didn't need a dragon. Hardly anyone does, come to that. Even other dragons, from what little I know of the matter. She needed a draft horse."

"So do I," Marta said wistfully.

"You do," Bone Tapper agreed. "Shall we go find yours?"

Marta nodded, though not with as much enthusiasm as she might have shown when she didn't yet realize what it was they hunted.

"You don't seem as keen," Bone Tapper said.

Marta rolled up her blanket. There wasn't much more to the camp to break up. "A debt is a debt. Dragon or king, it doesn't matter who owes it."

Marta told herself that more than once as they made their way through the forest. When they finally came to the first place where the new spring growth showed unmistakable traces of fire, she was still saying it. Bone Tapper, for once, kept his opinions to himself.

"Yssara's close," was all Bone Tapper said.

Marta eyed the charred foliage. "That's what you said yesterday."

"It was no less true yesterday. Remember that deer carcass I breakfasted on this morning? I forgot to mention it was a bit singed. It was obviously one of Yssara's meals that got away...at least until the unfortunate creature died of its injuries. I imagine Yssara was out of practice."

"Sympathy for your breakfast? Well, maybe Yssara just didn't eat it all," Marta said.

"Are you joking, Mistress? This is a dragon we're referring to—they swallow their prey whole."

Marta just nodded, but the truth was she didn't know much about dragons. They weren't exactly common creatures; in fact before now Marta wasn't really sure that they existed. Even now she wasn't totally sure, since she hadn't every seen Yssara as a dragon. Still, if this was indeed its nature, how this one came to be in her mother's debt was a tale she'd like to hear, if she ever felt like enduring one of Bone Tapper's rambling narratives long enough to get the meat of the story out of it.

Marta looked up from the burned place. "He's that way," she said, pointing north. "Fly ahead and see if you can find where he is."

The raven hesitated. "If my feathers are burned to nothing it'll be hard to report," Bone Tapper said. "You do realize Yssara doesn't want to be found?"

"What he wants is beside the matter, and the same goes for you. As for your feathers, I suggest you fly high enough that this doesn't happen."

Bone Tapper took off without more argument. Marta followed north at a brisk walk, though it was nothing compared to Bone Tapper's wings. He soon returned and landed on her shoulder. "You were right. There's a cave less than a league from here. Yssara's there."

"Did you see him?"

"I didn't have to. He's there."

Marta frowned, but didn't question the raven further. When they approached the line of rocky hills that held the cave, Marta saw what Bone Tapper meant; trees near the site were as charred as logs in a slow fire. The odd thing was, some of the burned traces were very old, looking more like the marks of long ago woodland fire that had since healed.

Bone Tapper perched on a branch well away from the cave's mouth. "Here's your cart-horse," he said sullenly. "In there."

Marta stood at the edge of the pines where they ringed the cavern entrance. Traces of charcoal and scorched earth showed the approach to the cave had not always been so clear.

"This place has been burned before now."

"Obviously it was his home long ago. If one has a home, wouldn't one go there? I would."

"Did you know where he lived all along? You were with Mother when Yssara was Indebted. You could have led me here directly!"

" I knew he was to be found here in these woods, and you knew the same, Mistress. I have served."

Which Marta already knew to mean he would speak no more on the matter unless ordered. Marta was getting tired of giving orders for every little thing that needed doing. It was draining, and just then she felt very drained. Were all Mother's servants as stubborn? No wonder she always looked so weary.

Marta took a close grip on her thoughts, reined them in, made them serve her for the task at hand like anything else that was hers by right. That was always what mattered; best not to forget. She strode out of the wood shadow like a queen before court, the sun finding red and gold sparks in her hair.

"What was your trouble?" she demanded of the darkness beyond the cave entrance.

There came a low hiss, then a wisp of steam appeared out of the darkness. "There are deer in the woods. My treasures are at my feet. Let me stay."

"By birthright and the Laws of Power you belong to me, Yssara. I will have what is mine."

Another hiss, this time followed by a jet of flame. "I want to stay!"

Marta kept her voice level, but the strain was great. "You are in my debt, and I need you."

"You fear me, Black Kath's daughter."

Marta opened her mouth to deny it, but then closed it again. It was a few moments before she answered. "I am afraid of you," Marta said, and knew the truth when she spoke it, "I'd be a fool otherwise. Yet my fear won't keep me from doing what I must do, Yssara. Your strength will not keep you from doing what you must do. Do we understand each other, Yssara? What you want doesn't matter."

"Not now. One day, Black Kath's daughter, you will find things very different."

Marta drew herself to her full height, though it was not so very much. "You will not threaten me."

A low chuckle that was like the fall of embers. "A threat? Say rather a prophecy. 'What Power Holds, Weakness Frees.' Oh, yes. I know that one. So do you, but I wonder about the limits of your understanding."

"I understand this much." Marta took a deep breath. "What was your trouble?"

Slowly, because there was no choice, Yssara answered. "Greed."

When the ritual was done, Marta led what was now a cart horse back from the mouth of the cave. Marta had won, as she knew she must, but it didn't feel like a victory. The day barely begun and she was already tired, and if she had the right of power over Yssara she certainly didn't feel very powerful. Marta had too much sense of things beyond her understanding, and visions beyond her sight. She felt... limited.

Marta knew Yssara was right to question her; she only knew one Law of Power, and it seemed to speak more of limits to power than potential, for all that it was fun to break rocks. Just then she was almost grateful for those limits, because the creature beside her moved slowly, every step begrudged, ears flat and nostrils flaring. Weary as she was, Marta kept a firm grip on the reins, and didn't allow the beast any slack at all.

Will it always be like this?

She shook her head. There was more to it. The craja in Amaet's cave had shown that. Yet that was just a glimpse of something beyond the simple destruction expressed in the First Law. A promise, really, that there was something more. Marta knew the deeper knowledge was there, but it was going to take time to find it. She hoped the superficial understanding of the Law would be enough, that and the rules of the Debt her mother had seen fit to document, because for a while that was going to be all Marta had to work with.

"What you have is what you use," Marta said aloud.

"Your mother was fond of that phrase," Bone Tapper said as he landed on Yssara's back. The creature shook himself, throwing the raven off like a fly. Bone Tapper settled grumpily on Marta's shoulder instead.

"You didn't have to do that," Marta said to the horse. It did not answer. She frowned. "Yssara, say something."

Yssara just glanced at her haughtily.

Bone Tapper sighed. "He won't speak, now that he's a horse again. He never did."

"Even for my mother?"

"Your mother never asked him to. At least, never in my hearing."

"Which probably means she never expected it of him." Marta thought about it. "Of course. Horses are good for bearing burdens, for running swiftly. Horses in war can be trained to attack and defend. Yet no one expects counsel from them. Yssara serves according to the nature of the form he's in."

Yssara looked away. Marta had the distinct feeling that, had he chosen to speak, Yssara would have said words that had nothing to do with counsel, except perhaps suggestions for actions either obscene, impossible, or both.

"Yet they do expect counsel of a raven?" Bone Tapper shook his head. "Not to my knowledge."

"Ravens are known to speak," Marta pointed out. "Or at least mimic a human voice. It stands to reason more would be expected because it can be expected."

"How fortunate for me."

"Stop complaining. We've got a long walk ahead of us before we can even begin the search for Treedle. Yssara has an appointment with my mother's wagon."

"Fine. Then which way will we go?" Bone Tapper asked.

Marta blinked. "Which way?"

Bone Tapper gave her an odd look. "Of course which way! North? South? You knew which direction to search for Yssara. You knew where I was, rightly enough. Where is Treedle?"

Marta had been concentrating so much on finding Bone Tapper and Yssara that this was the first time she'd taken a moment to think about it. She looked around her. "He's..."

Marta stopped, and let the words trail off to nothing. Her own surprise was such that she spoke the words aloud, not caring if Bone Tapper and Yssara knew the truth.

"I don't know."

Bone Tapper just stared at her. Even Yssara snorted a question.

"I said I don't know!"

"Mistress..." Bone Tapper began, but one look from Marta and he kept silent.

"We'll find him," she said, and that was all. They searched until the food ran out. Marta bought more in a village they passed and they searched until that ran out. They first snows held off and still they searched, but Marta knew the snows would not wait much longer. The money was running out quickly. Yssara remained sullenly fierce. Bone Tapper said as little as he could manage and Marta said almost nothing at all. Finally, because there was no other choice as winter descended on them, Marta turned her cart back toward home.

CHAPTER 7

"The Arrow Path is an honest transaction. Amaet gives us what we need to seek the Seven Laws and we owe her debt service in return. The Path of Solitude is a surrender. In which case the Power, whichever one it may be, uses you for their own purpose and gives nothing in return, save only that which serves their purpose. It is, bluntly put, a bad bargain."
— Black Kath's Tally Book

Morushe was a small kingdom nestled against the southernmost slopes of the White Mountains. Wylandia lay to the north on the other side of the mountains, Borasur to the south on the coast. Laras thought it a rather awkward place for a such a small kingdom, with greater powers to both north and south. Yet it had managed to keep its independence for nearly a thousand years, save a period when, for a few generations, it was bound after a marriage alliance to Borasur. Yet the more Laras thought about it, the more sense it made. Morushe was the gateway to both greater kingdoms, controlling the main trade pass through the mountains. Either Wylandia or Borasur would be foolish to allow the other to conquer it, and thus control the trade of both.

The balance requires uneasy alliances and a fragile peace.

It was the sum of the history of the twelve mainland kingdoms, so far as Laras could see. The marvel was not that there were wars; the marvel was that there hadn't been more of them.

The journey had taken two days longer than Laras planned; just getting a mount had taken more time than he felt he could afford, and in the end he'd been reduced to snapping a lock on a nearby stable. The mount he'd taken, though the best of the lot, was little bargain even at the price. The sorry nag cropped grass on the slope a few yards away while Laras sat on a rock and contemplated the city of Balanar in the valley below. Every now and then he would look away from the city to the book resting on his knees.

It's a rather plain thing.

It was well made, as most books were. Anything worth binding at all required the work of craftsmen, and the book Amaet had sent him to steal was no exception. The boards were covered with thin leather, the pages fine vellum. It was the book, no question. Amaet said he would know, and he did. The library at the Temple of Amatok was immense, well over two hundred volumes of esoteric religious practices, politics, history. Yet as soon as Laras had brushed his fingers across the cover of this particular book the image of Amaet flashed across his inner eye. She was smiling. Laras took the book and broke a lock on a side door; the priests were busy making ready for an unscheduled ceremony. Laras doubted they even remembered he was there. It was, he realized, incredibly easy.

Getting the book into the King's Library at Karsan would be a different matter altogether. He had been a messenger of the King; almost everyone at court knew his face. He was risking life and limb letting himself be seen in Lythos again. And for what? That was the thing that Laras couldn't understand; the thing that kept him loitering in the hills near Balanar contemplating the volume on his lap.

"I can't believe," he said for the third time and to no one in particular, "that the goddess required me to steal a wayfarer's guide!"

That's all the book was, despite a very clerical sounding title: "Centers of Faith in the Southern Mainland." It was just a listing of the primary shrines and temples south of the White Mountains. Basic directions, a bit of information about each, the best and safest inns to stay in on the way. All compiled by a rather detail-oriented monk some two hundred years earlier, so needless to say the accommodation advice was out of date. In all other respects as well a volume so trivial that, as far as Laras could see, no one had ever bothered to make any copies; there was just this one hand crafted volume. Handsome it was, if plain. Probably bound as a gift to some clerical patron and shelved and forgotten.

Don't make a habit of questioning me, Laras. Laras remembered the goddess' words exactly. He shrugged, and sighed. No, it wouldn't do to question. Yet he couldn't help but wonder. Laras finally rose, gathered his mount, and put the book safely away in his saddle pack. He didn't bother to shatter the rock he'd been sitting on; in truth breaking rocks was getting a little wearisome. There was more to the First Law, he knew, and would find it in time, but mostly he wondered what glories there would be in the Second Law.

Laras climbed into the saddle and turned the beast towards the west. It was a long ride back to Lythos. Not that Laras was in a hurry; the days of travel ahead would barely be enough time to figure out how he was going to fulfil Amaet's quest and still live long enough to collect the reward.

There's always a catch.

Laras knew there would be more. Getting the book had been tedious and time consuming, but easy. The next part would not be easy. It could not; there just wasn't that much good luck in the world. No matter; soon he would be able to reorder the world more to his liking. Laras's horse may have been pointed toward Lythos but his sights were on that distant, happy day. By the time Laras reached the border of Lythos he had an idea. A rather good idea, he thought, and just after he crossed the border he put his idea into practice. When Laras finally rode into Karsan he did so with his face covered with a black cloth, as one ill or disfigured. He got several dark scowls as he rode past the good folk, and there was much muttering. If there was a plague around no one wanted it in Karsan. Still, his former neighbors could think him malformed if they wished, or even unwelcome. Just so long as they didn't think of him as who he was. Laras heard more than a few names hurled at him, but he smiled. None of those names was "Laras."

Funny how predictable they are.

There was an undertone of judgment in the thought, Laras well knew, and he wasn't exactly proud of the fact even if he wouldn't deny it. Yet he was also genuinely astonished. His disguise was ludicrously simple; to his own way of thinking a child shouldn't have been fooled. Now he was beginning to think he shouldn't have bothered with a disguise at all. He had been one of the King's Royal Messengers, and if that was just a fancy way of saying "servant with a horse," it still meant something. Or at least he had thought it did. Laras was beginning to wonder if the townsfolk would have recognized or even taken any notice of him if he'd rode in at the height of the day.

I was never very important, but surely someone would have recognized me?

Maybe yes, maybe no. He did hope that one particular person could still recognize him. Everything depended on that. Laras found a stable willing to see to his mount once the stable keeper saw the color of Laras's silver. Laras took only the book from his saddle, bundled in a pack that made him look like a peddler. He wasn't overly fond of that impression, but there was no help for it. He left the stable and kept walking until he reached the grounds of King Alian's castle.

Karsan had no true palace, as did Borasur or even Morushe. Lythos was rather small as kingdoms went and even the king's dwelling had to do double duty as residence and fortress; Karsan itself had grown up partly under the protection of the old castle, partly as a pilgrim's shelter on route to the Shrine of Amaet. There was a ramshackle, hodge podge quality to the whole place that was missing in older, richer towns.

The courtyard gates were open, as he knew they would be. One of the guards frowned at him but did not challenge him; an illness mask might mean exactly what it appeared to mean. Then again, it might mean that here was someone on the king's business who did not want his identity known. Alian's guards, in Laras's experience, were an unimaginative lot and didn't use much initiative. Absent, of course, specific and detailed instructions on when and how they should do so. Laras had no doubt they had orders to arrest him if he showed his face there; King Alian wouldn't risk offending Black Kath when the price to stay on her good side was to sacrifice a mere messenger.

I'm not showing my face. Such a simple thing makes all the difference.

There was a good deal of activity in the courtyard inside the curtain walls surrounding the complex. Laras found a spot near the siege well and took some water, partly to rest but mostly to try and overhear what all the excitement was about.

The King of Junland is coming.

Laras smiled. He'd been quite surprised, soon after his start as a messenger, to discover that even kings had kings. Or at least, Alian did. He technically owed Junland fealty for several valley farmlands near the southern border, a land grant to a distant ancestor not, at the time, in the royal line. The lands weren't worth very much, but they were a considerable buffer between Lythos and its neighbor to the south and Alian had no intention of giving them up or giving Junland an excuse to repossess by force. All Alian had to do was put up with the bother of a rare Royal Visit and pay an annual token tribute. Doubtless it was more than a little galling to Alian's pride, but if so it was merely part of the price. Alian's court was in full preparation for the impending visit of the King of Junland and the chaos and confusion would make Laras's job a great deal easier. Or was it good luck at all? Was Amaet smoothing the way for him? And if she was, was it just to make certain that her wishes were carried out. Or was it more? Was it, perhaps, a sign of Favor?

Don't think of her. Think of the power she can give.

Laras tried. The power was what he'd wanted, the power that would make him anything he wanted to be, anything except just what he was. To serve something outside himself, indeed far beyond, was a new thing to Laras. This wasn't like serving a king; to Laras it had been no more than a position, like working in a stable or a smithy. Yet his mind kept forming images of Amaet's sweet shining face, and worshiping her was becoming easier and easier all the time. He would serve her well, whatever else he did or what rewards he commanded. It was something, he realized, that he wanted to do. Something he wanted besides power was Amaet's approval. To see her smile, and to know it was all because of him.

I think my ambition has just grown.

Laras found an inconspicuous place in the lee of a parapet stairway and settled down to wait for night. He finally dozed, despite the noise, and woke to find the shadows considerably lengthened and the clatter in the courtyard just as considerably reduced. When he was sure the evening meal was concluded he made his way through the tangle of outbuildings and stables built against the outer wall. There were tents in the courtyard now, as there had not been when Laras first arrived. That was a little worrisome; the only reason for extra shelter would be to have a place to bed down the servants and men at arms accompanying the king. The King of Junland himself and his closest nobles would sleep in the castle itself.

Laras checked a few of the stables and felt some relief to find no unusual number of mounts. Either the tents had been pitched in preparation only or, at most, a few of the king's knights had gone ahead to make sure of the preparations.

The guards will not be quite so relaxed once the king is here.

Laras didn't intend to still be around then. If he waited long enough, there was a good chance he could slip in through the kitchens; once the fires were banked no one would be there except a kitchen boy or two in exhausted sleep. He proceeded to the back door of the kitchens and peered in one small window then smiled and pulled the black cloth mask from his face. Perhaps he needn't wait after all. He rapped once on the door.

"Crust of bread for a weary traveler?" he said, when the door was cracked open.

The young woman who had opened the door just stared at him for a moment. Laras thought the dab of meal on her nose was utterly charming, though he had to confess that her red hair under its kerchief was a bit of a mess. In another moment her stare of disbelief was gone, and her entire face lit up like a Midwinter's Eve lantern.

"Laras!" She almost shouted the name, then looked about furtively and lowered her voice. "I mean...it's you! Where have you been? The Chamberlain has been looking all over for you!"

"I came to see you, Tarsy my lass. Of course. A mere witch couldn't keep me away."

The girl blinked. "What are you talking about? I said the Chamberlain. You've been gone for weeks! Where have you been?" she sounded fierce enough, though there was faint smile at the corner of her mouth that hinted that, perhaps, she would believe him if she chose. "Get your skinny arse in here before someone sees us!"

She pulled him inside quickly, then closed the door. There was no one else around. "Now, are you going to tell me the truth?"

"I'd ask the same of you. Where is everyone?"

"The Mistress is making all the kitchen staff sleep in the Great Hall tonight to make sure there is no one absent tomorrow when Junland arrives.

A few of the girls chose to meet their sweethearts last time and were late returning. Breakfast was almost ruined."

Laras smiled. Amazing coincidence, that, he thought, but what he said was, "And were you among those, Tarsy?"

The young woman blushed. "No, and I've got other tasks besides the kitchen... and who are you to ask me that? You haven't even answered my question yet!"

"I had business to attend." Laras said. "It kept me away for some time. Will you betray me?"

She looked confused. "Betray? To whom? The Chamberlain's likely to turn you out for going missing like that, but why should I tell that pompous ass anything? Now that you're back he'll find you soon enough."

Now it was Laras's turn to be confused. "Is he the only one looking for me? Are you sure?"

"Who else would be looking for the likes of you? Other than myself, that is. Why? Have you done something wrong?"

Laras looked carefully at Tarsy's face, but he couldn't see any signs of deception there. She was skilled at many things, but lying wasn't among them. Was it possible that Marta had not told her mother about what he had done? Or that Black Kath had chosen not pursue him? Neither notion made a bit of sense.

"Tarsy, when was Black Kath at the castle last?"

"That one? Not since the queen gave birth...weeks ago. The queen had a boy, you know."

"No, I didn't," Laras said. "That's wonderful..."

"You don't sound pleased. Have you tangled with that witch? Over her daughter, I bet. I saw her last winter. She's pretty."

"No, nothing of that sort. I have more sense than that," Laras said. The lie came easy, despite the fact that he felt a little annoyed that Tarsy had gotten so close to the matter. That was almost suspicious, yet he looked into her guileless face and knew that she wasn't hiding anything from him. She couldn't if she tried. "I've just got something on my mind...So. Have you got some time tonight for an old friend?"

She appeared to consider the question carefully. "That depends on how good a job you do of convincing me of your good intentions. And I still want to know where you've been."

He kissed her on the nose. "Feed me first. I'm too weak from hunger to say more."

Tarsy fed him and then they kissed some more. Later she led him to a hidden place off a back staircase where they kissed a lot and more beside. Later, when Tarsy was asleep, Laras slipped back up that staircase a few more floors to Alian's library, where he slipped the book into a little used section containing mostly folktales and legends.

Assuming the King's Librarian even notices it at all, I'll wager he enters it in the rolls rather than explain how it got here without his knowledge.

Laras smiled. He didn't understand what had happened or why, but clearly within the kingdom he was not a wanted man, save by his former master who doubtless meant no more than a good whipping and discharge. He'd skip the whipping, thank you kindly, and he hadn't planned to stay in any case. For whatever reason Kath and her daughter were keeping his crime secret, he had no doubt that it was so they might seek their own path to revenge without interference from the King's Judgment. Best that Laras remain a moving target, for now, and not make it any easier on them than he could avoid. And why not? He had no farther business in Karsan. His quest was completed, and with an unexpectedly pleasant bonus.

Laras thought of Tarsy and felt just a twinge of guilt. He hadn't lied to her much. Certainly no more than she had reason to suspect. Yet his tryst still felt like a betrayal to him, almost as if he'd been, well, unfaithful. The strange thing was that he wasn't sure who the injured party was.

Have I betrayed Tarsy, or Amaet?

Laras didn't know, or even understand why he was thinking the way he did. Yet even after he slipped back out through the kitchen early the next morning and calmly walked past the guards, the feeling would not go away. It stayed with him when he reclaimed his horse and left Karsan far behind. Later still, as carefully slipped back to the cave so close to Black Kath's home to claim his reward from Amaet, it was the image of Amaet's radiant smile that grew stronger and more vivid even as the memory of Tarsy's sweet face almost completely faded away. By the time he arrived, he could think of little else.

HAVE YOU DONE AS I ASKED?

"To the letter," said Laras.

IT GOES WELL. MARTA WILL PROGRESS RAPIDLY, I THINK.

Laras felt as if a cloud had formed over him. "I don't understand. What has the book to do with Marta?"

THAT ISN'T YOUR CONCERN. NOW CLAIM YOUR REWARD.

Amaet leaned close and whispered the secret of the Second Law of Power.

Laras frowned. "So simple..."

ANSWERS ARE OFTEN SIMPLE...ONCE YOU POSSESS THEM.

Yet Laras wasn't really thinking about that. He was thinking how easy it would be, with Amaet leaned so close to him then, to kiss her.

Doubtless I would be turned into a pile of blackened ash.

That didn't stop him from thinking about it. So intently, in fact, that he almost missed what Amaet said next.

--YOU LEAVE THIS PLACE, SEAL THE ENTRANCE.

Laras blinked. "Seal? But then I can't return!"

NO NEED. THIS PLACE'S USEFULNESS IS ENDED. WHEN I NEED YOU AGAIN, I WILL MAKE THE PLACE AND THE TIME OF OUR MEETING KNOWN TO YOU.

Laras thought to ask a question, but thought better of it. He simply bowed once and, when Amaet had again vanished, he stood there a time longer, staring at the cold stone shrine. He wasn't really thinking about the shrine, though he was determined to fix it in his memory. No, how focus was on what Amaet had said to him: When I need you again...

When.

I will see her again. She promised.

In the meantime, Laras had other concerns. Winter was coming, and he couldn't go back to Karsan now. Even if Black Kath was not searching for him, it was a safe wager that the Chamberlain was.

Shall I be a stable boy now, for a while?

The notion appealed to his sense of the romantic, if not to his sense of worth. He'd often found the two in conflict and had never quite worked it out.

I'm a magician now, he thought. Surely there was a way to make that pay? Black Kath certainly did, if the rumors Tarsy had told him about the price the king had paid for his wife's first illness were true. He wasn't quite out of Kath's shadow yet but, still, he was someone to be reckoned with. But how to take advantage? He needed guidance, and the one place he knew for certain to find it was now closed to him...and everyone else in the world. Plus, Amaet had made it plain that there was no point seeking her out until she was ready, and Laras had no idea at all of how long that would be or where it would be. He was on his own.

There are no magicians in Junland, so far as I know. I think I will go there.

No one knew him there, and that was a good thing. It was also further south on the coast, and almost never snowed. That was even better. He would make his way, and do better than get by. He knew it. There was no question at all.

CHAPTER 8

"Never confuse what's possible with what's true. For that matter, never confuse what actually happens with what's true."
— Black Kath's Tally Book

"It's hardly fair," Bone Tapper said.

"Be quiet," Marta said, as she added another log to the kitchen grate. Her hands were cold and sore from chopping the wood, and she paused there to warm them as best she could. The cold was soon gone, but the ache remained.

"Counsel is my duty. If you will recall—"

Marta glared at him. "You're not counseling—you're whining. And all I recall is that you've done little but complain of Treedle's absence for the past month. And yet you perch here in the warmth and Yssara lies snug in his stable and I'm the one who has to wield that sodding axe!"

The raven subsided, but it was a grudging, sullen sort of silence. Marta knew it well. It was the same sort of uneasy quiet she'd found herself sinking too readily into over the last few weeks. She glanced at her mother's account book, but didn't open it again. Whatever she needed to learn to solve her current problem, it wasn't in there now.

I'm not studying now. I'm brooding. Just like Bone Tapper.

Knowing that didn't help matters. Marta found herself at a loss. Treedle was still missing and she was no closer to finding him than that day in the forest when she first realized she had no clue as to his whereabouts. Why was Treedle different? He still lived and the Debt still held him, she knew both beyond question just as she knew to the day when his time of service would be at an end. So why couldn't she sense him? Compel him? Find him?

"I am not my mother," she said aloud.

"Hardly news," Bone Tapper said.

Marta glanced at him and he subsided again, chastened. "I wasn't talking to you, but since you will speak no matter what I say, put your tongue to good use. Why can't I find Treedle? How is he different from you or Yssara?" Marta had been turning the question over and over in her mind for weeks, and was no closer to an answer.

"He serves for a different reason, just as my reason for being here is different from Yssara's. Yet the Debt doesn't make those fine distinctions, so far as I understand, once the terms of service are set. I wish I knew, Mistress since—as I've said more than once—it isn't right or proper that Yssara and myself are serving you as required and he is not."

"No, it isn't," Marta said. "I have my mother's obligations but not all her power. Little more than a fraction, as you well know. More than enough where you are concerned," she added pointedly, "and that infernal dragon masquerading as a cart horse, but not, apparently, enough where Treedle is concerned. I'm failing, Bone Tapper. It's driving me to madness!" Marta sat back hard in her mother's chair in her mother's kitchen, and she closed her eyes.

"I doubt not Yssara and I will be right behind you," Bone Tapper said dryly.

"Doubt not what you want, but first take the Arrow Path and lose your guide, then perhaps you can speak of 'right and proper' so that I will listen."

"You're angry," Bone Tapper said.

"Hardly news," Marta said, in a rasping voice very much like Bone Tapper's.

The raven raised his wings in a shrug. "No, but who are you really angry at? Yssara and myself for being difficult?"

"Yes!"

"Your mother for being so inconsiderate as to die on you?"

"Yes!!" Marta practically shouted the word. "I confess it freely! I'm angry at all that's happened, all that will happen, all the things I cannot change, try as I might. Frustrated, scared and very angry! Do you have a point?"

"Just that your mother is not here and we are. If you won't grieve for her, at least take some pity on us."

"I'll do what I have to do," Marta said. "I'll have what is mine. Now be quiet; I need to think."

To Marta's considerable surprise Bone Tapper did fall silent for a good long while. The log Marta had used to feed the fire fell to embers and she replaced it with another before the coals died down; she added a little kindling and worked the bellows until the flame was restored.

I still can't make the flames dance —

The sound of the door's knocker clanged through the kitchen, muffled somewhat but not so much that they couldn't hear. "Whoever it is, send them away," Marta said.

"I might as well. I can't work the latch." Bone Tapper flapped through the open doorway and out into the hall beyond before she could say anything. Marta heard muffled voices, but didn't try to make out the words. She simply stared at the flames until Bone Tapper returned and landed on her shoulder. She started to brush him off, irritated, but it was too much trouble.

"I think you'll want to see this one, Mistress."

"Who is it?" Marta asked.

"A messenger from the king...and no, not that messenger."

Marta frowned, and then she realized that the king didn't know. No one knew, except herself, Bone Tapper, Yssara and, she presumed, Treedle. She had told no one else, and the harsh winter kept travel and news down to the point that Kath's absence hadn't been noticed, so far as Marta could tell. She did realize the time when Kath's death was common knowledge could not be far off. Marta left the kitchen and trudged slowly through the hallway to the heavy iron-bound front door, and pulled the latch.

She didn't recognize the man standing there. He was young, as messengers tended to be, barely older than Marta herself, she judged. Despite her suspicion there was nothing about him that brought anything like the instant and intense dislike Marta felt for Laras. He was shorter and more strongly built, dark haired, dark eyed. Though obviously cold and weary he smiled at her.

"Hello... Lady Marta?"

"Just Marta," she said, "Come in."

He stamped the snow off his boots as best he could and followed her inside. Marta shut the door against a stiff wind.

"My name is Feran. King Alian sent me with a message for your mother."

"Come into the kitchen and I'll see if I can find you something warm to drink."

Marta still had some of the cider that had been delivered from Molbrook the week before. The apples had been very fine that season, and the amber cider was rich and smooth. She realized she'd left a tin pot simmering by the grate and forgotten all about it. Marta poured out a warm mug of it for Feran while he looked around the room. Marta frowned at that at first, but finally let it go. It was just curiosity; try as she might Marta could read nothing sinister into it.

"Is your mother about?" Feran asked. "I don't think King Alian or anyone at Karsan has heard from her lately, but we didn't believe she was away."

Marta handed the mug to Feran, who accepted it gratefully. Then, because she didn't know what else to say, she told him the truth. "My mother is dead."

"Oh...I'm sorry," Feran said, and sounded as if he really meant it. "When did it happen?"

"It was soon after the queen's confinement. I believe that was the last office she performed."

Feran looked as if he wanted to question her further, but decided against it. He reached into the pouch at his belt and pulled out a roll of parchment bearing Alian's seal. "Well, then, I am sorry to impose on your grief, but I believe this message is for you."

Marta hesitated. "Not if it was for my mother..."

"It is for the Witch of Lythos. Unless I am mistaken, that title belongs to you now."

Feran held the scroll out to her and Marta reluctantly accepted it. Not that she thought the 'title' was appropriate, but still there was truth in what he said. She broke the seal while Bone Tapper flapped over from the windowsill where he'd been resting and landed on her shoulder. He perched there, reading along as she did:

"Send to the Witch of Lythos Warm Greetings.
I have need of you again, as we both knew I would.
Please come in speed, but not in haste."
— Alian

That was all it said. Marta rolled the message up again. She realized Feran was still standing and she bade him sit down while she considered what to do. It didn't take long since, to Marta's way of thinking, there wasn't much choice.

"It's too late to leave today. I'll set out for Karsan in the morning."

"As you will; I do not know what the message was, though I was given to understand the matter was important but not urgent." Feran started to rise, but Marta's mind was already somewhere else. "I'll leave you, then."

Marta blinked at him, uncomprehending for a moment. "It's almost dark. You don't want to be traveling now. You're welcome to stay here tonight if you don't need to return immediately."

Bone Tapper squawked, but Marta shushed him with a glance. Feran smiled hesitantly. "That's very kind of you. I'll escort you back to Karsan, if you'd like. No one will fault me if I bring you to the king personally."

"Thank you. Bone Tapper will show you where to sleep tonight. There's room for your mount in our stable, but I would keep him away from Yssara. He bites. We won't be having supper as such, but there's a decent pease porridge on the fire if you're hungry. Help yourself."

While Bone Tapper escorted Feran to the guest room Kath had occasionally used for just this purpose, Marta picked up her mother's accounts book and made her way up the stairs to her old bedroom. She'd slept a few times in her mother's bed, soon after returning home with Bone Tapper and Yssara, but not since. A little while later Bone Tapper joined her there.

"This isn't a good idea," Bone Tapper said.

Marta looked up from the book. "What isn't?"

" Letting that young man stay here, of course! Have you forgotten Laras already?"

"Feran's harmless."

Bone Tapper looked down his beak at her. "Such a judge of young men's character already, are we?"

"Of this one, yes." Marta turned the page, read for a moment, then turned it back. Bone Tapper was still looking at her. "Stop looking at me as if I were a lamb in a thicket! Will you please explain your concern?"

"That should be clear enough! You're practically alone, since there's very little I could do if it came to trouble."

"It won't," Marta said. "Kath did the same, sometimes. It's a long trip from Karsan."

"Kath had Treedle, who in his hob form was stronger than most oxen of my acquaintance," Bone Tapper said, but hurried on when Marta scowled at the name. "It's not proper! A young man and woman, unchaperoned save for a raven—"

"I'm not a young woman," Marta said grimly. "I'm the Witch of Lythos. He won't try anything."

"Perhaps he won't, but what if he does?" Bone Tapper asked. "What will you do?"

"If you must know, I'll shatter his spine like an icicle," Marta said. And to illustrate her point, she picked up an empty stone candlestick and invoked the First Law. In a moment the pieces rained down onto the floor. There wasn't a single one larger than a pea.

Bone Tapper stared at the debris. "Impressive. Just remember that you can't solve all your problems by breaking them."

"Duly noted. Good night, Bone Tapper," Marta said, in a tone that made it clear that this was not a suggestion.

Bone Tapper, with one last glance at the rubble, shrugged again and wished her pleasant dreams before flapping out the door. Marta then locked that door against all and sundry and spent the better part of the evening studying her mother's books, both accounts book and histories. For all that she had told Laras that the keys to power weren't in a book, she continued to examine these as she had been doing since her mother's death. Perhaps they wouldn't lead her to more power or understanding, but she had to try. As far as she could tell there weren't a lot of other options.

There are archives in the king's palace at Karsan. Perhaps they can be of help to me.

Marta had always assumed that her mother went there for pleasure, but it now occurred to her that, perhaps, there was more to it. That might be worth finding out for herself.

Marta continued reading until the candled burned down and sleep finally took her. By sunrise she was awake again, but her eyes were red and the morning sun, weak thought it might have been, was close to blinding. Feran found her leading Yssara out to the cart when he came to saddle his own mount. Smoke curled from Yssara's nostrils, but Marta was in no mood for nonsense and the beast behaved himself.

"Good morning, Mistress. That's an...interesting breed of horse," Feran said. "I'm not familiar with it."

"He's not really a horse," Marta said, and Yssara snorted another plume of smoke in emphatic agreement. Marta didn't elaborate. "Did you sleep well?"

Feran turned his gaze away from Yssara. "Much better than I would have in a cold camp in the woods," he said. "My thanks."

Marta shrugged. "My mother would have done the same," she said, thinking that it was probably true. She would be like her mother where she could. If all else was subject to doubt in her life there could be that one certainty. There needed to be at least one.

Marta slid the harness collar over Yssara's head. Feran stepped forward to help but Marta waved him back. "He won't let anyone touch him except me...and that grudgingly," she said, pausing to swat Yssara on the nose when he threatened to take a nip out of her thigh. Yssara submitted with bad grace, but Marta finally got him harnessed properly. She'd already packed provisions into the cart but she did let Feran help her load a bag of grain for Yssara. She took a little satisfaction knowing that the beast probably didn't like grain, but in his present form was not capable of eating much else save grass, and there wasn't much of that around this time of year.

Marta climbed up into the driver's seat and Bone Tapper perched on the peaked roof of the cart behind her. Feran mounted his big dun gelding and the set off. They had only ridden for a little while when Marta asked the question she'd been wanting to ask all morning.

"I don't suppose you have any idea why King Alian wanted my mother? If you wouldn't be revealing secrets, that is."

Feran shook his head. "I can't reveal any secrets because I don't know any. I didn't even know the message was a summons until you told me, thought of course I'd assumed so. I've heard no rumors; all at the castle are well as far as I know."

"Including the queen and her son?"

Feran nodded, smiling. "Especially them. A fine healthy boy and the queen is radiant. Motherhood suits her."

Marta was glad of that. She remembered too well what the poor girl had gone through the first time. Still, she was sorry that Feran didn't have any more information for her. She didn't know what to expect when they arrived at Karsan and considered the very real possibility that she would not be able to do whatever it was the king required. She had resolved to try, whatever it was. No point in letting the king think as little of her abilities as she herself did... Marta let the thought trail off into confusion.

What...was that?

The feeling was familiar, but it took her several moments to turn it into something coherent, something she understood on a conscious level and could express in words. The feeling was that of *recognition.* Something she recognized but that she didn't know. It seemed like a paradox, but it was more like remembering something she hadn't even known that she had forgotten. The last time she'd felt it was just before she'd found the First Law of Power.

I touched one of the Laws.

She was sure of it, but she didn't know which one and, try as she might to reconstruct the thoughts that led up to it, she couldn't quite get a grip on it. Something about not letting the king know her limitations. How could that be it? The notion was little more than sense, to Marta's way of thinking. Where was the recognition coming from? Marta sighed. Whatever it was, it was gone now. She knew it had been important, but whether in itself or as proof of Marta's ability to feel that connection, she didn't know.

Feran rode beside the cart on her right. "You look very serious, Mistress," he said.

"Marta," Marta said, distracted. The word felt wrong to her. Grating. As if he were accusing her of something she wasn't. There was nothing in Feran's tone or manner to suggest he was being anything other than polite, but she wished he would stop it just the same. "I was just thinking of something; it's probably not important," she said, though she knew better.

Feran smiled, looking sheepish. "It's very difficult for me to get used to the idea of addressing the Witch of Lythos by her given name."

"Even for a King's Messenger?"

"A glorified errand-boy, Marta. Yet it does get me out and into the countryside. I'm from Wittanplace, originally."

"That's east of Karsan, isn't it? I've never been there, though I think my mother spent some time in the area once." It was where Treedle had entered her service, if Marta remembered what her mother had told her aright. Marta blinked, and thought of something she hadn't before.

"Bone Tapper, you were with Kath when Treedle entered her service, not so?"

"Yes," Bone Tapper said from his perch on top of the cart. "Why?"

"Where did it happen? Was it at Wittanplace?"

"No, but very near to it. Averdale, I believe. Wretched little village."

"Yes, though I'm sure the villagers had a much higher opinion of you," Marta said dryly.

Feran looked from one to the other, clearly without a clue as to what they were talking about or what it meant. Marta wasn't totally certain of that herself, but when her duty to the king was done she thought she just might find out.

"You may have just done me a service, Feran."

He blinked. "I have? How did I do that?"

"By reminding me of something I should have thought of myself, and weeks ago at that. Don't concern yourself about that; it's private. I am grateful, though."

Feran shook his head, looking bemused. "On a first name basis with The Witch of Lythos and she's in my debt as well? This is starting out as an amazing day."

Marta blushed slightly, though for the life of her she didn't know why she should. "Well, a small debt...more than likely. Real enough, though."

Feran looked at her intently then. "You're serious, aren't you?"

"Yes," Marta said, though with more reluctance. There was a hint of calculation in Feran's eyes that she hadn't seen before, and she didn't like it at all. In a moment, though, he seemed back to normal, and in a little while Marta stopped thinking about it. Feran was a much more pleasant conversationalist than Bone Tapper tended to be, and the day passed very quickly. By evening Marta knew most of Feran's family history and much of his childhood, and she'd revealed more about herself than she'd really planned. Still, she couldn't see the harm in it, and it had made for quicker travel. It wasn't until they had camped for the night and Feran had gone off into the trees to pay heed to nature that Bone Tapper spoke again.

"You're thinking Treedle might have gone home."

"I am. Aren't you?"

Bone Tapper shrugged. "He's been gone for years. It wouldn't be his home now."

"It wouldn't? Surely he has some family left there."

"Who would stone him as a revenant or worse, more than likely, assuming they even recognized him."

Marta frowned. "They would? Why?"

"You didn't see me before I was changed back to a raven. You haven't seen Treedle in any form except a hob. You wouldn't know about this."

"About what?"

"When the body is changed for service it's as if the old form is put in storage...that's not how it really works, I know, but the effect is the same. When I was a man again I was exactly as I was the day I entered your mother's service, and not a day older. It will be the same for Treedle. He would return a young man, just as he was. If he returned a proper graybeard he could make up a story of running away to see the world or some other poppycock. What would he tell any family remaining when he returns a youth? That he was enchanted?"

"Well...wasn't he?"

"That's not the point! Would they believe him? Would anyone even recognize him? That's the point."

Marta glanced to heaven. "Bone Tapper, I swear by the Powers that if you found an emerald in a dung heap you'd complain about the smell!"

He cocked an eye at her. "Wouldn't you?"

Marta's mouth set in a hard line. "We will search around both Averdael and Wittanplace," she said. "When time permits, since even a hint of a direction is better than none, and I will not let Treedle escape his debt. So. What else do you wish to say? I know there's something else nagging at you."

"That boy, as if you didn't know."

"Feran? What has he done?"

"Nothing."

Marta scowled. "Bone Tapper, we've come a long way today, and I've probably spoken more than I have in a month and I really need some hot tea and supper. I'm tired. I'm not in the mood for a riddle."

"No riddle. You asked what he'd done and I told you. That doesn't mean he won't do anything. I saw that look on his smiling face when you talked to him about that niggling 'debt' you may owe him. I know that look, if you don't. He wants something."

Marta shrugged. Her head was starting to hurt. "Everyone wants something. It's not a sin."

"True enough, but what Feran wants he wants from you. Your mother understood what that meant but you don't. Until you learn you're like a lamb in a thicket, bleating for the wolf."

"Again, duly noted, and thank you once more for the reminder of how wanting I am compared to Black Kath of Lythos. Now be still; Feran's coming back, unless I misunderstand all that noise in the undergrowth. Have a look around the campsite to make sure no one else is about."

Bone Tapper flew off without another word. In another few moments Feran returned, bearing an armload of dead wood. He cut several shavings with a small knife in his tinderbox and had a fire going in almost no time at all. Marta brought an iron tripod from the cart and soon had a broth and water for tea simmering to go with their bread and cheese. Bone Tapper didn't return until supper was long done, but when Marta asked, the raven replied that there was no one for miles and he had dined elsewhere, thanks just the same. Marta, remembering the deer, didn't ask further. Bone Tapper fluttered off to the top of the cart and settled in to cleaning his feathers.

"I don't think I could ever get used to talking with a raven," Feran said.

"I should think it would be far easier to get used to speaking to one than to being one," Bone Tapper said, "but I'll admit all my experience is of the latter."

Feran looked embarrassed, but Marta just smiled. "I've been doing it all my life. I think it would be rather strange without Bone Tapper around."

"Here's hoping you have the experience," Bone Tapper said grumpily, "and that I still have a life to pursue elsewhere."

"I think I could bear that," Marta said. "Now go to sleep. We've got another long day before us tomorrow."

Feran finished his tea. "What did he mean by that?" he asked in a lower voice, clearly hoping Bone Tapper wasn't listening. Marta rather believed otherwise, but the raven didn't bother to comment.

"He means that he's looking forward to the day he's free from me," she said. "When his debt is paid. He'll resume his old form then."

"He's not really a raven? Like Yssara is not really a horse, even though he looks like one...mostly. Is that right?"

"That's it. They're both bond-servants under the terms of their debt to my mother...to me, now."

"Like slaves..." Feran reddened, looked away. "I meant no offense Mistress... Marta. I don't think I could do that."

"It's a condition of the Arrow Path," Marta said, remembering some of the words in her mother's account books. "I have almost as little choice in the matter as they do."

"Can't you free them?"

"Only if I want to bear their debts myself," Marta said stiffly. "You may think ill of me for that, but I've enough of my own without adding to it. They made their choices freely; I won't feel guilt for what I must do as a result."

"What if someone you cared about came to you for help?" he asked, after a while.

Marta met Feran's gaze squarely. "It would pain me a great deal," she said, "but it wouldn't make a jot of difference."

"I'm sure I wouldn't know," Feran said, and he didn't say anything else for a long time. For the first time since they had set out that morning the silence turned awkward. Marta took the kettle and pots and washed them out in a swift stream nearby, her thoughts colder than the water.

What does he expect of me? To be other than what I am?

No one had that right, and Feran least of all. She was thinking of telling him so, but when Marta returned, she found Feran already curled up in his blankets by the fire, eyes closed. She went to her own place in the cart and firmly closed the door. By the next morning her urge to say anything at all to Feran had diminished considerably. Conversations during the next few days were polite but no more than that. Bone Tapper, for his part, seemed almost unbearably smug. Marta was more than a little relieved when Karsan finally came into view.

Bone Tapper flew ahead to see about Marta's lodging, but Marta bade him fly on to the castle and meet her as soon as that was done. She had no idea of what to expect there and she wanted all the help that was hers to call. Feran escorted her to the antechamber near the main hall where the Chamberlain was to be found, then took his leave as soon as he had discharged his duty. Marta pointedly ignored him as he walked away from her, turning all her attention on the Chamberlain.

The Chamberlain was a small, balding man with a bit of a paunch and a nervous, distracted manner. He had been away from Lythos on Marta's last visit. Marta hoped it wasn't a diplomatic mission, because in just a few minutes she had come to the unescapable conclusion that the man was a complete and unredeemable fool.

"You are Marta? Yes you are. Who else would you be? Your mother? Did she not come? But the King specifically asked for her."

"He asked for the Witch of Lythos. My mother is dead."

"Dead? And no one told me? This isn't right, no not at all."

It was all Marta could do to keep from leaping at the man's throat. "I apologize for the inconvenience my mother's passing may have caused you," Marta said, though now she was having a hard time deciding which she wanted to do more, laugh or kill him. It was just too hard to decide.

He waved it away. "A tragedy of course; I don't wish to appear insensitive but the king will be...best not to think of that. I'll attend to that, of course, no need for you to worry. You'll have to do then, won't you?"

"That was my own conclusion," Marta said.

"Yes, of course. Please wait here. I'll inform his majesty of your arrival."

"Most kind," Marta said.

He hadn't been gone more than a few minutes when Marta sensed Bone Tapper's presence. She heard his questioning croak and whistled to guide him to her. He flew in through the open doorway and landed on her shoulder.

"All done at the Apple Branch," Bone Tapper said, "though I dare say Master Lokan was acting a bit oddly."

"Oh? How so?"

Bone Tapper shrugged. "Oh, he seemed a bit surlier than usual. Probably nothing more than a sour batch of wine. So. Where is the noble Feran?"

"In blue blazes and roasting merrily, for all I care."

"I told you so," Bone Tapper said.

"You told me he wanted something," Marta corrected. "I have yet to hear anything of that."

Bone Tapper nodded. "Not yet. You will."

"So tell me—when did you add prophecy to your limited skills?"

"The moment I saw the way Feran looked at you," Bone Tapper said. He had that smug look that Marta was beginning to roundly detest, but she didn't argue. She was too afraid that he was right.

CHAPTER 9

"Everything happens for a reason. If that reason proves elusive, create one."
  —From the Annals of Dommar the Beast

King Alian was a bit taken aback by the Chamberlain's news; that was plain enough. He sat in his chair by the table in his workroom. It was just as Marta remembered: books and scrolls and tally sheets in wild profusion. The only thing different was the Chamberlain standing at a discrete but very prominent distance from the king.

"When did it happen?" Alian asked.

"When my mother was returning from the birth of your son," Marta said. "I trust all is well with them?"

"Of course. Your mother was very helpful...I don't know what to say, Marta. I won't say your mother and I were always on the best of terms; you know more of that than we need discuss. Yet I am sorry for your loss. For my loss and the kingdom's as well."

Bone Tapper made a very faint sound, something like a snort, but Marta shot him a warning glance and he settled down demurely on her shoulder.

"I thank you for that, Majesty. As Kath of Lythos is no more, her obligations are mine now. That includes this present duty. I will try to be of service to you, as would she."

He smiled then, but the smile didn't quite reach his eyes. "For a price?"

She inclined her head in something like a bow. "The Arrow Path's stipulation, Majesty. Not mine. Nor," she added pointedly, "My mother's."

King Alian nodded. "Quite so."

The king studied Marta frankly for several long moments. Marta, feeling a bit like a suspect coin on a scale, fought the urge to fidget. Alian finally came to a decision.

"Let's see if you're up to the challenge, then. Chamberlain?"

The Chamberlain bowed deeply and hurried from the room. He returned leading a man Marta had never seen before. He was tall and thin, with strong features and hair trimmed and combed as carefully as a girl's.

"Marta, may I present Dalan Kom?"

She knew the name of course. Who in Lythos had not, and even further? He was the king's own bard, though it was probably only ties of kinship that kept the man in a backwater kingdom like Lythos. He was known from Wylandia to Calyt for the beauty of his voice.

"Say hello, Dalan," the Chamberlain directed.

"H-hello," the minstrel said, and Marta knew what her first service as the Witch of Lythos was going to be. The man's voice was a wreck: scratchy, hoarse, and it cracked worse than that of a boy with his first chin whiskers. A bard, especially one that was such an ornament to a court as this one, would certainly rate the services of an Arrow Path magician if that was the only way to save his voice.

Was this the only way?

Marta hoped not, since she wasn't too sure that there was anything of the First Law that would help here, save perhaps being able to tell how badly the man's voice was damaged. Marta tried to keep her uncertainty from showing. She held up her hands. "With your permission?"

The bard nodded and Marta stepped forward, reaching up—he was very tall—to place her hands on either side of his throat. She kept them there for a few moments, breathing slowly, trying to listen to what her hands told her and hoping there was a story for them to tell. There was. Marta almost laughed with relief.

"It's done," she said, lowering her hands.

"Done..?" Dalan Kom, said in a voice as bad as ever, "but I still sound like a weasel caught in a waterwheel..."

"And will for a week or so more, I fancy," Marta said. "I've done what I can but even so the healing will take time, Master Dalan. I suggest rinsing your throat with pickle brine twice a day...and don't talk at all if you can avoid it. Of a certainty, do not sing. It will be well."

Dalan Kom looked at her as if she were the only lantern in an eternity of night. It was as if Marta's own certainty overwhelmed his doubts. She believed what she said, and so did the bard. He smiled then, with tears of relief in his eyes and he bowed his head to her. "I am grateful. Name your price, Mistress."

Marta didn't hesitate. "A song will do. When your voice is fully healed I would love to hear you sing."

"Gladly..."

The Chamberlain led the bard away, probably in the direction of the nearest pickle vat, leaving Marta, for the moment, alone with the king.

"Pickle juice? A song?" A smile showed faintly on the king's face.

"Little enough to ask, considering that I didn't really do anything," Marta said. "His voice was just strained, not destroyed. I wager your own physician told him as much."

"You would win that bet, Mistress Marta," Alian said, smiling openly now. "Yet I could hardly deny him when he sought help from the Witch of Lythos as well. An inconvenience for which I apologize and yet I had little choice. And may I say: well played. So. What is your real price?"

Marta closed her eyes. There was no sense of the Debt, no hint of what the price would be. Which, remembering her time with her mother on their last trip here together, didn't surprise Marta at all. Still, she thought long and carefully and and all of a sudden she remembered an earlier notion. Not a payment, exactly, but something she thought might be useful. Marta realized there was no way to compel what she wanted, yet thought it might not be impossible to obtain nonetheless...

There it was again. That feeling. That almost but-not-quite sense of understanding. Had she touched another Law? No, not another one. The same one she had touched, briefly, on the trip to Karsan. But what was it? Marta blinked, noted the cloud slowly gathering on the king's brow, and forced her attention back to here and now.

"As I used no Power, there is no fee, as perhaps you may remember from my mother's visit before the last one. However, for the slight inconvenience...well, I do have a favor to ask."

Alian looked at her speculatively. "A favor? What is it?"

"Majesty, with your permission, I would like to have the use of the Royal Archive."

He frowned. "That dusty mass of histories and tax rolls? I know your mother was fond of it, but I have to ask--whatever for?"

"I've been neglecting my education in...certain matters. I think perhaps the Archive may be of help to me, though I confess I do not know that for certain. May I?"

He waved his hand. "Secrets of State are not so easily found, if that's what you're searching for, but otherwise I have no objections. It's certainly easier on my purse than most of your mother's visits, Mistress. I will so inform Brother Akaen."

Marta thanked the king and took her leave. Bone Tapper waited until they were out of the chamber and partway down the hall before he spoke.

"Should have asked for gold."

Marta shook her head. "Mother never used most of what she had. The last thing I need right now is more to carry around."

"You weren't just dancing around the bard's problem, were you?"

Marta glared at him. "Certainly not. He will be fine. I just hope the king doesn't ask for anything else for a while. I doubt the task will be as easy next time and the Second Law still eludes me."

"You think you'll find it in the king's archives?"

Marta remembered telling Laras that the secrets of Power were not to be found in books. She thought it was true then, and she still thought it was true. Even so, she had to look somewhere and she knew her mother had been fond of the archives. Besides, her mother's account book had been more than a little useful so it was at least possible... Marta shook her head. She knew better. "No, but perhaps I will find something I can use."

"What?"

"How will I know unless I've found it? We'll start tomorrow morning."

Bone Tapper scowled. "We?"

"I know you can read, you lazy thing. I'll need help."

"My curse to be so talented," Bone Tapper said.

"Your curse to be unable to control your impulses. Else you wouldn't be here."

They retrieved Yssara and the cart from the castle courtyard and drove over to the Apple Branch. The green tree on the inn's signboard was a welcome sight. When Marta had seen to the cart and Yssara's stabling, she went inside, Bone Tapper as usual riding on her shoulder.

It was just past mid day; the common room was filled with people and the murmur of voices. Mostly travelers this time of year, though there were a few who traded in horses or cloth. Marta saw more than one group of folk who were clearly pilgrims, come to visit the Karsanmon Shrine. Marta realized she'd have to pay her own respects to the Priestess of Amaet as common courtesy, but she wasn't looking forward to it. Listening to her mother's accounts of the woman had not endeared the priestess, at least by reputation. Marta doubted the reality would be any improvement.

Several people glanced at Marta as she walked in. She was aware of it but pretended not to notice. Let them get used to seeing her now, coming and going on her own business as her mother had before her. This was the way it had to be.

"Marta?"

Marta looked around to find Master Lokan coming to greet her personally. He was heavyset and florid, wearing the same fixed smile Marta had never seen him without. The publican wiped his hands on his heavy stained apron and gave her a small bow.

Marta nodded. "Master Lokan. How are you?"

"Oh, well enough," he said, with the same fixed smile never wavering. "I just heard about your mother. I'm sorry."

Then why are you smiling? Marta thought, but all she said was, "Thank you."

Lokan just stood there, wiping his hands, smiling. Marta frowned. "Was there something else?"

The smile did fade then, just a bit. Lokan wore an expression that, in anyone else, might have been taken for the prelude to telling a joke, but Marta knew that on Lokan it was more likely discomfort. "Well, there is a delicate matter I need to discuss with you."

Marta sighed. "Master Lokan, I've just come from the castle, and I went there directly after traveling half the morning. I'll be glad to speak to you about anything you wish after I've had a chance to rest for a bit. Can it wait?"

"I'm afraid not. It's about payment."

Marta frowned. "Payment? What are you talking about?"

"For the rooms you've engaged. Surely you know that's customary?"

"My mother had the use of that room at all times. It's part of your arrangement with her."

"Your mother is dead," Lokan said. "For which I am sorry, as I said. Yet, well, there it is."

"I have assumed my mother's obligations," Marta said. "Those she owed and," she added pointedly, "those that were owed to her. That includes many things, including that one room in your fine establishment."

"Marta, our arrangement was informal. As far as I'm concerned, it ended when she died. That is the custom. You're welcome here, certainly. More than welcome! But I will require payment. As I have friends in court I'm sure the king's writ will agree with me. Shall we take it to judgment?"

Marta was aware that, by now, almost all the conversation in the common room had faded completely. All attention was focused on her and Master Lokan. All listened. Some looked worried, some curious, a few whispered to each other in excited tones. Others smirked with such pleasure that Marta would have gladly killed them then and there, if she had the trick of calling lightning.

Perhaps one day.

Marta shook her head. "No, Master Lokan, we needn't trouble the king in this trifling matter. You're quite right: Payment is required."

Lokan's smile turned to one of pure triumph. "Do not fret, girl, my rates are quite reasonable. What about—"

"What was your trouble?" Marta asked.

Lokan blinked. "My what? I don't understand."

"Yes, you do."

Bone Tapper laughed, and then even the faintest whispering elsewhere in the room faded to dead silence. Marta repeated the question, a little louder, and with full intent. It wasn't a use of Power, exactly. It was the working of the Debt, which had power of its own. Marta remembered the image of a man turning into a raven, and a dragon becoming a cart horse. The Debt was the Debt, and Master Lokan was no different. There was no escape; not for Master Lokan. Not even for Marta herself.

I do what I must, Master Lokan.

"What was your trouble?"

Master Lokan's eyes widened even as his mouth opened to speak. He clearly did not want to speak. Under the power of the Debt, he had no choice, and his terror began to grow as understanding finally dawned. "Drink," he said, as softly as he could.

"A little louder please," Marta said. "What was your trouble?"

"Drink," Master Lokan said loud enough for all to hear, and he wasn't smiling now.

"What was my mother's promise?"

"To free me of the curse," he said, trembling slightly.

"And was it done?"

"Mistress Marta..."

"Was it done?" Marta repeated, as cold, remorseless and as inescapable as time itself. Because he had no choice, Lokan answered, clear and loud so that all could hear.

"Yes."

"How will you repay that? No, don't answer that part. I've already seen how you intend to deal with your obligations. I suppose it's up to me, then." Marta gave all the appearance of deep consideration. She turned to Bone Tapper. "What do you think?"

"How about a hob?" Bone Tapper asked, practically bouncing on Marta's shoulder in barely suppressed glee.

"I already have one of those," Marta said. "Or will again. A mule? No, Yssara would kill him... A hound, perhaps? Yes. Something useful for keeping watch and finding lost items. That might be an advantage indeed." She turned the full fire of her attention back on the shaking innkeeper, who went whiter than snow.

"So shall it be," Marta said.

Lokan began to change. A gasp traveled through the room as his arms and legs shrank, his nose and snout began to lengthen and sprout coarse hair. Now Marta was looking down on him as Lokan, falling forward, stared at his paws in horror.

"No!" he shrieked, close to hysteria. The word came out contorted; his lips were nearly gone and his tongue long and lolling.

Marta shrugged. "Your choice."

"I was...mercy! Oh, mercy..."

"Have you changed your mind about honoring your debts?" Marta asked.

"It was a jest! Yes, that's it. A jest. A poor one. Of course you may have your room. It's ready for you, as always! Please..."

"Well then," Marta said, and that was all. She didn't say anything else. In a moment Master Lokan was back to himself. The room was so quiet a feather falling would have sounded like thunder. Lokan ran his hands over his face, his arms, trying to assure himself that he was really back to his own self.

I think you would have made a better hound, Innkeeper. Marta smiled at him. "My room, Master Lokan? You may send up our meal as soon as we're settled."

The man almost fell over himself in his haste to show her the way, though of course Marta knew it well enough. She allowed him to proceed, though. As soon as she was inside Marta shut and bolted the door and then sat down on the bed and put her head in her hands.

Bone Tapper landed on one of the bedposts and giggled. "Oh...that was almost worth being a raven, to see that."

"Quiet," Marta said.

He frowned, which for a raven is very hard to do. "What's wrong? You don't look happy."

"Happy? I almost had that fool for a servant! Better a new enemy than such help."

Bone Tapper snorted. "Hah! You got that anyway, though a toothless one. I swear, for the rest of his life that man will faint if you so much look at him sideways! As for the rest of them..."

"The rest of them will take the tale of this day far and wide," Marta said. "I don't suppose it can be helped."

"Helped? Nay, you could not have planned it better! No one else will test you like that. I wondered who would be first. I expected the king, really, but then he's not such a fool."

"In a way the king has tested me already. He may do it again, and if he does, it won't be over such a trivial thing." Marta looked up. "That business with Master Lokan was necessary, Bone Tapper. The Debt must be honored, and that's all. That doesn't mean I enjoyed it."

"Yes, you did, and more than a little," Bone Tapper said. "Don't deny it."

"Enough! It's done, and there is much else to do. I need to think."

Bone Tapper held his piece, but remained in such a cheerful mood that Marta wanted to choke him. After a few minutes Master Lokan had a servant bring up food, and more than Marta could have eaten all day. She didn't eat much at all; Marta wasn't as hungry as she'd thought she was. In fact, she was feeling a little sick.

Damn you, Bone Tapper, but you're right—I did enjoy that. Marta decided she didn't want to think about that after all. Nor did she even want to see the room, or eat the food, and certainly not look at Master Lokan's terrified, smiling face if she could avoid it. "I'm going back to the castle," she announced after she'd rested for a while.

"What for?"

"For the archives, of course."

"I must say I share King Alian's question. What do you want with that musty mess?"

"How will I know that until I see what's there? Yet my mother saw some value in them and it would be foolish of me to overlook the possibility. Lythos is a small kingdom, I know, and books are expensive, so I doubt this will take long to sort through. I need to do this, Bone Tapper. The sooner I'm started the sooner we can go home."

Bone Tapper didn't argue, clearly seeing there was no point. "Must I go?"

"Must you ask?"

Bone Tapper sighed and flapped up to perch on her shoulder. Marta went back downstairs and was a little relieved to see that the common room was mostly empty now, and those who were there studied their drinks very intently rather than look up and risk her gaze. Master Lokan smiled nervously from behind his counter.

Marta nodded slightly in his direction. "I'll return this evening," she said, and that was all. Outside the sun was settling into mid afternoon. People came and went; Marta noticed a group of pilgrims on the north end of town moving slowly along the well beaten path leading up the Karsanmon Shrine. "I'll have to go too, I suppose, and pay my respects to the Priestess. Though I'd like to go when it's not so crowded," she said. "Do you know a time when that may be so?"

Bone Tapper shrugged. "Your mother always managed, though how she did so is a mystery to me."

"My mother did many things I don't have the knack for," Marta said. "Let's walk to the castle. It's a nice day and I don't feel like dealing with Yssara just now."

Bone Tapper didn't say anything for awhile, just rode on her shoulder. Now and then Marta realized he was looking at her, though he never had much expression and she couldn't see what little he had now.

Marta finally had enough. "If you want to ask me something I wish you'd get on with it."

"You were angry with your mother. Are you still angry?"

Marta took a slow breath, let it out. "I remember what I said. I was just angry at everything then. My mother is dead. Stop talking nonsense."

"But the way you talk about her—"

"Is to state the facts as I understand them, no more and no less. Don't go reading epics into a footnote."

Bone Tapper just shrugged and didn't say anything until they'd reached the castle. Unfortunately, they had to deal with the Chamberlain again. Fortunately, he was, by his own admission, "a very busy man" and assigned a page to escort Marta to the archives. They were located in the northeast tower. The boy led Marta through the courtyard. She noticed several pells and a quintain set up for training men at arms, but all were unused; except for a few of the castle staff doing laundry near the well, the courtyard was deserted.

"The kingdom seems a bit calm, of late," Marta said.

The boy escorting her, who couldn't have been more than nine, started as if she'd poked him. "Huh? Oh, pardon me, Mistress. You mean the training grounds? His Majesty had them moved outside the castle walls, on account of the noise was disturbing his son..." He looked away then, and almost cringed, as if he were afraid that speaking to her was a striking offense.

"It's all right...umm, what's your name?"

"Maky," he said, looking pale.

Marta smiled at him. "It's all right, Maky. I don't bite."

"Don't believe her," Bone Tapper said. "She eats children for supper."

From the look on his face, it was clear which of the two the page believed. Marta just sighed and let him lead her to a rather plain and unpretentious oaken door bound in iron. Marta thought it looked more like the entrance to a storeroom though, after thinking about it some more, realized that was more or less what it was.

"Please, Mistress, Brother Akaen who normally keeps the library is ill today, so he will not be able to help you. The Chamberlain expects him to be available tomorrow," Maky said. His voice squeaked like a nervous mouse.

Marta took pity on the boy. "I'm sure I can manage for now. You may go."

To the boy's credit he didn't quite break into a full run, but he left very quickly just the same. Marta watched him go and then turned to glare at the raven inches from her face. "Bone Tapper, was that really necessary?"

"No, but wasn't it fun?"

Marta ignored that. She grabbed the handle to the doorway and yanked it open. "By the Powers..."

The king's library, to say the very least, was far more than Marta had expected. The room was no mere partition of the ground level of the tower; it filled the entire floor. The walls were ringed with cubbyholes for parchment and shelves for books, or which there were far more than Marta had thought possible in one place. In the center of the room were books open on reading stands, and one long table with several volumes piled on top of it.

"I may need the services of the king's clerk after all," Marta thought, her eyes open wide in amazement. "I didn't know there were this many books in the entire kingdom!"

"And could not have cared less, I fancy. Why the sudden interest? You're the Witch of Lythos, not a sodding scholar."

It was the second time Bone Tapper had asked the question and she still didn't have a good answer. Oh, her answer made sense enough; she had been surprised to discover how much information had been in her mother's account book, and again disappointed that there was so little. She found herself wanting more, with no idea of where to get it except, perhaps, that maybe it was indeed in a book.

Laras would laugh at me now.

"Maybe the Witch of Lythos would do well to be a scholar, too," Marta said. "It's not as if there is aught else to do for a bit. If you think I'm going on the road after Treedle until spring, think again."

one Tapper hopped from her shoulder unto a book stand, glanced at the volume there, and shrugged. "All the same to me. He's your servant, not mine. Just don't blame me if he's halfway to Calyt by now."

"He's not," Marta said.

Now Bone Tapper looked at her again. "I thought you didn't know where he was."

"I don't. That doesn't mean the bonds of the Debt are no longer in place. If they weren't I would know," she said, and she knew it was true. "I don't understand why I can't sense him, but he remains within my reach, and I will find him, make no mistake."

Marta turned her attention back to stacks and stacks of books. Since books were expensive it stood to reason that a king might have more than the average scholar, but this was almost beyond Marta's comprehension.

Did I say 'in the kingdom'? I didn't know there were this many books in the entire world!

Marta sighed. For all that she apparently would inspire terror wherever she went, Marta knew that she was still a very provincial girl suddenly thrust onto a much larger stage. Sooner than planned, or expected, if indeed she had ever really expected it, or thought of the possibility at all.

I thought you would always be there, Mother. I'm sorry, but you raised a fool.

She looked at the volume that Bone Tapper had dismissed, and did likewise; it was a treatise on the armor used in the Lyrsan wars. She could imagine the knowledge being useful to someone, somewhere, but not to herself, not now. She looked at another one, a herbal, and it looked much more promising. She pulled it aside and kept looking. By the time she had pulled three books aside she had gone through all of the ones on the table, and Bone Tapper was asleep perched on a high shelf. She threw wadded piece of parchment at him to wake him up.

"Hmmph?"

"I want you to start on the western section of wall. Note any volumes of magic if you find any such, but I'm mostly looking for herbals and kingdom history right now."

"If you want. I suppose I can see the use of herbals—many plants make excellent poisons—but why history?"

"Because Arrow Path magicians have been around for a long time. I'd be surprised if their presence hadn't been noted more than once. I don't expect accuracy but there may be some accidental truths. Also anything of religion... Amaet or the Karsanmon Shrine, that sort of thing. That's more than enough for now."

"More than enough, indeed," Bone Tapper agreed, grumbling, but he flew off to do as he was bid. Marta opened the first volume in her pile and started reading. It was difficult, at first. Many of the words were strange to her and she had to sound them out with their companion words around them to winkle out their meaning, and she didn't always succeed. It was like a mystery in a way, extracting the meaning from such scant clues. When Marta looked up again the shadows were long through the one window and Bone Tapper was asleep again. She started to scold him again but yawned instead.

"Marta? Maky said you were here. I wanted to come sooner but I had duties. I'm glad you're still here."

Marta looked up from the book. Feran stood in the open doorway, smiling tentatively.

"Hello, Feran," she said. She really wanted to say "go away," and say it very loudly and clearly, but the words wouldn't come out.

Feran glanced around the room. "I haven't been in here before. Very impressive. I trust you found what you're searching for?"

"Not yet, but I'm managing well enough," she said. The silence after that stretched on for an awkward moment or two. *You'll have to do it yourself, Feran. I'm not going to help you.*

"There was...well, a matter I need to discuss with you."

"Yes, Feran," she said, and hoped it didn't sound like a question. It wasn't mean to be. She didn't want him to ask her anything, or for anything. Especially not that.

Feran sighed. "I know I shouldn't—"

"Then don't," Marta said suddenly.

Feran hesitated then, but finally shook his head. "I'm sorry, but I have to."

No, Feran. Please don't...

"I need your help."

Done. Said. Was that all it took? Couldn't she refuse, and send him away? No. She wanted to refuse, but she could not. It was like a geas laid on her. She was no different than that poor fool Lokan , or Bone Tapper, or anyone else caught in the web of the Debt. As Feran was about to be caught.

"What is it you want of me?" she asked.

"It's this."

Feran held up a small orb of what looked like iron; it was dull black with just a hint of what could have been rust or something like it. It gleamed slightly in the poor light. Feran slowly walked inside the room to the table and handed the thing to Marta. Upon closer inspection it was obviously what it appeared to be—a ball of iron, just a little wider than the palm of her hand. Heavy, too, but to Marta's thinking perhaps not as heavy as it should have been.

Hollow.

The weight of it would have told her that, but she didn't need it. Marta knew it was hollow the moment she touched it. She tried to hand it back to Feran, but he wouldn't take it.

"What do you want me to do?"

"There's a trick to it, I've been told, but I can't open it. I want you to open it, Marta."

Marta just looked at it for several long moments. After a while Feran spoke again.

"I should explain—"

"No need."

Feran shook his head. "No, I want to tell you. I need you to understand. I don't do this lightly, I would never. I understand what it means."

"Do you?" Marta asked softly.

Feran nodded, his expression set and firm. "I do. Your confrontation with Master Lokan is all over the castle...probably all over Karsan too, since we don't always hear things first here behind our walls. I understand I'll be in your debt, and I don't know how heavily. It's also true that I have little in the way of gold. I will do service, whatever it takes."

"Don't say that until you know the price, Feran."

He shook his head. "I'll pay it. Whatever it is."

"What if I made you into a dog?" Marta asked. "You say you heard what I almost did to Master Lokan. Do you think I wouldn't do as much or more to you?"

Feran met her gaze. He barely blinked. "That will be up to you."

"Yes. I suppose you're right." Marta just stared at the sphere. "I think I would like to know why, after all."

"It's about Kerasa," he said. "The girl I want to marry."

"Oh," Marta said.

"That's why I have to do this, you see," Feran told her. "Her father is a proud man, and I have so little to offer. He knows I have his daughter's heart, but that's not enough. So he gave me this test. I don't know where he got the thing and I don't care. All I know is that he won't consent to the marriage unless I can tell him what is inside this ball. He gave me two weeks, which end tomorrow morning. I've tried everything I could think of..."

"Did you try a blacksmith?" Bone Tapper asked, apparently awake and listening after all.

Feran smiled. "Good Raven, Kerasa's father is not such a fool as that. I have to return the blasted thing to him intact."

"Do you love her?" Marta asked.

"Do I..?"

Marta spoke the words again, slowly and carefully. "Love. Her. You said you want to marry Kerasa. I'm presuming her father is wealthy?"

"By my standards, yes," Feran admitted. "But not so much that Kerasa's portion will be much more than the price of an ox, and for better or worse I'm no farmer. I want the lady for herself. Yes, Mistress Marta, I do love her."

Mistress. They were not to be friends, but Marta already knew that, had known it since the day he'd escorted her into Karsan. Something about the Arrow Path and friendship didn't quite make a good weave together. So why was she even thinking about what she planned to do next?

Conscience is an inconvenient thing along the Arrow Path, yet it persists.

Black Kath's words came back to Marta with the force of a blow. She closed her eyes for a moment, then opened them again. "I'll name my price now."

Feran nodded. "I'm ready."

"For this service I request one from you. One you have already rendered."

Feran frowned. "What service have I done you?"

"You didn't realize it at the time, but you gave me a hint of where I might look for something I lost. It doesn't matter what, nor would I tell you if you asked. But it was of value to me, and for that I grant you this request."

"Mistress—" Bone Tapper began, but Marta shushed him.

"I have to concentrate for a moment."

Marta touched the sphere, felt it this way and that. It didn't take long. For someone versed in the First Law, finding the hidden keys and yielding places of the iron orb was less than simple. In a few moments the thing unfolded like a flower.

"A walnut, wrapped in cloth. A shell within a shell. I suppose the good father thought he was being profound." Marta put the orb back together and again it was a seamless mystery.

Tears were forming in Feran's eyes. "Mistress....Marta, I don't know how to thank you."

"One doesn't require thanks for a fair trade. Off with you and give your beloved Kerasa the good news."

In a few moments Feran was out the door. Unlike Maky, he ran immediately and made no effort to hide his haste. Bone Tapper flew down from his perch.

"Mistress, what did you just do?"

Marta shrugged. "What I thought would be obvious to anyone paying attention: I granted his request. I could not refuse."

"Perhaps, but anyone also paying attention would know that the bare hint he gave you was not even a fraction worth the price. You took his debt on yourself, didn't you?"

Marta glared at him. "Oh, be sensible. Would I, the scourge of little children and innkeepers everywhere, do such a foolish thing?"

Bone Tapper just looked at her for a several long moments, and all he said was, "Mistress, if we stay here longer tonight we will need some candles."

"I'm tired, Bone Tapper," Marta said, and she closed the book she had been reading when Feran appeared. "Let's return to the Apple Branch. Perhaps these books will make more sense tomorrow."

"If anything makes any sense here I'll be surprised."

Marta rather thought so too. So far she'd come for knowledge and mostly what she had found were possibilities and uncertainty. All except for one telling exception: Marta was quite sure that somewhere in the world or out of it, the Power called Amaet was laughing at her.

At least Feran will be happy. Marta's smile was grim. *For what he just cost me, he sodding well better be.*

CHAPTER 10

"As an Arrow Path Initiate your primary business is to seek the Seven Laws of Power. That is primarily to fulfill your obligations under the Debt, but also in part to prevent the Seven from seeking you."
— Black Kath's Tally Book

That night Marta dreamed of faces. Her mother's. The King and Queen's. Feran's. They passed in front of her mind's eye like masks. A rather vaguely female mask for Kerasa, a mask with a frozen, infuriating smile. Their eyes and mouths were empty as they passed in front of the light, flashing bright for a moment as the light came through the empty places. Only the light behind them all remained constant. Marta looked at the light, and it had a familiar shape.

Amaet.

"Is this a dream?"

The glow faded. Amaet stood, again looking not so much like a Power as a human girl. When she spoke, it was with a voice that Marta heard and understood with her ears and not just echoing inside her head as before. The power's voice sounded just like a human girl's.

Amaet shrugged. "Yes and no."

Marta put her hands on her hips. "That's no answer."

"You don't really want an answer. You want a meaning, and meaning is an interpretation. Mine will not be the same as yours. Make your own when you can, but for now come with me." Amaet held out her hand.

Marta didn't want to do any such thing, including touching Amaet's hand, but the Power's tone made it clear that refusing was not an option. Marta reached out, felt Amaet's hand close on hers. Marta wasn't sure what she'd expected, but the touch was a human touch, warm and dry. The Power led Marta away from the masks in her former dream but the masks followed, bobbing and floating along like will-o-the-wisps in Marta's wake.

"Your dreams are stubborn things," Amaet said.

Marta said nothing. She was trying to see the landscape Amaet was leading her through, but as far as Marta could tell there wasn't anything to see. It was a vast expanse of black nothing. No motion of animals or birds or anything else. No hills, no rivers. No moon, stars, or sky for that matter. There was no horizon, just a distance that faded into dark mist. There was a continuous stretch of something that could have been solid ground, but didn't feel like ground or anything else since Marta wasn't even touching it. She looked down, and was a little relieved that she still had feet, and hadn't managed to change into some drifting vapor or some such when she wasn't looking.

Marta was even a little relieved that the masks from her enigmatic little dream were following her like goslings in flight; they were comfortable, now. Almost familiar. Hers. Unlike everything else Marta was seeing now.

"Is this the home of the Powers?"

"This isn't anyone's home. It isn't anything at all, really, except a place that is not. It is a means, not a destination. Think of it as a road, though that's a rather puny word for it."

"If this is a road, then why are we walking when we aren't going anywhere? It all looks the same."

"Nowhere is the fastest road from somewhere to somewhere else. What else should nowhere look like?"

Marta had no answer to that, mostly because she didn't understand it. She did understand, however, when the scene abruptly changed.

Amaet and Marta stood at the base of a mountain so high that, try as she might, Marta could not see the top of it, so wide that either side looked more like a vertical horizon than anything else; there was even the slight distending curve that Marta would have expected to see from a true horizon. There were no other mountains nearby, nor trees. There was a blue sky above but it seemed a pallid thing, more sky by courtesy than the deep, vivid blues Marta knew. All this Marta took in with barely a blink; there was a part of her that considered this still no more than a dream, and likely to change without warning. What she saw next got all her attention, and put thoughts of dreams right out of her mind.

It was a cave. The darkest, deepest, least inviting maw of the earth that Marta had ever seen. Marta groaned.

"Why do the Powers who rule the heavens spend so much time in holes in the ground?"

Amaet just looked at her, expressionless. "As well ask why you dream of masks, Black Kath's daughter. I am not responsible for how you see this place. Or how you interpret the reality of what you know back in the waking world. As I said, your meanings are your own."

"Are you saying this isn't a cave?"

"If a cave is what you see, then that is what it is. Since you apparently don't like caves, that is unfortunate for you. However, it changes nothing."

Marta nodded looking glum. "We're going inside."

Amaet laughed then. "No, Black Kath's daughter. You are."

Marta stared at the hole. The rocks around it were broken and ragged looking; there was a faint whiff of rotten eggs drifting from the opening.

"I don't want to go in there."

Amaet just shrugged.

"Will you at least tell me why you won't go with me?"

"Because she would know, fool. That's why I have servants to act for me when needs must."

"Who would know?"

"My... enemy, for want of a better word. Astonei."

Marta had heard the name before. Another Power, though Marta thought that Astonei's cult was more common in the west and north. It was definitely the first time Marta had heard of a dispute between two Powers. So far as she could recall, Marta had never even heard of two Powers in the same context. There were no legends of 'Wars in the Heavens' or anything of the sort. She's thought of Powers like the Laws themselves: related yet separate. Aloof.

"What is the dispute between you two?"

"That is not your concern right now. It is enough that there is a point on which Astonei and I disagree. Naturally each seeks to destroy the other."

"Naturally. Yet you are immortal," Marta pointed out. "How can you destroy or be destroyed?"

Amaet shrugged. "I confess that point does make settling disputes a tricky matter, but not impossible. And 'destroy' does not necessarily mean 'kill,' you know. Just a point of fact that you needn't concern yourself with just now. Brace yourself."

Marta blinked. "Why?"

"Because I'm going to turn you into a craja."

Marta didn't even have to time to scream a denial before it was done. She held up her hands, staring in mute horror at the skeletal claws they had become. Marta almost reached up to touch her face, but she was too afraid of what she would find there, and hesitated, afraid to know and to not know all at once. Yet the transformation, abhorrent though it felt to her, was not the worst of it.

The worst part was the hunger.

Marta looked at Amaet. So close. So full of flesh and steaming, hot blood. Or at least, so it seemed to her. Without thinking, without being able to think, she leapt at Amaet. Amaet didn't move, or try to defend herself. There was no need. Marta's leap brought her to Amaet and through Amaet. Marta fell hard on the rocks beyond the form of Amaet, every touch of stone like a cold knife against her bare bones where they lay exposed by ripped, rotted flesh.

"You're not handling this as well as I'd hoped." Amaet produced a hunk of steaming red meat and it in front of the whimpering Marta, who didn't so much eat the morsel as engulf it.

Marta reached out with her bony hands. "More!" she croaked.

"Marta, look at me!"

Marta felt the voice as a distant thing, like a hunting horn calling from the depths of a forest. She shook her head, trying to listen, trying to hear anything except the sound of her own dry joints creaking together, and the grinding of her yellowed teeth, and the almost unbearable din of her hollow belly. Slowly, Marta forced her arms down to her sides, forced herself to breath slowly even though she didn't need to breath at all, not really. She started to hug herself until she realized what she was embracing, and quickly pulled her arms away. She fought back a sudden throatful of bile and looked into Amaet's cold blue eyes.

Amaet smiled. "Still in there somewhere, Black Kath's daughter? Hiding yet behind those bright red eyes and that lovely face?"

Marta managed to nod, but it was hard to think, or to know anything except the hunger. It was as if Amaet, having given her a new body, now was also giving her back enough of herself to keep the reality of the transformation from overwhelming her.

Barely.

"What have you done to me?!"

"What your mother did to Bone Tapper and Yssara and Treedle, no more and no less. I've transformed a servant into the form that serves me best. It's not a punishment, Marta. It's simple necessity."

Just as what I did to Master Lokan. Marta felt sick again. She didn't think she deserved to ask what she did ask, just then, but she had to. She hated the piteous tone of her voice, but she couldn't help it. "You'll change me back?"

"If you do as I say."

"Anything..."

Marta hated the smile on Amaet's sweet face, but mostly Marta hated herself, hated the word that came out of her mouth because she knew it for simple truth, hated herself for hearing as much from that fool Lokan and enjoying the sound too much. Yet, for all that he had brought it on himself, Marta understood Lokan a little better now, at least so far as his surrender went. If Amaet had asked Marta to strangle Queen Mysona in her bed or boil King Alian's heir with carrots and onions, right then Marta would have done either or both of those things without hesitation. Anything to change the horror she had become, but most of all to lose the hunger filling her soul and mind until there was little between herself and gibbering madness but Amaet's will turned on her, anchoring Marta to herself. Marta could almost hear the chains of that anchor groaning under the strain.

"...not much time," Marta managed to say, and Amaet nodded.

"True enough. Go into the cave. When you see what is there, you will know what I want you to do. Go. Hurry."

Marta wanted clearer instructions, but she went, and she did hurry. She ran over the stones, crouching like an animal, and dove down into the cave like a badger returning to its burrow. Once inside, Marta realized the darkness wasn't as absolute as it appeared. There seemed to be a faint reddish glow that illuminated all, but she couldn't tell if it was a characteristic of the cave or of her new body's night vision. Whatever the case, Marta had no trouble at all as she scuttled down deeper into the earth. It felt right to her, much safer and familiar that the vast bright open above. Down here it was quiet, and secure.

Hungry hungry hungry...

For a moment Marta was afraid the other inside her was asserting itself again, but after a moment or two Marta realized the thoughts were not hers, that she was not alone down in the earth. Marta scuttled down a steep slope of limestone, looking for the others. She saw no one at first, just a vast cavern that reminded her greatly of the one near her home where she'd found the shrine to Amaet. Except for the vast lake that lay near the center—and it was a lake so far as she could see, not a river. She didn't know what fed it, but there was no dark ribbon of water connecting it to the underground river system, if any. Perhaps a spring from underneath? And why did the place look so familiar? Was she affecting the reality of it by her perceptions, as Amaet seemed to hint?

Marta shook her head. *This place is nothing of me.*

So who did live here?

Marta still saw no one, and her own hunger was growing again. Perhaps she could find food there. Perhaps a blind fish, hard and boney but with flesh as well? Marta studied her hands. Her fingers were like hooked claws; she was sure she could fish with them, or anything else. She made her way down to the dark water.

She thought they were fish at first, those flashed of white near the surface, those furtive ripples, but of course they were not.

Craja.

The lake was filled with them.

So many...

Marta saw a pale white glow beyond the lake, but she did not go to investigate. Marta felt exposed there on the bank, vulnerable, but it was not the craja nor what lay beyond the lake that she feared. She slipped into the water itself, felt its cold embrace as the comfort she could not give herself. Down there in the water she found the darkness that was missing in the cave. Even her glowing red eyes could not see very far; hardly enough to reach all the other glowing pairs of eyes that saw her in turn, recognizing her, for now, as one of their own. The lake was a place to hide, and yet still be near her sisters.

Close to the One.

Marta blinked. She had no sisters. She was no craja, despite the curse of a ruined body that Amaet had bestowed on her. And who was this 'One,' anyway? She felt the thought, absorbed it as if through the communal water itself. After a little longer Marta believed she had absorbed something else. A little understanding that had been missing before, even after her own confrontation with the craja in Amaet's cave.

It's not flesh they...I, hunger for.

The craja were dead, in the sense they no longer lived. Yet proper death meant oblivion. And oblivion meant separation from the one they loved, worshiped, feared, adored. Like the woman in Amaet's cave, the woman who had once owned a name and a life of her own, and had given all to something she thought was greater than herself, more important, and had given all until there was nothing left, not even life itself.

They will not stop.

With that understanding, it was almost as if a little more of Marta's soul had returned to her. The pity that Marta had felt for herself now turned outward. She would find a way out of this ruined body and back to where she belonged, somehow. But these poor creatures, hundreds of them, were trapped forever. Doomed to a hunger that would never go away as long as there was that connection, and a place to hide. Marta wanted more than anything to set them free, but how? Even if each and every one wore some talisman to Astonei as the other had worn her image of Amaet, Marta could not overcome them all to break the image, the bond. There were too many.

I'll do what I can.

Marta found one craja who did not move in the main group, a straggler stalking an evil-looking blind eel near the opposite shore. The creature took no notice of Marta as she came close; all its attention was on the eel. Marta reached down to its ruined chest, feeling for what she thought must be there.

It was easier than she'd expected; there was no flesh at all on this one over the ribs. Marta reached in and her hand closed on nothing.

It's not there?

The craja hissed at her, absently, then reached out to snag the eel. In a moment it had chewed up and swallowed the entire thing. Marta watched the gobbets fall through the creature's upper ribs and float on the faint current. Eating clearly wasn't helping her, nor would it help Marta. Worse, what she thought she knew of the craja's nature was apparently mistaken. Her defeat numbed Marta for a moment. She had freed one craja, back in the waking world. She had been so certain that she could do it again.

Marta frowned. *Maybe I still can. There's something different here...*

The craja apparently thought so, too. Just as their thoughts had intruded on her, it seemed as if Marta's growing otherness, her discordant thoughts had finally gotten their attention. Marta realized that most of the other pairs of red eyes were turned in her direction.

Marta ignored them. *I think I know now what's different here.*

In the cave near her home, Amaet's shrine, even though the craja had known it was there, was not visible from the water's edge. Marta didn't want to leave the water, even when the other craja there started to creep toward her, slowly; their confusion leading toward something like fear, and anger. Marta remembered that the other craja back in Amaet's cave didn't want to leave the water either, yet it could. So she forced herself to walk up the sloping far shore until her head broke out of the blackness and she looked at the pale white glow she had seen before.

It was a woman.

The image of one, anyway. Carved from rock crystal at least seven feet high; it shimmered there in the darkness. Faint as it was, the glow made it hard for Marta to look at it directly. She could make out an upraised hand holding what looked like a water jug.

Astonei of the Springtime and Summer.

A fertility aspect, if Marta remembered right. Not that Marta thought there was much fertility or anything in the way of green, growing things in that place. Marta felt a touch at her back and she pulled herself out of the water, too fast for the touch to become a grip.

Marta heard a low moan, rising from a hundred ruined throats; she glanced back to see red eyes, row on row in the black water staring at her in fear. That fear didn't stop them from moving toward her. Quickly.

Marta ran toward the shrine. Even as the other craja sensed Mart's intent, the closer Marta got to the Shrine, the more she saw what the other craja saw, felt what they felt. Their worry, their fear, but most of all their anguish. How could she even think of doing what she intended? How could anyone be so vicious, so cruel?

How can I...?

Marta stopped just short of the shrine, sobbing. She heard the others closing on her, but she didn't care. She was with them, of them. She was craja. She was...

The first mask floated across Marta's field of vision. Her mother? Kerasa? It didn't matter. Marta had forgotten about them until then and yet they followed her, that little bit of dreamstuff that was hers, not Amaet's, not Astonei's, not of the craja approaching her, their clawed hands reaching out to rend and tear.

This is me. This is mine. I do what I have to.

Marta felt another touch then, but it was not the craja. It was recognition. She had touched another Law, but there was no time to think about that now, or hesitate. Marta reached out and her hand touched cold stone.

The First Law is mine. Whatever form I take or what I look like, I am Marta, Black Kath's daughter.

Marta broke the image of Astonei. There was one long howl from behind her, but Marta did not look to see. She did not need to see the result of what she had done, because there was no question. In another moment Marta was alone. Except for the masks. They followed her as she, still reluctantly, made her way out of the cave to where Amaet was waiting for her.

"I couldn't do it, Amaet. Whatever you wanted, I failed you."

Amaet smiled. "Hardly."

There was no other word spoken, but in an instant Marta was herself again. Her hands looked strange to her then, felt strange even as she ran her fingers slowly across her face and brushed her arms, gently, as if reminding herself what flesh felt like when bone is properly hidden.

"You wanted me to free those poor creatures? That was your task?"

"As you did at my own shrine, though I only had the one and so could spare the cost. I'm surprised you didn't recognize that at once. After all, it was you who gave me the idea in the first place, and thank you for that. Astonei has been weakened just slightly tonight, and you've taken a bit off your Debt. Hardly worth mentioning on both points, but Astonei will not be pleased and so it was worth doing. And frankly I wasn't sure such was possible. This knowledge is worth more than the small cost."

Marta shook her head. "Cost you? You did this to hurt Astonei somehow? I don't understand you."

Amaet shrugged. "It's simple enough: Powers tend to accumulate souls...a certain type of soul. The ones who long for something greater than themselves, those who see answers somewhere else, always, and never in themselves. Fools, basically. There's energy in a soul. Strength. Even in such wasted things. Astonei is older than I am and has been accumulating souls far longer than I have. Now she's lost a few. She was never keen on the idea and, since I didn't act against her directly, I doubt she'll notice."

Amaet took Marta's hand. The cave was gone. The vast mountain was gone. They were once more walking across the great nothing from which they had come.

Marta shook her head. "Older? But the Powers are eternal, unchanging..."

Amaet laughed at her. When she finally stopped laughing, she said, "Immortal? Yes. Unchanging? Hardly. Those who are Powers now may not always be so. Those who are not Powers at all may become so."

Marta's growing fury at Amaet's laughter was stopped cold. She could not believe what had been revealed to her. Marta didn't understand the full significance of what Amaet had just said, but she understood to the core of her being that a very great Mystery had been unveiled to her just then, and in such an offhand fashion that Amaet, for all the notice she took, could have been discussing the weather. Yet Amaet did not give gifts, and Marta knew it. "Why are you telling me this, Amaet?

The Power sighed with exaggerated patience. "Two reasons, Black Kath's daughter. The first is that, from time to time, I may have other errands for you to run in the places beyond your limited existence. Such knowledge may boost your strength here, and that is useful to me."

"And the other reason?"

Amaet turned on the full power of her beautiful, radiant smile. "The other reason is that, when you're awake, you won't remember a bit of it."

Marta got the full significance of that right off. She wouldn't be able to use this knowledge in her quest for the Laws. Or anything else that did not suit Amaet's purposes directly.

"You..."

"Hold your eloquence, girl. I'm not likely to be impressed."

One of Marta's dream masks drifted by, and Amaet paused to look at it. "What is a mask, Black Kath's daughter?"

"What is...?"

"A mask," Amaet repeated slowly, as if Marta were a simpleton. "You're so fond of them, apparently. Don't you know what they are?"

"Of course I do. They hide the wearer's face."

"So whose face do they reveal instead?"

Marta let out a gusting sigh. "No one. They are false."

"Are you sure?"

Marta shook her head. "You're mocking me."

"I don't think that's possible. One other thing, Black Kath's daughter, and I do want you to remember this when you wake up."

"Yes?"

Amaet was gone, but her voice returned, no longer human and real as it had been for just a little while.

COME TO THE KARSANMON SHRINE TODAY. THE BOOKS CAN WAIT.

CHAPTER 11

"Powers often tell the truth, though they don't always do it on purpose. The trick is to recognize the truth when you hear it."
— Black Kath's Tally Book

Marta woke then, morning seemed to stream into the window with the sun itself, bringing her back in an instant from whatever far place she had been. Marta only remembered her dreams fleetingly, something about masks, but she remembered the image of Amaet telling her to come to the Karsanmon Shrine. It was a dream, and Marta knew that well enough, but she didn't believe that a dream was all it was.

One thing it definitely was not, and that's a request.

Marta might not worship Amaet or accept her as a goddess, but Amaet was a Power and only a fool would risk angering one without cause. Besides, Marta was just curious about what Amaet had to say. Marta yawned, and stretched, then very reluctantly got out of the warm bed. There was a thin crust of ice on the basin that she had to break before she could wash her face. Fully awake now, she dressed warmly and went out into the hallway.

Bone Tapper was keeping watch, of a sort, on the post of the doorway outside. "Wake up, Bone Tapper, it's time to go."

The raven blinked, then ruffled his feathers. "To the dusty books? This early? The castle will still be asleep!"

"I doubt that," Marta said, "Alian's a notoriously early riser. But we're not going there now. We're going to the Shrine. I hope Master Lokan has tea ready."

Marta headed down the stairs and Bone Tapper finally got his wits about him enough to fly after her. The raven sighed the sigh of martyrdom. "Aleeta will be cross if she doesn't have any notice. I suppose I'll have to take word to her?"

"Let's worry about that after breakfast, shall we? I'm ravenous."

After they ate in the common room Marta sent Bone Tapper off on his mission and went back upstairs to get her heavy cloak. The foot of the mountain path leading up to the shrine was about two leagues from the north end of Karsan. Fortunately the road through the pass leading to that path was well-established, thanks to the constant stream of pilgrims to the Shrine. Even so, it would take her most of the day to make the trip and return on foot, since it just wouldn't do to take the cart through the pass and then leave Yssara unattended at the foot of the path to the Shrine. She wasn't afraid anyone would steal the cart, but she did think it more than likely that Yssara would take a possibly mortal bite out of someone passing by if he got impatient. Now, if she had someone to watch the cart….

Blast you, Treedle! Where are you?

Marta went back downstairs. Master Lokan practically beamed when she told him she was leaving, but the sunshine on his face eclipsed when she also told him that she would return by nightfall. Not that she blamed the man, but still Marta was getting royally annoyed that so many folk were glad to see the back of her.

I'm not a monster, whatever they may think. Marta smiled a wry smile then, remembering. Feran said that too.

Marta stopped by the stable to pack a small travel bundle from the cart with food for the day; she took a partially-empty wineskin and filled it with water from the well in the marketplace, then set off at a brisk walk.

The day was cold but clear; some clouds to the east promised a late snow, but for the moment the weather was as good as could be reasonably expected. Marta was actually a little warm in her cloak, but she knew that would change once she reached the pass. There were others on the road north but not so many as Marta had expected after seeing the group heading north toward the Shrine the day before. Mostly they walked in ones and twos, sometimes three or more but not often. One or two mounted groups rode by, but no more than that. The pilgrims kept to themselves for the most part as if they didn't notice Marta at all, which was more than fine with her. She kept up her pace until mid-morning when she reached the entrance to the mountain pass, where she stopped to rest.

Marta sat on one of several boulders that had tumbled down the hillside in some long ago rockslide. The nearest peak of the White Mountains rose on her left, while Mount Karsanmon was almost hidden in haze and distance on her right. Marta stared up at it until her neck started to hurt.

I'm glad the Shrine isn't quite that high up, she thought, rubbing her neck until the pain subsided. Still, it was far enough. She ate an apple she'd brought with her; there was dried fruit and meat for later and Marta knew there'd be a well at the Shrine itself where she could refill the waterskin for the hike back to Karsan. If she remembered aright there would be some merchants at the base of the path where she could have gotten food and water if she'd wished, but Marta didn't want to depend on them, or anyone, if there was an alternative. Besides, it had been five years or better since she'd been here last, and she wasn't entirely sure what, if anything, had changed.

Bone Tapper finally rejoined her just as she was finishing. "You're late. There's some dried meat in the pack if you're hungry," she said.

"No, thank you. I've eaten."

"Something dead, I suppose?"

"In the condition the creature was in one would certainly hope so. And no, it was not the reason I was detained. Aleeta would not let me leave until I had told her as much as I knew of your mother's passing."

"Nosey, isn't she? Yet that shouldn't have taken very long."

"It wouldn't, except she didn't seem to believe me when I told her how little I know. And I certainly wasn't going to explain the inner workings of the Debt, though it probably wouldn't have taken as long if I had just done so and got it over with."

"Longer, more than likely," Marta said, though she was pleased enough that Bone Tapper hadn't shared any more than he had to. "Let's go, then. I want to be back at Karsan before nightfall, and I'm afraid the inquisitive Priestess may make that difficult."

"Difficult" was hardly adequate. After Marta arrived she only had a few moments to admire the beauty of the Karsanmon Gate when two of the High Priestess' blue robed acolytes came hustling out to usher her into Aleeta's presence.

The Priestess sat on a throne of polished applewood in the main sanctuary, just below a statue of Amaet. The statue was just as gaudy and overbearing as her mother had described. The Priestess was much the same.

"My dear Child," she said, and magnanimously swept down from her throne to take Marta's hands in hers as the acolytes withdrew to a discrete distance. "I was so shocked when I heard the news, yet I think there may have been some delay; apparently word didn't come to Karsan for some time."

"I had...business to attend following my mother's death, as I'm sure you can understand," Marta said. "I only recently returned to Karsan. Are you well?"

She waved that away. "Oh, tolerable enough for someone whose bones have grown old. Your mother and I shared that, among so many things."

Marta almost bit her lip to ask what those 'things' could possibly be; Marta knew there could be no point or profit in asking. "Even now I won't be able to stay long, though of course I did want to pay my respects to Your Eminence, and to take some time for quiet reflection here."

"Thank you, Child, your mother certainly raised you properly. Yet to come into your own so young, it must be difficult for you."

Not as difficult as being called 'child' constantly, Marta thought, but she smiled and thanked Aleeta just the same. Marta wondered briefly why she was reacting so badly to the Priestess; Marta remembered her as a very kindly woman from her one and only prior visit. Perhaps it was the fact that her mother had never thought much of her. Perhaps it was the way she nattered on about everything and nothing. Still, Marta could see no harm in the woman. Irritation, yes, but not harm. Marta tried to hold up her end of the conversation, but it barely seemed necessary, as the priestess seemed to be doing more than well enough on her own. Yet after a time, longer than Marta wished but not as long she feared, Marta did manage to bring the subject back to one she wanted.

"With your permission, Eminence, I'd like to visit the grotto now."

Aleeta shook her head, and for a moment actually thought the woman meant to deny her, but no, it was merely a mild sort of bewilderment. "Honestly, Child, I still can't see what your mother and you see in that hole in the rock. The Sanctum is much more appropriate, and certainly more comfortable."

"Perhaps no more than habit, but it was my mother's favorite spot." Marta felt more than a little guilty invoking her mother's name and the sympathy it elicited, but it did get her what she wanted.

"Well, so be it. I have other supplicants to see, so I really should be about it. Do you know the way?"

"I think I remember...through that door and straight out the back, yes?"

"That's right. Fare well, if I don't see you before you leave. Go with Amaet."

Marta wasn't quite sure what to say about that, so she just nodded. It wasn't quite a bow, but it seemed to satisfy Aleeta well enough. She gave Marta's hand one final squeeze and then walked slowly and serenely from the sanctuary, the picture of saintly decorum. Marta left by the back door and found the entrance to the narrow defile behind it, just as she remembered.

Bone Tapper hopped off her shoulder and perched on a dead bush growing from a crack in the stone.

"I'll wait here, if you don't object. Powers scare me."

"Suit yourself," Marta said. Now that she was out from under Aleeta's distraction, she was more than a little nervous herself. Marta made her way slowly along the narrow path to where the large stone bowl sat on the rock.

I remember this part.

The problem was, she remembered little else. Marta hadn't been so very young when she'd been here before. She remembered Aleeta, she remembered the grotto with its stone bowl. Yet she remembered very little of what had really happened there that day.

Mother spoke to a white light. That's all I saw. I don't remember what the light said.

Even that part seemed more like a dream now. More so even than the real dream of masks that morning. Marta looked around, but there was no one there.

"Hello?" Marta's voice was barely above a whisper, but still it echoed back to her. Marta, feeling foolish, spoke again a little louder. "Hello?"

Nothing. No sound, no response. Marta crossed her arms, irritated. After all, it wasn't as if she'd requested an audience; Amaet had summoned her.

I'm forgetting something.

That wasn't a new thought, but now it seemed more important. Yes, of course she was forgetting something. She was forgetting many things, but which of them was the one that, right now, mattered the most? Something that had happened before, something her mother had done before the white light appeared. Marta stared at the stone bowl, and realized her mistake. Not just a bowl to catch rain; it was there for another reason.

Mother put something in it.

Gold.

Marta could have slapped herself for a fool. It was an offering bowl. Marta smiled grimly. "I suppose I'll have to bribe you to talk to me."

She fished a gold piece out of her purse and dropped it in the bowl. In that instant Amaet appeared, sitting cross-legged, floating in the air over the offering bowl. She smiled. That first time, in the darkness of the cave, Marta had not really noticed Amaet's eyes. The light still wasn't very good where they were now, but Amaet's radiance was not so blinding here and Marta could see a little better.

They're like ice... Marta didn't think ice was quite the right word, but just then she couldn't think of anything colder.

THE GOLD IS A SYMBOL, BUT AN IMPORTANT ONE. EVERYTHING HAS ITS PRICE, MARTA BLACK KATH'S DAUGHTER.

"I make mistakes, Amaet," Marta said grimly, "but I'm a fast learner."

OH? AND WHAT LESSON DID YOU LEARN WHEN YOU TOOK ON FERAN'S DEBT?

Marta scowled. She didn't question how Amaet knew about that; the answer was obvious enough if Amaet truly controlled all aspects of the Debt. "The service is paid to you either way. What does it matter?"

IT MATTERS TO ME BECAUSE IT DOESN'T SEEM TO MATTER TO YOU. DON'T YOU WANT TO BE RELEASED FROM THE DEBT?

"Of course I do!"

THEN WHY DID YOU DO IT?

"Because I chose to," Marta said. "That's reason enough."

IT *HAS* HAPPENED THAT AN ARROW PATH MAGICIAN GAINED THEIR POWER AND WON FREE OF THE DEBT...BUT NONE WHO MADE SUCH FOOLISH CHOICES. AND, AS YOU SAW, THE STAKES ARE HIGHER NOW.

"Did you summon me here for a lecture, Amaet?"

I CAN SUMMON YOU FOR ANY REASON I PLEASE. NEVER FORGET THAT, MARTA.

Marta shook her head. "That I will not."

GOOD. NOW, THEN. YOU HAVE PAID FOR A QUESTION, WHETHER YOU REALIZE IT OR NOT. DO YOU WANT TO KNOW WHERE YOUR HOB SERVANT IS?

"Certainly, but I'll find him on my own," Marta said.

ARE YOU SURE? DO YOU WANT TO KNOW WHY YOU CAN'T FIND HIM? I COULD TELL YOU THAT.

Marta did want to know the answer to that question too, but she suspected that finding the one would give her the answer to the other. At least, so she hoped. She didn't want to let her impatience get the best of her. There was something else she wanted to ask. Something that she knew she herself would never be able to answer. "My question is about my mother."

ASK.

"My mother was one of the most powerful Arrow Path magicians there has ever been. That is not my pride speaking, nor hers. I know this to be true."

ASSUMING YOU ARE RIGHT, WHAT IS YOUR POINT?

"My point is that she should have been able to free herself of the Debt! She could have done great service to you, equal to her obligations. I'm sure of it."

THAT'S NOT A QUESTION, BUT I WILL ANSWER ANYWAY--IT'S TRUE.

"Then answer this, because it is a question: why was my mother never free from you?!"

Amaet's expression didn't change by a flicker. BECAUSE SHE CHOSE NOT TO BE.

"You can't expect me to believe that."

BELIEVE WHAT YOU WISH. PERHAPS YOU WILL CHOOSE AS SHE DID, WHEN THE TIME COMES. PERHAPS I WILL REFUSE YOU THE CHANCE OF SUCH SERVICE AND NOT ALLOW YOU TO BE FREE OF ME.

"You can't—"

Marta stopped, knowing foolishness when she heard it. Amaet could do as she said. Right, wrong and fair didn't enter into the matter.

OH, YES—THE RULES DO APPLY TO ME AS THEY APPLY TO YOU...BUT DON'T FORGET I MADE THOSE RULES, MARTA, AND THE STRICTURES OF THE ARROW PATH UNDER WHICH THEY OPERATE. THE SERVICE REQUIRED IS MINE TO DECIDE, AND MINE ALONE TO REQUEST.

Marta nodded, understanding finally dawning on her. "My mother refused to do what you asked. That is why she was never free of you. You asked her to do something horrid."

I WILL ASK THE SAME OF YOU, MARTA. IF YOU BELIEVE NOTHING ELSE I SAY TO YOU, BELIEVE THAT. WHEN YOU'RE STRONG ENOUGH, IF THAT DAY EVER COMES. IT WON'T IF YOU KEEP CONFUSING KINDNESS WITH VIRTUE, AS YOU DID WITH FERAN. ONE OTHER THING —

"What is it?"

DON'T WASTE ANY MORE TIME WITH THOSE BOOKS. THEY CAN'T HELP YOU.

Amaet was gone, leaving Marta trembling with barely suppressed rage.

Mother, I had no idea of what you had to bear alone. Why didn't you tell me? A tear formed in Marta's eye. It might have been her rage. It might have been something else, but she brushed it aside, and clenched her fists so hard that they hurt, and she didn't stop clenching them until she was certain there would be no more tears.

Marta collected the raven and slipped along the outside rear wall of the sanctuary. She didn't trust herself to speak to Aleeta just then, but she did believe she understood why Aleeta was so much a trial to her mother, and why she would be the same to Marta.

"How can anyone worship that foul creature!"

Bone Tapper glanced at Marta speculatively, but apparently read the anger on her face and kept silent, for which Marta was grateful. She wasn't ready to talk about it. She was also very certain of one other thing—she wasn't ready to abandon the Royal Archive either, though whether it was despite Amaet's warning or because of it, she didn't know or care. Her business with Treedle would have to wait anyway, so it didn't matter that it might take the rest of the winter to finish searching the archive. If there was anything there that could teach her, make her better suited to understand and channel what power she had, Marta intended to find that something and make use of it. Amaet would not get the better of her!

I'll be as strong as you were, Mother. Stronger, if that's what it takes to beat her. You'll see.

Marta went back down the mountain path, Bone Tapper on her shoulder. Marta barely noticed when others on the path stood aside from her, averting their eyes, whispering to each other in various degrees of nervousness or excitement once she was past. When Marta reached the bottom, however, she stopped, and it was as if all the anger she'd built up over Amaet's injustice, now too much for her to control or confine, boiled away. Marta felt weak and unsteady, and found a place to sit and rest. It took a few moments for the feeling to ebb, but it left something behind.

"I'm hungry."

The provisions she'd brought with her didn't seem quite adequate then, despite her intentions. Marta looked around at the vendors clustered near the foot of the path. She mostly ignored them before, now at least one of the smells coming from the group was very appealing. Marta sought out a stout older woman selling warm bread. She looked up at Marta and her smile froze and died.

Marta, for her part, turned on a bright, friendly smile as if she hadn't noticed a thing. "I'll have one of those, please," Marta said. She didn't ask what the woman was afraid of; she knew. *I suppose she thinks I'm going to turn her into a rat or something.*

The woman almost dropped her wares, she was trembling so. Marta wanted to tell her that nothing was going to happen to her, but what could she say to cut through all that fear? Marta knew she'd been more than willing to use it against Master Lokan; she couldn't very well complain that she'd done the job so well. The baker finally managed to get a grip on one fine loaf and hand it to Marta.

"Thank you. How much?"

"N-nothing. Please take it."

Marta managed to keep smiling, though the effort cost her. She took a small silver coin from her purse. "If you'll take this in exchange." At that she almost had to force the coin into the woman's hands, but Marta finally managed to make the payment, and turned away before the woman tried to return it, leaving her standing there staring at the small metal disk as if it might bite her.

Bone Tapper glanced behind them as Marta walked away. "It seems foolish to turn down free food. I never do."

Marta took a bite, savoring the heady aroma. "If I had a taste for carrion I might agree, as who would pay for that? Yet this wouldn't have been free. Taking that bread would have cost me, somehow. I'm sure of it. This way is better."

The raven looked disgusted. "Easily three times what the loaf was worth and she'll probably just throw it away, the way she's looking at it. Like as not she thinks the coin is cursed."

"Maybe, but she owed me nothing and now I owe her nothing. I'm in debt enough."

Bone Tapper cocked his head at her. "Indeed? Forgive me for asking, but what about Feran? I'm not a fool, so don't deny what you did."

Marta took a deep breath. "Feran was a mistake I will not repeat. If you're really not a fool you won't mention that name again."

"Noted. What now? Back to the sodding archives?"

"First thing tomorrow," Marta confirmed. "Tonight, however, I will want a bath. As hot and as scouring as Master Lokan can make it. I've got something I need to wash off of me."

Bone Tapper tested the breeze. "Strange. I don't smell anything."

Marta remembered Amaet's cold gaze.

"I do."

CHAPTER 12

"History will remember me as a fiend and a monster. There are those who have a better opinion but, unfortunately, history will outlive them."
— From the Annals of Dommar the Beast

"Greetings to the house."

It was late afternoon. Treedle had stopped counting the days he had been on the road. The gold that Kath had given him had lasted long enough to give him lodging through the winter, but now it was almost spring and his purse was empty. He knew he wouldn't be able to run much longer anyway and this area, one he knew and had reason to think Marta didn't, seemed like as good a choice as any.

I hope I've chosen right, but I still have to survive here long enough to find out.

Treedle stood on the cart road where it passed a small farmstead. The cottage was small but well built. There were signs of recent neglect—thatch that needed mending, a split post on the windlass at the well—that seemed out of place. After a few moments a woman opened the door. She was small, and her dark hair was gathered in a pale blue kerchief. She wore a dress of the same cloth. She might be handsome; it was hard to be sure through the weariness Treedle saw in her face. She stood against the door frame, one hand out of sight. Treedle thought he saw movement in the darkness behind her, but couldn't be sure.

"Greetings, Stranger," she said.

"I've had a long day's walking, Mistress. Could I trouble you for a drink of water?"

She smiled faintly. "Easily given, but not easily done. The windlass is broken, as you can see. I'm afraid you'll have to haul up the bucket yourself."

"Little enough to ask." He stepped through the gate, keeping his movements slow and deliberate. He lowered the bucket on its rope and pulled it up full. He drank from the dipper, watching the woman from the corner of his eye. He could see the haft of the woman's ax partially hidden by the door, and nodded approval. She was kind enough to a stranger, but no fool. "There's plenty left in the bucket, if you've no mind to waste it."

She frowned. "That I have not. Jacky, fetch the basin."

Treedle heard footsteps from the house and a small boy appeared at the door beside the woman. Treedle guessed him to be about nine, give or take. His hair was as dark as his mother's. He stepped out past her and brought the basin, and if he was afraid of the stranger he didn't show it. Treedle carefully emptied the bucket into the basin and the boy carried it back to the cottage slowly, trying not to spill.

"I saw a marker for a village down the road, but the lettering was gone. Is it far from here?"

"Wittanplace," she said. "About a league down the road."

Treedle smiled. He'd come farther than he had thought. He knew it wouldn't be enough, but that was all as it must be, and there would be time enough to worry about that later. "I was born near Averdale. We used to come for the fair, years ago. Do they still have it?"

The woman's dark eyes seemed to lose a little of their hard edge. "Every autumn after harvest. How long since you've been home?"

Treedle smiled, and told the understated truth. "Too long. I doubt anyone will remember me. My name is Mattic Jerson. Everyone called me Treedle."

She frowned. "Odd name. And I don't know any Jersons."

"As I said, a long time."

"What's a Treedle?" asked the boy before his mother could shush him.

"Well, if my grandmother was to be believed, it's the old way of saying 'treadle.' Something that does useful work without complaining. She said it was my only virtue, and I dare say she was right. Still, you look as if you could tolerate some useful work done for you."

The suspicion was back. "We have friends who help out as they can."

Treedle was a little surprised that she didn't immediately claim a husband who was merely away for a bit and would soon return. Then it occurred to him that perhaps that particular lie might have been too painful for her to tell.

"Doubtless good friends, but ones who have their own land and families to tend, I wager," Treedle said. "Especially this time of year. Spring is a busy season. Still, I'm sure I can find something in Wittanplace."

"I'm sure you could..." she paused, and the struggle was clear on her face. Fear, suspicion, and need were waging battle royal. Treedle waited.

"We can't pay you," she said, finally.

"Food and a dry place to sleep seem like excellent wages to me just now. And I do good work; you'll see."

Need won. "I am so tired of lifting that infernal bucket... All right. If you can fix the windlass I'll give you supper and a place in the barn for tonight. After that, we'll see."

"Done."

"Jacky, fetch the tools."

There was no spare timber handy to replace the split post. Fortunately, it had split from the augur hole to the side of the post rather than down, and the windlass had been set a bit high for either the child or the mother's comfortable reach anyway. Treedle took the windlass apart and evened up the posts with the bow saw, then marked them for the auger. Jacky watched him openly, perched on the stone fence.

"How long since your Da died, Jacky?" Treedle asked as the wood curls from the augur piled up at his feet.

"Last summer. He took sick with the water fever. The barber bled him but it didn't help..." Jacky stopped himself and looked at Treedle. "How did you know about Da?"

"Men are known to stray, and that's no more than truth. Yet the sort of man who builds a home like this and has a wife like your Ma and a son like you—" The auger struck a knot hole and Treedle paused to give a little more twist to the crosspiece. "—doesn't just leave of his own will. Besides, I read it in your mother's face."

The boy frowned. "That's silly. You can't read a face."

The auger point nibbled through the opposite face of the post. Treedle moved it to the other side long enough to clean up the hole and went to the other post. "Faces are easier than books. I can read yours, if you'd like."

The boy's face went stony. "What does it say?"

Treedle smiled. "At the moment, nothing. A few minutes ago it told me there was something you wanted to talk to me about. Man to man, I think. Was I wrong?" He worked the auger as he waited for Jacky to answer.

"It's about the oxen," said Jacky, at last. "The plowing, I mean."

"Hmmm." Treedle kept working the auger.

"We share the oxen with Jolan Tol and his family. My Da helped him buy the pair, and they took turns for the plowing. Then Da died."

"And this Jolan fellow keeps the oxen for himself now?"

Jacky sat up stiffly on the fence. "He wouldn't do that! But Jolan's fields are bigger than ours and now that his Da is getting on he has all he can manage alone. And... and I'm too small! Another year, Ma says. Maybe two. Ma and I can do the planting, but we need someone to do the plowing now."

"It's a hard thing to be responsible for so much so soon, Jacky. It's not a sin to need help now and then."

Jacky took a breath. "I want to hire you."

Treedle kept his expression as serious as the boy's. "Have you talked to your Ma about this?"

The boy shook his head, looking solemn. "I'm my father's son. It's my place to see that the plowing and sowing gets done. We can't pay you money now, but Ma said we have food and a place to sleep, and *I* say when the harvest is in you'll have a share of what we sell at the market. A full share."

Treedle nodded, equally solemn. "A fine offer. Let me think on it." Treedle finished the new mount and set to putting the windlass in place. Another few minutes and the bucket was spinning merrily toward the water below.

"Try the crank now."

Jacky hopped down from the fence and worked the crank vigorously. The bucket rose easily from the well, brimming with water. "I knew you could fix it," he said. "I've watched you. You handle tools as good as Da, and I think you know how to do lots of things. Will you work for me?"

"I don't know how long I can stay, Jacky, and that's the bare truth," Treedle said. "But if your Ma has no strong objection to our deal I'll stay as long as I can."

Treedle took the boy's offered hand and they shook on it, as men do. Jacky went back into the house, and a few minutes later the woman emerged alone. She glanced at the windlass.

"Done, I see."

"As I agreed."

She didn't say anything else for a bit. "Jacky's a good son. This has been hard for him." She met his gaze squarely. "He told you about our need. Well, it's true enough. Yet I do not know you, Treedle. I'd be a fool to accept you blindly."

Treedle shrugged. "That's no more than sense. Yet as I don't know how we change that situation on such short acquaintance, I have no solution."

"Nor do I. But need has its own rules, and I may be willing to accept the risk. You heard Jacky's offer; frankly I was thinking of making it myself if you did fix the windlass. But there's something I need to know first."

"Yes?"

Silence. Then "Who's chasing you, Treedle? Have you done something wrong?"

He smiled. "How did you know?"

"I've watched you," she said frankly. "You're no tinker, no beggar, no peddler, nothing that speaks of a life on the road. You were made to be in one place and live your life as part of it. A man like you is not rootless without cause."

"I see all of Jacky is not from his father, fine man though he doubtless was."

She smiled too. "He was all that and more besides. Now answer my question."

Treedle took a deep breath and let it out slowly. "I've done many things wrong in my life, and made at least one very bad choice. But I swear to you that I've harmed no one save myself, and what follows me seeks only me. I'm no danger to you or your son, directly or otherwise. I'd like for you to believe that, because I would really hate to leave sooner than need be."

"I would hate that too," she said, "my name is Genfyr. Supper's waiting." She left him there without time or reason to say or do anything save follow her.

*

The King's Librarian was a monk, not a priest, and sworn to Amatok instead of Amaet. Perhaps that is why Marta had allowed herself to like him, despite her best intentions. That and the fact he was a friendly soul, more interested in his realm of parchment than anything else. Marta knew that he understood what she was, at least on a superficial level but, as he wanted no more than exactly what he had in life, this knowledge didn't affect him in the least. He had accepted both Marta and her obscure scholarly interests without hesitation, and in the weeks following her return from the Shrine had made himself extremely useful, if sometimes annoying. Partly, she knew, because the king had told him to help her, but just as much because he enjoyed what he did and it was rather hard to stop him from doing it even if one wanted to. The man's enthusiasm was nothing short of contagious. Come see! Read this, consider that. Marta had a hard time keeping up with him, and now and then had to be firm and say no until she had gleaned all that could be gleaned from her current project.

"Mistress, you have to see this."

Marta looked up from a somewhat fanciful history of the founding of Junland. "What is it, Brother Akaen?"

"Something that might of considerable interest to you. It's the earliest reference I've seen to something that might be the Arrow Path."

Marta yawned, and put her scrolls aside without much regret. Most of what had been recorded there she could now judge better in the light of other readings. The events that these particular records chronicled either couldn't have happened, or didn't happen to the people named, or did happen and the chronicler had forgotten to mention it. Marta usually found that the bits that were left out were the most interesting, but she had only just begun to realize how much work was required to even scratch the surface of what she needed to know, and how hard it was to see patterns with so little of the picture provided. She had made a good start, but that was all.

"I was done here anyway. What have you found?"

"A chronicle of the reign of Riegur I of Borasur, done soon after the coronation of his son Galan. That makes it...five hundred and sixty years old, give or take a decade."

Akaen held up a moldering volume. Marta peered closer and saw that the book actually was moldering, at least somewhat. There were dark streaks that had been mildew, as if the book had gone through several cycles of wet and drying. Akaen handled the thing carefully, obviously afraid it would fall to pieces on him. He placed it on the table and Marta rose, stretched, and walked over to look where he was pointing. "Read this bit starting...here."

Marta followed Akaen's finger and started to read. It mostly concerned a treaty agreed between Riegar and an unnamed Lord of the Five Isles which put an end to a period of raids and piracy against Borasur's ports and trading vessels.

"I don't see..."

"Keep going," Akaen said.

Marta obeyed, and finally came to a passage that caught her attention. "They suspected Dommar the Beast fomented the crisis," she said. "But my understanding is that he was suspected of nearly everything, from the murder of Duke Palot to the eruption of a volcano near the Blacklands. What has this to do with the Arrow Path?"

"You'll note," Akaen said, "that in each instance Dommar was said to have acted through intermediaries. People who, I quote, 'owed their very souls to the evil wizard.'"

"That's rather vague," Marta pointed out. "And I certainly don't own any souls."

"But telling, don't you agree? And you must admit that, to an outside observer, it certainly might at least seem the case?"

Oh, fine, Marta thought. *Now the Arrow Path will be linked to one of the darkest magicians in the history of the mainland.*

"It's interesting," Marta admitted, and that was all. "Not all magicians are Arrow Path, or so I understand, and what they owe the Powers is a matter I know little about. If the Arrow Path existed before my grandmother's time I've seen no direct reference. Still, it is interesting. Thank you."

Akaen beamed. "I thought you would see it thus..." Akaen suddenly frowned. "Speaking of souls, where's that bird of yours? I don't think I've seen him for a day or two."

"Bone Tapper? He's on an errand." Marta hesitated, then went on, "I wanted to see what shape the eastern road was in. I'll be leaving soon."

Akaen's face fell, and it was all Marta could do to keep from hugging the man. *At least one soul in Karsan will miss me.* It wasn't much, but Marta knew it was more than she had any right to expect.

"Why must you go now?"

It was the first time Marta could remember someone expressing sincere regret at the thought of her departure. "I have business to attend to, Brother Akaen; I've tarried here longer than I should have in any case. I...I do hope to return and visit on way home, if you have no objection, but I don't know how long that will be."

"Certainly not; you're always welcome." Akaen sighed. "I suppose it was inevitable, but it has been nice to hear a thought other than my own down here. Mostly the king sends for what he wants, and it's my job to find it. Well enough, but one does weary of tax rolls and ancient points of protocol. This search of yours has been invigorating. I hate to see it end."

"I don't think it's ended," Marta said, "I don't think it ever will. But if Bone Tapper returns this evening as he should I'll be leaving in the morning."
"Well, then. Let's do what we can while we can, yes?"

Marta didn't have much hope that they could complete an understanding in a few hours what she'd failed to finish in as many weeks, but there was no point in not trying. There were references to magicians aplenty, and some of the information was accurate, at least so far as Marta could judge. Some was hateful. Much more was just rumor, speculation, and gossip. Marta had heard of dark magicians of course, names like Tymon the Black and Dommar the Beast weren't unknown to her—even her own mother had used them to frighten her into good behavior as a child. Yet she'd never associated them with anything her mother was, and she certainly didn't see anything of them in herself.

At least, not much. She hadn't forgotten Master Lokan, and what Bone Tapper had said about her enjoying what she had done to him.

Perhaps that's how it starts. I must be careful.

Marta wondered if being careful was enough. By most of Karsan's opinion she was well on her way to full sisterhood with The Beast as it was.
"Akaen, I need to ask you something. I don't want to create a debt-bond between us, yet I really would like to know."

"I don't know what you mean by 'debt-bond' unless you're talking about the obligations of supplicants to an Arrow Path magician. Yet you're asking me."

"Well, debts are serious matters and I don't pretend to fully understand them at this point. I have to be cautious."

Akaen shrugged. "My charge from the king is to help you with your search. I'm sure your question will fall under that."

"It's more personal."

"Even so," Akaen said.

Marta took a deep breath. "How did people view my mother?"

Akaen stopped smiling for a moment. "The truth? Yes, of course the truth. What else is of any use in the long run? They feared her, Marta. Even the ones who were fond of her."

Marta frowned. "Fond? You mean anyone was?"

Akaen laughed. "Well, a few certainly. Mistress Thornap for one. For another, the king... though in His Majesty's case perhaps 'fond' isn't quite the right word. Better to say they understood one another. He respected her, I know, even if their dealings were not always without friction."

Marta had personal witness to one of those less affable dealings, but it hadn't seemed to go anything beyond that, even then. She hoped she could earn as much from Alian, since sooner or later he would seek something from her.

The king is always reluctant to ask. That's to his credit.

"Then there was me," Akaen said.

Marta blinked, not certain if she had heard right. "You were my mother's friend?"

"Of course. She often visited the archives when she was in Karsan." Marta shook her head. "Yes, of course I knew that. No offense, but she didn't speak of you often. Or the archives, come to that, though I know she was fond of them."

Akaen shrugged again. "She seldom mentioned a meal at the Apple Branch either, I fancy, nor Master Lokan's fish soup. Yet I think she was rather fond of that, too. It was just something she did."

Marta nodded. That sounded like her mother. "What was she looking for?"

Akaen closed the book very carefully and took it back to the shelves for storage. "I was never certain. I don't think she was sure herself. Anything, really. She had very broad interests. I think she wanted to visit the library at the Temple of Amatok at Morushe, but I don't think her health or duties permitted it... oh."

Marta, deep in her own thoughts, didn't notice what had brought that reaction from the monk. "What is it?"

"This book." Akaen held up a different, newer volume. "I've never noticed it before."

"There are so many. Perhaps you'd forgotten?"

Akaen shook his head, looking slightly affronted. "I most certainly would remember..." He opened it, read a bit. "Curious."

Marta left the table and joined him by the massive shelves. "What is it?"

"A listing of the major Shrines on the mainland...plus one or two in the outer isles. Routes, some facts—at least, one hopes they are such—about each one. I didn't know anyone had ever compiled such a list. See? The Karsanmon Shrine is listed."

Marta read what was there. "The author had an eye for beauty. I share his opinion of the gate...though I think he rated the temple much too highly."

"As do I. The newer Temple of Amatok at Borasur is much finer, though of course it was after that man's time. Still, the rest seems accurate enough, so far as I know. There are a few sites I've never heard of. But how did the book get here?"

Marta was barely listening. "I don't know... May I see it?"

"Hmmm? Oh, certainly. You have an interest in places of worship?"

"Not as such," Marta said dryly. "But the subject? Yes."

"Like your mother," Akaen said.

Marta didn't say anything else for a while. She took the book back to the table and settled back into her chair. She skimmed the section on the Karsanmon shrine again and found a reference to the grotto. It didn't say much other than speculate a bit about the site probably being at least part of the location of the original shrine, but the fact that the anonymous author had mentioned it at all gave Marta more confidence in the narrative. Certainly the current Priestess thought the place of little concern, but Marta certainly knew better.

This is new...

Marta read intently for a while. When she looked up again it was later than she'd thought, though Akaen was still there, deep in a history of the Lyrsan Wars.

"Akaen, have you ever heard of a Power called 'Astonei'?"

"Certainly. She has two major shrines. One's in Wylandia and the other..." he frowned in concentration for a moment, then brightened. "Of course. Near Westas, far south and east of here before you reach the coast." He looked over her shoulder at the book. "Yes, just as I thought. It was on the old pilgrim route through Sendale."

Marta frowned. "I've never heard of Sendale."

"It no longer exists. A Sea-King raid destroyed the town and it was never rebuilt; it was already in decline." Akaen pulled another volume off the shelves, opened it to a page he well knew. "It's here in the Chronicles of the Wind-Singer."

Marta read the passages quickly, then looked up. "But the shrine is due south of where Sendale was?"

Akaen nodded. "Right enough. It's usually just called the Basilisk Shrine; I almost forgot Astonei was the patron. Why do you ask?"

"Is it true about the skull?"

"Depends. What does the book say?"

"That whoever sleeps in the basilisk's skull will have one true thing revealed to them. This privilege is very hard to win, naturally."

"Both are true, or at least that's the rumor. I don't know anyone who's actually done it."

Marta frowned. "You don't sound as if you believe it's true."

Akaen shook his head. "No, it's just that I don't really care if it's true or not. I do believe that's the sort of question one shouldn't be asking a dead monster, Marta."

"I suppose you're right..." Marta said, but her thoughts were elsewhere. A Law of Power could be a revealed truth...well, maybe not directly. But perhaps it could point the way... Marta didn't notice that Bone Tapper had returned until he landed on her shoulder.

"I'm returned," Bone Tapper said.

"So I see," Marta started to turn back to her book, but something caught her attention and looked more closely at the raven. "You're bleeding!"

"Not now but I was, and thanks for noticing. A goshawk tried to eat me."

"Are you all right?"

"Why do you ask? Afraid I'll die and avoid my debt?" Bone Tapper's voice fell off to a low grumble, but he submitted to Marta's examination meekly enough. Akaen brought a bit of damp cloth and Marta cleaned the wound on the raven's back.

"Just a scratch and a few feathers," Marta said finally, trying not to let her relief show, "Don't carry on so."

"You were the one getting upset at the blood," Bone Tapper said. "Whereas I—"

Marta closed his beak firmly between two fingers. "When I let you go, tell me what you found, without additional commentary. Can you manage that?"

"Mrwrp," said Bone Tapper and Marta, taking this for assent, released his beak. Bone Tapper opened his beak and closed it again a few times as if to make sure it wasn't broken. He finally gave his report: "The road is fine; there's no snow to speak of save for a few patches in the deep woods and the northern slopes."

"What about our friend?"

"No definite word, but strangers have been passing through Wittanplace. I would have asked, but people tend to be too startled to make coherent responses when I speak to them."

"No matter. I would have to go in any case." Marta closed the book reluctantly. She wanted to read more about the Basilisk Shrine, but enough that she knew where it was. Once they had resolved their business in Averdale it seemed the logical next step. Or at least worth pursuing. For now there were more pressing matters, business that had been left unresolved for far too long.

"Mistress..." Bone Tapper hesitated.

"What is it?"

"At the risk of 'further commentary,' I have to say that you don't look well."

"I'm fine," Marta said.

"I have to agree with your friend," Brother Akaen said. "Marta, you look tired. Almost feverish. I was about to suggest you go get some sleep."

"I will, before tomorrow. Good bye, Brother Akaen...and thank you."

"So it's certain, then? You're leaving us for now? That's a pity—you'll miss the wedding."

Marta went a little numb. "Wedding?"

"Feran and Kerasa, of course. It's tomorrow, in the king's own chapel. People have been in preparation for days. You didn't notice?"

"No," Marta said.

"Lovely couple. Have you met them?"

"I've met Feran," Marta said softly. "I hope... I hope they will be happy."

"As do we all. Go with Amatok," Akaen said. "Good luck on your journey."

Marta just smiled, and thanked Akaen for his good wishes, but any Power's blessing was the last thing she wanted now. She would do what she had to do, and sod the Powers or anyone else who got in her way.

Enjoy your freedom, Treedle. It's about to end.

CHAPTER 13

"It's a wise king who loves sad songs. Melancholy reminds all men of what they share."
— Bruga the Deliberate

The breeze stirred Duke Kon's thinning red hair. "We know they're coming," he said. "Why don't we just kill them all?"

Laras kept his eye on the pass. The raiders weren't visible yet, but the scouts said they were on their way and there was no reason to doubt them. "Because it's not enough to kill a desperate man, Your Grace, because there are always more desperate men. We have to frighten them, and that's much more difficult. Yet I will do it."

Kon's duchy of Fellmark was almost a little kingdom in itself, on the northeastern border between Morushe and Calyt. Though Kon by law and custom owed fealty to the kings of Calyt, in practice he was left alone to do as he saw fit.

Duke Kon was not a particularly stupid man. He knew that this state of affairs had both advantages and disadvantages, as he had been quick to point out to Laras when Laras first entered his employ: "The raiders come mostly from the eastern borders of Wylandia. The Chiefs of the Eastern Highlands owe fealty to the kings of Wylandia as I do to Calyt, but Wylandia does not control them. So, when they raid south, Wylandia rightly says it was none of their doing, and in any event which of the many chieftains is responsible? I have no answer for him. If I ask my sire of Calyt for aid, it comes at the expense of the precedent, and he takes too much interest in my affairs as it is."

Laras, for his part, blessed his good sense in leaving Junland before the spring thaw, despite his dislike of the cold. It had been easy enough to become accepted at court there, in the sense that his presence was tolerated. Yet Old Junland hadn't trusted the young magician for a moment and, far worse, had no particular need for him. "Whenever I think I have need, I see the pendant you wear, Laras, and it gives me pause." Laras could not bring himself to admit that he had no idea what the king was talking about. Junland, for his part, had never felt any need to explain. So their relationship had gone for a month, until Laras had been able to gather enough news from the court gossips to realized that Duke Kon would make a far better patron. Fellmark wasn't overly wealthy, but the Duke needed help and was willing to pay for it. This was all Laras required of a patron, and so far it had worked out very well indeed.

Laras gathered his new rich blue robes about him then walked to a flat rock overlooking the narrow valley below. It had taken him less than an hour to find what he needed among the rocks on either side of the valley leading out of the White Mountains, and now all he had to do was wait. When he released his grip on the edges of the cloak it billowed around him in a fresh spring breeze quite dramatically. Laras could only imagine the effect on anyone in the valley below.

Fortunately the warriors of the eastern highlands aren't known for their archery.

Not that this was a great fear in any case, but Laras didn't want any distractions, and certainly no twanging of arrows to spoil his dramatic moment. It was important that it play out just as he planned, both to observers in the valley and those standing behind him on the ridge.

One of the scouts slipped down out of a line of trees on the high ridge. He was a wiry and scarred little man from Kon's northern holdings, of the same stock who had suffered most of the raids. He reported to Duke Kon, but of course Laras was listening.

"Your Grace, if any are wearing a chieftain's insignia I haven't seen it, though I doubt any of the Lords in the highlands would be fool enough to show their hand."

"Doubtless they're all at fault, at one time or another," Duke Kon said, "though it would certainly help to find one to single out for blame. A show of force on my part might be enough to make the others turn on him as like as not. There are a lot of old feuds unsettled for want of an excuse."

"Perhaps, Your Grace," Laras said loud enough to be heard, "yet after today it won't much matter. All will get the word and your men needn't lift a sword."

"Magician," said one of Kon's barons, "some men like lifting their swords now and then. Keeps the arm strong."

Laras sighed. "There will always be a need for swords, Lord Polas. Just not today."

"So you say," Polas replied, but let the matter go at that.

Laras took no offence. He knew the time had come to prove what he said. He looked into the distance. "So I will show," Laras said. "They are coming."

The scout hurried off for a closer look, but Laras ignored him. The man had been warned of what areas to avoid; if he didn't listen it wasn't Laras's problem. Laras stepped back from the edge of the cliff; he didn't want the raiders to see him until they were well into the pass. The cliffs on either side made any other approach unlikely, but once they were through this next section they'd be able to send scouts out over the ridges, and doubtless they would. Timing was everything, so Laras waited well back and out of sight until the first faint sounds of men on the march came drifting up. Laras stepped back into view.

"Greetings," he shouted.

The man in the lead held up his hand and the armed men behind him suddenly stopped. As one all their swords were drawn, except for the few carrying spears. There were one or two archers among them but those moved uncertainly, arrows on the string, but their eyes were on the leader. Laras's quick count put the number of men at just over a hundred. They were a rough looking lot, and their equipment and armor was a mishmosh of different styles and origins, everything from rough scale brigandines to a full set of plate. The leader was mounted on a small mountain pony and so was lightly armored, and he was the only one riding. He was also showing his apparent contempt for danger by being several yards ahead of the main body.

They'll assume it's an ambush, Laras thought, and waited until they did just that, but before they could form anything like either a charge or a defensive formation, Laras brought the cliffs down on them.

It was as easy as thought, indeed it was a thought. Not a word, not a shout, not an incantation. Laras had found that these worked well enough but, in a pinch, weren't really needed. There was light, and sounds of thunder, and a blue balefire that seemed to spear out from Laras to the sides of the valley, but those were all just for show. Laras liked the tricks that came naturally to him now; they intensified the effect. He knew that's all they were: tricks and drama. The Laws were what mattered, and here he only used the First.

The stones on both side of the valley roared down the hillside and met at the bottom where the raiders, much against their will or preferences, were waiting for them. It was over in seconds. In a moment nothing was stirring in the valley below save dust.

And the former warband's leader. He sat on his pony, staring in shock and disbelief at the mess of rubble and dust that had been a formidable raiding party. Laras was fairly sure the man was trembling. Probably with rage, now, but the fear would come.

Laras called down to him. "My name is Laras. If anyone brings more men to raid south next time I'll drop the whole mountain on them. Tell your chieftains."

Laras stepped away from the cliff, he didn't wait for an answer. The Duke was beaming like summer but, as Laras had instructed, he kept silent, as did the rest of his nobles, although with sullen resentment clear on the lot of them.

"Well done, Your Grace. They'll get the message more strongly if they think one man alone did this."

"Well," Duke Kon said, "that is more or less what happened. I see you are not all boast, Magician."

Laras bowed slightly. "I am no boast at all, Your Grace. What I say I can do, I can do, and more beside."

After a little while the scout returned to make his report. "Maybe seven in all escaped the rocks, including the chief. I got my first good look at him. It was Jarban; I'd swear to it!"

Now Duke Kon did laugh. "Old Patan's son, and none other! This is even better."

"Yes," Lord Polas said eagerly. "If we seize him now, we'll have proof of who is raiding!" The man looked as if he was halfway to giving the order, but the duke stopped him.

"Lord Polas, bless you, but that isn't what I meant. They've all had a hand in it, from time to time. If we seize this boy his father will just claim a bit of youthful high spirits in joining a band from another chieftain. He'll pay a token ransom or not—he has other sons—and the tale will be stale by the time it all sorts out. Let him go home to his father as he is now, in shame, his warband shattered, and no loot! Eh, Master Laras?"

Laras nodded. "He'll fall all over himself relating the power of the great magician that Fellmark has in its employ. In fact, I wager by the time he returns there'll have been a battle with a horde of demons and who know what else, raised at my command. If there's half a brain left the highlands there won't be any more raids to amount to more than cattle theft."

"Suppose you're wrong?" Polas said.

"Then, as I said, next time I will drop the sodding mountain on the lot of them."

"That would seal the pass," Duke Kon pointed out. "There is some legitimate trade with eastern Wylandia and the Highlands."

"Quite so, Your Grace, and even more reason Wylandia should pay some attention. They don't want this pass closed any more than you do. If their king doesn't have stern words with some and the edge of his sword for the others, I'll be astonished."

"I am often astonished at what happens contrary to my expectations," Polas said dryly.

It took a bit of doing, including a word from the Duke, but Lord Polas was dissuaded from tracking down any other survivors. He wasn't such a fool that he couldn't see the sense of Laras's plan. The more people spreading the tale of this day's business, the better. Still, the man was clearly put out about donning all his armor and not getting to kill anyone. Laras knew that resentment of his presence, influence with the Duke, and his raw power would make Lord Polas and the rest of the nobles see him as a threat and move against him, sooner or later. Laras was pretty sure he could defend himself if it came to that, but the Duke would never tolerate a war between his magician and his nobles. In that sense, his loss was inevitable so he tried not to dwell on it.

I'll have to leave. The only question is when.

Laras, for all his triumph over the raiders, felt a little sad. Being a magician was proving a lonely profession. He wouldn't trade it for anything, but that didn't change the fact. More, he knew that the Third Law was waiting for him, and he'd never gain it as Duke Kon's servant.

Amaet, why haven't you summoned me?

That evening, Laras got his answer while he slept and dreamed of destroying mountains.

THERE'S MORE TO THE FIRST LAW THAN BREAKING ROCKS, she said.

Because it was a dream, and the presence of Amaet filled Laras with great joy and happiness, he was moved to answer her with more truth than tact. "Blessed One, I like breaking rocks."

She smiled at him then, and Laras's joy was complete. WELL, THEN. PERHAPS I CAN FIND SOME NEW STONE TO BREAK. YOU'VE BEEN PATIENT, LARAS, AND IT'S TIME I REWARDED THAT. IT'S TIME TO SEEK OUT MARTA, BLACK KATH'S DAUGHTER.

"Marta..." The name was familiar, in the sense that a fact that you once knew and forgotten is familiar. Then he remembered. "What do you want me to do with her?"

I WANT YOU TO DESTROY HER.

"Oh."

IS THAT ALL YOU CAN SAY? I THOUGHT THIS YOUR FONDEST WISH.

"Blessed One, I was angry with her and no denying it. Yet everything that has happened to me since she shut me in that cave...well, the joy of knowing you, the power I've acquired... It's all I've ever wanted! In a way, I think I should thank her."

YOU MAY THANK HER IF YOU WISH. BEFORE OR AFTER, IT MAKES NO DIFFERENCE TO ME.

"If this is your wish, then of course I'll obey," Laras said.

A RELUCTANT SERVANT IS A POOR TOOL, LARAS.

Laras shook his head firmly. "I am not reluctant. Whatever you wish, that is what I wish also. Yet it hardly seems fair. Unless much has changed, she is no match for me now."

SHE HAS THE FIRST LAW, LARAS, AND WHILE YOU HAVE THE SECOND AS WELL, IT WOULD NOT BE WISE TO UNDERESTIMATE HER.

"I will not," Laras said. "How do I find her?"

NO NEED. WHEN THE TIME IS RIGHT SHE WILL FIND YOU, IF YOU GO WHERE I TELL YOU AND DO AS I SAY.

Laras listened very carefully to Amaet's instructions. They seemed simple enough and, he had to admit, there was a certain irony and justice to what Amaet had in mind. When she smiled at him, all seemed right and wonderful. Yet, in the back of his mind and buried so deeply that the Laras who worshiped Amaet would never see it, there was another Laras. One who couldn't help feeling that, whatever justice there was in Amaet's request, it did seem a little pointlessly cruel. It was the same Laras who, that day at the cave near Black Kath's home, had struggled to keep from becoming a fiend and would have lost in the final test. He lost now.

"Whatever you wish, Blessed One."

Amaet leaned close, so close Laras could feel her honeyed breath, and whispered the Third Law.

*

Marta and Bone Tapper and Yssara were three days out of Karsan. Wittanplace was still a few days away, but the weather remained mild and the last lingering traces of snow were gone even from the deeper parts of the woods. Marta had taken the cart far off the main road to make camp at the edge of an empty meadow as evening approached. Darkness closed in around them, turning the trees into shadows. Now Yssara chewed the remnants of his supper. Bone Tapper perched on a dead chestnut tree near the campfire, just looking at her. Marta brewed tea and pretended not to notice.

"How do you do that?" he asked.

"Make tea? It's fairly simple, for all that it needs to be done right."

Bone Tapper flapped down from the tree and landed across the campfire, just out of reach. "I wasn't speaking of tea. I want to know how you stay so angry."

Marta frowned. "What are you talking about?"

"What I said. During your time with Brother Akaen in the archives I thought perhaps you had calmed down but, no, you were simply distracted. And you still don't look well. Are you sure you're not feverish? I think something is eating at you."

"I am not angry," Marta said, very slowly and clearly, "and I'm not feverish, and nothing is 'eating at me.' Though I will admit to being distracted for while. That's over now."

"No, Mistress, you were angry before your mother died and you're angry now. Oh, I'll admit that you don't rage, you don't shout—often—but you're still in a slow roiling fury. How do you do that? I've never been able to stay angry for more than a day or two, regardless of the provocation."

"Speaking of provocation..."

Bone Tapper just sighed. "You don't want to talk about it."

"There's nothing to talk about." Marta strained tea into an earthenware mug. "Do you want some tea?" Bone Tapper just shuddered and Marta smiled. "I'll assume that means 'no.'"

She sipped the drink, enjoying its warmth and the relative silence once Bone Tapper settled back into sullen quiet.

I am not angry...

Marta looked around, suddenly. "Bone Tapper, did you hear something?"

The raven shrugged. "No. What was it?"

"I'm not sure." Marta lowered her voice to a whisper. "Go take a look around the camp."

Bone Tapper launched himself into the air without further discussion and disappeared into the dark sky. Marta took the rest of her tea and moved away from the campfire so as not to be quite so visible to any lurkers. She considered moving closer to Yssara but then she'd never really associated the obstinate beast with safety. She let her eyes adjust to the greater darkness and scanned the trees on the edge of the meadow.

I should never have camped out of the open, even so far from the road.

Marta kept listening, and she heard the sound again. Indeed, she was pretty sure that she'd never stopped hearing it, not since they'd made camp. It was faint, fading into the background until, on some level, she'd paid it no more mind than the crickets singing around them. Yet this sound was not singing.

Someone is crying.

As soon as she put the feeling into words, she knew she was right. The sound was clearly that of someone weeping, so faint that it barely reached her consciousness, but it was there. Marta turned her head this way and that, but couldn't find a direction to the sound, try as she might. Bone Tapper finally returned and settled grumpily on her shoulder.

"Sensible precaution, but needless," he said. "There's no one out there. Not on the road, not in the woods for nearly half a league. I'm certain."

Marta shook her head. "Someone is. I hear weeping," Marta said. "Don't you?"

Bone Tapper looked at her. "I don't hear anything. Perhaps you're just tired."

Marta shrugged. "I am tired. Very tired. That doesn't change what I hear."

Marta walked across the clearing to the opposite side. There were a few stumps there, and upon closer examination Marta saw clear signs of an axe. "This isn't a natural meadow. This land was cleared at one point. A farm?"
Bone Tapper shook his head. "Too small. And if these stumps say true, there'd be a sign of a house or something if such had ever been built here."

"Then why would someone go to all the trouble?"

Bone Tapper shrugged again. "Why does anyone do anything toward an idea that doesn't become real? Maybe someone thought this would be a nice place to farm and then realized there wasn't enough water nearby. Or some local lord wanted the land for hunting and made them change their minds. Maybe someone died. Pick whatever answer you like; likely you'll never know the real one."

Marta thought perhaps Bone Tapper was right. She made two circuits of the clearing and was no closer to finding the source. She did decide that, if something close to an echo of a whisper could be measured at all, the sound was easier to hear by the area where the stumps hadn't been completely cleared. Marta walked by what appeared to be the stump of a large cedar and then stopped, frowning. She stood there for a very long time.

"Bone Tapper, this stump is crying."

"That's not possible."

"Unprecedented," Marta said, "at least in my experience. Impossible? No. I tell you it's so."

Bone Tapper hopped down from her shoulder and cocked his head at the stump. "I'm trying, Marta. My hearing is more than passable. I hear nothing."

"Maybe it's something you can't hear with your ears."

Marta kneeled down beside the stump and placed her hands on each side of it and invoked the First Law, but it told her nothing she didn't expect to find. Places where the rot had taken hold, places that the axe had damaged the wood but left it in place, a thousand places that the remainder of the stump could be shattered.

There was one place only where it could not be broken.

Marta felt for that spot, tried to understand what the wood was telling her. What it told her that this was not wood, part of the tree and yet not part at all. A separate thing, and yet not. It made no sense, Bone Tapper was right about that, but Marta finally understood that it was this thing, this one unnamed, indestructible thing that was crying.

Not knowing what else to do, Marta got cross. "Stop that! I'm trying to help you."

The crying stopped. If it was a sound she no longer heard it. If it was a feeling she no longer felt it. The crying was replaced with words Marta could understand, not loud but clear enough.

Who are you?

"My name is Marta, Black Kath's Daughter," she said aloud. "Who are you?"

What came then was not a word, but rather sound and feeling together, the sound and the feel of two tree limbs rubbing together in a high wind, the touch of bark on bark, the creaking of wood and the rustle of thousands of leaves. It was the 'feel' part that made Marta shiver in a mixture of nervousness and excitement. For that one instant Marta felt what the creature felt, to be a part of something large and alive. To know what it knew then. To know what it knew now. A stump, slowly rotting away.

"You're a leata, aren't you?"

Yes.

A wood-spirit, for want of a better description. Something that shared the life of certain kinds of trees, even though it was not a tree. Born of the tree and dying with it. Marta had heard the fairy tales, of course but, as with the craja in the cave, Marta was finding more truth in old stories than she had ever suspected. Here was a leata and, also like the spirit revenant in the cave, it was trapped.

The tree is transforming. Not rot away!

It took Marta a few moments to comprehend what the creature was telling her. Marta touched the stump again. She risked the use of Power again, since this was for her own understanding. The leata had not asked her for anything. Yet.

"There's a great deal of resin in the stump. It's hardening. It may lie in the ground for a thousand years or more. Not gone but not a tree, either."

Trapped!

Marta nodded. In the normal course of things, when a tree died its body would rot away, releasing its spirit companion. This tree stubbornly refused, and its spirt might not be freed for years...if ever. "Let me think—"

Help me!

Marta swore, softly. Now it was no longer a matter of curiosity and kindness. She had been asked for help. That carried a price and, because Marta had no choice, she knew the price.

Bone Tapper had been watching what, to him, must have appeared a one-sided conversation for several minutes. "Mistress, what is going on here?"

"There's a spirit trapped in this stump. She's asked me for help." Until she said the word 'her' Marta hadn't even realized that she knew the spirit was female.

"Can she afford you?"

Marta didn't answer right away. Her mind ran through a list of possibilities, each quickly considered and quickly discarded. She finally shook her head. "Absent gold—and where would a leata get money—the price is service for twenty years, in physical form. She couldn't do that even if she wanted to."

"So turn her into a cat or something."

Marta glared. "Turn what into a cat? The stump isn't her body!" She addressed the spirit again. "I'll try to help you, but I want you to tell me something: have you seen a man pass this way, traveling alone, within the last season?"

"What would she see with?" Bone Tapper asked.

"What does she hear with, cry with?" Marta snapped. "She sees, she hears, she feels! More than you do, I think. Be of some use and describe Treedle in his human form. I've never seen it."

Bone Tapper eyed the stump suspiciously, but he did as he was told. "A large man, fair, curly red hair. Well favored, I think. I'm no judge of that."

I did see that one, or one much like him. No more than three turnings of the sun gone.

Marta blinked. If that was true, they were much closer than she'd hoped. "Three days ago?" she said aloud, mainly for Bone Tapper's benefit. "He must have found a place to winter before Wittanplace, if that's where he's gone."

Will you help me? The creature repeated, pleading.

"Yes," Marta said. "I will help you."

Now Bone Tapper glared at her. "Marta, have you taken leave of your senses? This creature's debt, and so soon on top of Feran's? Have you learned nothing??"

Marta shrugged. "I haven't learned as much as I need to learn. Yet I do think I know what I'm doing."

Marta walked back to the campfire. It had died down to embers in her absence, but it only took a few moments to get it going again. She gathered up several of the remaining small branches and shavings that she'd used for tinder, and took them with her back across the meadow and piled them at the base of the stump. She peeled back several strips of the cedars rotting bark and added that to the mix. Then she took a small knife and carefully shaved several pieces of the resin-rich wood, and added that to the pile. She could feel the leata's presence, watching her intently.

"Just what do you think you're doing?" Bone Tapper asked.

"I would think that would be obvious, even to a feather brain like you. I'm going to burn the stump. It only has to be destroyed. There's no rule that says I have to use Power. For this favor, the information she gave is quite enough...not that I wouldn't have done it anyway—"

Marta stopped. She'd touched a Law. The same Law she'd sensed twice before. She knew it. She felt it almost like a physical presence, very close. Marta tried to reach out for it, to understand as she had that day at the cave, in a time that now seemed like ages past though she knew it hadn't been that long. Marta tried, but she couldn't quite reach it, couldn't hold it in her mind and say its proper name. Something given, something taken? Yes, it had to do with that, she was certain. But what? The understanding would not come, the meaning remained hidden. It was a glance, an encounter, but not a meeting. Marta almost screamed in frustration, and when Bone Tapper spoke again she very nearly screamed at him.

"Won't this hurt the thing?"

Marta forced her attention back to the here and now, forced herself to keep her mind clear. She turned back to the forlorn spirt. "Will it?"

Yes...very much. Please hurry.

Marta didn't hesitate, for she knew that if she did she might not be able to go through with it. She gathered a new bundle of dead wood, just large enough to fit well in her hand, and she set the end ablaze in the campfire. In a few moments the tinder by the stump had caught and was burning hot.

Ahhh...

The feeling washing over Marta was pain, pleasure, impatience and gratitude all muddled together. Marta found another stump to sit down on, no longer trusting herself to remember to stand, or not to fall, or not to cry, beg, or scream. She hugged herself as hard as she could. The spirit released its pain just as the fire released the spirit. Slowly, inch by flaring, sparking, blackened and smoking inch.

I can't stand it...

Marta didn't know if that was her thought or the leata's. The two seemed to be blending together so far as Marta could tell. She worried, a bit, if she would be able to find herself again in all the confusion in her mind. The confusion lasted a long time, but not forever. Marta sat there as the fire spread though all the exposed surfaces of the stump. After a time that could have been minutes or hours the flames appeared to die out, but Marta wasn't fooled. The fire still lived, smoldering in the deep parts of the stump. The breeze caught sparks and blew them away to die cold in the night but the fire still lived. It kept burning hot and spreading until it reached the last of the heartwood about the taproot and began to burn that as well. Marta felt it as extreme pain and great comfort all at the same time. The balance was the only thing, she knew, that kept her from collapsing in agony, and it barely did that.

"Almost over," she said aloud.

The smoke billowed up. In that moment Marta came back to herself, fully, and saw with her eyes alone, felt no more than she should feel, sitting there by a smoldering stump by the first light of dawn. In that moment Marta saw the leata for the first time, an image of leaves and twigs forming a small, sharp-featured face that smiled at her with thorny teeth. In a moment it was gone, as if it had never been, and the last of the stump collapsed on itself like the remnants of a burning house.

Marta put her head in her hands. "It's done."

Bone Tapper said nothing, but merely kept watch as Marta staggered off to find her blankets and sleep well through the morning.

CHAPTER 14

"The wonder is not that a snake bites. The wonder is that, from time to time, it does not."
— Bruga the Deliberate

It was late morning on the second day of plowing. The sun was high and, despite the early season, almost uncomfortably warm. Genfyr brought Treedle a cold drink from the repaired well. Treedle accepted the bucket gratefully and drank deep. Neither said anything for a time. Treedle just stood for a moment, enjoying a moment's rest in the freshening breeze. That, and the sight of Genfyr trying not to look at him.

Genfyr looked around the field instead. The earth showing where the plow had broken it apart was dark and rich; the smell was heady. "It's going well," she said, and that was all.

Treedle nodded, more patient than the pair of yoked oxen stolidly chewing their cuds. "The bulk of it should be over by evening. I'll be able to help you and Jacky with the sowing tomorrow...maybe." He waited for what he sensed would follow, though he wasn't yet sure what that might be.

"Are... are you leaving us? I was thinking you might be."

"I don't know, Genfyr. As I told you, there is a good chance of it. I will do my best to finish this field, come what may."

Genfyr nodded, again not looking at him. "Well then..." she started to say something else, hesitated. "I need to think about supper," she said, and left him there without another word.

Treedle smiled faintly and got back to his plowing. The work was hard; his back ached and his hands were sore. The field seemed to go on forever, and yet each course, to Treedle's way of thinking, was over far too soon. Treedle almost wished that were really the case. Every long course down the field was like a borrowed bit of paradise. Treedle couldn't remember the last time he had been so happy.

It's not the work. It's the purpose.

A purpose of his own, freely chosen and even better because it was shared by others. There was poetry in Treedle's plowing, and music and laughter, all things very real to him, very much in the moment, as opposed to the uncertainty that was waiting for him on the morrow. He fervently wished the day would never end yet, after the usual amount of time, the day did end. That night Treedle washed off the sweat and dust in the cold stream that ran between the house and the first field. After supper and despite his weariness he took a brief walk, enjoying the night air and the freedom he knew might soon end. When he returned to the barn Genfyr was there waiting for him. She was wearing a dress he had not seen before, and her hair was unbound. It was the first time he had seen that, too. He rather liked it.

"I believe what you said about not being dangerous, Treedle," she said. "I've come to talk to you about staying on. With Jacky and me, I mean. I know you say it's not up to you, but what if it was? Would you want to stay?"

"It may be that you've come to talk to me about staying, but that's not the only reason you're here," Treedle said. "We could have the whole of the matter with a little work. Shall we try?"

Genfyr reddened slightly. "How dare you!"

Treedle frowned. "Speak the plain truth, you mean? Then what would you have between us, Genfyr, if not that?"

She didn't look at him. "Why did I come, then?"

"I think you sought to trade what you have for what you need. Only you're not quite sure what either of those is yet."

She met his gaze steadily. "Not sure? Treedle, I've borne three live children, buried two of them and my husband in the bargain. Say what you will of my judgment—I'm no callow girl."

"And I'm no blushing boy, but I'll say fair that the coin I spent to lose that state didn't purchase very much. How about you, Genfyr? Do you understand any of it any better now, for all your experience?"

Genfyr smiled a little sadly. "No."

Treedle smiled, too. "There's your truth. Here's mine: Tomorrow I may have to leave. Or the next day. I don't know, but I think I will find out soon. That's neither threat nor entreaty nor spur to your purpose or mine. It's just what I know. What I fear, because I don't want to leave."

"I'm not very happy with any of our truths," she said. "Except that last one."

He shrugged. "It may not seem so now, but between a man and a woman, truth is usually the best place to begin."

"You're a strange one, Mattic Jerson," she said. "Truth is an unsentimental sort. It strangles most beginnings in the crib and laughs to do it."

Treedle smiled. Fond as he was of the nickname his grandmother had given him, it felt both strange and very good to be called by his own real name again. Especially when Genfyr said it. "All the more reason. If I have to leave you, I'd rather you not remember me at all than remember me unkindly."

Genfyr's mouth set in a hard line. "Most men wouldn't care, once they were gone. Why does it matter to you?"

He shrugged. "As for other men, well, some wouldn't care and good riddance to them. Yet I'm not so rare a creature as you might think. As to why it matters...because it does. How can I say it more plainly than that?"

Genfyr smiled at him then. "You could say it much more plainly, and certainly with more poesy and flowery words in it," she said. "But as it is, that'll do just fine."

She kissed him on the mouth then, full and sweet. Treedle kissed her back, clumsily at first, but after a while he remembered what he knew and started to learn the rest and in time he made a match for her in every way he could. It wasn't her first time nor his, but it was now.

*

"You'd think I had the blessed plague!"

Marta raised the bucket from the well in the market at Averdale. For all she could tell, she and Bone Tapper might have been the only two living creatures in the entire town. Yet Marta knew that wasn't so. Every now and again she would catch a pair of eyes watching her from beneath a window shutter, or a darkened doorway. Bone Tapper just shrugged, saying nothing. He'd said very little that afternoon ever since Marta had awoken after sleeping most of the morning away.

Let him sulk.

Marta didn't care. At least now she was spared his sarcasm when she stated the obvious. Avedale, a lively and industrious place when she'd first walked down the main street, had suddenly turned into something more like the Kulgan ruins at Lyrsa, for all the life showing. Marta had taken care to unhitch Yssara and stash the cart in some woods nearby, and had even cautioned Bone Tapper to keep his distance while she went in to find out what she could. None of that had mattered. Averdale knew immediately who she was, and what she was, and wanted no part of her. Marta, for her part, couldn't be as angry as she wanted to be, at least not about that. She considered the attitude much preferable to the alternative; she was roundly sick of the two servants she did have, yet she had no choice but to look for the third, and being shunned wasn't helping her find him.

Marta used the dipper to take a drink from the bucket, then left the rest of the water there.

More than likely they'll dump it out and cap the well once I leave, for fear of poison...

"It was like I said, Dela. He was the one. I knew it. That's why she's here."

Marta looked up. The words weren't addressed to her. Two old women were approaching the well, bundles of washing balanced on their heads. Wisps of white hair escaped the kerchiefs on each old head to shine faintly in the morning sun. Marta wondered at first if it was just the equalizer of age, but Marta realized it was more than that. The women were either sisters or else very close family.

"I remember his father. He was a handsome man in his prime, do you remember?" said the one called Dela to the other. The other nodded.

"It's a fact...oh, hello child."

The first one noticed Marta standing there and smiled at her. Marta smiled back, tentatively.

"Good day to you, Grandmothers."

The first laughed. "Both of us! How sweet. How long has it been since anyone called you that, Dela?"

"I forget," Dela said, smiling with what teeth she had left. "And Onlee, love, you never were, poor dear."

"I had my chances, and don't you go saying otherwise," Onlee replied haughtily. "There was Kygo and Amaran. Oh, remember him? Never mind. She's a polite thing. So few children are, these days. New here, aren't you?" Onlee dropped her washing on an old bench by the well basin. She took the water left in the bucket and poured it in, then lowered the bucket again on its rope. Marta hurried to help her haul it back up.

"Very polite," Dela said. "You know she's not from here. Where are you from, girl?"

"My name is Marta and I'm from Karsan...west of here."

Onlee looked up from her bundle. "Karsan? I'll dare say it's west! Very far west indeed."

"Very far," Dela agreed. "And far too young to be on your own like this. Are you an orphan?"

"Orphan..." Marta said. She hadn't really put a word to it like that, one simple word to sum up all that she was and wasn't, without Black Kath. Marta knew that she must have had a father, because she had noticed other children usually had them and asked her mother about it. Black Kath had confirmed that, yes, she had a father. Marta hadn't seen any point in asking further at the time. There had never been anyone except her mother at the very heart of her world, and Marta had never felt that state as any kind of absence or loss, something that should have been but was not. Still, she was a bit curious, now that she thought about it.

I'll ask Bone Tapper, if there's time later. He was with mother then.

Marta finally nodded and gave the only answer she knew. "I'm alone now. Yet there is someone I'm trying to find... perhaps you can help me." She described Treedle as best she could, though she thought that any stranger would summon enough attention that they might have heard of any.

Onlee perked up. "A relative?"

"Not exactly," Marta said. "More like an old friend of the family. He would be a stranger here himself, maybe around for a few weeks, I'm not sure."

"She's not sure," Dela said.

"Surprising," Onlee said.

Marta frowned. "I don't understand."

"Well, you'll forgive us, Marta, but we expected an Arrow Path witch to know everything. I suppose that's just a legend. I think your description was accurate enough, though. You are a pretty thing... or more so, if you'd smile more."

Marta was too surprised to be either embarrassed or annoyed. "You knew? But I thought..."

" That we were a pair of dotty old women with barely one coherent thought to share, perhaps on the odd Holy Day?" There was a twinkle in Dela's eye. "Why else would we be jabbering with you while the rest of these fools cower like a flock of blessed sheep?"

Marta blushed. "Well...yes."

"Honest, though," Onlee said. "And has the decency to be a little ashamed of herself. I think I like her."

"I do, too. Very well and fair enough," Dela said. "The truth, Marta, is that it's our Washing Day, and this is our washing place, and we will do our washing together as we have for the last forty years."

"Unless it's raining," Onlee said. "More to the point, a lot of these same fools will have as little to do with us, most of the time. Mostly because we know a fool when we see one and don't hesitate to point this out. Doesn't make us loved, does it, Dela?"

"No. It does not. Still, there is also the fact that we don't want anything from you and, we hope, you don't want anything from us. Aside from some polite talk and news if you have any. How fares the queen? We heard somewhat of her troubles."

"Very well," said Marta. "Mother and babe strong and healthy. My mother helped at her confinement."

"And more beside, if the rumors are true," Onlee said. "That was well done."

"Yes," Dela agreed.

Marta didn't say anything else for a while. For their part, Onlee and Dela didn't seem to expect it. Marta almost suspected the two old friends were conversing, discussing, weighing, and all without saying a word.

"The one you're looking for is near here. You won't harm him, will you?" Onlee asked, finally.

"We have business to settle," Marta said, matching the honesty of the old women as best she could. "And I will claim him. I must. But harm him? No. I won't do that."

"There's harm and there's harm," Dela said.

"Genfyr will be devastated. I can't say she's my favorite person in the world, but she deserves a little happiness."

"I don't know this person," Marta said.

"It doesn't matter," Onlee said. "You being what you are, you'll find him sooner or later. If I hadn't met you, I'd be inclined to let you hunt and be blasted for it. But we like you."

"She's not a bad girl," Dela agreed. "Though she'll do bad things if she's not careful. We did."

"We weren't always careful, were we?" Onlee said.

Marta started to ask about what those bad things' might be, but decided she was better off not knowing. Onlee turned back to Marta. "Walk north of here on the road. Genfyr's farm is about two leagues away. There's a well in the front yard, and the roof is well-thatched. You can't miss it."

"Do what you must. Be kind if you can. Smile, if you can find a reason to be happy," Onlee said.

Happy? Marta wasn't even sure if the word meant anything. She just said "Thank you."

"Don't," Dela said. "Just go, before some idiot in the tavern across the way drinks his courage up and does something foolish."

"I know you're not afraid," Onlee said. "But there's fear and there's sense. No shame in listening to either at times."

Marta nodded, and left Averdale without looking back. In a few moments Bone Tapper landed on her shoulder.

"Did you hear any of that?"

"All of it," the raven said. "I was in the persimmon tree behind the well."

"Were you? I didn't notice," Marta said. She was still a bit distracted, trying to get some sort of grip on the two women she had met in Averdale, but not really succeeding.

They were no witches, she thought, *but I wouldn't cross either of them for love nor gold.*

Whatever her mother had been, there was more than a little of it in Onlee and Dela, though she was ashamed to say she would never have suspected that if she hadn't spoken to them.

"Fly ahead," Marta said. "We know where Treedle is staying. I want to know what he's done there. Don't let him see you."

The raven took off, dwindled to a black speck, and vanished. Marta, still deep in thought, walked steadily on. There was a lot to think about, and in the press of it she forgot all about the question she'd meant to ask him.

*

Bone Tapper landed on the limb of an oak tree just above Marta's shoulder. "Those gossips in Averdale had the right of it. There's your hob. Plowing the land, and no doubt the widow, too."

"So I see." Marta stood behind the windrow separating one field and another. If she didn't count the days spent in the archives at Karsan, tracking Treedle down had taken less time than she'd expected. She was inclined not to count them, since it had seemed necessary, or at least a reasonable course at the time. Yet after her first failure she hadn't expected it all to end so soon, or be as easy as it seemed it was going to be. Marta was almost disappointed that her search was over, but couldn't say why, and despite her impatience she hesitated. What she sensed wasn't danger, exactly, but Marta couldn't escape the feeling that she stood a risk of losing something important, and she had no idea what it might be.

"So take him back and let's be gone," the raven said. "He might as well be waiting for you."

It's almost as if he is.

Yet that didn't make sense. Marta kept her eyes on Treedle all the time she spoke to the raven. "Are you in a hurry, Bone Tapper?"

The raven glared at her with his beady black eyes. "Yes! Why aren't you? It's been 'Bone Tapper, find my horse' and 'Bone Tapper, tell me where my hobgoblin slave has gone off to' and 'I will have what is mine' over and over as if no one was ever listening, even as you take pity on hopeless, hapless, brainless lovers and sobbing stumps! Well, where's your pity for me? Where is it for Treedle? He's a man now and no hob at all, and what of it? I too was a man before you forced that bit of two part harmony recitation on me and made me a raven again."

Marta was still looking at the man called Treedle. She had never seen him as a man, indeed never thought of him as one. She had known the hob all her life but the man? Never.

I'm beginning to understand why mother made him a hob. I wouldn't want him around me as he is. Her mother had understood about distractions. After Feran,

Marta was beginning to understand, too. Yet there was something going on now and, she realized, had been from the day her mother died. Something she didn't understand at all. She wasn't sure if she needed to understand, but she certainly wanted to understand it.

"Are you just talking, or is there a point?" she asked Bone Tapper.

"Just that he is the last one, the scab you pick when you complain that 'you are not your mother' and feel worthless and angry. Have done and back to witchery with all that your mother owned. Have what is yours, since that is all that seems to matter to you."

Marta's voice was a harsh whisper. "Don't attempt to dictate what I do and don't do, or presume to tell me how I feel or what matters! You've been sullen and silent since yesterday. Why have you found your tongue now?"

"Because now my words trouble you where my silence troubled you before," the raven said. "Even a slave finds pleasure where it can."

"Enjoy it while it lasts, Bone Tapper. The cost may be dear."

Bone Tapper apparently thought better of it, since he said nothing else for a time. Marta just watched the man plowing the field, looking almost as stolid and content as the oxen, though the day was sweltering and the sweat soaked his body. She watched as the day lengthened, she watched while a boy and then later a woman brought Treedle water, tarried briefly, then left again. Marta took some water herself, and a bit of dried fruit, but she watched, and kept watching, and the only thing beside the crushing weariness readable on her face was a frown that deepened until it overwhelmed all else, even the pain and weariness there.

The sun was setting before she said or did anything else. "Why?" she asked aloud. It was the question she really wanted answered. Not 'how,' though that was next on her list. 'Why' was the key, and what mattered now.

Bone Tapper cocked its head and eyed her quizzically. "I don't understand," he said, finally annoyed enough to speak again.

"Neither do I," Marta said. "I wonder what it will cost me to find out?"

Treedle turned the oxen at the far end of the field, starting up the final row. Marta emerged from the windrow and the lengthening shadows and strode purposely toward her mother's servant, the one who must in turn be servant to her. Treedle calmly finished the final row and then waited for her there. He didn't try to run. Marta almost wished that he had run. That at least would have made some kind of sense.

"I have found you at last," she said, trying her best to look grim.

Treedle just smiled. "When you look like that I can see Black Kath in you," Treedle said. "I never could before, but she's there now. Somehow you've managed to harvest her pain and carry it with you in these last few months. Or have you grown your own to match?"

Marta didn't say anything for several long moments. Then: "What was your trouble?" she said.

Treedle answered her without hesitation. He didn't try to resist, or argue, or plead as both Bone Tapper and Yssara had done. "Grief, Marta."

There was no surprise, no fear showing on his face, nothing but the same infuriating pity Marta saw there from the first. Marta realized that Bone Tapper, whether he knew it or not, was exactly right. Treedle was waiting for her, had been expecting her to find him, no, had been *certain* that she would find him, and that was more than Marta had been. More, as far as Marta could see he was still waiting. For what?

"And what was Mother's promise?" was all she said.

"That my grandmother, who raised me when my parents died and who I loved more than life, would not die of the Red Fever. And before you bother to ask, yes, the promise was kept. She died of plague instead a month later when I wasn't there to help her, but that wasn't your mother's fault. It was mine. I recognize my debt, Marta. Impose your rights and let's be gone, if we must."

Marta hesitated. "I want to know something first."

Treedle shrugged. "When I am your hob again you can ask what you will."

Marta looked grim. "I can ask. But my power over my servants doesn't extend to all things."

"Is that so? Why do you think that is?" He sounded like innocence itself. Marta was young, and frightened down in the deep places where she couldn't pretend she was not, and very lonely. But she was not a fool.

"I don't know," she said. "But I think you do. There's something strange going on here, yes, and more than one thing. First there is the fact that you were able to elude me. That should not have been possible. The second is this place, and you in it."

"You want quite a bit, Marta."

Marta worked her will. Treedle was a hob again. He looked up at her with big brown eyes set in a squat, ugly face, but otherwise nothing changed, including Treedle's expression. He still seemed to be waiting.

Marta took a deep, slow breath. "This is a reminder, Treedle. I could command you to follow me now," she said. "And I swear my yoke will be much lighter than the one you've found here. Why, Treedle? Why do you who toiled for so many years for my mother spend your short freedom toiling so much harder for others? Was it simply for food? Or the woman?"

Treedle laughed at her. Marta's hands balled into fists. She started to speak, but held her tongue. She waited until he was through.

"Oh, Marta... it's your time. Spend it guessing if you will. Or lose patience and haul us all off to be to you as we were to your mother. Or..." He didn't finish.

"Or what?"

"Or first you can answer a question of mine. I can't compel your answer, any more than you can compel mine. Will you answer, or will you command first and let the mystery go hang? Your choice."

"Ask," Marta said.

"Why did your mother have so many servants?"

Marta frowned. "Why? Because all debts must be paid, and not everyone had gold to pay. You didn't."

He shrugged. "Certainly not true of Yssara. But Black Kath transformed each of us into something she needed, rather than let us serve her as we were. Bone Tapper, to replace her weak eyes. Me, to serve far better than her own arms. Yssara, to be her legs. Now, your eyes are clear, your arms and legs are young and strong. So tell me—why should we serve Red Marta as we did Black Kath?"

"I..." Marta stopped. The shock of recognition rooted her to the spot. It was a Law, and the same one she had touched before. It was right in front of her, if only she could see it, if only she didn't think too hard or clutch too tightly. Like a butterfly that would only land if she did nothing wrong, held her breath, remained still. When Marta spoke again, she gave the answer to herself as well as Treedle. Her constant frown smoothed into amazement. "You shouldn't, should you?"

Treedle grinned broadly. "Your mother said you were a bit slow, but not deadly so. I see she was right."

Marta looked at him as if she were seeing him for the first time in her life. "It was you, Treedle. You buried her."

"Yes."

"Why?" she asked again, and it was all the questions rolled into one: Black Kath's grave, the plowing, everything.

Treedle leaned forward and beckoned. Marta leaned close and he whispered the answer: "Because all that," he said, "was my choice."

Marta stared. "That's it?! That's the sum of it? What neither my mother nor this woman could command, you did of your own will?" She didn't speak for a moment, and when she did speak again there was wonder in her voice. "That is the sum of it. I've been an idiot."

Treedle the hob grinned ear to ear, which in a hob is something to see. "Your mother said it was a Law of Power, Marta. She couldn't teach you but she thought, perhaps, she could lead you to it. You had to earn it, and I agreed to help. That's why you couldn't find me right away—I was already in your service, and honoring your mother's last wish."

Marta didn't say anything for a long time. She finally looked up again, her eyes glistening. "I have the words now: 'What Can't be Taken, Can be Given.' It's the Second Law of Power."

"Fine words, but only words, to me," Treedle said. "Though I understand them as true enough. I imagine they mean something more to you."

"Clever, Mother," she said softly. Then she smiled, faintly. "And clever Treedle." Marta closed her eyes for a time, then nodded. "I thought as much. Your freedom served me better than your obedience ever could. Your debt is paid, Treedle. You're...you're free of me. I hope you'll be happy."

Treedle stood as a man again. He was smiling, but there was still pity in his eyes. Marta could not wipe it away nor could she bear the weight of it. She turned abruptly to get away from him, to go anywhere that pity was not, but Treedle reached out and put his hand on her shoulder. She started to pull away from him, but Treedle's grip was firm, if gentle. "You'll have enough trouble making your own way, Marta. You'll have enough pain of your own. You shouldn't carry your mother's, too. She loved you, if she loved anything in this world; she wouldn't want that."

Marta stared at the ground, her hands still clenched tight, gripping hard on nothing at all. "You don't know, you can't understand. Mother..."

"She's dead, Marta. I do know—I buried her, remember? Past time you did the same."

"I'm sorry....I can't. I won't—"

"Remember what I told you on the road to Karsan? Well, now I'm a free man once more. Free to be your friend again, if you need a friend. I think you do."

Marta had no more strength to stand or to fight the tears, and this time she lost. And won. Treedle put his strong human arms around her and she didn't resist as the first racking sobs overwhelmed her.

"It's all right, girl. Let it go."

Marta didn't stop crying for a very long time, and Treedle held her safe until she could stand on her own again.

CHAPTER 15

"The sun sets whether the day is done or not. It rises, regardless of the business of the night."
—From the Annals of Dommar the Beast

Marta couldn't remember the last time she had slept so well as she did on the hay in Genfyr's barn. She woke just as dawn showed as a pink glow in the east. The boy called Jacky looked tentatively around the door.

"Mistress Marta? Are you awake?"

Marta yawned. "Yes, Jacky. Good morning."

"'morning. Mother says breakfast will be ready soon, if you're hungry."

"Thank her for me. I'll be along shortly."

Bone Tapper still had his head tucked under his wing. Marta started rolling up her blankets and shaking out the hay. "Wake up. Time to be up and about."

Bone Tapper stretched his wings. "This is not the way I expected this meeting to go."

"You sound disappointed."

"Disappointed? No. Envious. Treedle's free from you and I'm not. He has also apparently acquired a farm and a new family in the bargain. I wish I had that kind of luck."

"Luck had little to do with it. He earned his freedom. I daresay he earned the rest, too. He deserves some happiness," Marta said, remembering what Dela and Onlee had said.

"If true it's totally beside the point. Many who deserve joy never get it."

167

"Do you include yourself in that group?" Marta asked mildly.

Bone Tapper shook his head. "Say what you will, I know what I am. I know what I deserve and what I've gotten is probably half of what's owed me, at best. That doesn't mean I won't envy Treedle just the same."

Marta stowed the blankets in the cart. Yssara was still asleep and Marta didn't disturb him. There was no point, at least not yet. "Then why do you constantly whine about your lot?"

"Because it irritates you, and comforts me. I may not deserve comfort but, like any other living creature, I still want it."

"Fair enough," Marta said, trying not to smile. "Are you coming to breakfast?"

Bone Tapper shuddered. "Oat mush and bread? No thank you. I'll find my own meal."

"Suit yourself."

Marta slipped into the near woods to deal with nature then drew a bucket from the well to wash in. After that she joined the rest for breakfast in the farmhouse. Bone Tapper was right about the oat mush and bread, but for her part Marta had no complaints: the meal was warm, filling, and delicious. Genfyr accepted her thanks with a smile, but kept a bit of distance. Marta didn't blame her for that; unlike the townsfolk at Averdale, Genfyr had reason to be suspicious of her. No doubt Treedle had told Genfyr the whole story by now and she must have known how close Marta had come to taking Treedle away from her.

When all was done Marta went with Genfyr back to the well basin to wash the crockery. When all was done Genfyr spoke to her just as Treedle emerged, dressed for the fields. "We'll...we'll be off to the fields in a moment to finish the planting. You're welcome to stay if you'd like," Genfyr said.

Marta knew the offer was sincere enough, yet even as the Second Law spoke of offers, that did not mean that all things given should be taken. She smiled. "Thank you, but no. I'll need to be on my way this morning."

"Where are you going?" Treedle asked.

"To correct a mistake," Marta said. "I think you know the one I mean."

"I suspect," Treedle said. "Something to do with Yssara?"

"Yes."

Genfyr looked from one to the other. "Who is this 'Yssara' person?"

"My horse," Marta said. "It's rather hard to explain..."

"That's all right," Genfyr said. "I doubt I would understand. I need to be in the field."

Treedle smiled at her. Marta wondered if anyone would ever smile at her just that way. "I need a word with Marta, Genfyr. Don't worry; I'll be along."

"See that you are," Genfyr said. "Goodbye, Marta."

"Goodbye, and thank you."

Marta watched her go. "You're going to marry her, I assume."

"No time now, but as soon as we finish the planting, yes. There's a priest of Astonei in Wittanplace. We've told Jacky, in case you wondered. He took to the idea better than I thought he might."

Astonei?

Marta thought for a moment. It was the name of a Power and sometime goddess, just as Amaet was. She'd heard the name, or read it, not too long before. Something about a shrine? She couldn't quite remember. So much had happened in the last few days.

"You seem to know what you're doing, Treedle. What you want and how to get it. I envy that, I have to tell you."

Treedle shrugged. "You're doing fine, Marta. I think even your mother would have said as much."

"There Arrow Path may be a path, perhaps literally, but there are no road marks," Marta said wistfully. "I wish it were otherwise." She smiled then. "And you won't be around to lead me to the next one."

"You'd have to find it on your own in any case. Just as you did the Second Law. Are you going to be all right now?"

Marta knew what he meant. She wasn't sure what the answer was, but she said, "I think so. My tears didn't change anything that I have yet to do, though. Nor perhaps even the way I have to do it, since I'm working this out as I go."

"That wasn't what the tears were about."

"I suppose... You know, I thought I was being strong, not giving in to grief," Marta said, marveling at her own thick headedness.

Treedle put his hand on her shoulder. "Fare well, Marta. If you ever need a place to run to, remember us."

Marta watched Treedle go off towards the fields where Jacky and Genfyr were waiting for him. Marta finally went back to the barn, where Bone Tapper and Yssara were waiting for her. Bone Tapper landed on her shoulder and she got a sniff of his breath.

"Whew...I don't want to know what you had for breakfast, Bone Tapper, so don't tell me."

"As you wish, though it was lovely. What now? Are we going home?"

Marta shook her head. "I won't find the Third Law at home."

"How do you know that?"

"I don't. But I do remember something my mother said: You find the Laws of Power to prevent them from finding you. I don't want the Laws to sneak up on me. I think that would be very dangerous."

"So you seek them," Bone Tapper said. "And it's a life on the cold hard ground for us. Why am I not surprised?"

"You perch in trees," Marta pointed out.

"I was speaking figuratively. So, and all right then: where are we going?"

"Bone Tapper, do you remember reading about a Power called Astonei at the archives?"

"Astonei...yes. Her main cult is centered on a place called the Basilisk Shrine, south of the Longbone River. What of her?"

Marta blinked. That was it. How could she have forgotten?

"Yes. The Basilisk Shrine. That's where we're going."

"That's at least twenty leagues from here! What makes you think the Third Law is there?"

"Nothing at all. I choose to go there, since it may be. And I hate to tell you, but it's considerably farther than twenty leagues, since we need to head back toward Karsan first."

"Karsan? I thought you said we weren't going home."

"We're not. Or at least, not to our home."

Bone Tapper didn't ask what she meant, though he clearly didn't understand. It was only when they arrived at their destination some days later that Bone Tapper saw what she had meant.

"This is Yssara's home," Bone Tapper said.

"Yes."

Yssara frowned. Marta had never seen a horse do that before. Not even one that was really a dragon. Marta had Yssara pull the cart into a thick grove of oak trees nearby. Then she unhitched Yssara from the cart and led him out and toward the cave. For once he obeyed her pull without trying to bite her. He seemed more confused than anything.

"Yssara, I know you can hear and understand me. I want a real horse," she said to him.

The entrance to Yssara's cave was clearly visible. He looked at her with as much astonishment as a horse can show, but only briefly. He started quickly for the opening, and Marta grinned.

"Not as easily as that. You still owe a debt."

A horse's throat and lips are not well suited for human speech, but he managed. It was the first time he had spoken since Marta reclaimed him from the same spot months ago. "What do you want?"

"You will bring me gold from your trove to the value of twelve crowns...and don't deny you have it. I know better. I said I want a real horse and I meant it. A *good* horse. You're going to buy your freedom from me, Yssara."

"You can afford a good horse without my gold, and twelve crowns would buy an entire herd!"

"Certainly. But it has to be your gold, or it doesn't count. And replacing the cart horse is just part of the debt, translated into gold. To settle all debts I want twelve crown weights of gold from you, plus for being such an ill-tempered brute I will add to the price two more conditions: I want you to guard my wagon and all that's in it until I return and on top of that I want you to give me an honest answer to one simple question. That is my price and those are my conditions. Keep arguing and I might add to both."

Yssara couldn't resist, despite his eagerness to be free. "Twelve?" Yssara looked ill at the very thought. "Not six? Or even five?"

Marta started to respond angrily, but something caught her attention, like a child tugging at the hem of her jerkin.

"Ten. It's ten, not twelve. Why is it ten?" Marta asked aloud.

Yssara smiled then with all his teeth. "Because I, too, agreed to help your mother in this one small matter: to be as difficult a servant as possible, so that, perhaps, you would question the nature of your relationship with your servants, and the forms we assumed. She wanted you to think for yourself, and not blindly follow what she had done. It didn't work so thoroughly as Treedle's game; you are a bit slow at times. Yet I did my part."

"That you did," Marta said. "And gladly, I imagine."

"Why not eight?" Yssara said.

"Ten," repeated Marta. "Or do you really want to pull that infernal cart for another fifty years?"

Yssara obviously did not. "Done for ten," he said hastily, and disappeared into the cave. When he returned there was a dried, rotting yellow leather bag in his mouth which he dropped at Marta's feet. Marta counted out the contents then nodded. "Very well."

Yssara snorted once, and smoke drifted out of his nostrils. "Now then, let's have it all done: What did you want to ask me?"

Marta put her hands on her hips. "You told my mother you wanted to be free of your greed and, by your own admission, it was done."

"Yes."

"So why, when I asked you to buy your freedom—a chance my mother never offered you, so far as I know—why were you so blasted reluctant? You're no more free of greed than a miser!"

Yssara grinned. "Oh, it's true. I had no greed about me when I entered your mother's service. Sometimes I wonder if that's why she didn't ask for gold; gold meant nothing to me then. It took me many years to relearn the knack, the desire for hoarding. Especially with no means or opportunity to indulge the urge. That was hard. Yet I did it."

Marta shook her head. "So you were bonded in my mother's service to lose a trait which you in turn worked to regain?? That makes no sense!"

Yssara demurred. "Black Kath's Daughter, it makes perfect sense. My problem really wasn't greed, you see. Oh, I thought it was, truly. I believed greed was a burden, an oppressive overlord that controlled my existence. I would have done anything to free myself of it, as witness what I did do."

"And greed wasn't a burden? Your master?"

"No. It was who I was. Without greed I was no longer a dragon, so it didn't matter to me what I looked like. Changing my appearance changed nothing about me, but losing greed? When I finally reclaimed my greed, I reclaimed myself and it began to matter again. That was what I didn't understand when I asked for Black Kath's help."

Marta felt that sense of *recognition* again. There was a Law afoot in something that Yssara had said, but it wasn't clear and, after a moment, the feeling was gone as if it had never been. Marta thought that, perhaps, she was mistaken. She forced her attention back to what Yssara was saying.

"And now you do?" she asked.

He nodded. "It took me a long time pulling your mother's cart, but I finally figured it out. You'll forgive me if I don't exactly thank her for that, yet I know she played her part as well." He grinned again, showing sharp pointed teeth. "Goodbye, Black Kath's Daughter. Your wagon and whatever's inside it will be waiting for you when you return, but better for us both if we don't see each other again."

Yssara hurried back to his cave, changing with every step. Marta got just a glimpse of golden scales as he disappeared into the darkness of the cave.

Marta glanced up at Bone Tapper on his perch. "Are you going to claim you were in on my mother's scheme as well?"

Bone Tapper sighed. "I would and gladly, but then we both know she wouldn't have trusted me that far."

Bone Tapper flitted down from the trees to perch on her shoulder. "Still, as you must know," he said, "I'm really a quite clever thief, when needs must. I could buy my freedom too."

Marta looked at the raven, and she smiled a deceptively sweet smile. "I don't want gold from you, Bone Tapper."

"What then? There must be something I can do!"

"There is. Unlike Yssara, you're going to be a better servant. You're going to carry out my wishes cheerfully, give me counsel when I ask and in sum be much more pleasant company."

The raven glared at her. "Oh? Why should I do this?"

"Because I'll make you this bargain: for every year you manage as I say, I will count three against your debt. What I cannot command, you will give— your cheerful obedience and help. What you cannot command, I will give: time. Perhaps even enough to salvage some of your own wretched life, if you learn enough of wisdom to strive for it. What is your answer?"

Bone Tapper hesitated, but his answer was firm. "Done."

Marta had never seen a raven smile, but she could have sworn he was trying. "Shall we return to Karsan to buy a horse?"

Marta walked to the grove, opened her cart and tossed Yssara's gold inside. "No." She gathered what she thought she would need into a travel bundle, which she hoisted onto her back.

"But you said..."

"That we were going to the Basilisk Shrine and I meant it. Now that matters are settled with Treedle the thing I need more than anything else, including a horse, is a direction. I've got one. If we find a horse to my liking on the way we'll buy it. For now, I walk. Besides, I've had enough of towns and cities and all the folk in them for a while."

"And beds, too?"

Marta sighed. "If I could have one without the other, I would. There are some things even the Laws of Power can't fix."

Marta had another of those faint touches of recognition that she had learned to expect, from time to time. She'd touched on a Law, perhaps, but how could a Law reference something outside itself? The recognition was gone, too, like a dream forgotten, leaving only the memory that there was a dream, but nothing of it save that one thing remained. Just like when Yssara spoke earlier, though Marta was pretty certain of two things: One, that they were not the same Laws. As for the second...

If I touched a Law, I barely did.

Or perhaps her understanding was just too limited now to even have a chance of grasping it. Perhaps it was a Law that she was not meant to find yet? Was there an order to them? Marta had always referred to them as First Law, Second Law, and, if she ever found it, the Third Law, and so on. Yet she didn't know if those were their real names or not, and whether the order of finding would change as the seeker changed. Her mother had never said, but then Marta had never thought to ask. Add in one more thing undone, and no point fretting about it now.

"We've got a lot of ground to make up before nightfall. Let's go, Bone Tapper," was all she said.

*

There was a dead village by the banks of the Longbone, just as Amaet had said. Laras did not know what it was called; there was no other settlement for several leagues and no one to ask. It had been a large, prosperous town by the look of it. Maybe even the seat of a minor lord; there was at least one crumbling tower standing and the round foundation of what might have been another; the pile of debris nearby suggested it had fallen, and not been carted away as new building material by nearby crofters. Apparently there were no nearby crofters; so far as Laras could tell the area was totally desolate.

Perhaps everyone in the town and for leagues around had been destroyed in one of the outbreaks of plague. That had happened in the south, he knew, though fortunately never so far north as Karsan and the White

173

Mountains; perhaps the Sea Kings had raided upriver and taken what folk they hadn't killed immediately as slaves, and done their normally complete and efficient job at destruction. The Sea Kings hadn't raided in more than a generation, but the level of decay and the encroachment of the forest nearby seemed about right.

Laras, his curiosity aroused, wanted to know what had happened here. Pity there was no one to ask. Or was there?

"If whatever happened was quick and thorough enough," Laras said, reasoning aloud, "as it certainly seems to have been, then there would have been no one left to bury the dead."

Laras decided to search the standing tower first. He reasoned that, if it had been war, then a last defense would have centered on the towers. If plague, there would have been folk going about their normal business when they were struck down. In this he was proved right almost immediately. He was barely inside the empty arched doorway when he came across human bones scattered in the debris and filth on the floor. Laras considered them for a moment, then shook his head. Too Scattered. Not much in the way of personality remaining, so far as he could see. Nothing in them that spoke much of a person; it could have been the remains of a roasted ox for all he could tell. Laras went up the winding stone stairway on the wall of the tower and found what he was looking for higher up.

She lay on the remnants of a bed. Not composed, not as if sleeping. There was nothing peaceful about her, even now. Animals had not been at her, not like they had apparently been on the poor sods at the bottom, but perhaps something else. She lay sprawled, half-on and half off the collapsed bed frame. Laras knew it had been a woman, from the rotting remnants of what had been a rich blue dress to the few wisps of long blonde hair still clinging to the skull.

What Law do I use for this?

It occurred to Laras that he didn't really know. It also occurred to him that it didn't really matter. All he had to do was make his will known, and it would happen. It always had, ever since the first day he had met the Goddess Amaet. Whatever he wanted was his to command, and he understood or didn't understand about his power was beside the matter. Now he commanded the dead woman to speak, knowing beyond any doubt or question that she would obey him.

"Wake," he said, in a stern voice brooking no argument. "Speak to me, Woman."

The bones stirred, then ordered themselves back into something approaching their living structure and function, sliding across the dust and rot as if each was a living thing itself, bent on its own purpose. Laras watched, fascinated at the effect of his own voice.

Could Black Kath's bastard daughter do this? Laras didn't think so. Whatever puny magic she had managed to acquire, it was nothing compared to the gifts Amaet had given to him. He touched the pendant she had given him. "Arrow Path" some had said, upon seeing it. Laras had just smiled, saying nothing but enjoying, just a little, the envy and fear in the eyes of those who said the words. Amaet had never said the words themselves, so far as Laras could remember, but he liked the sound of them. Arrow Path. It sounded like something straight and sure. Powerful. Deadly.

The dead woman sat up and tried futilely to compose the remains of her dress into something more concealing of her pale bones. She looked at Laras with her empty eye sockets. Laras felt his gorge rise just a bit and he commanded her again. "I know what you are now. Remember what you were. Show me."

Her memory wasn't very strong, it seemed. The best she could do was a flickering phantom of a body, only a little more substantial than mist. Laras built on what little she could show him, creating the illusion of a living woman out of nothing but a few rags and bones. It was hard not be pleased at the final effect: a very pretty young woman looked up at him.

"Where is he?" she asked.

Laras frowned. "I don't know who you mean. I summoned you to answer my—"

"Where is he?" she demanded again. "He was coming. I heard him shouting below. He heard my screams!"

Laras nodded, believing that he finally understood. "Oh, that. He's dead. They're all dead."

She looked at him, and Laras finally realized that he'd been fooled by his own illusion. She wasn't really looking at him. Those eyes were a memory cloaked in appearance; the woman did not see anything nor look for anything except other memories living in a time long gone.

Laras reached out, felt his hand close on nothing but bone as he took what appeared to be a young woman's wrist. He pulled gently, not so much afraid that he would hurt her—since he knew that was impossible—as he was that he might rip her apart and have to start all over. He willed her to see him, to see the ruined tower and room for what it was. "What happened here?"

"Gone," she said. "He's not coming...I remember."

"Who's not coming? What happened?"

"Kynan. Beautiful Kynan. He's not coming. He's dead. They killed him." The woman looked around herself, slowly. "They're all dead. I'm alone. No one to stop them now."

"The Sea Kings? Were you raided?"

She didn't seem to hear him, at first. The face flickered in and out of focus like the mirage it was, from flesh to bone and back again. She reached down to her waist, appeared to be trying to grasp something he couldn't see. "Lost..."

"What have you lost?" Laras felt his frustration mounting. One thing to bring the miserable creature back to life—of a sort—quite another to make her pay attention to anything beyond the memory of her last moments of life.

What can't be taken, can be given.

Laras released the bones and stepped back. He remembered the Second Law, as Amaet had given it to him. Yet how could he persuade this silly woman to give him what he wanted? Forcing her wasn't working; there wasn't enough of either mind or substance left to force, so far as he could tell. What could he do to persuade her to listen?

"Lost," she repeated, still groping for something that wasn't there. She looked around, confused, then reached down into the tangled debris that had been a bed. She picked up a rusty dagger. The hilt was tarnished, the blade badly pitted and dark brown from rust.

"They're coming. Lost..." she said again, and Laras realized that it wasn't the dagger that was lost. The woman was lost. Everything was lost. She'd never be able to see beyond her own pain, and her own way out of it. She took a bony grip on the dagger and Laras saw that she meant to act out the tawdry tragedy again. He enveloped her will with his own and stopped her, but that left the problem.

"Kynan," he said, musingly, and to his surprise the woman repeated the name.

"Kynan? Where are you?"

Of course. He knew what she wanted now, and would have known earlier if he'd been paying even a little bit of attention. Well, easy enough to arrange...

"Kynan," Laras said, only this time it was a command. He repeated the name, louder, and heard a faint scrabble and then one rasping groan from far below. Laras nodded. He'd guessed right about the fragments on the bottom floor. He hoped there was enough left to work with.

"Kynan?" the woman called, piteously.

"Alaea..."

So that was her name. It was more than Laras had known before, and so far well enough. Oh, it wasn't so much a true sound as an echo, but it was clear enough for all that. The shambling horror that once had been—or so Laras presumed—a handsome young man rose up the stairwell. Laras grimaced, then helped Alaea's memory recreate the missing bits. It wasn't perfect, but apparently the likeness was good enough. Alaea stepped past

Laras as if he wasn't there, indeed Laras wondered if had ever actually been there at all, for her. She reached out to her long dead lover.

"The Sea Kings...I thought—"

"Ah, so it was a raid, not the plague," Laras said. "And since I'll never get a straight answer about anything else, Thank you, and farewell."

The two ghosts' fingertips had not quite touched when Laras was finished with the both of them. In a moment all was undone, and the bones fell down to lie in two separate piles once again.

You could have let them touch, you know. One last time.

Laras blinked. Where had that thought come from? It was a foolish notion. They were dead, and had been for centuries. It couldn't possibly make any difference at all, not now. All he had wanted to know was whether there was a chance that a plague was still lingering about the site. Something well worth knowing if he was going to be waiting there for he wasn't sure how long. He had Amaet's mission to consider, and that was all. He had no time for useless sentiment.

Still, as he walked back down the tower considering how best to set his trap, try as he might Laras couldn't quite escape the feeling that he had done something wrong.

CHAPTER 16

"People often talk of their life's purpose but the truth is that no one really knows what they're seeking until they find it."
—Black Kath's Tally Book

Bone Tapper returned from scouting the woods and landed on an aspen branch. "The Longbone is just over that line of hills."

Marta, resting on a rock, nodded. She rubbed her eyes, wearily. "What's the water like? I could use a bath," she said wistfully.

Bone Tapper shrugged. "Not feeling dainty?"

"Sarcasm is against our agreement."

"Sorry. Sometimes I can't tell what is and isn't. I thought I was phrasing the question rather delicately."

"For you, perhaps," Marta conceded. "The river?"

"A bit high from the mountain runoff, but clean enough and I noted a quiet pool here and there. It'll be cold, but managable."

"Good." Marta got back on her feet, leaning heavily on the cherrywood staff she'd cut for herself the day before. She was beginning to regret not buying a new horse first, since there had been no chance at all to buy one. She hadn't even seen a town, or even a farm, for days. "I had no idea this area was so empty."

"Well..." Bone Tapper hesitated.

"What is it?" Marta asked.

"I think this place isn't so empty as it seems."

Marta sighed. "Bone Tapper, stop circling the carcass and land, will you?"

"Pardon?"

"Say what you mean!"

"I could counsel you to do the same," Bone Tapper said dryly. "But never mind that. There's an empty village by the river. I saw no one, and believe me I did look. I hate surprises when I'm not the one arranging them."

"Yet you think someone is there?"

"I may be wrong—as I said, I saw no one—but I don't think I am."

Marta considered. "Is that Sendale? It was described in the book."

"I believe so. The only town I saw was a ruin, and right by the river. How old was that book?"

Marta sighed. "Old. Yet if it was accurate for the time, Sendale is the only river crossing for leagues around...not that many folk choose this route these days, it seems, but it was more common when Sendale still existed, else our worthy cleric would have talked about Makor instead. Still, I'm not swimming that far and I'm not going to march halfway to Junland just to get across. What about boats?"

"I thought of that," Bone Tapper said modestly, "and there isn't one to be found. You'll have to build one, if you want to get across that way."

"Then we go through Sendale, whoever is waiting for me there. Unless I learn how to sprout wings like you have."

"You can't just turn yourself into a raven? Or some less worthy bird?"

Marta laughed. "Transformation is an aspect of the Debt. I'm not in debt to myself, Bone Tapper. If I could, why do you think I'd have walked this far??"

"If that's true, then Amaet could do it for you."

"You think I'm fool enough to ask?"

Bone Tapper shrugged. "What use is your magic then? And I'm not being sarcastic, I swear. I really would like to know."

Marta shrugged too. "My 'magic' only works to the extent that my understanding of the Laws works, and at that I have only two of them. I'm doing the best I can."

Bone Tapper looked resigned. "I had to ask... Well then, and failing that, I would advise caution."

"Always good advice," Marta said, and Bone Tapper seemed pleased with himself. In fact he was preening, which so far as Marta knew was the same thing.

Counting the time removing itself from his debt, no doubt. Still, so far Bone Tapper was keeping up his end of the bargain, or at least making an attempt. It was a pleasant change. Yet now and then Marta found herself missing the sarcasm. She hadn't enjoyed it, exactly, but it was such a part of their relationship that it's absence was noticed, and more than she would have thought. Her life had changed so much in the last few months, yet she was still surprised time and again by the things she missed, and the things she didn't.

When Marta got her first good look at Sendale, she knew that 'cautiously' was the very best way to proceed, if at all. It was the first real ruin Marta had ever seen. It wasn't just age at work here, as in the Karsanmon Gate. Sendale was like a corpse. That was Marta's first and second impression. Something that had been alive and now was not. Marta sat down on a stone atop the ridge for a moment, to rest and get a better look, but mostly to delay entering the place.

Bone Tapper landed beside her.

"Cheerful thing, isn't it?" she said, without looking at him.

"Very. So, what do you think? Did this place just die or was it murdered?"

"Murdered," Marta said without a moment's hesitation. "The Sea Kings were raiding far upriver at the height of their power. Several towns were destroyed, according to the chronicles. Sendale was one of them."

"So those weeks in the archive weren't a total waste. I'll pose another: why wasn't it rebuilt? Makor was further down river and surely got the same."

"Just a guess, but I'd say there was no reason. It was a backwater even then, according to Brother Akaen; any outlying families that survived either died off or moved away. Makor was closer to the main pilgrim and trade routes anyway and they have an actual bridge. More than one, I hear. By the time the Sea Kings found Sendale there more than likely wasn't much left to tempt them."

Bone Tapper studied the heaps of ruined stone where once a great tower had been. The other was still standing, though barely. "Which doubtless added to the Sea Kings' annoyance. They were very...enthusiastic."

Marta didn't say anything about that. There was no need to. When Marta got closer she was even surer that she was right. If plague had done for Sendale there might have been a few fires as the first homes stricken were burned to try and prevent the spread, but if it had spread, soon there would be nothing to gain from the burning. Yet Sendale had been burned, very systematically and thoroughly. The lone tower still standing as they approached the river seemed to be the one exception. Marta's curiosity was focused on that to such an extent that she almost didn't see the man calmly sitting in the middle of the fallen second tower's round foundation, waiting for her.

"Hello, Marta," Laras said.

For several long moments, Marta just stared. "Laras! What are you doing here?"

He grinned at her. "None other. Why do you ask? Could it be that you didn't expect to see me again?"

"Not really," Marta said frankly.

His smile faded. "No. You expected me to die in that damned hole in the ground!"

Marta dropped her bundle and then stepped up on the stone flooring and walked partway across toward him, but not too close. Laras was carrying no weapons, so far as she could see. Not even a knife. "Don't be more of a fool than birth made you, Laras. Of course I didn't expect you to die!"

That seemed to genuinely surprise him. "Are you going to tell me that you sent me into that cave just to meet Amaet?"

Amaet. Marta remembered the shrine.

Oh, blast.

Marta kept her voice calm and reasonable. "No. I didn't know about the Shrine then. I expected you to find the other way out! After getting a good scare, mind you, which is only fair for the one you gave me, and a poor price at that for what you were planning."

He dismissed that. "We do what we must go achieve our goals. You're no different from me there, Marta, so don't give yourself airs. That those unfortunate events worked out well for me—for both of us, I gather—was pure luck."

Marta was barely listening. Amaet. Laras found Amaet in that cave, just as Marta found the First Law. It was only then that Marta noticed the small golden pendant Laras was wearing. Not silver, as hers was. Gold. She took a deep breath and stated her question very slowly and clearly. "Laras, what did you do?"

He frowned. "Do? I've done many things. You'll have to be more specific."

"Did you join the Arrow Path?"

He laughed. "At first I didn't even know what that was. Those who buy Amaet's power like merchants when she gives it so freely? That sorry lot? Certainly not."

Marta pointed at his pendant. "Then why are you wearing that?!"

"This? Amaet gave this to me, as a token of my obedience, and her favor. Yes, you understand that. I can see it in your eyes. I am doing the Goddess's will. For instance, I placed that book in the Royal Archive, the one that spoke of the Basilisk Shrine, on Amaet's orders. It brought you here."

That was something to consider, but later. At the moment Marta had room for no consideration other than pity, though she was equally certain that Laras would never see it for what it was. "You worship that lovely bag of offal? That was a very stupid thing to do, Laras."

Laras turned red with anger. "I'll caution you not to blaspheme my goddess! It was she who freed me from the cave, she who bade me plant the book that would lead you here and she alone who gave me the Laws of Power which I will now use to destroy you as she commanded."

Commanded? The book...? Marta shook her head. There were so many contradictions and nonsense in what Laras had said that she could barely keep track of them all. She grabbed the one that seemed the most wrong. "Gave? Laras, no one can give you a Law of Power! It doesn't work that way."

"Foolish girl. You haven't a clue of how power truly works. Yet you did me service, though that was not your intent, when you brought me to Amaet. For that, let me show you power. It's the least I can do."

Laras stared to glow. He seemed surrounded by red fire as if he had doused himself with pitchboil and set himself alight, yet Marta could see that the flames were not touching him.

How in the name of the Seven Powers is he doing that??

It made no sense to Marta. It was nothing that she knew, nothing that the first two Laws had even hinted. If anything, they spoke as much of what power could not do as what it could. Was he really so far ahead of her now? Yet how could this be, if everything she had been told, everything she had learned wasn't a lie?

"Laras, what are you doing?"

"Second Law; I know you have it...but don't understand it. 'What cannot be taken, can be given.' I'm giving myself a halo of fire."

Marta started to repeat that this was wrong, that it had nothing to do with the meaning of the Second Law, but the words died in her throat. How could it be wrong? She was seeing Laras's proof, right before her.

"Don't be jealous, Marta. I'll give you one too."

Marta was on fire. She screamed at the sudden pain, fell and rolled to try and put it out. In a moment it was gone as if it had never been. The flames had left no mark, only the pain, and that, too, was fading now. Marta stared up at him.

"Pity you weren't touched by a goddess, Marta. Then perhaps you might could stand a little fire. I can see my lesson is wasted on you; I am sorry. It was never my intention to torture you. I'm not a cruel man, whatever you think of me."

Marta got up slowly. She wanted to tell Laras exactly what she thought of his character, but she was too stunned at what was happening.

Laras sighed. "Basics, I think. Let's go to the First Law."

He broke the stone beneath her. He didn't touch it. He barely looked at it. But in an instant the stone was breaking, and not just cracking. It fell away completely from under her and Marta only had the briefest glimpse of darkness before she fell into the pit.

A piece of stone cut her cheek but she barely felt the pain for terror, and in another moment it was over. She hit the water almost as flat as the stone that smacked into the water all around, barely missing her; the impact knocked the breath from her body and the shock nearly knocked her senseless. It was only the icy coldness of the water itself, gathered in the deep pit below the tower, that kept her conscious. She thrashed, feebly, as total darkness closed on her and she heard the hiss of bubbles escaping overhead. She couldn't see, could barely feel, and it was only the sound of the bubbles rising that told her, however faintly, which way was up. The ache in her lungs made her gasp, only to swallow the bitter cold water. Stars swam in front of her eyes. She more clawed than swam to the surface; she broke through and tried to draw breath even as she tried to cough out the water she had swallowed. She almost slipped under the surface again and it was only the certain knowledge that if she did so she would not be coming up again that kept her fighting to stay afloat, kept her breathing the dank chill air that, for all its faults, tasted wonderful.

"Help..."

Laras's face was a small pale circle in a patch of light far above her. He could barely shout for laughing. "Me? Help you? I think you're still missing the point here, Marta. Actually, I didn't know about the water. I expected the fall to kill you."

She shouted up at him. "Why...why are you doing this? Revenge?"

"Weren't you listening? Amaet commanded your destruction. I simply obeyed. I'd be lying if I said I took no pleasure at all in what I'm doing, but for what little it may be worth to you I'm not enjoying it as much as I expected to."

Amaet. Marta remembered now. One of the contradictions. It hadn't seemed the most important at first, but Marta's priorities were rapidly changing. "You can't just leave me here!"

"Why not? You left me in somewhat similar circumstances, remember? It's either that or throw stones at you until you drown. I told you once I wasn't a monster. I meant that, but surely you can see that helping you is not an option? Goodbye, Marta. For what it's worth, I am sorry. But only a little. What's happening to you now is no more than justice."

Laras disappeared. Marta shouted a curse at him but didn't follow with more; she needed all her breath to stay alive and afloat. Marta wasn't the best swimmer in the world; she'd never swum more than fifty yards in her life nor had to, and staying afloat was even further beyond her experience. She was beginning to get her wits back, but she wasn't happy about it. Her wits told her that if her situation didn't change and very soon, she was going to die. Her eyes had adjusted somewhat to the weak illumination; at least the break in the stone flooring above let some light in. She looked around for a way out, or anything she could use, and found neither. The stone walls were of smooth-fitted stone with scarcely the width of a fingertip's grip on any of the stones showing. Nor was there any wood of floating debris she could cling to; Marta wondered if the buried section of the tower had been intended as a well, or whether the water level of the nearby river had risen to flood it. She didn't know, and didn't think it much mattered. She swam to the edge, forcing herself to be calm, to feel for a weakness that might speak of a hollow or some fissure in the earth that she could break the stone wall to reach, but she felt nothing, and the effort of swimming was sapping her strength quickly.

The cold water was already affecting her. She could barely feel her feet and her fingers were numb and stiff. Marta shivered. She slowly became aware of the weight around her waist and realized it was her purse, with its weight of gold and silver coins, pulling her down. Marta almost laughed.

At least I didn't bring Yssara's gold too.

It took a few moments of fumbling, but she finally got the pouch free from her belt and she let it sink into the depths with barely a moment's hesitation. Losing that weight made it a bit easier to stay afloat, but the water was still little short of freezing and would kill her all by itself even if she didn't drown first. Was this what all her searching and pain had come down to? To die alone, drowned like a stupid rat, at the bottom of a cistern?

Alone...?

Marta could have kicked herself, if the effort wouldn't have pulled her under water. She settled for kicking the water itself, keeping her head out as far as it could reach. "Bone Tapper!" She shouted the name once and then again, commanding, "Bone Tapper!"

No reply at first, and for a sick moment Marta was afraid that Laras had killed the raven before he'd left...assuming he had left. Marta had no way to be sure, but there was nothing left to try.

"Bone Tapper!"

She heard his answering croak with sweet relief. In a moment a black speck appeared at the hole above her and quickly resolved itself into the raven's familiar form. "I'm here, barely," he said.

Marta's nose crinkled as she got a sudden whiff of him as he perched precariously on the edge of a stone block nearby. "What is that smell?"

"Burned feathers, and thanks for asking," Bone Tapper replied. "I tried to scratch that wizard's eyes out and he threw fire at me! I barely got away."

"I didn't get away," Marta said ruefully. "I need something I can float on until we figure out how to get me out of here. Did you see anything out there?"

"There may be some rotten beams or something in that other tower. Yet how am I to get anything down here? I can't carry it."

"Throw it. Just don't hit me when you do."

The raven just stared at her for a moment. "Has the cold got to your brain? How am I supposed to lift anything bigger than a twig?"

Marta grimaced. "Bone Tapper, I may not have whatever powers that Laras has, but I'm still more than I was. Fly back to solid ground and I'll tell you."

Bone Tapper obeyed, and when she was sure he was out of the shaft she changed his form with barely a thought. All she needed to do was focus on her current need, and the form that would suit it best. Something that looked very like Treedle glared down at her from on high.

"What have you done?? Just look at me!"

It occurred to Marta that she could have done the same, back when she needed to chop wood. She would have cursed herself for a fool, but she had larger problems. "I need a hob's strength, blast you! Now hurry before I drown or you'll stay like that forever!"

Marta didn't really know if that was true or not, but Bone Tapper was clearly taking no chances. He yelped with sudden horror and disappeared. In a very few moments he was back. "I'm sending something down! Ware below!"

Something large and dark sailed down to smack into the water a few feet away. Marta turned her face to avoid the splash, then groped blindly for whatever Bone Tapper had sent to her. Her fingers closed on something solid and, with the near the last of her strength, she pulled herself up on top of it. She floated there, precariously, and she felt it sink enough so that she was not completely out of the cold. Yet at least she no longer had to tread water to keep afloat.

"Are you all right?" Bone Tapper called down.

"For the moment. Bone Tapper...is this a bed?"

"What's left of one. I found it in the other tower...beside a pile of bones. I don't think the owners will be needing it. It's full of dryrot, but it'll float for a while."

Marta felt a slat crack beneath her and moved off it, carefully, trying to find a spot that floated higher and wouldn't break. The wood beneath her creaked ominously, but held.

"Now what?"

"Now we need a rope...or something."

"It will have to be 'or something' unless you have one tucked in your bundle."

Marta perked up. "My bundle is still there? Laras didn't take it?"

"The sod barely glanced at it. Too much pride in him to make a proper thief."

The Powers know Laras has enough failings. Bless All that he didn't have that one too.

Marta called up. "Listen, Bone Tapper. Open the bundle. There's a knife in there...or should be. Get that and the bundle and bring it back here. I'm going to tell you what to do." Marta shivered; her teeth were starting to chatter and it was hard to talk. "And blast you, hurry!"

Bone Tapper quickly cut the bundle itself into thin—not too thin!—strips and braided it as Marta directed. It seemed to take forever, though Marta knew Bone Tapper was working as fast as non-humanly possible, which in a hob was pretty fast indeed. Marta felt the bed slowly sinking below her, drinking in water quickly in its dried out state, becoming waterlogged. Just as she thought it was going down a coil of braided cloth landed in the water beside her.

"You'll have to tie it off yourself! The sodding thing will never hold us both."

Marta took the rope in her stiff cold fingers and pulled the end around her and underneath her armpits. It was slow going, and the knot she managed did inspire much confidence. Marta wrapped the end around her arm as many times as she could managed. "The bed's going under! Pull me up!"

The rope stretched taut and, bit by bit, Marta pulled off the remains of the bed and out of the water. The cloth creaked and squeaked and protested with every yard gained, but it held. Just as she was sure it was about to snap Bone Tapper's strong hands grabbed her wrists and hauled her out like a bag of flour. Marta could very well have been a bag of flower, for all the help she was able to give him.

"For a skinny wisp of a girl you're surprisingly heavy," Bone Tapper said.

Marta lay on the stone, gasping for breath, but she managed to get the words out. "If...through ...about my person, get me a blanket!"

Grinning, Bone Tapper obeyed.

"Now turn around!" When Bone Tapper had likewise obeyed that command Marta quickly stripped out of her wet clothes and wrapped herself in the blanket, holding it tight and letting it and the spring sun drive the cold from her at last. It took a while, and to speed up the process Bone Tapper gathered wood and got large campfire going."

"Won't Laras see it?" Bone Tapper said.

Marta sat as close to the fire as she could, and leaned closer. "It won't matter if I don't get warm," Marta said, her teeth still chattering. "More than likely he'll just think he set something on fire besides you."

"I hope that's true. And your concern is touching, by the way."

"It's hard to be sympathetic when you're drowning! Yet now that I am not... thank you," she said.

"You're welcome. I don't suppose this settles my debt by any chance?"

"Settles?" The possibility hadn't even occurred to her. Marta took a moment to consider it, asking the question and waiting for the answer. "No," she said at last. "Yet it's taken a score of years off."

"I should rescue you more often then," Bone Tapper said, and Marta glared at him.

"You'll pardon me if I hope that's not necessary." She paused to look Bone Tapper up and down. "Return," she said.

In a moment Bone Tapper was a raven again.

He gasped in surprise. "What did you do that for? I was just getting used to being a hob. Not so bad, really. Ten fingers, ten toes...it was almost like being myself again."

Marta shut her eyes, feeling the sheer luxury of the fire's warmth on her face. "You reminded me too much of Treedle. Besides, I don't need a hob now. I need you to find Laras for me. Stay out of sight if you can, but find him. Go."

Bone Tapper went. Marta used the time to dress herself from the extra clothes she'd had in her former bundle. She wouldn't be able to carry as much now, but then there was less to carry. Now that the immediate problem was out of the way, the loss of her purse nagged at her a bit. Still...

Better it than me.

She would manage. Even that wasn't what worried her most.

"Exactly what happened here today?" she said aloud.

"You almost died. Don't you remember?"

Bone Tapper had returned, flying as silently as an owl to land beside her again.

"That's not what I meant," Marta said.

"I know...and Laras is nearly a league north of here, and moving briskly away from us. If he noticed the smoke he made no account of it. Seems to be in a hurry."

Marta wrapped the blanket around her shoulders and stared at the fire. "Good." Neither said anything for several long moments, and Marta finally looked up again. "What I meant," she said, and more to herself than Bone Tapper, "was that it shouldn't have happened. It makes no sense."

"Perhaps Laras is just a better magician than you are. That's why Amaet chose him as her assassin"

Marta shook her head. "That appears to be true, but even so it's beside the point. Why would Amaet want me killed? I can hardly repay the Debt that way. I don't even have a child of my own to pass it on to."

"Perhaps she thought being rid of you was worth the loss."

"If so, why?"

Bone Tapper shrugged. "I'm just a servant, and not one to move in the circles of power. I don't know."

"Neither do I. But that's not the worst."

The raven blinked. "It's not? I'd certainly consider the situation bad enough if a Power was lusting for my blood."

"Amaet gave Laras the Laws of Power. At least two of them. Perhaps all."

"Rather unfair of her to play favorites like that."

Marta shook her head. "You don't understand--everything Mother taught me, everything I've learned since, all say that this is not possible. The Laws of Power cannot be taught, only learned. They certainly cannot be placed in one's hands as a gift."

Bone Tapper shrugged again. "Why not? The Arrow Path was created by Amaet, they say."

Marta nodded. "She created it, but the strictures apply to her too. Or they don't apply at all."

"You saw what he did," Bone Tapper pointed out. "More to the point, you felt it. He could have crushed you like an insect. It's only luck that you survived."

"No," Marta said. "It was not luck at all."

"Well, no," Bone Tapper agreed. "I helped you."

"Exactly. If he were truly Arrow Path, Laras would have known what you were, and known that he had to destroy you as well else you would have given me aid, which you in fact did. That fact that he only drove you off, and that because you were annoying him, makes no sense either."

Bone Tapper sighed. "You've swallowed well water instead of air, Mistress. You're weary. Did it occur to you that you're thinking about this too hard? You say all this is impossible, that it makes no sense. Yet it did happen. It is possible, and saying otherwise is what makes no sense."

"If you're right, then the Arrow Path is a lie, as is everything I know and everything I believed myself and Black Kath of Lythos to be."

Bone Tapper shrugged. "I have no answer to that, Mistress."

"Neither do I, but I'm going to find one." Marta gathered up the remnants of her belongings as best she could.

"Where are we going?" the raven asked.

"To the Basilisk Shrine," Marta said. "I thought you knew."

"Knew? Weren't you paying any attention at all? Amaet ordered Laras to place that book in the Archives! That explains why the good brother Akaen didn't know it was there. Somehow she knew you would seek the Basilisk Shrine!"

"That a person on a quest might follow any lead she might find doesn't take omniscience," Marta said dryly.

"My point is that this was clearly a trap from the beginning!"

"I know that." Marta started toward the river.

The raven flew after her, still arguing. "You know? Then why go on?"

"Bone Tapper, if Amaet meant me to die here, then she never meant for me to reach the Basilisk Shrine in the first place. Well, I didn't die, so making the trip despite her is reason enough."

"That's not your reason, is it?"

"No. I'm going because it still feels right to me. If I can't trust what I know, then I will trust what I feel. I will use what I have."

"Do you really think you will find a Law of Power there? Or anything except more lies?"

"The book was real, whatever purpose it served. The Basilisk Shrine is real too, and the virtue of the Basilisk Oracle is this: The First Night, Truth. The Second Night, Lies. The Third Night, Death."

"I imagine very few people seek the second and fewer still the third of its oracles," Bone Tapper said.

"The chronicler said more people sought the Third than he would have believed, and in that I tend to trust his word. No matter, I seek only the First. If anyone in this world is owed some truth right now, that person would be me."

CHAPTER 17

"A philosopher offered me the Truth once. However it turned out to be his truth, not mine, and thus of no use at all."
— Tymon the Black

"That is not a temple to Astonei or any other Immortal Power," Bone Tapper said. "That is a hole in the ground."

They stood at the top of a line of hills, looking down at the valley snaking by below them. Marta was thin, dirty, and weary beyond belief, but they had reached the Basilisk Shrine. They could see it now, a dark maw of a cave at the base of a rocky cliff on the far side of the valley. Silently Marta agreed with Bone Tapper's 'hole in the ground' comment, at least to that point. The Basilisk Shrine was indeed a hole in the ground, whatever else it might be. Marta had developed an active dislike for the deep dark places where the Powers that she knew of tended to manifest. Even the grotto on Mount Karsanmon could have been a hole in the ground, as cold and dark as it tended to be.

"Are you forgetting our agreement?" was all Marta said, despite that. Her tone was deceptively mild.

The raven was quick to demure. "I serve you in all things, as my debt to your late mother and thus to you requires. I try to be as pleasant a servant and companion as you could wish. But fear has a way of smothering tact, and I am afraid. I don't like caves."

Marta nodded, reluctantly. "Me, either. That doesn't change what we're here to do."

"My confidence knows no bounds," Bone Tapper said, but Marta ignored him.

They stood just within the shade of the forest, looking out over a large grassy valley and across to where the line of cliffs thrust up abruptly from the grassland. At this distance the temple was just a darker patch near the base of the cliffs and, if Marta did not see as well as the raven, she certainly noticed more. For instance, the broad, beaten path that ran from the far end of the valley floor and up to the cave and the one small figure trudging along toward the entrance, doubtless a supplicant on the main pilgrim trail from Makor to the west. Then there were the faint lines across the top of the cave mouth, recognizable as Westan glyphs even at that distance. Marta remembered several illustrations of them in the Archives, though she had yet to learn to read them. Marta regretted that now; Akaen had offered to teach her but she hadn't thought there was time enough. Perhaps she'd been right, but if she ever got another chance...

"We'd best be going," was all Marta said.

"I could stay and keep watch from here," Bone Tapper said, obviously trying to make the suggestion sound like the most sensible thing in the world. Marta wasn't fooled.

"And do what, if it came to doing? Besides, I may need you. Come on."

Bone Tapper obediently perched on Marta's thin shoulder, and together they started down toward the pilgrim trail. By the time they reached the path, the figure Marta had seen from the opposite ridge was well past them; it was easily identified now as a vigorous old woman keeping a smart pace along the trail, her staff preceding each step like a herald. Marta quickened her step just enough to close the distance without appearing to hurry.

"Blessings of the day to you, Good Mother."

The woman turned back to look at them. Her face was lined by the wear of life and more than a little sun; she pulled off her hood to reveal gray hair still carrying a memory of black. She wore her hair long, and tied back with a red cord. She ventured a faint smile. "And to you, child, though in truth it has been many years since anyone called me mother."

"Have you come to visit the shrine?"

"Most certainly, there being precious little else to draw a body's attention hereabouts."

Marta bowed slightly. "Well struck, well deserved. I had assumed as much and was hoping you could tell me something about the shrine. This is not my country."

The woman smiled at her. "I had assumed as much. Folk from as far away as Torsa come to worship here, but I think you come from farther still."

"Just a bit," Marta said, though it was more than a bit of understatement. "Karsan."

"Far indeed. What do you want to know?" the old woman asked.

"Does this shrine contain the Oracle of the Basilisk? I've come seeking a divination dream."

The woman wasn't smiling now. "I would speak that name softly if I were you, child. The Oracle is only consulted at great need, and the price for a Basilisk Dream is high."

"My need is great," Marta said. "And I will pay whatever I am asked."

Marta wasn't sure how she was going to pay for anything at the moment; all the gold she'd had with her now lay at the bottom of an ancient cistern at Sendale. After all that she had been through, it still seemed a trivial matter. She would pay, somehow.

"The price will be a steep one, I assure you. The priestess of Astonei will take great pains to dissuade the curious and the foolish. You might be asked for more than you can give for the privilege of oracle."

"I see I was fortunate to meet you today, Good Mother. Your knowledge of the priestess's whims seems very intimate." Marta smiled then, and met the old woman's gaze squarely. "Even more than intimate, I dare say." Marta waited.

The old woman nodded with evident satisfaction. "I can't speak for the quality of your curiosity, but you are certainly no fool. Yes, child—my name is Lornis. For the past forty years I have been Priestess of Astonei, Mistress of the Basilisk Oracle. Well, then. I think we need to speak more. Shall we go?"

Lornis's quarters were in a room off the main entrance to the cave. It looked like a natural opening that had been refined by a mason's hand into a very comfortable space. There was even a serviceable fireplace carved into the stone of one wall, with a working draft. Lornis brewed tea while Marta sat on one of the priestess' chairs, watching her. Bone Tapper had been given free rein of the quarters with Lornis's permission. He flitted from table to chair to mantel to bed, looking at everything with his cold black eyes. He finally lit on Marta's shoulder.

"I trust your friend is satisfied for your safety?" Lornis asked, not looking up from her preparations. "What is his name?"

"Bone Tapper," Marta said.

Lornis did glance back at her this time. "I meant his real name. He must have had one before he was changed."

Marta didn't speak. It was Bone Tapper who broke the silence. "Dyras," he said. "As best I can remember." Bone Tapper looked at Marta and shrugged, clearly indicating that he thought denial pointless.

Marta had to agree, but her heart sank a little. She felt no animosity from the woman, but it was never a good idea to reveal too much at first meeting, even among those who might be friends. Lornis had pierced her mask a little too easily, a little too casually, and with apparent unconcern for what it revealed about herself.

Whatever power I have, I'm no threat. She clearly knows that. I wish I could be as sure of her.

"You are an adept, I see," Marta said. "Not Arrow Path, but adept nonetheless."

"The tea is ready," Lornis said. It wasn't an answer, but then Marta hadn't really asked a question. Lornis served the tea in stoneware mugs. She placed one cup and a bit of cake on the mantel for Bone Tapper, then took her place on a willow-work chair across from Marta. "So tell me, Marta, why have you traveled so far to seek the Basilisk Oracle?"

Marta thought of her options and decided on the truth. "I'm seeking a Law of Power," she said.

Lornis nodded. "I suspected as much. Which one?"

It wasn't idle curiosity, Marta knew. She'd started with the truth, and clearly Lornis wanted all of it. But it went against every instinct Marta had to surrender everything without at least token resistance.

"Why, the next one," she said. He face was innocence itself given shape and countenance.

Lornis smiled. "So be it, child. Just be aware that there is an order to Laws, and learning one out of turn can be worse than not learning it at all."

"My mother said the Laws come in their own time and their own choosing; I think that part is out of my hands in any case."

"Most likely," Lornis said. "Your mother is a very wise woman."

Marta looked away. "She was. She died a few months ago." She hadn't mean to say it; a sudden painful memory pushed it out. Marta knew it was a mistake but it was too late. Lornis proved that Marta was right.

"Then young as you are she could not have had time enough to teach you more than a fraction of what you need to know," she said, looking thoughtful. "She couldn't even have begun, really, until you'd achieved the First Law."

Marta felt pinned to her chair by the truth in what Lornis said. She hadn't known that. She'd thought that, perhaps, it all had to be learned alone, with the barest guidance. Black Kath had never even seen Marta after she'd gained the First Law. Marta remembered Laras, and all the power that he had under Amaet's patronage and guidance, all the understanding that she herself clearly did not have. Yes, that explained much. So far as her true understanding went, she could have been an infant.

"You've achieved at least one Law of Power. Perhaps two...yes, your eyes betray you, child. You seek the Third Law."

Marta nodded, beaten. "Yes."

Marta knew that she had lied earlier when she said that she'd sought the next Law of Power, when what she really sought was the truth about the Arrow Path. Yet here Lornis had handed her that truth, it seemed. Marta was untrained, and likely to remain so. No match for Laras when he discovered she lived and came after her again. Somehow Amaet had given him the Laws. It went against all Marta knew, but did that matter? She knew so very little...

The priestess smiled, echoing her thought so clearly that Marta almost gasped. "You know so little. For one who owes soul-debt to one of the Immortal Powers, that is a serious matter. So. What have you brought for an offering?"

Marta had wondered how long it would be before they came down to talking terms. She was almost relieved, but now her lack of gold was going to be a problem. "What is customary?" she asked, vying for time to think.

Lornis shrugged. "A copper or two for the local villagers and the humbler pilgrims. Silver for a scholar, gold for a noble, though both are rare in these parts. You are none of those," she said. "Show me the sign."

Marta looked blank for a moment, then remembered. She reached down the front of her blouse and pulled out the small golden pendant hanging from its leather thong. The emblem of the Arrow Path. "My mother gave me this." "Is this all she gave you? I think so." Lornis said primly.

Marta kept her tongue with an effort. She was being challenged again, she knew, but she didn't dare respond. Lornis nodded in evident satisfaction and leaned forward. She took the pendant in her hands, examining it carefully. "Novitiate of the Arrow Path, Servant of Amaet," Lornis said. "The price will be high indeed."

Marta took a deep breath. "Priestess of Astonei, I must tell you truly—I have no money. It was lost on the way."

Lornis smiled, and try as she might Marta could find little of the sweet old woman that she had met on the trail in that smile. "No matter. For such as you there is a special price, and only the little bit of silver you brought with you."

"But there is no coin at all. I told you—" Marta stopped. She understood. "My pendant? But I can't..."

Lornis dropped the pendant and sat back, taking a long sip of the bitter tea. "You can," she said. "The pendant isn't the price; it's merely the token of it."

Marta took a deep breath. She suspected what Lornis meant, but she hardly dared to form the thought. "Please name your price."

"You will forswear the Arrow Path. You will allow Astonei to remove your Debt to Amaet and you will bow to her, becoming a Novitiate of her order."

"Forgive me, but that's not possible." Marta felt foolish saying the word, but yet she said it.

"You don't know what's possible," Lornis said. "That is why you are here."

"Mother taught me..."

Lornis smiled. "What, child? That it was foolish to worship a Power? That your freedom is worth more than all the favor of any Power?"

"Well...yes," Marta said.

"And what has your freedom bought you, girl? A life of hard travel and danger? And what of her? She could not have been so very old when she died. You may have thought of her that way but, no older than you are, she could not have been so ancient as you thought. She died young in my view, however her life had aged her, and I'll wager it wasn't something as simple as an accident or murder. Am I right?"

"Yes," Marta said again. She felt totally out of her depth, subject to powers and abilities she had barely suspected, never mind attained.

"So. Since there is so much you don't understand, let me explain it to you: Astonei can free you from the Arrow Path, absolve you of your debt. You will be safe, cared for, and your service to her will bring the sort of good and blessed work that this world needs. When has the Arrow Path done as well for you, or brought any peace or joy to those who seek your power?"

Marta didn't answer her. She couldn't. "May...may I have some time to think of what you offer me?"

Lornis rose. "Some, but not much. I have some business to attend, and some preparations to make. Finish your tea, and when I return I will require your answer."

The priestess left the room, leaving Marta and Bone Tapper alone. Marta stared at her mug of tea but she didn't touch it. Bone Tapper kept silent for several long moments, but at least he could no longer contain himself.

"Mistress, by everything holy in this world, why do you even hesitate??"

Marta leaned forward and put her head in her hands. "I don't know."

"I'll tell you truly, though you didn't ask: the Arrow Path has certainly brought no peace or joy to me."

"It saved your life. That was your choice. I have to make mine."

"Yes, and thank the Powers you have this chance! The Arrow Path has brought you little but grief, Mistress, and the same for anyone else, just as Lornis said. And now your Power wants your life! How can you remain on the Arrow Path now? Be rid of it."

Marta thought of those folk she had seen who had something approaching a normal life. She remembered the envy she felt now and then. Even so.... "Amaet's intentions are not as clear to me as they appear to be to

Laras. As for abandoning the path, it's not as simple as all that. At least, I don't think it is."

"Wiser heads have counseled you otherwise. I'd listen."

"I *am* listening," Marta said. It was true. She'd heard a great deal, seen a great deal. She was being offered escape, but not understanding. Safety, but not her own will. Did it matter? Marta felt like seven kinds of fool, but she still wanted to find out. She said nothing until the priestess returned.

"What is your answer, child?"

"I am willing to do as you say, but I have a condition of my own. A small one."

Lornis seemed amused. There was a twinkle in her eye, but she did not smile. "What is it?"

"Just this: First grant me the Oracle. If it does not tell me what I need to know, then I'll take that as a sign that I was not meant to follow the Arrow Path. I will forswear it and vow to serve Astonei for the rest of my life."
Lornis barely hesitated. "Granted. You will make a fine Novice."

*

Marta followed Lornis down a long tunnel. The priestess wore long black robes that would have made her nearly invisible except for the stars embroidered on the cloth with silver thread. The uneven floor sloped downward about fifteen degrees. Lornis moved with serene confidence while Marta had to concentrate on her footing, which was hard to do with Bone Tapper riding nervously on her shoulder. Even harder when he leaned toward her ear every few minutes to whisper: "Have you taken leave of your mind?"
Marta bit her lip and kept silent. In a moment Bone Tapper was distracted by the sight of a large bone embedded in the walls of the tunnel. The marks of a chisel were clearly visible around it as someone had clearly worked to expose as much of it as possible.

"Upper leg bone. And of a very large animal." Since Bone Tapper's ravenhood began, he had become quite the expert on bones, and the sweet bits of carcass still attached to them. A little farther they spied another, then another. Bone Tapper identified each with professional interest. "Lower leg. Right shoulder. Right front paw...ooh, consider the length of that claw." Bone Tapper shuddered delicately.

"Were these all from the same animal?" Marta asked.

Bone Tapper shook his head. "At least three...probably more. And before you ask, no. I don't know what sort of creatures they were. Nothing I've seen living, that's for certain, and that includes Yssara."

The tunnel ended abruptly in a large round room that seemed part cave and part charnel house. The floor was littered with bones. Bones protruded from the walls. Bones were half-sealed in stalagmites or covered with delicate lacework crystals, clear as ice.

"Oh," Marta managed to say.

"These were the Companions of the Basilisk," Lornis said. "Like the few in the tunnel, their nature is unknown. So is the basilisk's, for that matter. Truth to tell, it's called a basilisk, but we don't really know that for certain. On this point, Astonei is silent."

The Powers are silent often when they could be of help, Marta thought and quickly suppressed the thought. It felt a little like blasphemy in this place, even though Marta yet worshiped no Power, Amaet or Astonei alike.

Still, when the time came to swear her oath to Lornis, Marta had no doubt it would be heard. She could afford no doubt because she was sure Lornis would require her to swear by Astonei. If worse came to worse and Marta failed, there was no way she could break her oath without risking far more than her life.

Lornis stopped in the center of the chamber, pausing to light two torches mounted on tall stalagmites. "As all things are measured, so are all things given value. The value I give the Oracle is this: Marta, if the Oracle gives you your answer and you have the wisdom to see it, you depart with what you sought. If you do not, you will remain here as my novitiate. You will surrender the Path of the Arrow for the Path of Solitude and take your place in time as Priestess of Astonei. Swear to this now or depart as you came, with neither honor nor blame."

Marta took a deep breath. "I swear it," she said. Even as she did so, Marta had the feeling that something was missing from the oath, but her mind was racing ahead to what lay down the far tunnel, and it left mere vague doubts behind quickly.

Bone Tapper shook his head. "I've said this before—"

Marta reached up and pressed Bone Tapper's beak firmly shut. "Enough."

Lornis left Marta and Bone Tapper alone among the Companions of the Basilisk. Marta found a smooth bit of stone and sat down, facing a circle of greater darkness on the far wall. It was the mouth of a tunnel, and the end of it was the basilisk's skull. She looked at it for a moment, then closed her eyes.

"Are you praying?" Bone Tapper asked.

"In a way. I'm thinking."

"About what?"

"About how to recognize a Law of Power when I see one."

Bone Tapper shrugged. "You'd be better off praying."

Marta smiled a grim sort of smile. "You're the one who should be praying, Bone Tapper, and that I'll fail. If I do fail, your debt to me is transferred to the Shrine along with the cart and the gold in it and everything else that is mine. If you harbor the illusion that Lornis would be a gentler mistress than myself, I think you're mistaken."

"I think you're right. And, since there's nothing I can do about it either way..." Bone Tapper yawned and hopped to the top of another stalagmite. He put his head under his wing.

"You could come with me, you know," she said. "The price serves for two."

Bone Tapper untucked his head from his wing, glanced at the tunnel and shuddered. "This is too close to being entombed as it is, so I'll stay here in the relative open if it's all the same with you. I doubt there's anything a basilisk has to tell me that I need to know."

Marta didn't say anything, and in a moment Marta was certain the raven was asleep. She envied him that skill, often demonstrated, of quick slumber. She didn't even know if she could sleep now, and sleep was the one thing she had to do now.

Time to hunt the night and basilisk dreams.

Marta rose and started down the tunnel. She thought of taking one of the torches with her, but the way was too narrow, and a strong draft blowing through the tunnel was likely to push the flames into her face as not. She moved half bent over, feeling her way as she went, using the weak light from the chamber behind her as much as possible. The way grew progressively dimmer until Marta was moving almost completely on feel when she came to the end of the tunnel.

Or not quite the end.

Marta's fingers touched smooth stone. The tunnel opened abruptly so that now she could stand to her full height again, such that it was, but her fingers now passed through another opening in the stone. There was a faint light from above; Marta glanced up and saw stars.

That explains the breeze.

The tunnel was open to the sky where the shaft ended. The starlight was faint but it was enough to see the pale ghostly outline surrounding the hole in the wall. It wasn't a new tunnel—it was the basilisk's skull, embedded in solid rock. Marta traced out an outline of a horned beak and a crest of bone. The opening was its left eye socket.

"Now what?" she asked. "Do I meditate on a skull locked in stone?"

There was no answer but the soft moan of the wind. Marta shuddered, hugging herself against the chill. She certainly couldn't sleep here—she'd freeze. She reached out to the eye again, feeling the bone of the upper rim, hard and rough now as the stone it had become. Lower down, the rough texture smoothed out, became almost glassy. She smiled.

"Marta, you are a silly bit of fluff, aren't you?" she said ruefully.

Marta crawled inside the basilisk's eye. There was plenty of room for her to crawl through, and once inside she found herself passing through a smaller hole where the inner bone had fractured. Now Marta was in true darkness, feeling her way through a space that was larger than she had expected but still fairly close. It felt more like being shut in a box than being in an open room. Marta felt the walls closing in on her in a way she had not any time before within the Shrine. She mastered an attack of panic through sheer will, forced herself to breath slowly and deeply until the feeling abated. She stretched out her hands again, taking the true measure of the inside of the basilisk's skull.

Once outside the short passage leading from the eye socket, the interior measured about seven feet long, almost as much wide, and about four feet high. There was no draft blowing in there; the air was mostly still and slightly warmer than in the fissure outside. The surface where she rested was slightly curved, like the bottom of a bowl. It was almost comfortable.

Marta nestled down into the curve of the basilisk's skull like someone settling into a hammock. She didn't get to sleep quickly—her mind was too noisy a place to allow *that*—but she managed it at last.

CHAPTER 18

"Judge what I say against what I do. Only then call me dishonest."
— From the Annals of Dommar the Beast

"Hurry up! She's waiting!"

Bone Tapper pecked Marta back to awareness. She was not in the basilisk's skull now. She sat with her back to one of the stalagmites in the Hall of Companions, with Bone Tapper perched on her shoulder and pecking her not so gently in the head. It didn't seem such a strange thing for him to be doing. What was strange was why she was there in the first place.

"How did I get here?"

"I assume your mother had carnal relations. It's the usual way. No time for this nonsense!" Bone Tapper left her shoulder as Marta struggled to her feet. "She's waiting for you," he repeated.

"Who is? Lornis?"

But Bone Tapper was already gone. Marta heard his croaking call echo from the tunnel leading back to the main hall of the temple. "Hurry!"

Marta didn't understand what all the rush was about. If she'd returned from the basilisk's skull, she'd done it without any oracle or dream that she could recall, never mind that she couldn't remember returning to the hall either. She had failed, that was what mattered. Marta followed Bone Tapper up the tunnel.

This time the tunnel opened on Lornis's private quarters.

This isn't right.

Marta knew the tunnel from the Hall of Companions didn't lead to Lornis's chambers, but this time it did. Marta was certain it was the same room but now very different, very changed. The chairs Marta remembered from earlier that evening were not present. The crystals on Lornis's mantel had been replaced by dried herbs in bundles. Even the bed covering and fireplace tools were different.

Bone Tapper perched on a peg by the doorway. "Will you hurry? You have no time to waste!" Then he was gone again, flying out the door and toward the main audience chamber. Marta started to follow because she didn't know what else to do, but she was certainly in no hurry to admit defeat. She paused to glance into a mirror hanging on the near wall, one of the few furnishing that hadn't changed.

I must look a fright—

Marta stopped. She didn't look a fright, she looked like someone else. A woman maybe a year or two older than herself, no more than that. A woman with long dark hair and rich clothes, and a face of casual authority. There was something familiar about the face but Marta couldn't place it. She examined the clothes in the mirror, then Marta looked down, saw the same fine robes in place of her own blouse and breeks, soft cloth shoes instead of her own sturdy leather boots.

"Who are you?" she asked aloud, then she felt talons on her shoulders, impossibly strong. Bone Tapper perched on her shoulder, grinning. Marta knew that a raven couldn't grin, but Bone Tapper was doing it anyway.

"You will come to audience hall. Now."

Marta was too stunned and confused to protest, or do much of anything except move as the raven directed her. She went out the door and followed the tunnel to the audience hall. Lornis was already there. Except, of course, it was not Lornis.

The woman was very old. The ceremonial robes of a Priestess of Astonei hung off her body like clothes on storage pegs with no form beneath to support them. Bone Tapper didn't release his painful grip until Marta marched herself before the dais and bowed to the seated priestess.

"Have you found what you were searching for?" the woman asked.

"No, Priestess. I have not." It was true enough, but why did the words feel so empty, as if she were speaking lines from some unknown play. And why did her voice sound so strange? With a little thought, Marta knew the answer to that part, at least.

Because here, now, I am not Marta. But who am I?

"Then by your own word and the Goddess' price, you now belong to the Basilisk Oracle. Have you anything to say?"

"Just that I will serve, as my word has bound me. May it please Astonei."

"So..."

Marta shivered, and the words seem to fall away from her like echoes across an impossible gulf.

"...Be."

Not impossible. She was there. Had been there...

"...It."

Marta shivered again, and the stone against her back felt as if it were set with a thousand needles. In a moment she was fully awake and back in the darkness of the basilisk's skull. The dream was over.

*

Marta did not go back to Lornis's quarters this time, but she did find a mirror along one of the tunnels near the baths. She looked into it for a good long time, but all she saw was herself.

"Vanity doesn't suit you. Where have you been?" Bone Tapper lit on her shoulder. Marta winced instinctively; the raven's grip was no worse than usual.

"I could ask the same of you. You weren't in the Hall of Companions when I returned."

"A hole in the ground is no place for a raven. I went out to get some air. Come along, Lornis is waiting for you in the audience chamber."

"Aren't you going to tell me to hurry?" Marta asked, but the raven just blinked at her, uncomprehending. Marta sighed. "Let's not keep her waiting."

"What did you find?" Bone Tapper asked, trying to sound unconcerned and not quite managing.

Marta thought about the question for a moment. "I'm not sure yet," Marta finally said. "But I can't wait to find out."

Bone Tapper had no reply. He rode her shoulder into the audience chamber, as vast and grand as Marta remembered it. Only now it was Lornis sitting in the High Priestess' chair on the dais. Marta stopped suddenly as the shock of recognition hit her.

It was Lornis in the mirror. Much younger, but it was her. Of course, I should have known.

"Have you found what you sought?" Lornis asked. Her voice seemed to fill the chamber.

Marta just looked at her for several long moments. "You came to the Shrine once, long ago, just as I have now," she said. "You took the place of the former Priestess."

"Yes," Lornis said, frowning. "Everyone who stays here, came here at one point or another. What of it? You haven't answered my question."

"You're not an adept," Marta said, as if she hadn't heard. "You recognized Bone Tapper by simple observation; the signs are there for anyone with wit to read them; I'm so used to Bone Tapper as what he is that I no longer see them."

Lornis's smile was all teeth. "I never said I was an adept, child. You did."

Marta nodded. "You're right. I went beyond the respect that is your due. I gave you power that you did not have."

"The Second Law, child: 'What cannot be taken, can be given.'"

Marta shook her head slowly. "A misinterpretation of the Second Law, which really has more to do with the limits of pure force. Force had nothing to do with this."

Lornis's face looked like a dark cloud considering a storm. "Enough delay! Did you find what you sought?"

"Yes," Marta said. "I did."

Lornis laughed at her. "Marta, that is not possible."

"Why?" Marta asked.

"Because—" Lornis stopped, and Marta smiled.

"Go on. You were going to tell me how you know that I did not find the Third Law. Yes, that is the one I was searching for, I admit it."

"You did not receive the Third Law from the Oracle!"

"You're right," Marta said. "I did not. Because, as you said yourself, it's not possible! The Laws cannot be taught, they cannot be earned, they cannot even be revealed, not by my mother, not by the Basilisk Oracle, not by Astonei, not by Amaet, not by anyone! That's true, isn't it?"

Lornis glared at her. "Yes, it's true, and what of it? You did not receive the Third Law and so you are sworn to Astonei, now and forever."

"No. I am not."

Lornis was stunned to silence, but she soon found her voice again. "Marta, have a care! Astonei will protect you for forswearing the Arrow Path, but break faith with her and no Power on earth or above it will protect you."

"I am having great care, Lornis, and I have not forsworn the Arrow Path. I told you—I found my answer. It wasn't the Third Law. I did not ask the Basilisk Oracle for the Third Law! I never said I had. What I sought from the Oracle was truth, just one bit of truth about something that I thought I understood. I received it, though it took me a little while to understand what it meant. It was only then that I acquired the Third Law. For both, I thank you."

"Prove it, then. What is the Third Law of Power?"

"I can't tell you," Marta said.

"You mean you don't know!"

"I mean," replied Marta firmly, "that you don't. I can't tell you because it would mean nothing to you. Words. I can't tell you because many years ago you came here searching for the Third Law and you didn't find it."

Lornis was silent for several long moments, then said, "You're wrong."

There was a seed of doubt in Marta's mind, as perhaps there always would be, but it did not grow. "I don't think so," she said. "Show me the sign."

Lornis just stared at her. She shook her head, slowly, but Marta was as merciless and inevitable as the tides, and she held her gaze. "Show me. You wanted proof, and proof is here, only it is you who will provide it. Show me."

Lornis reached inside her robe and slowly, reluctantly, pulled out the pendant she wore around her neck. The Arrow Path. Marta wasn't even a little surprised.

Lornis looked weary beyond her years, but she managed a smile. "You're still wrong...about part of it, anyway. I already had the Third Law when I came here. I wasn't searching for the Fourth Law or any other. I asked for no Law of Power when I slept in the Basilisk's skull. I didn't ask for anything."

Marta blinked. She struck down the denial forming on her lips; she only had to look at the old woman to know she spoke the truth. "But...why?"

"Why? How can you even ask that? I can't say what is right be for you, but for me The Arrow Path was a mistake. I was weary of the traveling, of the searching, long before I came to the Basilisk Shrine. And I found a very weary, very ancient Priestess with a settled life and a high office, and both looked very good to me. All I had to do to make it mine was one little lie. So that's my soul debt to Astonei. It'll be paid soon enough. I have a better offer for you, Marta—stay with me. You won't even need to lie. It could be your choice."

Marta shook her head. "You are a very fine servant of Astonei. I think your choice to stay served a greater truth than the fact you hid to preserve that choice. But if I tried to stay, that would be the lie, and would not serve Astonei at all. Or you. Or me. This is not my way, Lornis. For better or no, the Arrow Path is mine. I will follow where it leads."

"Suppose it leads you to nothing but death?"

Marta bowed. "All roads lead to death sooner or later. I believe how we make the journey is what matters. Shall I tell you the Third Law?"

Lornis shook her head. "No need. I believe you, Marta. Go in peace. I think you may yet regret your choice, but it is yours to make."

Marta nodded once to the priestess and then left the Basilisk Shrine without another word, and soon stood in the sunlight again in the grassy valley.

"That was quick thinking," Bone Tapper said, and it was the first thing he'd said since they took their leave of the Shrine. "Pity."

"What was? And why a pity?" Marta asked.

"That story about finding the Third Law, of course. You were convincing, I must say. So was she. I'd swear Lornis actually had found her Law and just chose to stay, as she said."

"She did, and she did."

Bone Tapper blinked owlishly. "She could have been pretending, just as you could have...and I thought you were. How could you know otherwise?"

"If I had actually failed, I would have stayed. I would have had to. Lornis knew that."

"I repeat: How?"

"If I still believed that Lornis was an adept at the end of the oracle, it would mean that I had not found the Third Law as I said I had. I made her produce the pendant to prove that I knew her secret."

Bone Tapper ruffled his feathers. "Fine, I give you that one. But what did finding or not finding the Third Law have to do with knowing that Lornis was an adept?"

"That was the bit of truth I asked of the Shrine. My oracle let me live a piece of Lornis's life, enough to suspect. I had assumed that Lornis was a powerful adept because I didn't consider the other option. Which is that she merely 'appeared' to be. That her experience and natural intuition together with what few of the Laws she did possess allowed her to seem more than she was. But if you always accept what you see at face value, how can you distinguish between it and the truth?"

Bone Tapper frowned. "I don't think you can."

Marta nodded. "Just so. At that point it no longer matters, at least in practice. 'The Appearance of Power, Once Accepted, is Power Itself.'"

"Is that the Third Law?"

"Assume what you will," Marta said. "I'll say no more on the matter."

Bone Tapper took his place on Marta's shoulder and she steered the wagon back the way they had come. "And how has this knowledge increased your abilities?"

"It allowed me to escape from the Shrine, didn't it?"

"There was nothing holding you there!"

"I believe that was the point," Marta replied dryly, then she smiled. "Now then: why is it a pity? Because you wanted to serve Lornis instead of me?"

"Because we were safe in the Shrine, Mistress! What happens when Laras discovers, as he will sooner or later, that you did not die in Sendale?"

Marta smiled. "Oh, that. Amaet surely told him by now."

"And you come out here, knowing Laras is looking for you?"

"Yes, Bone Tapper, I do. Out into the world where I belong. I'll either share it with Laras, or one of us will die. Whatever happens, this matter will be settled."

"Then I think it will be settled now. Look there!"

Marta looked up toward the ridge on the northern edge of the valley, the way they had come. She saw a figure made of fire.

"Laras," she said softly. She wasn't surprised; in fact it was no more or less than she expected. It made perfect sense that he would be waiting for her, somewhere if not here. Amaet would not be so easily fooled as Laras himself had been. And this had been her idea all along hadn't it?

She's going to answer for that. I just have to live long enough to make that happen.

"Let's have it done then," Marta said simply.

"I've asked it before, I'll ask again: are you mad??"

"Shall we go find out?"

"Umm... I'd rather not."

"I know," Marta said. "Yet you will come with me anyway."

Bone Tapper didn't argue further. He rode Marta's shoulder as she walked up the hill to meet Laras. There was neither haste nor hurry in her stride.

"One thing, Bone Tapper," Marta said as they approached the living flame. "Doubtless he will burn me. Feel free to fly to a safe distance when that happens."

"And leave you to die? Is that what you really want? It certainly explains your attitude."

"If I die, your Debt belongs to Amaet. She will see how to collect it and even if she does not you're no longer my problem."

Laras waited for her in all his glory there on the hilltop, the flames that framed his body flickered from red to blue to gold and back again. He looked like a god. Marta thought this appropriate, considering he had the power of one. Almost literally. Marta shrugged. If she had misread the situation, if she was wrong about the nature of Laras's power and what it meant, she would die. If she was right she might die anyway; the risk wasn't exactly slight. Yet she had made her choice, and she would live or die by that choice because it belonged to her. That and the Laws of Power that were her heritage, and her destiny.

"I'm glad you choose not to run, Marta," Laras said as she approached. "I serve Amaet, and her ways are harsh and unfathomable, but I am no monster. I have no wish to make this any harder than it has to be."

Marta nodded. "I believe that's true."

"Well then—" Laras raised his hands, but Marta stopped him.

"If it's not too much trouble, Master Laras, before you kill me there is something I would really like to know."

"Ask, and please be quick. My patience is not without limits."

Marta bowed slightly. "Of course. So. You told me that Amaet gave you the Laws of Power. Is that really true?"

Laras glow changed from a flame to a roaring inferno and then back again. "Do you doubt it?"

"Yes," she said. "I do."

Laras smiled a grim smile. Sparks flew from his hair. "Then I guess I will have to prove it."

Laras burned her. Flames speared out from Laras's open hands and enveloped her. Bone Tapper had already flown clear, croaking in fear and horror. Laras glanced up. "Oh, off with you, carrion-eater. Amaet gave no instructions concerning you. Don't give me a reason to kill you, too."

"You need a reason? Perhaps you're not really a monster after all. Merely a deluded fool."

Bone Tapper and Laras both stared in disbelief. Marta stood calmly in front of them, still enveloped in fire. She regarded the flames with some curiosity; the grass at her feet began to smolder but Marta herself could have been standing in a pleasant glow of sunset for all that she took note of them.

Laras's mouth set in a grim line. "So...trickier than I suspected, aren't you? No matter."

This time he called lightning. It struck out of a clear sky with a flash of heat and roll of thunder. The ground at Marta's feet smoked and steamed. Marta smiled at him. "Nice trick. Could you teach me that one?" Laras just stared, and Marta finally sighed. "No, I guess not. You really don't know, do you?"

Fear and confusion warred across Laras's face. For a moment, confusion got the upper hand. "You can't be standing, you can't be alive! No one could withstand that!"

Marta shook her head. "There was nothing to withstand, Laras. These flashes of light and sparkle have nothing to do with magic. You burn the grass because you believe otherwise. They do not burn me because I know what you do not know."

"What? What do you know?"

"That they are false flames. Tricks. Just like your mastery."

"Amaet gave the Laws to me!"

Marta shook her head slowly. "No. The Laws of Power are not hers to give, or anyone's. That is not the way of the Laws. I told you that before. It was true then and it's true now."

Marta made the flames around her go away. Laras took a step back. "I've shattered stones!" he said, a note of hysteria creeping into his voice. "I broke those beneath your feet at the ruins!"

Marta shook her head. "The stone was indeed broken, but you didn't do it, not really. You don't know how."

His hands balled into fists, but his flames were beginning to look starved and ragged, like a dying campfire, unattended. "I do! 'What Power Holds, Weakness Frees'! It's the First Law!"

"No it isn't," Marta said. "That is merely the expression of the First Law. That is all that Amaet gave to you. They are not the Laws themselves, or anyone who heard their names would know them. No true Arrow Path initiate would make that mistake." She smiled then. "At least, not a second time. But then you are not Arrow Path, are you? Despite the pendant you wear. You are Amaet's dog."

"I've shattered stones!" Laras stubbornly repeated. "I caused landslides with a thought!"

"It may have been your thought, Laras, but it was Amaet's will, and her power alone. She doesn't want me dead. She wants something else."

"You're lying! I will show you."

Laras looked at his hand, then slowly began to reach out. Marta understood the danger. That much of his belief was true—he did have access to the First Law, or at least the effects of it. Unlike the false fire and lightning, there was danger in his touch. She smiled at him and Laras froze, uncertain.

"I'm telling you the truth," Marta said to him. "It's past time someone did. If you really want to understand Power, then let me show you what it is."

Marta spoke no spells, since she knew none save the Ritual of the Debt. She neither called lightning nor conjured fire. All she did was reach out, suddenly, and with her own bare hand she snatched the symbol from Laras's neck. She held the gold pendant in her fingers and, with her own strength and the gold's malleable nature, she crushed it.

Laras's fire went out.

"I thought as much," Marta said. " Amaet channeled her power through this." Marta held up the crushed pendant. "You have no power and never did. She taught you nothing. She gave you nothing. No Debt incurred, or at least not a fair, proper one, because you never used Power on your own. There was no understanding on your part required, and she let you believe what you wanted to believe. It's over now."

Laras shouted improvised incantations that had no effect. Laras gestured to the heavens and received no answer. Marta simply waited until Laras finally fell to his knees, sobbing. "She promised...she lied! She lied to me!" Laras looked at Marta, his eyes overflowing with pain. "I loved her!"

Marta heard it all in those few words, choked out in rage and pain. What Laras had hoped, what he dreamed, what he sought to make real. All gone. Or rather, never existing at all except in Laras's own mind. Yet that clearly wasn't the worst that Amaet had done to him.

"Loved...Amaet? Oh, Laras..."

It was only then that Marta truly understood the completeness of Amaet's corruption of Laras. Then, too, she finally realized, as she had not before, that Treedle's earlier refusal to be her friend was something like a compliment. *Treedle may have been my mother's slave, but he never loved her, nor me. At least, not for allowing him to become a slave.* The same could be said of anyone who served Kath and now Marta. Perhaps it wasn't so great a difference, but it was a difference, between herself and the Power called Amaet. Marta felt surprisingly grateful for that difference now.

"Choose better next time, Laras," was all Marta said. "Goodbye."
She heard his scream of incoherent rage even before she sensed Laras springing forward. Later, Marta would think of all the things she could have done. Break his arm, or a leg. Crush his shoulder. Anything except what she did. Yet in the moment there was only that moment, and no time for second choices. As Laras's fingers closed about her throat, Marta touched his chest. There was purpose in that touch. Not anger, nor even fear. Just purpose, and then followed, as always, the consequences. Marta's touch wasn't a blow. It was barely a caress, yet there was death in it. Laras's cry of rage and madness choked off into silence and he crumpled like a rag doll onto the grass.

Marta just stood there for several long moments, staring first at her hand, then Laras's limp body, then her hand again.

"Wrong to the end...Damn you, Laras, and Amaet in the bargain," Marta said, and that was all. She left Laras's body where it fell and started walking north. In a short time she found where Laras had left his hobbled mount. Bone Tapper flew down to perch on her shoulder as she untied the lashings and freed the reins.

"You seem to be making a habit of taking horses from that poor sod." Bone Tapper saw the expression on Marta's face and changed the subject. "Laras beat you the first time because he believed he had power?"

"No. He won because *I* believed him. I doubted what my Mother taught me, and everything I knew to be true. I won't make that mistake again."

"Did you have to kill him?"

Marta nodded slowly. "Yes, because I only had time to think of one thing, and this was the result. I will learn better. Next time, perhaps, I will consider another option first. Not that this will help poor Laras. It might help some other fool in times to come."

Bone Tapper sighed. "Back to the Archive, I suppose?"

Marta heard the sarcasm in the bird's tone, and she did not protest. If anything, she was grateful. "Anywhere I can," Marta said. "Everywhere I can. One other thing, Bone Tapper, and I want you to pay close attention to what I say."

"Yes?"

Marta worked a change, and Bone Tapper was a hob again. "We have no spade, so you're going to help me carry Laras to Sendale and raise a cairn for him. If you try to slip back there later, or if you so much as glance at Laras with thoughts of a fuller belly, I will turn you into a garden slug and leave you to get home on your own. Do you understand me?"

"You needn't worry," Bone Tapper said, sounding the very soul and voice of wounded virtue. "Despite what you may think, I'm pickier about my food than that."

Together they returned to drape Laras's body across the saddle and then carried it across the Longbone, and there in the shadow of the standing tower, together Marta and Bone Tapper buried him.

It was not until the cairn was finished that Marta let herself feel the full impact of what she had done, and the tears came. Marta knew Bone Tapper was watching her but she didn't care. Nor did she fight the tears this time, for they were not, as she had once thought, an enemy. She wept for herself and what she had done, for Laras and what he might have been, and for one last bad choice on both their parts, neither of which could be undone. It was only when there were no more tears to shed for Laras or herself that Marta climbed into the saddle and began the journey home.

EPILOGUE

Marta dropped a gold coin in Amaet's basin.

"I am here, Amaet. I have paid for my question. You will answer me." Marta crossed her arms as if daring the Power to say otherwise.

There was a flicker in the air above the basin, and Amaet was there. After a fashion. There was no bright flash of pure white, no radiant Amaet hovering there and smiling at Marta with that infuriating smile that Marta had come to loathe. Amaet was no more than a shadow, hardly as substantial as a ghost. Marta frowned, but she kept silent. The shadow that was Amaet did smile then.

YOU WON'T ASK WHY I APPEAR THIS WAY. YOU'RE WISE NOT TO WASTE YOUR QUESTION ON TRIVIAL THINGS.

"I'll decide for myself what is trivial, Amaet," Marta said. "And whether you tell me the truth that I've paid for."

SUCH AN ANGRY LITTLE THING YOU ARE. IT DOES NOT SUIT YOU. AND WRONG, TOO. YOU PAY FOR A QUESTION. WHETHER YOU CAN BELIEVE THE ANSWER IS UP TO YOU. IT ALWAYS WAS AND ALWAYS WILL BE.

Marta dismissed that. "Why did you send that poor fool Laras after me? If you'd wanted me dead, I would be dead."

QUITE RIGHT, BLACK KATH'S DAUGHTER. IF YOU BELIEVE OTHERWISE YOU'RE MORE THE FOOL THAN LARAS.

"Then why?"

THERE ARE MANY QUESTIONS WRAPPED UP IN THAT ONE. SINCE YOU HAVE BEEN THROUGH SO MUCH, I WILL INVOKE THE SECOND LAW AND GIVE YOU SOME OF WHAT YOU'VE ASKED. INCLUDING THE QUESTION YOU WILL NOT ASK: I

LOOK THIS WAY BECAUSE MY ATTENTION IS NOT WITHOUT LIMITS, MARTA. RIGHT NOW YOU ONLY HAVE A VERY SMALL PIECE OF IT.

"I'm grateful for the explanation, since I was curious. Yet that isn't what I asked. I want to know about Laras. The man I killed."

THAT'S ONLY ONE DEATH. THERE WILL BE MORE. YOU'LL SEE.

Marta clenched her fists, then slowly opened them out again. She took a deep, shuddering breath of the clear, cold mountain air. "Tell me," she said.

Amaet smiled. NO.

"Will you tell me why not?"

BECAUSE WHAT WEAPONS I USE AND HOW I CHOOSE TO HONE THEM IS ENTIRELY UP TO ME. THAT'S THE REAL ANSWER, BLACK KATH'S DAUGHTER. MAKE OF IT WHAT YOU CAN.

Marta frowned. "Weapons? Are you at war?"

Amaet smiled at her. YOU'RE FINDING A GREAT DEAL OF MEANING IN ONE WORD.

"I would not think you would be careless with your words, Amaet. Words have power, too."

YOU WHO UNDERSTAND SO LITTLE SHOULD NOT PRETEND TO UNDERSTAND MORE. YET I WILL SAY, AFTER SUCH A SLOW BEGINNING, YOU HAVE PROGRESSED WELL. THREE LAWS? TO CELEBRATE, THERE IS ONE THING I WILL TELL YOU. CALL IT FAIR WARNING.

"What is that, Amaet?"

FROM NOW ON, THE ARROW PATH WILL ONLY GET HARDER.

Amaet's presence, slight though it had been, was gone.

Marta smiled a grim smile. *You may not realize this now, Amaet, but that goes for both of us.*

Marta was alone. Later she would rejoin Bone Tapper and the rest of the world below Mount Karsanmon and resume her search for the Seven, but not just yet. Perhaps it was only coincidence, but when the Priestess of Amaet next entered the Sanctuary of the Karsanmon Shrine she found the lovely new gilded statue of the Goddess Amaet smashed into pieces beyond counting.

Aleeta sighed. "Blazes. Not again!"

The End

ABOUT THE AUTHOR

Richard Parks' stories have have appeared in Asimov's SF, Realms of Fantasy, Fantasy Magazine, Weird Tales, and numerous anthologies, including several Year's Bests. His first story collection, *The Ogre's Wife*, was a finalist for the World Fantasy Award. He is a native of Mississippi and, despite several attempts to leave, still lives there with his wife and a varying number of cats.